Blackhawk
Desires

Three exciting and enticing romances from
one adored Mills & Boon author!

Blackhawk
Desires

BARBARA McCAULEY

First published in Great Britain 2011
by Mills & Boon, an imprint of Harlequin (UK) Limited,
Eton House, 18-24 Paradise Road, Richmond, Surrey TW9

BLACKHAWK DESIRES © by Harlequin Enterprises II B

Blackhawk's Betrayal, *Blackhawk's Bond* and *Blackhawk's*
published in Great Britain by Harlequin (UK) Limited in se
single volumes.

Blackhawk's Betrayal © Barbara McCauley 2006
Blackhawk's Bond © Barbara McCauley 2006
Blackhawk's Affair © Barbara McCauley 2007

ISBN: 978 0 263 88346 6

05-0511

Printed and bound in Spain
by Blackprint CPI, Barcelona

ROM
Pbk

Barbara McCauley, who has written more than twenty novels for Silhouette Books, lives in Southern California with her own handsome hero husband, Frank, who makes it easy to believe in and write about the magic of romance. Barbara's stories have won and been nominated for numerous awards, including the prestigious RITA® Award from the Romance Writers of America, Best Desire of the Year from Romantic Times BOOKclub and Best Short Contemporary from the National Reader's Choice Awards.

BLACKHAWK'S
BETRAYAL

This book is dedicated to Jennifer Stockton, Chef Extraordinaire! Thanks for all your help and expertise, sweetheart. Your secret for chocolate mousse is safe with me.

One

She should be in Paris.

Sighing, Kiera glanced at the yellow-lit dial on her rental car dashboard. Nine thirty-two, Texas time. If she had got on her plane this morning, she would have landed at the Charles de Gaulle Airport two hours ago. At this very moment, she would be checking into her room at the hotel Château Frontenac. Ordering room service. Sipping espresso while she nibbled on a *navettes*. Sinking her exhausted body into a Louis XVI four-poster bed.

Instead, she sat in the cracked asphalt parking lot of Sadie's Shangri-La Motel and Motor Lodge.

Welcome. Park Your Cars Out Front, Your Horses Out Back, flashed the pink neon vacancy sign.

She didn't know whether to laugh or cry, so she dropped her head into her hands and did both.

"Damn you, Trey," she said through clenched teeth. "Damn you, damn you, damn you."

She let herself rant for a full ten seconds, then wiped her tears and flipped the visor down to study her face in the lit mirror. *Scary,* was her first thought—*deal with it,* her second. Mumbling curses again, she dug through her purse and pulled out a compact of cover-up, then carefully blotted the fading bruise beside her left eye. Not perfect, but the best she could do unless she put on her sunglasses, which, considering the fact that it was pitch black outside, just *might* draw attention to herself.

And *that* she certainly didn't want to do.

Adjusting her bangs and the sides of her hair to hide the fading bruise, she stepped out of the car and stretched her stiff muscles. She was too tired to care that her skirt, a pristine white ten hours ago, now looked like tissue paper pulled out of a gift bag. Nor did she care that her sleeveless blouse, a clean, crisp green when she'd left the ranch this morning, currently had the appearance of wilted lettuce.

It is what it is.

A double-trailer big rig rumbled past the motel, jarring her out of her thoughts. She slung her purse strap over her shoulder, sucked in a breath, then made her way to the motel's front office. Heat from the sweltering day lingered, and the humidity clung to her like wet plastic wrap. *Shower,* she thought, drawing the heavy, damp air into her lungs. She needed one desperately. A long one to wash off the grime and sweat of the day's travel.

When she opened the glass door, a buzzer sounded

overhead and the scent of coffee hung heavy in the air. The desk clerk, a well-endowed petite blonde with Texas-size hair, stood behind the counter, hands on her voluptuous hips and her gaze locked on the screen of a small corner television.

"Be right with y'all," the woman said without even glancing up.

Kiera held back the threatening whimper. Born and raised Texan, she knew what "be right with y'all," *really* meant: sometime between the near future and next Christmas.

Living in New York the past three years had made her impatient, she realized. She'd become accustomed to the frantic rush of people, the swell of city traffic, skyscrapers and closed-in spaces. A delicatessen on every corner.

The thought of food reminded her she hadn't eaten today. She'd kill for one of those deli sandwiches right now. A ten-pound ham and cheese, with lettuce and tomatoes and—

"No!"

The shout made Kiera jump back and clutch her purse. The desk clerk threw up her hands in disgust, which set the strands of silver circles on her earlobes swirling.

"I *knew* I couldn't trust those two," she exclaimed, gesturing angrily at the TV. "For eight weeks she carries Brett and Randy's scrawny, lazy asses and what did it get the poor girl? What?"

Kiera wasn't certain if the woman—Mattie, according to the plastic badge on her white polo shirt—really wanted an answer, but she doubted it.

"A boot in her butt, that's what. Lower than manure, that's what those two jerks are." Shaking her head, Mattie grabbed the remote and lowered the volume, then turned and stretched her bright red lips into a smile. "You checking in, honey?"

Kiera hesitated, briefly considered taking her chances that she might find a room at a hotel in town. Someplace not quite so far off the beaten path. Someplace…safer. Then she remembered how much cash she had and shook off her apprehension. "The sign said you had a vacancy."

"Sure do." Mattie moved to a computer monitor behind the counter. "Single or double?"

"Single."

Mattie's long, glossy red nails clicked over the keys. "Kitchenette?"

Kiera didn't really plan on cooking, but, then, she hadn't planned on being here, either. "Sure."

"How long y'all staying?" Mattie asked.

"I—I'm not sure." God, this was a bad idea, she thought. A *really* bad idea. "Maybe a week or so."

"Name?"

Kiera shifted uneasily. She didn't dare use her real name. At least, not her *last* name. "Kiera Daniels."

The desk clerk entered the name into her computer, then printed out a form and slid it across the counter. "Credit card?"

She thought about the name on her credit card, the fact that she could easily be traced back here if she used it, not to mention the fact that the name might raise questions. "I'd, ah, like to pay cash."

Lifting one penciled brow, Mattie glanced up. "I'll need two night's deposit."

"All right." She pulled out her wallet and opened it, felt her heart sink as she remembered most of her money was in *francs,* which obviously wasn't going to help her now. She counted what usable money she had, then tentatively laid out the amount that the desk clerk had entered on the printed card. If she was very, very careful, she might last two or three days before she ran out of cash.

Mattie stared at the bills Kiera had so carefully and reluctantly counted out, then looked up again. Kiera shifted uncomfortably when the other woman studied her face.

"Husband or boyfriend?"

"Excuse me?"

"Honey, I know it ain't none of my beeswax," Mattie stated flatly. "But it's hard not to notice that shiner you got there."

Instinctively, Kiera reached up and pulled her hair forward. *So much for makeup.* "No—I— It's not like that. I fell off a horse."

Sympathy softened the harsh edges of Mattie's eyes. "Like I said, it's none of my beeswax. But a woman comes into my motel late at night, alone, looking like she's been chewed up and spit out, and I can't help it, it's my Christian duty to ask."

Do I really look that bad? Kiera thought, biting her lip. She glanced down at her rumpled clothes, knew her eyes were probably still red from crying, and she realized that she *did* look that bad.

"If you need an ear or a shoulder..." Mattie went on "...I know a few things about men. I hear there's a few good ones around, but, honey, my experience is most of them are asses."

At the moment, Kiera might tend to agree with that assessment but decided against encouraging the topic. "If I could just get my key."

"Sure." Mattie shrugged a shoulder, dropped the money into a drawer, then held out a key. "Room 107."

"Thanks."

"You know," the desk clerk said when Kiera turned. "If you decide to stick around for a while and need a job, they're hiring at the hotel in town."

"Thank you, but—"

"I could put a good word in for you," Mattie offered. "My sister, Janet, is head of human resources. I'm sure she could find a spot for you."

"I'm really not—"

"You don't even have to have any experience," Mattie continued. "They got all kinds of jobs open since they expanded. Between conventions and conferences and the new wedding chapel, the place is packed most of the time. I hear the new owner, Clair Blackhawk is great to work for."

Blackhawk?

The name sucked the breath out of Kiera's lungs. She stared at the desk clerk, had to swallow before she managed a weak reply. "Blackhawk?"

"Well, that *was* her name, but she got married a few weeks ago, so I'm not sure what her last name is now. Oh, wait—" Mattie snapped her fingers "—it's Carver. Clair Carver."

With her heart clamoring so loudly, it was hard for

Kiera to concentrate. The name Carver meant nothing to her. But Blackhawk… *God, was it possible?* It was all she could do not to grab the desk clerk's arm, ask her point-blank if—"

"You okay, honey?"

Kiera blinked, watched Mattie's face come back into focus. "What?"

"You look a little pale. You feelin' okay?"

"It's just been a long day." *The longest of my life,* she thought, and forced a smile. "I appreciate your concern, but, really, I'll be fine."

Mattie nodded. "You're the last room on the left, just past the ice and vending machines. You need anything, just give me a call."

"Thanks."

Knees shaking, Kiera turned and walked back to her car. She wasn't certain how long she sat there, dazed, staring blankly into the deep shadows of the poplars edging the motel. As a child, she'd always been afraid of the dark, knew that ferocious monsters lived there, waiting to swallow children whole.

At twenty-five, maybe she was still a little afraid of the dark, she realized.

When she walked back into the motel office, Mattie glanced up from the TV.

Kiera closed the door behind her. "About that job…"

When Sam Prescott made his morning rounds through the lobby of the Four Winds Hotel, bellmen straightened their shoulders, desk clerks smiled brighter, valets hustled. The entire staff of Wolf River County's largest and most luxurious hotel knew that nothing slipped past the general manager's penetrating gaze. The white marble floors and vast expanse of glass windows had better sparkle, the chic black uniforms be crisp, the massive floral arrangements fresh.

The sharp, sculpted planes of Sam's face and the hard angle of his jaw played well with his thick, dark hair and deep brown eyes. It was a combination that made grown women sigh and young girls giggle. Even with his football player's chest and lean waist, Sam's six-foot-four inch frame wore Armani well.

A few lucky women knew he wore nothing at all even better.

Joseph McFearson, the Four Winds doorman, tipped his hat when Sam approached. "Mornin', Mr. Prescott."

"Mornin', Joseph." Joseph was one of the few employees whose height—and eyes—directly met Sam's. "How's Isabel?"

"On a rampage our boys don't call more often," Joseph groused. "Says they got their father's cold heart."

Sam grinned. Everyone knew Joseph had a heart of gold, just as everyone knew that his wife adored him. "Give her my best."

"Will do." Joseph nodded, then added when Sam walked by, "Call your mother."

I probably should, Sam thought, realizing he hadn't talked to her for a while. Maybe he'd just send flowers. Last time he'd called her, all he'd heard was, "Samuel, you're thirty-two years old, when are you going to stop living in hotels and give me more grandchildren?"

"Soon as I meet a girl like you," he'd say to placate

her. He had no intention of changing his bachelor status any time soon, but he knew his mother needed hope, so he gave her that much.

His rounds complete, Sam stepped into a mirrored elevator, noted the quiet, instrumental version of McCartney's "Band On the Run" playing overhead. He had a ten o'clock briefing with Clair, an eleven-thirty lunch meeting with the publicist for the Central Texas Cattlemen's Association, then a two o'clock appointment with the city council and the Department of Building and Safety. The Four Winds had already outgrown its original tower, and the proposal for a second, taller tower and conference center had been submitted two weeks ago.

The elevator doors had nearly closed when a hand slipped in to stop them. Long, slim fingers, no rings, short but neat unpolished nails. Automatically, he pushed the open door button.

"Sorry," the woman muttered a bit breathlessly and stepped inside, her head down while she rummaged through a white purse.

She was taller than average, maybe five-nine, slender. Shoulder-length hair, shiny as polished coal, swept softly across her shoulders. Her suit was pale pink, the lace-edged camisole under the jacket lime-green. She'd turned away so he couldn't see her face.

Damn, she smelled good.

"What floor?" he offered, lifting a hand to the button panel.

"I've got it."

She started to punch a button on her side of the elevator, then pulled away when she saw it was already lit.

"Six?" *Turn*, he thought. *Just a couple of inches this way...*

She didn't. "Yes, thank you."

There was no smile in her voice. More of an I-can-handle-it-don't-bother-me polite tone.

Discreetly, he watched her in the mirror—it was, after all, he reasoned, part of his job to notice the people in his hotel. She seemed tense. Her shoulders and back just a little too straight, the grip on her purse a little too tight. The sixth floor was all offices, which probably meant she was here for business of some sort.

He started to introduce himself when the cell phone in his jacket pocket buzzed. He pulled it out and glanced at the caller ID. Clair.

The elevator doors opened smoothly and the woman hurried away. Sam stepped out, watched her walk down the hall, enjoyed the gentle sway of feminine hips and purposeful stride of long, sexy legs. When she paused at the door to Human Resources, he sighed. Too bad. If she was here for a job, his fantasy of soft black hair sliding over his naked chest was shattered.

Rule Number One: He did not date employees.

When his phone vibrated again, he flipped it open. "Mornin', Boss."

"You can be boss today, Prescott. In fact, I think I'll just give you the Four Winds and crawl back to my bed."

Sam frowned. "What's wrong?"

"I think the bug my nephews had last week decided to visit me, too," she said weakly. "Will you ask Suz to reschedule my appointments?"

"Sure." He noticed the woman was still standing

outside Human Resources, though it seemed a bit odd she had put her hand on the doorknob and not moved. "You need soup or something sent over?"

"Please," she groaned, "don't mention food. And Jacob's home today, so if I—oh, God, not again. Bye."

The line clicked dead. *Poor kid,* Sam sympathized, slipping his phone back into his pocket. He could think of much better ways to spend a day in bed.

That thought drew his glance back down the hall. The woman was gone. He could still smell her, though. A soft, pretty fragrance that seemed to whisper in his ear.

Damn.

He'd never even seen her face.

Heaving a sigh, he glanced at his watch and headed for his office, hesitated briefly outside of Human Resources, then kept going. Since Clair had cancelled their morning meeting, this would be a good time to get a jump on the end-of-the-month reports. At the rate the Four Winds was growing, he could barely keep up with the paperwork. He didn't have time to traipse after beautiful, mysterious women.

Halfway down the hall, he stopped.

Oh, hell, why not?

Even if she was applying for a job, she wasn't an employee *yet,* he figured. He turned back around and headed back for Human Resources. He might as well satisfy his curiosity while he had the chance. No harm in putting a face to that sexy body.

He stepped into the office and glanced around. Janet's secretary was not at her desk, and the door to the inner office was closed. The waiting room was empty.

Damn. He'd already missed her.

Slipping his hands into his pockets, Sam wandered closer to the closed door.

"I see you've had some restaurant experience, Miss Daniels," Sam heard Janet say. "Anything in particular?"

"Hostess, waitress, bussing," the woman replied. "Some kitchen training."

"Are you available nights, weekends and on call?"

Sam waited for the woman to mention a husband or children, but she didn't, simply answered that she was available whenever she was needed.

"Miss Daniels—"

"Please, call me Kiera."

"Kiera, you haven't listed any references on your application. Could you give me your last place of employment?"

"No, Mrs. Lamott. I—I'm sorry, but I can't."

No references? Sam lowered his brow. Janet couldn't possibly hire the woman without references.

"Kiera." Janet's voice softened. "My sister explained your situation to me, which is why I'm meeting with you so quickly."

Situation? Sam leaned closer to the door. What situation?

"I appreciate it, and I assure you, I'm a hard worker and learn quickly." Desperation edged the woman's voice. "I'll work any hours you ask, do whatever you need me to do, but please just give me a chance."

Sam narrowed his eyes and frowned. He didn't care what the woman looked like, or what her "situation" was. The Four Winds was not a charity. It was a business. They hired people based on qualifications, not because they said *please*.

Rule Number Two: Hotel policies applied equally to the *entire* staff.

Sam wished like hell he could see what was going on inside the office. He could hear both women speaking, but they'd lowered their voices and he couldn't make out their words. His ear was all but touching the door when he heard Janet speak again.

"Can you start tomorrow?"

What? Sam raised his head, then stared at the door and frowned. Janet had actually hired this woman without any references at all?

"Yes, of course I can start tomorrow. Thank you." The woman's voice trembled. "Thank you so much. You won't be sorry, I promise you."

"Go downstairs to the lower lobby employee entrance and ask for Francine. She'll fit you for a uniform."

He rarely interfered with the head of a department, but there were times it was necessary. Anything that took place here at the Four Winds was ultimately his responsibility, and that included hiring and firing. He straightened, set his jaw and prepared himself to face both women. Janet might not like it, but if he had to supersede a decision, then she'd just have to—

The door opened, and his mind simply went blank.

Her face was everything he'd imagined and quite a bit more. A sensuous, delicate sculpture of high cheekbones, straight nose and wide, full mouth. Smooth, sun-bronzed skin against deep, smoky-blue eyes. Eyes that considerably widened when they met his.

The faint tinge of black and blue next to one of those bewitching eyes was like a sucker punch in his gut.

"Sam, I didn't know you were here." Smiling, Janet moved to the door. "This is Kiera Daniels. Kiera, Sam Prescott, general manager of the Four Winds."

"Mr. Prescott." Kiera's smile never made her eyes. "How do you do."

He took the hand she offered; it was as soft as it was warm. "We're not formal here, Kiera. Just Sam."

"I hired Kiera for the lunch shift at Adagio's," Janet said. "She's on her way downstairs to see Francine."

"Welcome to the Four Winds." He realized he was still holding the woman's hand and reluctantly let go. "I'm headed in that direction. Why don't I show you the way?"

"I wouldn't want to trouble you." Kiera hitched her purse a little higher on her shoulder. "I can find my way."

"I'm sure you can." He kept his gaze steady with hers. "But it's no trouble at all."

He saw the resistance in her eyes, knew she wanted to refuse his offer but, under the circumstances, couldn't. He'd cornered her, and she countered with a lift of her chin and a nod.

Janet looked at Sam. "Was there something you needed?"

Something he needed? Oh, right. He *had* been lurking outside her office, hadn't he? "I want to take some stats into my lunch meeting with the Cattlemen's Association. I'd like to reassure them we have the staff to handle a convention their size."

"No problem." Janet's gaze shifted to Kiera and softened. "If you have any questions, or if you need anything at all, please don't hesitate to call me."

Sam set his back teeth. Obviously, Janet had let her heart rule her decision, not her head.

Rule Number Three: Do not get emotionally attached.

Which he wouldn't. But what he *would* do, at least for the moment, was trust Janet's decision.

And keep an eye on Miss Kiera Daniels himself.

"I know how busy you must be," Kiera said politely when he walked with her in the hallway. "I hate to trouble you."

"No trouble." He pressed the elevator button, slipped his hands casually into his pants' pockets. "My ten o'clock meeting was cancelled."

Her lips pressed into a tight smile before she turned away to adjust the strap of her purse. With her attention elsewhere, he allowed himself the pleasure of drawing her scent into his lungs, held it there for a long moment.

And for reasons that had nothing to do with hotel policy, wished like hell Janet *hadn't* hired her.

"In fact—" he followed her onto the elevator when the doors slid open, made a decision he was certain he'd regret "—since I'm free for the next hour, why don't I give you a tour?"

Two

Kiera was certain she hadn't heard him right. She cleared her throat and calmly met his eyes. Dark, intense eyes, that seemed to bore straight through her. "A tour?"

"Every person on the staff needs to know their way around the hotel." He pushed the elevator button. "But if you haven't the time…"

"Not at all." Why would he do this? She'd worked in hotels before, knew perfectly well that the general manager didn't take new employees on a tour. She also knew perfectly well she couldn't refuse. "Now is fine."

"Good."

The smile he gave her made her pulse jump. Something told her that very few people—especially women—ever said no to Sam Prescott. He had a…*presence,* she thought. Not just his height, or the broad stretch of shoulders. Not even those lethal eyes, strong jaw and thick, espresso-brown hair.

No, it was much more than the way he looked. The first time she'd stepped into the elevator with him, she'd *felt* it.

Power.

The air inside the elevator had sizzled with it. She'd intentionally kept her gaze turned from him, even when she'd felt the gripping pull to look. Perhaps for self-preservation, perhaps to prove to herself that she *could* resist. She hadn't even been able to breathe until she'd stepped out of the elevator.

And here she was again. Same elevator. Same man. Same sizzle.

Trey had told her on more than one occasion that she was naive. When they'd argued before she'd left the ranch, he'd told her again. So maybe she was. But she wasn't *so* naive to think that Sam Prescott standing outside Mrs. Lamott's office door was an accident. And she wasn't so naive to think that this *tour* he wanted to take her on was hotel policy.

She certainly hadn't done anything to attract this man's unwanted attention. As far as he knew, she was simply a new employee—a waitress. There was nothing about her that should warrant interest from a general manager.

Unless he suspected she wasn't being completely honest…

Oh, good grief, Kiera, she silently chided herself. *You're being paranoid.* Of *course* he doesn't suspect anything. How could he?

This has to be the slowest elevator I've ever been on.

"You're not from around here," he said flatly.

She hesitated, decided that the best way to avoid questions was to offer information. It might be useless information, but she hoped it would alleviate any apprehensions he might have about her. "I was born and raised in East Texas. Have you heard of a town called Rainville?"

"Can't say that I have."

"It's not exactly a tourist spot." It wasn't *exactly* where she was from, either, though it was close. "Unless you're interested in honey."

"Honey?"

"Rainville's claim to fame." When the elevator finally slid to a stop, she stepped forward. "They raise bees."

"Really."

When he pressed the button to keep the doors closed, then leveled those piercing eyes at her, Kiera's stomach twisted.

"What happened to your eye?" he asked.

Her eye? Confused, she stared at him. Oh, her *eye*. She'd forgotten about that. She released the breath she'd been holding, waited a moment for her pulse to slow down. "I fell off a horse."

His frown darkened. "I'm not asking to be nosy. If you have a problem that might become this hotel's problem, I need to know."

So *that's* what he was suspicious about, she realized. Not because he knew who she was or that she lied but because of her black eye. Relief poured through her. "Everyone has problems, Mr. Prescott," she said evenly. "But I assure you, whatever mine are, they will in no way affect my job or this hotel."

He stared at her for a long, nerve-racking moment,

then removed his finger from the button. "Sam," he said and straightened.

The elevator doors opened and he stepped out.

On unsteady legs, she followed.

The decor at Adagio's Ristorante was elegant and contemporary. Crisp white linens, airy palms and high ceilings invited diners to relax, while the menu invited them to indulge. Homemade fusilli, a carpaccio sauce that made even the most hardened critic shed tears and "the best crème brûlée on the northern continent," according to one reviewer, had made the restaurant legendary in the few short years it had been open.

The fragrant scent of warm spices and fresh bread mixed with the clink of tableware. The lunch crowd was always louder than dinner, and the animated voices of hotel guests and local business owners filled the softly lit room.

Sitting in a corner booth, Sam speared a bite of the steak he'd ordered, chewed attentively while Rachel Forster, publicist for the Central Texas Cattlemen's Association, discussed her schedule.

"I'll be sending out a press release to all the local newspapers within a hundred-mile radius, and I have a photographer coming out next Tuesday," Rachel said. "I'll have him call to set up an appointment."

It was more information than Sam really needed, but the blonde sitting across from him, young, extremely efficient and heavily armed with pages of notes, seemed determined to go over every minute detail of the upcoming conference.

"I'd also like to write an article for *The Dallas Register* on the Four Winds chef. I understand he's won the Hotelier's Choice Award three years in a row. I thought maybe I could tie that in with some kind of a Texas beef angle."

"Chef Bartollini is on hiatus for the next six months." Actually, he'd flown home to Italy for a family emergency, and, unfortunately, no one knew when, or if, the man would return. "Chef Phillipe Girard is with us until then."

"Would it be possible for me to meet him?" she asked.

Not a good idea, Sam thought, but simply smiled. "I'll see what I can do."

"I'd appreciate that, and oh, I was wondering—" she pushed her black-rimmed glasses up the bridge of her nose and scribbled on her notepad "—I'd like to meet the new owner and get some background so I can write a story about her, as well."

"She's out of the office today." Sam doubted that Clair would consent to an interview. Even though most of the people in Wolf River knew her family history, Clair wouldn't want it printed in newspapers across the state. "Why don't I have her secretary call you?"

When the publicist moved on to the next item on her list, transportation issues, Sam listened patiently. Well, *half* listened, anyway.

He glanced across the crowded restaurant to the serving station, where Kiera busily filled water glasses with ice. Francine had already fitted her with Adagio's standard uniform: white, long-sleeved shirt and tailored black slacks. The only variation the restaurant allowed for the servers was their personal choice of tie. Kiera's was silver, with thin stripes of white and black. She'd knotted her dark hair on top of her head and secured it with shiny red chopsticks. The style not only revealed her long, slender neck but gave her an exotic look, as well.

Unwanted, restless, something stirred in him.

The tour he'd taken her on had included the lobby, conference rooms, employee gym and wedding chapel. She'd paid attention and asked several questions regarding hotel policies but had kept a stiff, polite demeanor. In itself, that wasn't odd, he reasoned. New employees were usually nervous around him. But with Kiera, she hadn't seemed nervous as much as simply reluctant to be anywhere near him.

Especially when he'd questioned her about her eye.

I fell off a horse.

Who the hell did she think she was kidding with that line? She might as well have said she'd walked into a doorknob, for God's sake. And why the hell should he believe her problems wouldn't follow her here? Because she'd said so?

She was hiding something, that much was obvious. For now, he decided he'd simply keep an eye on her.

Which was exactly what he was doing, he thought, watching as she hefted the tray of water glasses. When she moved smoothly toward a table of noisy businessmen, the silver in her tie shimmered.

Dammit. Why the hell did he think that tie looked so damn sexy?

"Will that be possible?"

Sam realized the publicist had asked him a question,

something about the banquet meals, and he snapped his attention back to her. He had no idea what the woman had said, so he flashed a smile. "I'll personally work with the catering department to see that your every need is met."

"Oh—" Flustered, Rachel's face turned rose-pink. She fumbled through her papers. "Well, thank you. Ah, now if we could go over the local publicity I've planned, I'd like to be sure it meets with your approval."

"Of course." With a silent sigh, Sam dragged his mind off the woman serving water several feet away and back to his job.

"Hey, babe, I need two iced teas and one soda at table six, one coffee, one soda at eight, refills at ten and eleven."

Kiera quickly memorized and filled the order, didn't bother to take the time to be annoyed that Tyler, the server she'd been paired with her first day, had pretty much called her everything except her name. She understood there was a pecking order in every restaurant, and as the new girl she was going to have to take her share of hits. She'd been there before and she could handle it.

What she couldn't handle, she thought, hefting the tray of drinks, was Sam Prescott.

He'd been watching her from that corner booth for the past hour. He hadn't been obvious about it, but, nonetheless, she'd been very aware that he'd been keeping track of her. As if it wasn't difficult enough that this was her first day on the job and she had to not only learn the staff's names, the layout of the restaurant and the stations, but keep her orders straight so Tyler-honey-baby-sugar-darling wouldn't be on her back.

While she smiled and dropped off the first order of two iced teas and a soda, she casually glanced in Sam's direction. He sat with a cupid-faced blonde who wore thick-framed glasses and a tailored pantsuit the color of buttered toast. They appeared to be having a serious conversation, although the woman was doing most of the talking, while Sam simply listened and nodded.

She knew he didn't trust her, and that tour he'd taken her on had been more of a fishing expedition than anything else. Even his questions hadn't been all that subtle.

Have you been in town long? Not really.

Will your husband be joining you? No.

So what brings you to Wolf River?

She'd wanted to say, "A car," but managed a response that was much more vague and certainly more polite. Her answers hadn't satisfied him, but something told her that Sam Prescott was not a man who was easily satisfied.

She knew all about men like that.

His gaze suddenly lifted and met hers. The knot of stress in her stomach twisted a little tighter, but she managed to curve her lips into what she hoped looked like a smile, then moved on and finished delivering her drinks. She hadn't even dropped off the tray in her hands before Tyler thrust another one at her.

"Take these salads to table ten. One chicken barbecue and one Caesar. And hurry it up, will you, toots? Table six is waiting for more bread."

Toots? Kiera ground her teeth, bit the inside of her lip, then turned with the tray.

And froze.

Trey?

Kiera stared at the man talking to the hostess. His back was turned to her, but it *had* to be Trey. Same wavy devil-black hair, same broad shoulders, same bronzed skin. That all-too familiar stance of arrogant authority.

Oh, God. She felt the blood drain from her face. *How had he found her?*

"Move it, sweet cheeks."

Startled at the sudden voice behind her, Kiera swung around too quickly and knocked the tray into Tyler. To her horror—and Tyler's—the food went down the front of him. The tray and salad plates crashed to the ground.

"You *idiot!*" Tyler hissed under his breath while he swiped at the bits of shredded lettuce and diced tomatoes clinging to his white shirt and burgundy tie. Barbecue sauce dripped from his collar.

Every head in the restaurant turned her way, but Kiera only cared about one. She glanced back toward the hostess desk, locked her gaze with a pair of curious dark brown eyes.

Oh, thank God.

It *wasn't* Trey.

Even as Tyler continued to berate her, overwhelming relief swam through her. Relief that quickly dissipated when Chef Phillipe Girard stepped through the double kitchen doors.

Her first thought was he looked like a rutabaga, round at the top, narrow at the bottom. Fleshy cheeks framed an oversized nose and underscored pale, deep-set eyes. A tall, black chef's hat sat like an exclamation point on top of a sand-colored ponytail. He had a knife in one hand and an onion in the other.

Kiera had heard about the man from a couple of the other servers. She'd been warned, "Stay out of his way," "Don't make him mad" and double-warned, "Don't mess with his food."

In the span of less than thirty seconds, she'd managed to do all three.

Based on the chef's ominous frown, Kiera had the feeling he'd like to dice and chop more than onions. He glared down his large nose at her.

"Clean this mess up immediately," he snarled, then he turned and swept back into the kitchen.

Releasing the breath she'd been holding, Kiera bent and picked up the tray and broken salad plates.

"You've done it now, miss butterfingers," Tyler hissed, still brushing bits of green and red from his shirt. "He'll take it out on all of us and God only knows what hell he'll put—"

"Tyler, that's enough."

Kiera looked up and met Sam's somber gaze. She couldn't quite read his expression, but when he shifted his attention to Tyler, Sam's mouth hardened.

"It wasn't my fault." Tyler pursed his lips. "I was just—"

"Never mind. Go change your shirt. Christine can cover for you until you get back."

"Yes, sir." Tyler tossed a look of annoyance at Kiera as he flounced off.

A busboy appeared with a trash bag and hand broom. When Sam cupped a hand on her elbow, Kiera pulled away. "I'll finish here," she said anxiously, still picking up chunks of broken plate. "I can help with those tables, too."

"Not necessary." Sam wrapped his fingers around her arm, tighter this time, and pulled her up. "Come with me."

Every bone in her body, every *cell,* vibrated in protest. *Terrific.* Just what she needed. One more lecture. He released her arm and turned away. Because she didn't want to make a scene—again—she followed Sam through the restaurant, down a hallway of offices, then outside to a shaded back alley.

An air conditioning motor whirred and blew hot air over her feet; in the distance, church bells chimed the three o'clock hour.

She lifted her chin, prepared herself to be fired. *A perfect end to the perfect day.*

"What happened in there?" he asked.

"I tripped."

He frowned at her. "Has anyone ever told you that you're a lousy liar?"

Trey, she thought. And Alexis and Alaina. But she sure as hell didn't need *this* man telling her. Still, common sense overrode defiance, and rather than speak she pressed her lips firmly together and stared blankly at him.

"You didn't trip, Kiera," he said evenly. "I was watching you. Something spooked you."

"Maybe it was you watching me."

He lifted an eyebrow. "Do I make you nervous?"

"It's not unusual to be nervous when the boss is staring at you."

"You have an interesting way of avoiding a direct answer to a direct question." He studied her face. "Do *I* make *you* nervous?"

Yes, dammit, she thought. But she had no intention

of admitting it. She glanced over her shoulder. "I really should be getting back to work."

"You turned white as your blouse when you looked at Rand," Sam replied, ignoring her comment. "Do you know him?"

"Rand?" she asked calmly, but her heart skipped a beat. Sam had obviously seen her staring at the man who looked so much like Trey. "Who is Rand?"

"There you go again." Sighing, he shook his head. "Rand Blackhawk. He moved back to Wolf River a few months ago, got married. He's rebuilding the family ranch outside of town."

She gave him her best I'm-really-not-interested expression, but her heart was beating fast. "Fascinating story, but I've never seen him before."

Sam moved closer. "But he looks like someone you know, doesn't he? Someone you're worried might find you."

He was too close, not only in his estimation of her situation, but physically. Close enough she could see the subtle but fierce striations of deep brown in his irises, the web of lines at the corners of his eyes, the thick fringe of lashes. His scent was pure male, and the female in her reluctantly responded.

"No one is looking for me, Mr. Prescott." For once, she could answer a question truthfully. At least, she *prayed* it was true. "Now if you're going to fire me, then fire me. Otherwise, I'd appreciate it if you'd let me get back to work."

He stared at her for a long moment, then stepped back. "I'll speak to the chef. I know he can be difficult."

She knew that Chef Phillipe would only dislike her all the more if Sam said even one word to him about her. "Thank you, but that's really not necessary."

Somehow she managed to walk away without stumbling or without looking back. In the employee restroom, she let out a long breath, shook off her jitters, then washed her hands and returned to her station. The spill had been cleaned up and Tyler had changed into a clean shirt and tie. His surly attitude, however, remained the same. He glared at her and gestured to a pitcher of iced tea.

"Refills at ten and twelve, miss grace, if you think you can manage without spilling anything."

Enough was enough.

Narrowing her eyes, Kiera moved in close to the server, stuck her face nose to nose with his and pressed a fingertip against his bony chest. "My name is Kiera. Got that? *Kiera.* Next time you call me anything else, next time you insult me, next time you even look at me with disrespect, you're going to be wearing more than a few scraps of lettuce and barbecue sauce."

Smiling, she smoothed a hand over the startled server's clean tie, then turned and picked up the iced tea. Red-faced, Tyler moved out of her way.

So much for keeping things low key, she thought while she refilled glasses. Rand Blackhawk. She glanced at the man now sitting in a booth with a pretty redhead, then quickly looked away before she did something stupid.

Too late, she thought with a sigh, then watched Sam walk back into the restaurant.

Way too late.

Three

With the Fourth of July only two weeks away, the town of Wolf River had already tuned up to celebrate. Red-white-and-blue bunting adorned the two-story brick store-fronts down Main Street, patriotic slogans welcomed tourists, posters announced an upcoming rodeo and carnival. The holiday would bring in tourists from across the country and locals as far away as Houston.

It might be a small town, but it was a busy small town.

And growing every day, Sam noted as he strolled down the sidewalk. On Main Street, the city council had carefully kept Wolf River's country charm through strict building ordinances, but off the main drag they had slowly allowed the big city in. Three-story office build-ings, two fast-food restaurants, a small water park, a multiplex theater and the most recent addition, a country-western dinner house with live entertainment and nightly line dancing. Sam had heard the rib-eye steaks were as thick as a phone book and tender as warm butter. He made a mental note to check it out for himself soon.

"Gonna be a hot one," Fergus Crum said dryly. The old man had been pushing a broom across the sidewalk in front of the hardware store, but he stopped and rested his arthritic hands on the broom handle when he spotted Sam coming his way.

"Come by the bar after work," Sam said as he passed. "Have a cold one on me."

"I'll do that." Fergus was never one to turn down a cold beer. Or any beer, for that matter. "How 'bout some of those onion thingies, too?"

"You got it."

Sam nodded at a local rancher coming out of the barbershop and the man touched the brim of his cowboy hat. Even though Sam knew most of the locals, he didn't come into town very often. He had no reason to. Most everything he needed he could get at the hotel. Food, clothes, even a car. He had few personal possessions, considered them a hindrance when it was time to pick up and move on. He kept his life—professional and personal—simple.

Exactly how he liked it.

His two-year contract with the Four Winds had been up for two months now. Clair had been pressing him to sign a new one, but he'd put her off. He figured it was about time to start putting out feelers for his next job. His entire life, he'd never lived more than three years in one place. He had no intention of breaking that record any time soon.

"Hey, handsome, where you headed?"

Sam smiled when Olivia Cameron pulled her sleek red Camaro up to the curb alongside him. The stunning redhead owned Vintage Rose, one of the antique stores in Wolf River and she'd also done the interior design on the lobby in the Four Winds.

He leaned into her open car window and gave her a kiss on the cheek. "On my way to the courthouse, gorgeous."

Her green eyes sparkled. "You finally going to apply for our marriage license?"

"Just say the word, Liv." They'd gone out on a couple of dates, but the chemistry hadn't quite been there between them, so they'd settled into a more comfortable, flirtatious friendship. "We could buy one of those tract homes they're building in Oak Meadows. Have a half dozen kids and join the PTA."

Olivia winced. "I'll get back to you one of these decades. Want a ride?"

He straightened and patted his stomach. "Walk will do me good."

"As if you need it. Every woman in this town knows you work out from five to six-thirty every morning in the Four Winds gym." Olivia gunned her engine. "Why do you think there are so many females in there at that ungodly hour?"

With a wink, Olivia shot away from the curb.

Grinning, Sam watched her disappear around the corner, wished there had been chemistry between them. Like him, the woman wasn't looking for a commitment or a picket fence. They could have simply enjoyed each other, without worrying about the theatrics or complications of a messy breakup. Olivia could have been an enjoyable distraction.

And Lord knew, right now he certainly needed one.

He'd spent the past three days watching Kiera. Watched her effortlessly memorize the menu and wine list. Watched her skillfully serve a heavy tray of dishes without fumbling or getting an order wrong. Watched her astutely make recommendations, then offer suggestions for a complimentary wine. Already, she not only had people asking for her station but actually waiting for her.

He'd never seen anything like it.

But—to his annoyance—he hadn't just been watching her. He'd also been *thinking* about her.

At the most unexpected times, he'd suddenly find himself wondering what the woman's story was, who or what she was running away from. If she was in some kind of danger.

The bruise next to her eye had nearly disappeared, but he couldn't get the image out of his mind. Couldn't stop the raw fury that knotted his gut every time he thought about it. The idea of some man raising his fist and—

Realizing he had balled his own hand into a tight fist, he stopped in front of the barbershop, stared at the swirling red-white-and-blue pole. He loosened his fingers, then shook off the anger bubbling through his blood. Dammit! A walk through town on his day off should have cleared his mind and relaxed him, and here he was, barreling down the sidewalk as if he were looking for a fight.

Maybe I am, he thought with a sigh. Lord knew the woman had frustrated him enough. It was obvious she had a problem, obvious that she'd been scared to death when she'd looked at Rand Blackhawk. Obvious she was lying about something. When he'd asked her if Rand looked like someone she knew, the answer in those smoky blue eyes of hers had obviously been *yes.*

And *obviously,* she hadn't wanted his help.

So fine. Why should that bother him?

He waited for a truck to pass, then crossed the street leading to the courthouse. As long as her problem didn't become the hotel's, then he'd keep his nose out of her mess. Lord knew he'd already given Kiera Daniels way too much time and thought. He was a busy man. With the upcoming conferences and events, not to mention the impending construction on the hotel, his focus needed to be on his job, not a pretty waitress.

And then suddenly that pretty waitress was walking out of the glass courthouse doors.

Surprised, he stopped beside a hedge of white blooming roses. Good God, he thought with annoyance. He couldn't even get away from her here.

Head bent, loose-limbed, she moved down the courthouse steps, her eyes focused on a piece of paper in her hand. She wore denim as if it had been invented just for those endlessly long legs of hers. Her jeans, low on her hips and snug, were faded in all the places a man liked to look. And touch. Her white tank top dipped demurely across her collarbone and hugged her breasts, then rose just high enough from her hips to show the barest hint of smooth, flat stomach.

A drought settled in his throat.

It took a will of iron to drag his gaze upward from that enticing glimpse of skin. A frown drew the delicate line of her eyebrows together and settled into a somber line across her mouth. Her hair flowed like a black river down her shoulders. The sun glinted off the dark strands.

For a split second, he didn't even know where he was.

He blinked hard, watched her fold the piece of paper and shove it into a black tote bag as she turned and walked in the opposite direction.

He argued with himself, lost, waited a full twenty seconds, then followed her.

The mouth-watering scent of grilling hamburgers drew Kiera toward the coffee shop on the corner. The exterior of the restaurant, shiny chrome, sleek lines and wrap-around windows reminded her of the '57 Chevy that Mr. Mackelroy, her high school principal, used to drive. Even the color was the same, she thought. Sorbet-blue.

When she stepped inside, life-size cardboard cut-outs of James Dean and Marilyn Monroe greeted her with a sign that said Welcome To Pappa Pete's. Kiera closed the door behind her, barely heard the jangling of the bells over the drumming of a Beach Boys song playing on an overhead speaker and the lively conversations from the lunch crowd. Locals, Kiera thought, noting the mix of families, town workers and ranch hands.

A tall, thick-boned, platinum blonde carrying four plates of burgers on one arm and two plates of French fries on the other bustled by Kiera. "Set yerself down anywhere you like, honey. Something to drink?"

Kiera smiled. "Lemonade, please."

"Hey, Madge, what about me?" A slumped-back cowboy sitting at a counter stool held up his coffee cup. "I'm still waiting for a refill."

"You're still waitin' for brains, too," Madge shot back. "Everyone knows you were in the basement when they got handed out."

"Yeah, well, everyone knows you were at the front door when tongues got handed out," the cowboy quipped, which brought a round of laughter from the patrons.

"Least I got something in my skull that works." Madge plunked the fries down on a table. "If your thinker was a mattress, an ant's feet would stick off the sides."

"That's not all I heard was ant size," someone in the front hollered, setting off a fresh round of laughter and a volley of replies. Red-faced, the cowboy got up, snatched a coffeepot from behind the counter and served himself.

While the wisecracks continued to fly, Kiera sat down at a Formica-topped table next to a window in the back. A teenage boy who hadn't quite grown into his long legs and arms set a glass of pink lemonade in front of her. She smiled and thanked the busboy, who turned beet-red, then turned and stumbled over his own big feet. One of the ranchers teased the boy, which set in motion a new volley of quips.

If she closed her eyes, she could almost imagine she was in her own hometown, sitting in the Bronco Cafe, adding her own two cents to the banter and good-natured fun. Even the smell was the same. Burgers, grease and pressed wood paneling. A good smell, she thought. Familiar. Comfortable. Since graduating college, then working her fanny off at restaurants across the country, she could probably count on one hand the times she'd even been back to the Bronco in the past six years.

Living in a small town could be difficult, she knew. The gossip, the politics, certainly the lack of privacy, all of it was a major pain in the butt. The closest city with a mall had been three hours away, the only theater showed movies two months old and the few dates she had been on had felt more like going out with a best friend or a brother.

But the camaraderie, knowing that there were always people who would pull together and help if you needed them, people who really gave a damn, was worth not only the isolation she'd often felt at Stone Ridge Ranch, but the aggravation of everyone knowing her family's business.

And now the question was, *did* everyone know?

She certainly hadn't.

With a sigh, she pulled the piece of paper out of her bag and spread it on the table in front of her, stared at the obituary, felt every word etch into her brain like acid.

> William Blackhawk…local rancher, business-man and community leader…died in a small plane crash…survived by his son, Dillon Black-hawk…services to be held Thursday at Wolf River Community Church…

That was two years ago.

Two years.

She closed her eyes against the fresh wave of pain coursing through her. If she'd known then what she knew now, what would she have done?

She honestly didn't know.

"Mind if I join you?"

Jolted out of her thoughts by the question, the terse "yes" on the edge of her tongue nearly slipped out. Her pulse jumped when she looked up.

Sam.

She prayed her hands weren't visibly shaking as she folded the piece of paper and slipped it back into her bag. Despite the fact that she would have preferred to be alone at the moment, she couldn't very well tell her boss to take a hike.

And since he had already slid into the booth across from her, he really hadn't given her much of a choice, anyway.

When she glanced around the room, several curious eyes quickly looked away. Terrific. No one in the diner knew who she was, but everyone in the place surely knew who Sam Prescott was. Before the day was over, Kiera had no doubt that rumors of the Four Winds general manager having an afternoon rendezvous with an unknown woman would be burning up the phone lines.

Sam followed her gaze. "You expecting someone?"

"No." She looked back at him, took in the street clothes he wore. She'd thought him handsome in a suit. Confident. Absolutely unwavering and completely sure of himself. But it had nothing to do with clothes, she realized, taking in the stretch of black T-shirt across his broad shoulders and muscled arms. Apparently, the rumors she'd heard about him working out in the gym every morning were true. "I was just running errands and stopped in for something to eat."

"You picked the right place." He leaned in close and whispered, "Best hamburger in town, though if you tell anyone I said so, I'll deny it."

The smile on his mouth disarmed her, had her whispering back, "I think I can manage to keep a secret."

"Yeah." He studied her for a moment. "I think you can."

She stilled at his comment, arched an eyebrow and settled back in her chair. "You sure you aren't here for fish, Mr. Prescott?"

Smiling, he settled back in his chair, as well.

An unseen cook in the kitchen dinged three times on a bell to signal an order was up.

Round one, Kiera thought absently.

"So how's it going?" Sam asked.

"I assume you're referring to my job."

"Of course."

She picked up her lemonade, sipped. "Why don't you tell me?"

"Okay." He folded his hands on the table and straightened his shoulders. "Your ratio of tables to gross and time are in the ninetieth percentile and an initial review of customer comments is exceptional."

In spite of the deep, official tone of his voice, Kiera saw the glint of a rogue in Sam's eyes. "Sounds like I should ask for a raise."

"I'm afraid that request would be denied. You've had two complaints filed against you."

"What!" Lemonade sloshed over the rim of her glass and ran down the front of her tank top; a sliver of ice slid under the cotton neckline and into her bra. Frowning, she grabbed a napkin.

He signaled for the busboy. "Tyler says you're difficult to work with."

Tyler's an ass, she nearly said, but managed to bite
her tongue. She'd worked with jerks like him before. He
was a good waiter, but he kissed up to the manager and
chef, patronized the rest of the staff and gossiped worse
than a tabloid columnist.

She had nothing to gain by defending herself or ac-
knowledging the waiter's complaint had even the tiniest
bit of merit. Nor did she have anything to gain by retaliat-
ing. Sooner or later, Tyler would have to face retribution.

Too bad she wouldn't be around to see it.

"Hey, Mr. Prescott." The busboy appeared beside the
table. "You want coffee or—"

Sam watched the dazed expression fall over the
teenager's face when his eyes dropped to the front of
Kiera's damp tank top. The boy's jaw went slack.

"Eddie," Sam prompted.

No response.

Sam sighed. It wasn't that he blamed the kid for
staring. Hell, it was all he could do not to stare himself.
Kiera was too busy dabbing at her chest to notice that
she'd attracted the attention of most of the men in the
restaurant.

"Eddie," Sam repeated.

"Huh?" The busboy blinked and looked at Sam.

"The towel?"

"Oh, sure, Mr. Prescott." Eddie grabbed the towel
from the waistband of his apron and reached out as if
to wipe the front of Kiera's chest.

Sam moved quicker than the boy and grabbed the

towel away. Realizing what he'd almost done, Eddie blushed deeply.

"I think we can manage now, thanks." Sam handed the towel to Kiera. "How 'bout you just bring me that cup of coffee?"

"Sure, Mr. Prescott." Eddie glanced at Kiera and swallowed hard. "You, ah, need anything, miss?"

"I'm fine, thanks." Kiera managed a smile. "I just spilled some lemonade, that's all."

"I—I'll get you some more," he stammered. "You need some water, too? 'Cause I could go get that, case that might stain or something, or maybe you want some club soda—"

"Edward Morrison!" Madge stormed up behind the boy. "Stop drooling over that girl and go get Sam here some coffee."

"Yes, ma'am." Eddie cast one last, puppy-dog look at Kiera.

"Sometime before Christmas?" Madge barked, then shook her head when the boy shuffled off. "What do you think, Sam? You're the big business expert here. Should I fire him?"

"Absolutely."

Kiera's mouth dropped open.

"I'll give him the boot after he brings your coffee." Madge grabbed the pencil she'd stuck over her ear. "The boy's a pain-in-the-butt, anyway. So what'll you have today? The usual?"

"We both will," Sam replied. "Extra cheese."

"Wait—"

"You got it." Madge scribbled on her order pad, then

stuck her pencil behind her ear and snatched up the menu on the table.

Kiera called after the waitress again, but Madge was too busy hollering the order to the cook to hear.

"How could you do such a thing?" Kiera said through clenched teeth. "He's just a kid, a sweet kid, who was just trying to be helpful."

The "sweet" kid reappeared with a mug in one hand and pot of coffee in the other. If he'd been looking at the mug instead of Kiera when he poured, Eddie might have even managed to get some of the coffee in the cup. He jumped when he realized he'd missed, reached for his towel, only to remember he'd given it to Kiera.

"Sorry, Mr. Prescott," Eddie apologized. "I'll be right back."

"I've got it." Kiera was already wiping the spill up. "It was just a drop."

"I'll get another towel," Eddie said and hurried—well, for Eddie it was hurried—off. Sam stared at his empty coffee cup, the mess on the table, then looked back up at Kiera. He gave her an I-told-you-so look.

"Don't you *dare* get that boy fired." She put her hands on the table and leaned forward. Outrage sparked in her blue eyes and flushed her cheeks pink. "You call the owner back here right now and tell her you were just kidding or so help me I'll—"

Kiera stopped suddenly, pressed her mouth into a thin line.

Sam raised an eyebrow. "You'll what?"

He could almost hear Kiera doing battle in her brain.

Her need to defend a slow, clumsy busboy warring with her need to tell her boss off.

"You'll what?" he asked again, lowering his voice. He was dying to know.

"Please." Her fury dissipated like smoke in a breeze. "Please, don't."

He might have strung her along another minute or two, but the desperate look in her eyes, the soft, pleading tone in her voice, took all the fun out of it. "Kiera, Eddie is Madge's son. She fires him at least once a day. Sometimes twice."

"Madge's son?" Kiera glanced at the busboy, who'd already forgotten about bringing a towel and was busy posturing for a cute teenage girl who'd just walked in the front door.

Sam nodded. "The youngest of six boys."

Kiera's eyes widened. "She has *six* boys?"

"Yep." He watched Madge come up behind her son and grab his earlobe, then drag him into the kitchen, lecturing him the whole way. "And she can say whatever she likes about any one of them, but if she hears someone else say anything close to criticism…well, let's just say you wouldn't want to be within ten yards. When her temper's up, the woman moves a lot quicker than you'd think."

"I believe you," Kiera said, then met his gaze. "I…I'm sorry. I guess I got a little carried away."

It struck him how incredibly beautiful she'd looked a moment ago—her face animated with anger, her chin lifted with indignation—and he couldn't stop himself from wondering what all that intensity of emotion and energy would be like in bed.

His bed.

The image of Kiera naked, underneath him, her body arching upward into his—

Madge slid a mug of steaming coffee in front of Sam and frowned. "What is it about teenage boys and hormones that makes them dumb as a post?"

And then she was off again, shaking her head as she walked back to the kitchen, obviously not looking for an answer.

Teenage boys have nothing on us big boys, Sam thought, thankful to have his mind diverted from his fantasy of Kiera. When he glanced at her, he could see she was smiling while she sipped on her lemonade.

He couldn't figure her out. The day she'd dropped the tray of drinks, she wouldn't say one word to defend herself, but today, when she thought that a busboy was going to get the axe, she'd wanted to reach across the table and rip out his liver.

The woman absolutely fascinated him.

"So are you going to tell me?" she asked.

"Tell you?"

"You said there were two complaints."

"Oh, right." In spite of her cool tone, he could see the tension in the rigid line of her shoulders. "Chef Phillipe said you questioned his authority."

"Did he?" Her lips pressed into a thin line.

"Did you?"

She shrugged. "I simply suggested he might have put too much thyme in his chicken kiev."

Sam wasn't certain he'd heard her right. In the two months the replacement chef had been with Adagio's, no one on staff in the restaurant had *ever* questioned him. They wouldn't dare. When it came to his kitchen, the man was a tyrant. "You told Chef Phillipe that he put too much thyme in his chicken?"

"I'm sure it was a mistake," Kiera said.

"You bet it was a mistake."

She frowned. "I meant the chef's mistake."

He stared at her in disbelief. "How do you know he used too much thyme?"

She hesitated, took a long sip of her lemonade. "I could smell it."

"You *smelled* it?" He was amazed that the chef hadn't stuffed Kiera in the pantry and put a double padlock on the door.

"I have an extraordinary sense of smell and taste."

She definitely had an extraordinary smell, Sam thought. From the first moment she'd stepped into the elevator, he'd been captivated by her scent. And her taste…his gaze dropped to her mouth. Right now she'd taste like pink lemonade, and dammit if he didn't want to lick that tart sweetness off those enticing lips. He tried his best not to think about the path the spilled lemonade had taken under her tank top. Tried not to wonder what it would feel like to taste that lemonade on her skin, her breasts…

He tossed back a gulp of coffee, though what he really needed was a tall glass of iced water—poured directly below his belt.

"I'm sorry," she said quietly, carefully setting her glass on the table. "I shouldn't have said anything to Chef Phillipe. I was out of place. I assure you, it won't happen again."

Her contrite tone bothered him much more than anything else she'd said or done. He'd caught a glimpse of the fire simmering just under her surface, an intensity that she clearly kept tamped down.

He wanted to know *why,* dammit. Wanted to know what it was she was so obviously running away from. Why she needed to keep herself so controlled and distant.

It might not be today, he mused.

But he intended to find out.

Four

"Mrs. Carver is just finishing up a phone call, Miss Daniels. Why don't you have a seat?"

Kiera managed a smile at the middle-aged brunette receptionist, then sat stiffly on the tan leather sofa. Afraid that her knees might start knocking, she gripped her thighs and held them tightly.

She was about to meet Clair Carver.

Clair *Blackhawk*.

A knot the size of a trucker's fist twisted in her stomach.

She'd been setting up her lunch station not even ten minutes ago when the restaurant manager, Christine, gave her the message to report to Clair's office. Kiera's first thought was that there'd been more complaints filed against her. Tyler had lightened up a little, but Chef Phillipe had been storming about the kitchen since she'd called him on his faux pas. She'd done her best to keep her opinions to herself, be polite and stay out of the chef's way, but if he wasn't barking orders at her, he was muttering under his breath about mindless, insipid waitresses.

Obviously, the man held a grudge.

Still, Kiera seriously doubted that Clair would handle a problem between a chef and a waitress. Normally, owners didn't get involved in the day-to-day operations of a larger hotel. They had staff for that.

Which led to her second, and definitely more frightening, thought.

Clair knows who I am.

The fist in her stomach twisted tighter.

But how *could* she?

Sam?

As careful as she'd been to cover her tracks, if he'd been curious enough, if he'd dug deep enough and made the right phone calls, it was possible he might have learned who she was. Maybe even why she was here. But it was doubtful. And he certainly hadn't *seemed* curious. Or even interested, for that matter. In fact, for the past four days, since they'd had lunch together at Pappa Pete's, he'd barely even looked at her. She wasn't certain if she was relieved or disappointed.

Both, she decided.

There was no question she was attracted to the man. Butterflies-in-the-stomach attracted. Can't-stop-thinking-about-him attracted.

Fantasy attracted.

When she least expected it, they'd sneak up on her. Those insidious little erotic daydreams. Bare, hot skin against bare, hot skin. Arms and legs intertwined. Busy hands, rushing lips. Sometimes her fantasy involved a bed, sometimes an elevator. In his office—on his desk—was her personal favorite. Sizzling, no-holds-barred sex. Wild. Frantic. Spontaneous. He was as mad for her as she was for him, reaching, gasping…

"Miss Daniels?"

She jumped at the receptionist's voice, blinked quickly. "Yes?"

"Are you all right?" A frown wrinkled the woman's brow. "You look a little flushed."

Darn it! Kiera touched a hand to her cheek, felt the warmth there grow warmer still. "Do I?"

The receptionist nodded. "I heard there might be something going around."

Knowing the effect Sam had on women, Kiera didn't doubt there was a lot of what she had going around. "I'm fine, thank you. Really."

"Miss Daniels, I'm so sorry to keep you waiting."

Kiera froze at the sound of the feminine voice behind her. It was one thing to *imagine* meeting Clair, quite another to actually *do* it.

Breath held, heart pounding, Kiera slowly turned.

Thick, dark brown hair skimmed the shoulders of her lime-colored jacket, framed her high cheekbones and wide mouth. Her skin had the barest kiss of bronze, suggesting her obvious Native American heritage wasn't full-blooded. And her eyes—Kiera stared at Clair's smiling gaze—they were blue. Deep blue.

"Thank you for coming." Clair moved into the room. "I'm Clair Carver."

Kiera watched the woman close the distance between them and felt a moment of panic. *Trey was right. I never should have come here. No good could possibly come of it.* She rose too quickly, awkwardly accepted the hand Clair offered.

"A pleasure to meet you, Mrs. Carver."

"Mrs. Carver," Clair repeated dreamily, her lips curving wider. "Even after six weeks of marriage, I haven't quite gotten used to the sound of it. But please, call me Clair."

Kiera managed a weak smile and nodded. "Kiera."

"Mary—" Clair glanced at the slender gold watch on her wrist "—why don't you take your lunch now? I can handle things by myself here for a little while."

"Mr. Carver told me not to—"

"Never mind what Jacob told you." Softly scolding, Clair tilted her head. "I'm feeling fine now and you both need to stop worrying about me."

Shaking her head in defeat, the receptionist slid her glasses off and picked up her purse. "I'll be back in thirty minutes."

"You'll be back in one hour, not one minute before, or I'll tell Albert in Shipping that you have a crush on him."

"I most certainly do not!" Mary puffed up like an agitated hen, then lowered her brow with worry. "You wouldn't, would you?"

"One hour," Clair said firmly, then smiled at Kiera. "After you."

The spacious inner office, a mix of contemporary and

Western decor, was warm and welcoming. Native American–themed watercolors and bronze statues decorated the walls and shelves. A smooth granite fountain bubbled softly in one corner, and two ficus trees flanked the floor-to-ceiling glass window that overlooked the pool and courtyard.

"Please, sit." Clair waved a hand toward one of the tan leather armchairs in front of a glass-topped cherry-wood desk. "Can I get you something to drink? Some coffee or water? I have some tea, if you like chamomile."

Kiera took the chair closest to the door. "No, thank you."

"I'm sorry I pulled you away from your shift." Clair sat at her desk. "I know how busy the restaurant gets at lunch."

If she's going to lecture or fire me, Kiera thought, *she certainly is being polite about it.* "Not for another half hour."

"Normally, I would have come down and introduced myself to you right away, but I've been a little under the weather for the past few days."

She did look a little tired, Kiera thought, and her cheeks were slightly pale. "I hope it's nothing serious."

"I seem to be over the worst of it now." Leaning back in her chair, Clair narrowed her eyes. "Have we met before?"

Kiera tensed, but managed to keep her tone calm. "Have you ever been to Rainville?"

"Rainville? I don't think so." Clair shook her head thoughtfully. "You look so…familiar, though I'm not sure why."

"I probably just look like someone else."

"Maybe." There was still doubt in Clair's voice, but she shrugged it off. "Anyway, I don't want to keep you, so I should get to the point. I received a phone call regarding you this morning."

Oh, God, she *does* know, Kiera thought. But with her throat closing up on her, she couldn't have spoken if she'd tried.

"Apparently," Clair said, "you've impressed my sister-in-law."

"Your sister-in-law?"

"One of them." Clair smiled. "Grace is married to Rand. She comes here for lunch quite often. You've waited on her a couple of times this past week. She couldn't stop talking about how terrific you are. I decided I wanted to meet you myself."

That's why Clair had called her here? Because her sister-in-law had said something nice about her? Kiera felt a bubble of hysterical laughter threaten to rise, but she quickly swallowed it back down. "I—I appreciate that. But really, I'm just doing my job."

"According to Grace, you were doing much more than your—"

Clair stopped suddenly, raised a hand to her temple and closed her eyes.

"Mrs. Carver?" Kiera leaned forward. "Are you all right?"

"I—I thought I was," she said breathlessly. "But maybe not."

Kiera stood. "I'll get your receptionist."

"No!" Clair opened her eyes and held up her hand. "No, please."

"I really should—"

"Just give me a minute." Clair laid her head back. "It's nothing, just a little wave of nausea. I'll be fine."

"You don't look fine." Her own nervousness forgotten, Kiera spotted a pitcher of water sitting on a console, hurried over and filled a glass, then quickly moved to Clair's side. "In fact, you're quickly approaching the color of your jacket, which I love, by the way. Vera Wang?"

Clair smiled weakly and nodded. "I did a little shopping on my honeymoon."

"Just sip." Kiera held out the glass, studied Clair's face for a moment, then, without thinking, asked, "How far along are you?"

"Far along?" Clair stared blankly at her. "What do you mean?"

Darn it! Why did she have to always speak before she thought? One more thing Trey was right about.

"Nothing. Here, just sip on this."

"You thought I was pregnant?"

Afraid to answer, Kiera shifted uneasily.

"I'm not pregnant." Clair laughed and shook her head. "I just had a little bug last week and I can't seem to shake it. My nephews had it, too."

Mentally kicking herself, Kiera forced a smile and started to back away. "It probably is just a bug. There's always something going around." *Like foot-in-mouth-disease.* "I appreciate you inviting me up here, but I should probably get back to work now."

"Wait." Clair reached out and grabbed Kiera's arm. "Why—what made you think that?"

"I was way out of line," Kiera said, wishing she could

be anywhere but here at this moment. "Of course you'd know if you were pregnant. Just forget I said anything."

Clair's hand tightened on Kiera's arm. "I'm not upset or offended. Really, I'm not. Please, just tell me what made you think that?"

Since it was too late to take the words back or escape, Kiera simply sighed and resigned herself to her fate.

"Well," Kiera said hesitantly, "I've been around a lot of pregnant women. The last restaurant I worked in, three of the servers there were expecting at the same time. They all had that same pale-green tint in their face as you do, the same unexpected wave of nausea that would come and go. I guess I just got pretty good at recognizing 'the look.'"

"And I—" Clair bit her lip "—I have that look?"

Kiera slowly nodded.

"Oh, my God." Clair sank back into her chair. Wide-eyed, she stared blankly out the window. "It's possible. There was that one time…"

Clair's gaze flashed back to Kiera. "Please don't say anything about this to anyone. I want to be sure, and if I am I have to tell Jacob first."

Kiera nodded, couldn't help but note the irony of the situation. "Of course."

"Oh, no—" the green tint in Clair's face deepened "—here it comes again." She slapped her fingers to her mouth and jumped up. "I'll be right back, don't leave. Please don't leave."

Clair didn't wait for an answer, just hurried to a door at the back of her office and ran through it.

Kiera rolled her head back and groaned softly. The

last thing she'd wanted to do was call attention to herself, but, between doing her job well and having a loose tongue, she'd practically screamed to be noticed.

With a heavy sigh, she started to turn and sit back down, but a grouping of silver framed photographs on Clair's shelves caught her attention.

Family photos.

Almost afraid to look, but knowing she had to, Kiera moved closer. There were several pictures, but one of them practically leaped off the shelf at her. Her pulse quickened as she picked up the photo and stared at it. Clair sat on the top rail of a corral fence; two men stood on either side. One of the men Kiera recognized—Rand Blackhawk. They were all smiling, not a posed smile, but one of those shots where someone with a camera sneaks up and captures the essence of the moment on film.

Kiera's fingers tightened on the frame. All three shared the same golden, bronzed skin, the same high cheekbones. The same thick, dark hair.

So familiar. So incredibly familiar.

Beyond William Blackhawk's obituary, Kiera hadn't been able to find out anything about the Blackhawk family. It wasn't as if it was a subject that came up with the few people she'd had contact with in this town. If she started asking questions, there was no doubt in her mind she'd draw unwanted attention. Of course, she'd *already* done that in spades.

"Hi."

Kiera whirled at the sound of Sam's deep voice close behind her. The photo slipped from her hands as she turned, and she could do nothing to stop its descent. She watched the frame bounce off the plush carpeting, then fall open, spilling the glass, the back cover and the photo onto the floor.

Horrified, Kiera dropped to her knees.

"Sorry." Sam knelt beside her, reached for the frame as she reached for the photo. "I guess you didn't hear me knock. I thought Clair was in here."

"She is—she was—she'll be back shortly." Carefully, she lifted the overturned photo, stared at the names hand-written on the back: Rand, Lizzie, Seth, at the Double B.

"Lizzie?"

She hadn't meant to speak out loud, but the name slipped out.

"Clair's birth name is Elizabeth Blackhawk." Sam slid the glass back into the frame. "Her parents died when she was little and she was adopted by a family in South Carolina."

Her parents died when she was little... Kiera let the words sink in. "Clair was adopted?"

"It's a little complicated." Sam took the picture from her, dropped the picture and backing into the frame and held it up. "There we go. No damage done."

No damage done? If only that were true. She couldn't seem to stop the sudden, uncontrollable shaking. She had another piece of the puzzle now, but the picture still made no sense.

"Hey." Frowning, Sam set the frame back on the shelf and took hold of her arms. "It's all right."

It wasn't all right, she thought. Nothing was right. It had nothing to do with a dropped frame, but she couldn't tell him that.

And why did she suddenly want to?

Because she was weary of the charade. Of the lies. Of feeling so damn alone.

Through the fabric of her blouse, she felt the warmth of his large hands, felt his strength. This was crazy. More like *insane*. Kneeling on the floor in Clair's office, Sam's fingers wrapped around her arms. So close…so damn close…

Lifting her gaze to his, she met the intensity of his eyes.

His hands tightened on her arms, his mouth flattened into a hard, thin line. She couldn't breathe, was afraid if she did she'd lose this moment she so badly needed.

Time slowed; her heart raced. She heard everything around her: the quiet ripple of water from the fountain; the faint tick of a desk clock; the distant laughter of children by the pool downstairs. The sounds surrounded her, enclosed her in a world of her own. A world where nothing else existed but her and this man she'd been fantasizing about for days.

Of course, none of her fantasies had been on the floor in Clair's office, she thought dimly. But even that didn't seem to hinder the response she was having to Sam's touch.

This was *so* wrong, so *completely* inappropriate, and even that didn't seem to stop her from wanting this. From wanting him.

Sam's hands tightened even more firmly on her arms; a muscle jumped at the corner of one eye. He made a low, angry sound, then dropped his mouth on hers.

The moment his lips covered hers, right or wrong or

inappropriate was no longer an issue. Nothing mattered, nothing at all, other than the feel of his mouth on hers.

She tasted his frustration, his anger. His need. He crushed his lips over hers, demanding, insistent. Sensations ripped through her, overwhelming, intense. Her hands clutched his suit lapels, fisted. She leaned into him, into the sheer desire gripping her. Her fantasies had been *nothing* compared to this. Not even close. How could they have been?

Sam jerked his head back and loosened his grip on her. "Kiera."

Dazed, and definitely confused, she slowly opened her eyes. His face appeared to be cut in steel, his narrowed gaze fierce. He rose, pulling her with him, then dropped his hands from her arms.

She stared at him, struggled to gain the control that he'd so easily attained. Knowing that she'd practically begged him to kiss her, she felt like a fool.

"I—I'm sorry," she said, but her heart was still pounding hard, her breath still frayed. "I—"

"Sorry I took so long." Clair stepped back into the office, stopped short. "Oh, Sam, you're early."

"I didn't realize you were with someone." Calmly, he bent and retrieved the frame still lying on the carpet. "I'll come back."

"That's not necessary." Kiera felt the heat of her blush on her cheeks, watched Clair glance curiously between her and Sam. "I was just leaving."

"Actually, Kiera…" Clair said, her tone reserved "…if you don't mind, I need another minute of your time."

Dammit! Kiera bit the inside of her lip. As if it wasn't

bad enough she'd made a fool out of herself with Sam, she was about to get a reprimand on employee-employer relationships. "All right."

"Thank you." Clair glanced at Sam. "We won't be long."

He hesitated, then reluctantly turned and left the room.

Kiera squared her shoulders and faced Clair.

"You said you lived in a small town, didn't you?" Clair asked.

Not exactly what Kiera had expected Clair to say. "Yes."

Clair moved to the window and stared down at the pool. "Working at the Four Winds, being here day in and day out, it's just like a small town. We all get to know each other very well. Maybe a little too well."

Here it comes… Kiera held her breath.

"It's not easy when everyone knows your business," Clair said. "Sometimes even before you know it."

How well Kiera understood—and agreed with—that. But she simply nodded.

"I realize this is an imposition." Biting her lip, Clair turned. A mixture of fear and hope lit her eyes. "But I need to ask a favor of you."

Five

Sam sat in his car and stared at the Shangri-La's brilliant pink neon sign. Like the beat of a song, the last two letters flickered steadily, blinking in and out...*La...La...La*...grating on his nerves. He tapped impatiently on his steering wheel.

Where the *hell* was she?

It was seven-fifteen, for God's sake. He knew her lunch shift had ended almost two hours ago. On the hotel security monitor, he'd watched her walk to her white sedan in the employee garage and drive away. Even with a traffic jam—which was virtually nonexistent in Wolf River—it wouldn't have taken her more than five minutes to drive here.

Dammit.

Heat lingered from the blistering day and radiated off

the asphalt parking lot, cutting a sharper edge on his foul mood. *You've gotten soft, Prescott,* he told himself irritably. When he'd been in the Army, he'd run reconnaissance in a South American jungle, where mosquitoes were big enough to throw a saddle on and the humidity was so thick you could drink it. He'd lain patiently in bug-infested swamps for hours, even dodged a few bullets.

If he could, he'd take those swamps and bullets over sitting here in this damn car, in this damn parking lot, any day.

He swiped at the sweat on his brow, thankful he'd at least changed into a T-shirt and jeans before he'd driven over here. Even after eight years in the hotel business, he'd never completely got used to the daily suit-and-tie routine. But, like the Army, he knew it was the uniform for the job so he dealt with it.

He glanced at his wristwatch again, was annoyed that only two minutes had passed since the last time he'd looked.

La...La...La...

He tapped harder, gritted his teeth, then looked up when he heard the crunch of gravel under tires. A white sedan had pulled into the motel driveway. *About damn time.* He reached for his keys, swore when he saw the driver of the car. Male, balding, thick glasses. Big nose.

Wrong white sedan.

With a heavy sigh, he settled back again, seriously considered leaving, going back to the motel and having a good stiff drink at the bar. Forget that today had ever happened.

Right. Nothing short of death or complete amnesia could make him forget he'd kissed Kiera.

It infuriated him he'd lost control like that. Stepped over—hell, *jumped* over—all boundaries. He'd been so damn careful to stay away from her the past few days. Had made a point not to speak to her, or even look in her direction, for that matter. And then in the blink of an eye, he'd blown his hard-won restraint to smithereens.

What the hell was he supposed to do when she'd looked up at him with those sexy blue eyes? When she'd softly parted those enticing lips? When she'd swayed toward him. Walk away?

Hell, yes.

That's *exactly* what he should have done.

Frowning, he raked his fingers over his scalp. In spite of what some people thought, he *was* human.

And *stupid,* he thought darkly. Not only because he'd kissed her, but because—of all places—he'd kissed her in Clair's office.

Clair hadn't said word to suggest she'd seen, or suspected anything had happened between Kiera and him. But during their meeting with the Four Winds architect, when they'd been studying the blueprints for the new tower, Sam had caught Clair—more than once—staring blankly across the table. As if her mind were somewhere far away.

Sam knew his lack of protocol could potentially put Clair and the hotel's reputation in an awkward situation. Sexual harassment claims and lawsuits were hardly good for business. Because he'd never stepped over that boundary before, it had never been an issue for him.

Until Kiera.

He wished he knew what it was about the woman that intrigued him to the point of distraction. She was pretty—beautiful, even. And sexy, for damn sure. He wished the attraction were as simple as that. If it were, it would pass quickly enough. But something, some little, annoying itch between his shoulder blades, told him it was more than that. Much more.

He sighed, sank down farther in his seat. Maybe it was the mystery surrounding her, he thought. Maybe when he'd seen that black eye, some primal need to protect had been awakened. Or maybe he'd simply been without female companionship longer than he was accustomed to. Of all the reasons, he preferred that one. It was the easiest to rectify.

He straightened suddenly, spotted her across the parking lot, getting out of her car, her arms loaded with brown grocery bags. She'd driven right past him and he hadn't even seen her!

So much for his reconnaissance expertise.

By the time he came up behind her, she had her key in her hand and was juggling the bags in her arms while she reached to unlock her door.

"I'll get it."

With a gasp, she jerked her head up and stared wide-eyed at him. "Sam!"

He took the bags from her, nodded at the door when she just stood there, staring at him. "You going to open it?"

"What? Oh, yes." It took her a moment to fit the key into the lock. When she opened the door, she turned and blocked the doorway, reached for the bags. "This really isn't a good time, maybe you can—"

"I'm coming in, Kiera."

She hesitated, then stepped to the side.

The room was spacious, with a small kitchenette, chrome dining table, box-shaped tweed sofa and a rust-colored armchair. Over the sofa, a large, framed print of a sunny, palm tree–lined beach attempted—unsuccessfully—to brighten up the drab room. An open door to the right of the sofa led to the bedroom.

He jerked his gaze away. The last thing he wanted to think about right now was the bedroom.

He set the groceries on the Formica kitchen counter, caught the scent of fresh herbs wafting from one of the bags, noticed two wine bottles in another. "Are you expecting company?"

She stood by the still-open door, white-knuckling the doorknob. "Why do you ask?"

"Why are you answering a question with a question?"

At the sound of a car pulling into a parking space close by, Kiera quickly glanced outside, then shut the door. "Just because I'm cooking doesn't mean I'm expecting anyone."

Again, she hadn't answered his question. "You have two bottles of wine."

She arched an eyebrow. "Are you the wine police?"

When he frowned at her, she sighed, then moved into the kitchen and lifted a bottle of cheap Bordeaux out of the bag.

"One's for drinking, one's for cooking." She plucked a corkscrew out of a drawer. "Why don't you just tell me why you're here."

"All right." He watched her effortlessly open the bottle. The dark, tangy scent of the red wine drifted across the counter. "I want to know if you'd like to file a complaint."

"Yes, I would." She pulled a frying pan out of a cupboard under the stovetop. "This frying pan is too small."

"Dammit, Kiera." He narrowed his eyes. "You know what I mean."

"Assuming you're referring to our little breach of conduct this afternoon, of course I don't want to file a complaint." She set the pan on the stove and met his gaze. "Sam, we're both adults. What happened…just happened, that's all."

"That's all you have to say?" he said tightly. "'It just happened?'"

"What do you want me to say?" With a shrug, she fumbled in one of the bags, pulled out fresh herbs, butter and an onion.

What *did* he want her to say? he wondered. Her answer should have relieved, not annoyed him. If he had half a brain, he'd be done with this, with *her,* and get the hell out now.

Apparently, he wasn't that smart.

"I kissed you, Kiera," he said, stating the obvious. "I shouldn't have."

"Because you're my boss?"

"Of course because I'm your boss." His annoyance increased when she didn't answer him but grabbed a knife instead and sliced off a chunk of butter, then dropped it into the pan.

"And what if you weren't my boss?" she said casually, then reached for the basil.

His pulse jumped at her comment. He couldn't tell if she was playing one of those coy, female games, or if she was seriously asking him a question. He watched her chop the basil, smelled the pungent scent of the spice filling the room. *Dammit! Why can't I read her?*

"If I wasn't your boss," he said slowly, evenly, "I'd have done a hell of a lot more than kiss you."

In spite of her resolve to be nonchalant, Kiera couldn't stop the winged stutter in her heart. She shouldn't have asked him that, knew her question was playing with fire. But somehow the words had just slipped out, and there was no taking them back now.

And if—for once—she was going to be truthful, she didn't want to take them back.

Her stomach jumped when he moved around the counter toward her. She didn't look at him, didn't dare. If she did, he'd certainly see everything she was thinking. Everything she was feeling. She wasn't ready for that. *Not yet,* she thought. It was too soon.

"Are you thinking about quitting?" He moved closer. "Or are you suggesting something else?"

Something else? She glanced up sharply as she realized what he meant, felt her cheeks warm. She supposed her question *did* sound like some kind of a proposition to have a secret affair or be a kept woman. She lifted her chin. "Of course I'm not suggesting anything else."

"What if I did?"

She stilled at his words, not certain if she should be insulted or excited. "What if you did what?"

"For starters—" he reached down and took the knife from her hand, laid it on the cutting board, then reached for her "—this."

His mouth covered hers. A hot, hungry kiss that stole her breath, sent her pulse racing and her mind spinning. And there it was again. Absolute pleasure, intense need. It streaked through her like liquid lightning, setting her skin on fire. She met the moist heat of his tongue with her own, slid her hands up the rock-solid wall of his chest. A moan rose from deep in her throat, hummed through her entire body. She was powerless to stop it, so she gave herself up to the feeling, let it melt through and consume her.

Wonderful, she thought, wrapping her arms around his neck.

So wonderfully wonderful.

He dragged her closer, deepened the kiss, maneuvered her between him and the Formica counter. She reveled in the feel of his hard, powerful body pressed tightly against hers. No one had ever kissed her like this before. Had ever made her feel such raw, wild need. It frightened and thrilled her at the same time. The kiss this afternoon had simply been an appetizer, she realized, a precursor to the main course.

She clutched at his back, rose on her toes to get closer.

Shifting his weight, he slid his hands down her spine and cupped her bottom. She heard a deep, low growl in his throat, then gasped when he suddenly lifted her up onto the counter and stepped between her legs. The paper bag behind her spilled over, and through the blood pounding in her head, she vaguely heard the oranges she'd bought roll onto the floor and bounce. She didn't care. With Sam's kisses spinning her world out of control, how could she?

His mouth left hers and she whimpered, drew in a sharp breath as his lips blazed kisses over her jaw to her ear. She rolled her head back, bit her lip when his teeth nipped her earlobe, then moved to her neck. Fire raced over her skin, pulsated at the juncture of her thighs. His lips and teeth teased and explored, but his mouth wasn't the only part of him that was busy. His hands worked her shirt from her waistband, then quickly slid underneath.

She quivered, lost herself to the mind-numbing sensations of his skin on hers. His palms were rough and when they cupped her breasts, she arched her back. He mumbled something, lowered his head to nuzzle. Gasping, she braced her arms on the counter behind her, and in some dim recess of her mind felt the small, plastic-wrapped box under her fingers.

And remembered what she'd bought.

When she stiffened, he raised his head.

"What?" he asked, his voice husky and deep.

"Nothing." She closed her hand around the box, tried to push it back into the paper bag, but the bag moved away and fell on the floor.

Oh, hell.

With a frown, he straightened and glanced behind her back.

She watched his eyes narrow, then his mouth press into a hard line when he saw what was in the box.

A pregnancy test.

His gaze shot back to hers. "You're *pregnant?*"

If the situation—and the look in Sam's eyes—hadn't been so intense, she might have laughed at the absurdity of his question. She certainly didn't want him to think the test was for her, but she couldn't very well tell him that Clair had asked her to buy it, either. No matter what Sam thought of her, Kiera wouldn't break that trust.

When she didn't reply, he stepped back and dragged a hand through his rumpled hair. "Dammit, Kiera, I can't help you if you won't talk to me."

She slid off the counter, picked the bag up from the floor, then dropped the box inside. "I didn't ask you for help, Sam."

His eyes dark with anger, he stared at her for what felt like a lifetime.

"Fine."

He ground the single word out through gritted teeth, then turned and headed for the door. He yanked it open, stopped, spun around and leveled his gaze at her.

"Just tell me this," he said tightly. "And dammit, tell me the truth. Are you married?"

That she could honestly answer. "No."

A muscle jumped in his clenched jaw. She watched him turn and slam out the door. Slowly, she released the breath she'd been holding, then leaned against the counter and closed her eyes.

She heard a car engine rev, then the squeal of tires.

Men!

With an irritated groan, she pushed away from the counter and bent to pick up the fruit that had rolled on the floor. Why should *he* be mad at *me?* she thought, picking up an orange and tossing it back onto the counter. And why were the men in her life who mattered to her most so damn demanding?

She scooped up another orange and glared at it. "I *refuse* to be bullied."

Why the hell did she have to fall for a guy who had the same ornery, the same intolerable, the same insufferable temperament as Trey?

She spun around at the sudden knock on the door. So he'd come back to interrogate her further, she thought and marched toward the door, ready to argue if that's what he wanted. She threw open the door.

But it wasn't Sam standing there. It was Clair.

"I—I'm sorry," Clair said hesitantly, obviously startled at the unexpected force of the door opening. "I must have come at a bad time."

"No, no. Of course not." Kiera felt the heat of a blush scurry up her neck onto her face. "I'm sorry. I thought you were—never mind. Please, come in."

Kiera closed the door when Clair stepped inside, then moved to the counter and picked up the box sitting there. "I hope I bought the right one. There were several to choose from and I really hadn't a clue."

"I wouldn't have known, either." Clair stared at the pregnancy kit with a mixture of wonder and amazement on her face. Tears suddenly filled her eyes. "Oh, I hope you're right. I really, really hope you're right."

"Then I really, really hope I'm right, too," Kiera said, then stiffened when Clair moved forward and hugged her. Just a brief hug, a simple, I'm-just-so-happy-I-want-to-share-it hug.

But to Kiera it was so much more.

It was a hug that had the power to topple defenses. To break through walls. To answer questions.

If there was anyone she dared trust, anyone who might be able to answer those questions, Kiera knew it was Clair.

But she couldn't. Not only because it was terrible timing, but because now that she had established this connection she was terrified of losing it, afraid that the joy shining in Clair's eyes would turn to doubt. Maybe even to hatred.

When the time is right, she thought, praying it would be soon.

"I'm sorry." With a sniff, Clair stepped back and wiped at the tears in her eyes. "I've just been so emotional these past couple of weeks."

"That's another sure sign." Kiera blinked back her own threatening tears, then shifted uneasily, not sure what to do now. "Can I—ah, would you like something to drink? Some water or iced tea?"

"Iced tea would be wonderful," Clair said distantly, still staring at the box in her hands. "I think I might need a couple of minutes to calm down before I drive home."

"Sugar?" Kiera asked, pulling a pitcher out of the fridge.

"No, thanks." Clair moved to the counter, glanced at the groceries and the chopped basil. "You cook?"

"I like to," Kiera said, filling a glass from the cupboard. "Do you?"

"Never learned, and now I'm too busy." Clair nodded at the pan with butter in it. "What are you making?"

"Chicken marsala." Kiera handed the tea to Clair,

then threw caution to the wind. "You're welcome to stay and eat if you're hungry."

"Just the tea, but thanks for the offer. Maybe a rain check?"

"Sure."

"Don't let me keep you, though," Clair said, sipping her tea. "I would enjoy watching you for a few minutes. It fascinates me how people can take a bunch of different ingredients and turn them into something exotic and delicious. Unless you'd rather not have someone hanging over you—"

"I don't mind." Kiera moved back to the stove and flipped on the burner. If there was one place she felt most comfortable, it was in the kitchen. And besides, if she was cooking it would keep her mind off being nervous around Clair—off all those questions she so desperately wanted to ask.

"So where did you learn?" Clair settled on a counter bar stool. "Your mother?"

Kiera shook her head. "Cookie Roggenfelder."

Clair raised a questioning eyebrow.

"I was raised on a ranch in East Texas." Kiera opened a package of chicken breasts she'd had the butcher pound thin for her. "When I was eight, I spent most of my time following after the cook."

"Named Cookie," Clair added, grinning.

Kiera nodded. "I'd beg him every day to let me help and every day he'd say no. I guess I finally wore him down, because on my ninth birthday he gave me an apron and told me if I still wanted to help, I had to start at the bottom. The bottom being peeling potatoes, shucking corn, chopping onions. It was nearly six months before he let me actually cook anything. I made corn fritters."

"How did you do?" Clair asked.

"They were hard as granite and burned, to boot." While she opened a bag of flour, Kiera smiled at the memory. The kitchen had smelled like smoke for three days. "Cookie insisted I bake them every day until I got it right. Took me three weeks straight, but now I can honestly say I make the best corn fritter you've ever tasted."

"I've never had one." Clair swirled the ice in her tea. "But you're definitely making me want one."

"I'll make them for you sometime," Kiera said, then dusted the chicken with flour. "You'll be spoiled for life."

Clair studied Kiera's face for a moment, then took another drink. "Does that mean you'll be staying in Wolf River?"

Kiera's heart jumped a beat. "What do you mean?"

"Like I said before, small towns are brutal on a person's private life." Clair gave an apologetic shrug. "There's been some talk."

"Oh?" Somehow, Kiera managed to keep her hand steady. Butter sizzled when she dropped the chicken into the heated frying pan. "What kind of talk?"

"What you'd expect," Clair said. "Where you come from, why you're here. Why you're living in a motel, by yourself. If you're married."

"I'm not married." But she'd answered a little too quickly, Kiera realized, especially for someone who was trying her damnedest to be calm and collected.

"I'm sorry if I'm prying." Clair's voice was truly contrite. "But I do have an interest in you beyond idle curiosity. I'd like to know if the best waitress my hotel has ever hired plans on sticking around for a while. And besides, I like you. This may sound weird, and it's probably just my hormones going crazy, but I feel as if we have a connection, somehow. I realize we just met, but I'd hate to lose you, as a Four Winds employee, and as a friend."

"I—" Kiera had to choke back the lump of emotion in her throat "—thank you. I don't know what to say."

"Tell me that chicken you're cooking will be done soon," Clair said with a grin. "I wasn't hungry a minute ago and now I'm suddenly starving."

Kiera and Clair looked at each other. Together they said, "Another sign of pregnancy."

They laughed, then Clair folded her arms and leaned forward on the counter. "I promise I won't pry anymore, but I'd love to hear more about Cookie and the ranch you grew up on. It sounds wonderful."

It *had* been wonderful, Kiera thought. Until two weeks ago, when she'd found out everything had been a lie. For the moment, though, she would pretend she didn't know the truth. Meeting Clair had helped ease the pain somewhat, but there was still so much to learn. So many questions to be answered.

And besides, after her incredible lapse of good judgment with Sam, she needed a distraction. Cooking and talking with Clair would certainly be a welcome one.

"My favorite Cookie story—" Kiera said while she

turned the chicken "—has to be the day one of the new ranch hands inadvertently commented that his mama made the best ribs in the entire state of Texas…."

Six

It seemed as if everywhere he turned, Sam saw an expectant mother. In the lobby. On the elevator. At the pool. An hour ago he'd seen *two* of them, walking together into the hotel spa. Then there was Christine, Adagio's manager, three of the women in Housekeeping and two of the desk clerks. Was it some kind of cosmic joke being played on him, or had he just suddenly become excruciatingly aware of their presence?

Scrubbing a hand over his face, he leaned back in his desk chair and stared at the report on his monitor. He'd been staring at the same page, at the same figures, for the past half hour. The way his day was going, he might finish this simple accounting statement around one or two in the morning.

But why should today go any better than last night?

It frustrated—and irritated—the hell out of him he couldn't get Kiera out of his mind. Or the burning question: was she pregnant?

It had taken a will of iron today not to seek her out and force the issue. If she'd thought she was pregnant, it might explain why she'd been so secretive since she got here, especially if she was running away from the father of her child. She'd told him she wasn't married, so the father would most likely be a boyfriend. He remembered the black eye she'd had when she'd first arrived, and his hands tightened on the arms of his chair.

Five minutes, Sam thought, narrowing his eyes. That's all the time he'd need with the guy. Hell, that would be taking it slowly. He could mess the jerk up big-time in under two without breaking a sweat.

He shook his head and sighed. Something just didn't jive here. Not that he knew anything at all about pregnant women. He didn't know a damn thing.

He couldn't put his finger on it, but he had a feeling that what he was seeing, what she'd *let* him see, was all wrong.

Or was that just what he *wanted* to think?

He swore, then rose and walked to the window in his office, stared down at the crowded pool. It was late afternoon, a popular time for guests to swim and stretch out on the lounge chairs. There had to be at least thirty people down there. Kids splashing, old men in shorts with white legs and socks sitting under umbrellas. Gorgeous women sunbathing in bikinis. And where did his eyes end up?

On a pregnant woman.

Dammit!

He turned and started to pace. Kiera was just as attracted to him as he was to her, there was no question about that. She'd been just as wild for him as he'd been for her. God, he could still taste her, still feel her body pressed against his.

He dragged both hands through his hair and linked them behind his head. What the hell was she hiding from him? he wondered. Or, more likely, *who?* Why wouldn't she tell him anything? And why wouldn't she let him help?

She was driving him crazy.

I don't want this complication, he told himself. *I like my life just the way it is.*

So why couldn't he stop thinking about her? Why couldn't he stop worrying if she was all right, if she needed anything?

If the test was positive…

He continued to pace. In spite of his lack of knowledge regarding "female stuff," he just couldn't believe she was pregnant. Kiera hadn't missed a beat since she'd been hired at Adagios. She worked as hard, if not harder, than any other server on staff. Weren't pregnant women supposed to throw up a lot, turn green and sleep all the time?

Shoot, Clair was acting more like she was pregnant than Kiera, he thought. Just yesterday she'd fallen asleep in the middle of a presentation by that publicist for the Cattlemen's Association, and she'd had that bug she hadn't been able to shake—

He stopped, furrowed his brow.

Clair?

Where the hell *had* that thought come from?

Clair *had* been acting strangely the past two days. He'd assumed because she'd suspected something had happened between him and Kiera.

But what if he'd had it all wrong, and she'd been distracted for another reason? Lord knew nothing had been as it seemed since Kiera had shown up. Why should this be any different?

Why indeed?

He squared his shoulders and set his back teeth. Enough already. He wanted answers.

And he wanted them now.

"Imbecile!" A loud clash of pots and pans followed Chef Phillipe's ringing insult. "This is repulsive. *Mon dieu,* I would not feed this slop to the pigs, let alone people."

A plate of grilled salmon in her hand, Kiera listened to Chef Phillipe berate Robert, Adagio's sous-chef. Phillipe was on his usual daily rampage and poor Robert was his most recent victim.

"This is what I think of your so-called food." Phillipe picked up the pan and turned it over, spilling the sauce onto the floor. For good measure, he then tossed the pan on the floor, as well. "You are a disgrace to chefs everywhere."

Red-faced, Robert glanced from the mess to Phillipe. "But I did what you—"

"Silence!" Phillipe bellowed. "Your brain is like a *petite* pea. Who taught you to cook? The man who cleans out your plumbing pipes?"

Kiera winced. While she was grateful that Phillipe's

anger hadn't been turned on her for once, she couldn't help but feel sorry for the young man. He was fresh out of culinary school and from what she'd seen, quite talented, though still unsure of himself. Kiera figured any confidence that Robert had would quickly be beaten out of him by Phillipe.

Stay out of it, she told herself. *Just turn around and walk away.*

"Must I do everything myself?" Phillipe towered menacingly over Robert, who was visibly shaking. "You are incompetent."

She clamped her teeth together and turned away. *Haven't you got enough problems of your own? This is your last order of the day. Just keep walking…*

"You will never be a chef," Phillipe continued. "You are not even fit to serve the food that I prepare."

Unable to help herself, Kiera glanced over her shoulder, saw Robert's eyes welling up.

Oh, hell.

She sucked in a breath, let a heartbeat pass, then dropped the plate in her hand. Well, more like *threw* the plate, she supposed. It landed with a loud, satisfying shatter.

Phillipe spun around, his eyes bulging with fury.

"Sorry," she said innocently. "It slipped."

Launching into his native language, Phillipe rounded on her, his fists clenched. Kiera spoke, and understood, enough French to know that his insults were as vile as they were insulting. The man was an ass, and she knew she should probably back away—or at least be afraid—but anger overrode her good sense.

And the expression on poor Robert's face—a mix of horror and relief—was enough to make her stand her ground.

If there was one thing Trey had taught her, Kiera thought, it was how to drop a man—any size—to the floor. When Phillipe strode toward her, she waited for the man to even lift a finger. Almost hoped that he would. With all the frustration that had been building in her since she'd left Stone Ridge Ranch, she was certain her knee would pack quite a wallop.

When Phillipe moved into her space, she tightened her leg—

"What the hell is going on here?"

Kiera froze at the sound of Sam's voice behind her. Dammit! Would this man forever be sneaking up on her?

Still, she didn't turn, didn't take her eyes off Phillipe, who looked as if he was about to pop a blood vessel in that thick neck of his.

"What is *wrong?*" His chest heaving, Phillipe glared at Sam. "I will *tell* you what is wrong. I am surrounded by complete idiots."

From the corner of her eye, Kiera watched Sam's jaw tighten. He glanced at Robert and the mess at his feet, then the plate she'd dropped. When he lifted his gaze back to her, she saw the controlled anger there. Her spine stiffened. *Believe whatever you want,* she thought. He'd already tried and convicted her yesterday when he'd seen the pregnancy test. What possible difference could it make to add one more crime to her long list of offenses?

"He is a buffoon." Phillipe pointed a sausage-thick

finger at Robert, then narrowed his beady eyes at Kiera. "And she is a clumsy, insolent—"

"That's enough."

The chef puffed up his chest. "You cannot expect me to work with such dim-witted, *abruti*—"

"I said, that's *enough*."

Stunned at the steel-edged tone in Sam's voice, Phillipe clamped his mouth shut and gave an indignant tug at the hem of his shirt. "I will return in fifteen minutes. I expect them both to be gone."

Phillipe turned on his heels and stomped out of the kitchen. Sam turned his gaze to the trembling sous-chef. "Robert, go over to catering and help Andrew with the anniversary party in the ballroom."

"I'm not fired?" Robert asked incredulously.

"You're not fired." A muscle jumped in Sam's clenched jaw. "Just don't let Phillipe see you until I straighten this out."

"Yes, sir." Robert hesitated, then cast an anxious glance at Kiera. She smiled reassuringly at him. He smiled back weakly and hurried out of the kitchen.

When Sam turned his dark gaze on her, Kiera pressed her lips firmly together. She refused to make excuses or apologize. "I dropped a plate."

"Did you?" He looked down at the broken china and food, then back at her. "Come with me."

Her heart sank. *Damn you!* she wanted to scream. How could he have kissed her like he had—twice!—and suddenly treat her with such cold disregard? Did he even care what had happened here?

Did he care about her?

Apparently not.

"What about my customer's order?" Kiera glanced at the salmon she'd intentionally dropped on the floor, then thought about the sweet, white-haired woman who'd ordered it. "I can't just leave."

"I'll have a menu and apology sent over and comp the meal."

"It took her twenty minutes to decide on the salmon." Kiera knew she was goading him, she was beyond caring. "I doubt that will make her happy."

"Fine." He could have ground glass between his clenched jaw. "I'll comp a meal for two and if she's a guest here, I'll comp her room, too. Will that make her happy?"

"I'm sure it will." Delighted that *something* good was going to come of this debacle, Kiera gave a satisfied nod. "You sure you don't want me to finish up my shift, because it's almost over and—"

"No, Kiera, I don't want you to finish up your shift. One of the other servers can cover your station. Now *come with me.*"

He turned and slammed through the kitchen's double doors. On the other side, the entire lunch staff scattered like a herd of frightened deer.

Kiera yanked her apron off and threw it on a counter. He wanted to talk to her? Fine.

She'd *talk* all right.

Pushing through the doors, she grabbed her purse out of the employee closet. After she told Sam Prescott exactly what she thought of him, it was pretty much a done deal she'd get canned. The last thing she wanted was to have to come back here and deal with the you-poor-thing-you-didn't-deserve-it condolences. Strangely enough, even Tyler was looking at her with sympathy.

She caught up with Sam after he'd paused long enough to give instructions to Christine, then followed him through the restaurant.

He didn't say one word to her.

In the elevator, she stared straight ahead, refused to even glance at Sam, determined to hold her tongue until they were in the privacy of his office. She'd been holding in too much for too long. She was ready—past ready—to let it out. No doubt she'd regret it later, but she'd simply deal with that when the time came.

Tension crackled in the tiny space, and the overhead music sounded like a muted roar. When the doors slid quietly open, Sam strode purposefully into the hallway without giving her so much as a glance. Part of his intimidation method, she figured, stalking after him. She kept her gaze lasered to the back of his head, every step heightening her already strained emotions.

He stopped outside an unmarked office, slid a card-key into the door and opened it, then stepped aside. Head high, she marched in. When she heard the door close behind her, she dropped her purse onto an armchair and whirled on him.

"Chef Phillipe is a bully," she said furiously. "He insults every member of the staff and refuses to acknowledge any mistake on his part, though let me tell you, he makes plenty."

Arms folded, Sam simply stared at her.

A tiny little voice told her to put a sock in it, but she

squashed the voice like a bug. She was on a roll and had no intention of slowing down.

"The man hasn't a creative bone in his body," she ranted on. "Everyone knows he's hanging on the skill and reputation of your last chef. Everyone but you, obviously, or you wouldn't put up with his arrogant nonsense."

Sam lifted an eyebrow. "Is that so?"

"Yes, that's so." She slammed her hands onto her hips and moved closer. "Robert is a wonderful sous-chef and he has tremendous potential. He just needs a little guidance, which he'll never get from Phillipe. You know why?"

"I have the feeling you're going to tell me," Sam said evenly.

"Yes, I am going to tell you." Why not? she thought. She'd already cooked her goose, why not serve it on a platter while she was at it? "Because any sign of talent threatens him so he beats it down. Because he knows he lacks the *je ne sais quoi* that a truly great chef is born with. And because, sooner or later, he knows that he'll be found out, and when he is he'll be flipping burgers and slinging hash in a coffee shop somewhere."

Lord, but she was riled.

Sam watched Kiera throw her arms out in exaspera-tion. Her cheeks were flushed and sparks flew from her eyes like tiny blue bolts of lightning. He was certain he'd never met anyone like this woman before. She abso-lutely fascinated him.

She absolutely dazzled him.

"I don't know why I'm trying to explain this to you.

You wouldn't understand working in a kitchen, what it means, what it takes." She spun on her heels and flounced away. "And why should you believe anything I say, anyway? You're too busy making assumptions and passing judgments."

"Kiera—"

"You're management, I'm just a waitress. What the hell do *I* know?"

"Kiera—"

"I'm done talking. So what are you waiting for? Fire me already." She whirled around and faced him. "Never mind. I'll make your job easy. I quit."

"Kiera," he said patiently. "I believe you."

That stopped her. "What?"

"I said, I believe you."

"You do?"

"Yes."

Still unsure, she tilted her head. "Which part?"

Sam folded his arms and sighed. "Chef Phillipe is a bully riding on the previous chef's coattails," he repeated her words. "He hasn't a creative bone in his body and Robert is a good sous-chef. I already knew all that."

"You did?"

"Yes, I did."

She frowned. "So then why did you let me go on like that?"

Grinning, he leaned back against the door. "I was enjoying the show."

Her frown darkened, then she suddenly went still and scanned around the room, confused. "This isn't your office."

He was wondering how long it would take her to notice. "No, this is not my office."

She took in the living room area of the large suite and the kitchen. "This is your…ah, where you…"

"Live," he finished for her.

She glanced back at him. "I don't understand."

"I wanted privacy." He saw her breath catch when he pushed away from the door.

She shifted awkwardly. "I hardly think dragging me out of the kitchen in front of the entire staff is private."

"Would you have come up here with me if I'd told you where we were going?"

"I—no."

The beat she'd waited to answer was just long enough to make his pulse jump. She wouldn't have said no, and they both knew it.

Yet still, he could see the inner war waging in her eyes: stand her ground or bolt. She was already running away from something or someone in her life. He had no intention of letting her run away from him.

Not anymore.

But she didn't bolt, just stood still, kept her gaze level as he closed the distance between them until he was less than an arm's reach away.

"You're not pregnant."

She jerked her head up. "What?"

"You're not pregnant. You bought that test for someone else."

"And why would I do that?"

She was on guard now. He'd come to recognize the look in her eyes when he approached a subject she clearly did not want to talk about. "Because Clair asked you to."

"She *told* you that?"

He shook his head. "She didn't tell me anything. It's more of an uneducated guess. You just confirmed it."

Her eyes narrowed sharply. "You tricked me."

"I didn't trick you," he stated. "I'm simply trying to understand why Clair would ask someone she's just met to buy a pregnancy test for her."

"I really don't see where that's any concern of yours."

"Fine." He shrugged and started to turn. "I'll just go ask her myself."

"No!"

Sam turned back, watched her chew on the inside of her lip while she struggled with the proverbial rock and hard place situation.

"She had all the signs," Kiera said finally. "I just sort of suggested she might be pregnant. She hadn't considered the possibility until I asked her how far along she was."

He raised a questioning eyebrow. "And she asked you to buy a pregnancy test for her?"

"If she'd bought it herself, how long do you think it would take for the entire town to find out?"

"Probably not even long enough for the stick to turn blue."

"Exactly."

"So did it?"

She started to say something, then quickly pressed her lips together.

He grinned. "Now *that* was trying to trick you."

"Whether she is or she isn't, and who she wants to tell

when, is Clair's decision," Kiera said primly. "And I'd appreciate you not mentioning this conversation to her."

"Geez, I don't know." He shook his head doubtfully. "This is pretty big news. It just might innocently slip out, you know, when I'm distracted or caught up in work."

"Sam, please," she said anxiously and reached out. "Don't joke about this. Clair trusted me to keep this quiet."

He glanced down at the hand she'd laid on his arm, wondered how the hell such a simple, innocent touch could make his blood rush. "I think I can manage to refrain from spreading gossip and rumors."

Relief washed over her face, then she quickly pulled her hand from his arm and stepped back. "I—I'm sorry. I didn't mean to imply you would be anything but discreet. Obviously, you've already proven that you are."

He knew she was talking about herself now, not Clair. "I've also proven I jump to conclusions."

Linking her hands together, she glanced down at the floor. "If I *had* been, I mean, if I *were* pregnant, would you have, would it…"

When her voice trailed off, he moved closer, lowered his voice. "Would it have mattered?"

She lifted her head. "Yes."

"You don't know?" he asked quietly.

She shook her head. "The only thing I know is that I'm attracted to you, and I think you're attracted to me."

Attracted? He let the word roll around his brain for a moment. It seemed like such a mild description for what he felt toward her. Other words came to his mind…*need, desperate, insane.*

He lifted his hand and cupped her chin in his palm,

felt her tremble at his touch. "I have three rules I live by," he said softly, watched her eyes slowly close when he ran his thumb over her soft cheek. "Three rules I promised myself I'd always keep."

Her eyelids fluttered open, and she met his gaze.

"Rule number one." He traced her mouth with the pad of his thumb. "Don't date employees."

"Rule number two." He cut her off when she opened her mouth. "Hotel policies apply to the entire staff."

"Sam—"

"Rule number three." He placed his index finger on her lips. "Don't get emotionally involved with an employee."

When she parted her lips, heat slammed into his gut. "I've known you less than two weeks," he said, "and I've already broken every damn one."

"You know," she whispered, "since I'm no longer an employee, those rules don't really apply anymore, do they?"

"No, I suppose they don't," he said, then grabbed hold of her shoulders and dragged her mouth to his.

Seven

Crazy.

Unbelievably, undeniably, wondrously crazy.

His mouth on hers, his arms crushing her against him, drove every rational thought from her mind. She didn't want to think, and how could she, with her heart thundering in her head the way it was?

She was too damn tired to fight her emotions any longer. She wanted, *needed,* as she never had before. When his lips moved to her ear, she rolled her head back on a soft moan.

Pressing closer to him, she wrapped her arms around his neck, felt giddy with the excitement rushing through her. But somewhere, far away, on the edges of her mind, she heard a tiny voice. *Are you insane? You're in the hotel. The entire kitchen staff watched you leave with Sam!*

"Sam," she managed a weak protest. "This is—"

"I know." He nipped at her earlobe.

She shivered violently. "We shouldn't—"

"No," he agreed, and blazed kisses down her neck.

There, right there, she thought when his mouth nuzzled the base of her throat. "Someone might—"

"They might."

She sucked in a breath when his teeth sank into her skin. "Will you stop being so damn agreeable?"

"Okay," he murmured.

His mouth caught hers again, kissed her long and hard. A hot, wild meeting of tongue and teeth and lips. Her pulse raced; heat swept through her veins like a firestorm, turning her insides to liquid. Certain her bones were melting, she clung to him, afraid she might slide to the floor.

But the carpet *was* soft, she thought dimly. Soft and cushioned.

And so close…

So decadent…

She arched up into him, felt the full length of his solid body against hers, the hard press of his erection. Her breasts tingled with anticipation, her skin tightened, and the intensity of the sensations might have been painful if she hadn't been so completely and utterly aroused.

Her fingers hurried up his neck, curled into his thick, smooth hair. The texture shivered from her fingertips all the way down to her toes. She breathed in the scent of his skin, a heady mix of pure male and hot passion, then rushed her hands down again, slid under the lapels of his suit jacket and slid it off his broad shoulders.

Through the rolling haze of desire, she felt him backing her across the room. Toward the sofa? she wondered. The bedroom? It didn't matter, just as long as they got there *soon*. As long as he never stopped kissing her.

She fumbled with the knot of his tie, cursed her inability to make her fingers work faster. Finally, with a *whoosh* of silk, the tie slid from her hand and dropped soundlessly to the floor. She worked at the top button of his shirt, felt his low growl against her fingertips when she opened buttons and slid her hands inside. The feel of his muscled chest under her palms, the heat of his skin, sent ripples of white-hot need coursing through her.

So it *was* the bedroom he was directing her toward, she realized when she bumped into the doorjamb. She opened her eyes just enough to catch a glimpse of smoke-colored walls, a mahogany armoire and late afternoon sunlight streaming through the open, dark blue drapes. She couldn't see the bed from this angle, but she knew it was there, and the thought of making love with Sam, of having him inside her, made her shudder fiercely.

His kisses swept like liquid fire across her jaw, over her chin, down her neck. Certain she couldn't take any more, she raked her fingernails down his chest, moved her hands toward the buckle of his belt.

"Sam…" She heard the desperation in her voice, his ragged breathing, her heart slamming against her ribs. The sounds swirled in her head, melded together. She kicked her flats off, then rose on the tips of her toes and wantonly moved her hips against him.

On a groan, he tugged her blouse from her slacks

and slid his hands underneath, rushed his fingers over her rib cage.

"So damn soft," he murmured.

As if in slow motion, she felt herself falling backward onto the mattress, the descent steep and long and exciting. His hands covered her breasts, and she sank into a river of erotic sensations, let herself be swept away in the swirling waters.

"I've been crazy wanting this," he said huskily. "Wanting you."

Crazy. There it was again. The word that seemed to say it all. She looked at Sam, saw the fierce desire glinting in his narrowed eyes as he stared down at her. Crazy or not, how could something that felt this right be wrong?

When he lowered his head to her bare stomach, she simply didn't care anymore.

It surprised Sam how fragile Kiera felt under him. She was tall for a woman, but her bone structure was delicate, her curves soft and smooth, her breasts firm and round. Her fingers moved restlessly over his back when he touched his lips to the hollow of her belly. When he swept his tongue over her warm, silky skin, she squirmed under him.

The sweet taste of her nearly sent him over the edge, but he held back, wanting, needing to draw that sweetness out. He nipped at the edge of her rib cage, heard her sharp intake of breath. She arched upward, and he slid his hands underneath her, unclasped her bra and shoved the lacy garment up.

When he took one hardened nipple in his mouth, she gasped and raked her fingers over his scalp. He suckled one breast, then the other, teased the peak of each nipple with his tongue and his teeth. The need he felt for her rocked him to the core. *Slow it down,* he told himself. *Get yourself back in control, dammit.*

Then she moved her hips against him and whispered his name.

Oh, to hell with it.

Flipping open the single button on her slacks, he blazed kisses along the underside of her breast while he tugged the zipper down, then slid his hand inside to cup her. Soft lace pressed against his palm. When he tightened his grip, she groaned.

Every breath burned his lungs, sweat beaded on his forehead. If he wasn't inside her soon, he thought he might go mad.

He slid between lace and skin and slipped a finger into the wet heat between her thighs. She bucked upward, and when he stroked her, he felt the bite of her nails across his shoulders.

"Take…off…your…clothes," she gasped and hurried her hands to his belt buckle.

He brushed her hands away, knew he didn't dare let her touch him yet. "You first."

In one fluid sweep of his hands, he had her slacks and underwear off and tossed them aside. She rose up, managed to undo the knot on her own tie and yank it off, then reached for him. But he moved too quickly, tugged her blouse downward, pinning her arms and dragging her closer while he dropped his mouth down on hers.

She couldn't move, could barely breathe, and she thought she might die if he didn't hurry. Heat coursed through her, coiled between her legs. She wanted desperately to touch him, but he'd trapped her arms, frustrating her. Exciting her. Thrilling her as no man ever had before.

"I can't stand it," she said raggedly, dropping her head back when his mouth moved to her neck. He sucked lightly, then used his teeth. Flames raced over her skin. "Sam, *please.*"

Hopelessly and wonderfully lost in the sensations battering her, she couldn't think, could only *feel* as he moved over her with his mouth and teeth and tongue. She trembled with need, wantonly arched upward, frantic for him to be inside her.

When he released her arms, she fell backward and lay naked under him. He unbuckled his belt and unzipped his pants. She drew in a breath when he shoved his pants and black boxers down. He was hard and fully erect.

And large.

Her eyes widened, and she felt a moment's apprehension. He slid his hands up her legs, her thighs, his gaze dark and fierce and primal. He spread her legs and she gripped the bedclothes as he moved over her.

He entered her, moving deeper with each thrust, then deeper still, until he was fully sheathed inside her. She released the breath she'd been holding and wrapped her arms and legs around him, felt the rippling sinew under her limbs.

And then he began to move.

Slowly at first, his rhythm building gradually. Exquisitely. Moaning, she clung to him, every thrust of his hips coiling the pleasure inside her tighter, then tighter still. Blood pounded in her temples, raced through her veins, until she burst apart.

She cried out, bit her lip as the shudders tore through her like shards of colored glass. When he groaned and thrust deeper, harder, she held him tight, felt his muscles bunch under her hands. He moaned, deep in his throat, then his body convulsed with his release.

He collapsed on top of her, pressing her into the mattress. Closing her eyes, she slid her arms around his neck and smiled.

It took a few moments for Sam to regain any sort of order to his brain. With his breathing still ragged, he rolled to his back, bringing Kiera with him. She lay over him like a rag doll, her head on his shoulder, her warm, soft breath fanning his chest. A fine sheen of sweat covered their bodies.

Reality slowly came back. They were in his bedroom, on his bed, their clothes tossed on the floor. He could still hear his blood pounding in his temples, though not quite as loudly as a few minutes ago.

He stilled when he saw the impressions on her arms left by his hands.

"Dammit," he said through clenched teeth. "Did I hurt you?"

"Hurt me?" she mumbled without moving.

"I was a little rough." He felt like an idiot, losing control like that with her. "I should have been more careful."

"Did I act like I wanted careful?" She slid her hand up his chest.

Gently, he traced a fingertip over the marks on her arms. "You may have a bruise or two."

She raised her head and rested her chin on her hand, gave him a sultry smile. "You may have a few yourself, mister. Maybe *I* should have been more careful with you."

He grinned at her. "Bring it on, darlin'."

"I love a challenge." She slid her hand down his chest, then his belly. Her smile turned wicked. "You may live to regret those words."

He hadn't a chance to answer, couldn't have come up with anything witty even if she *had* given him a chance. But the second her hand closed over him, his brain locked up and his body took over. When she brushed her lips across his stomach, he sucked in a breath through clenched teeth.

"I see we're off to a good start," she murmured, touching her tongue to his skin.

He couldn't have agreed with her more.

When he woke, the room was dark, the bed beside him empty. His brain was thick as mud, his throat dry and coarse. He rose on one elbow and winced, realized he must have pulled a muscle in his bad shoulder.

But at least he was alive.

Barely.

Frowning, he sat, scrubbed a hand over his face, then shook the cobwebs from his brain and waited for his eyes to adjust to the dark. He glanced at the bedside clock: 8:57. He swore, irritated that he'd lost over an hour sleeping.

And given Kiera an opportunity to escape without an argument.

Any other woman, any other time, he wouldn't have been annoyed. Hell, it had always been easier if he'd been alone when he woke up. Usually, after he made love to a woman he didn't have a great deal to say, and he sure didn't want to deal with the emotional expectations some women built up in their minds.

But this wasn't any other time, and this sure as hell wasn't any other woman. Without question, Kiera was one of a kind. Sexy, funny, confident, and yet strangely innocent at the same time. He'd never met anyone like her in his life. He rotated his shoulder, preferring the sharp pain of a tweaked muscle to the strange, dull ache in his chest.

Tossing the bedcovers off, he sat on the edge of the mattress, spotted his slacks at the foot of the bed, had barely yanked them on when he stilled. The amazing smell of warm chocolate wafted in from the other room. His first thought was one of relief that she hadn't left, but then he frowned, couldn't imagine that under the circumstances she had ordered room service.

Dragging a hand through his hair, he moved to the bedroom door, felt his heart slam against his ribs when he caught sight of her.

She stood in the kitchen, wearing nothing but his shirt. She hummed softly, her arms elbow-deep in dish soap bubbles. He leaned against the doorjamb, took in the endless length of sleek legs, the curve of her bottom, her shiny black hair tumbling down, resting on her shoulders. How could he want her again so soon? he wondered. They'd fallen into bed nearly an hour ago, and all he could think about was dragging her back.

But he wouldn't. Not yet, anyway. At some masculine level, he felt a profound sense of satisfaction simply watching her. He glanced at the oven, couldn't imagine what she was baking in there, especially considering how little food he kept stocked in his cupboards. But if there was a kitchen in heaven, he thought he'd just stepped into it, complete with his own gorgeous angel.

He pushed away from the doorjamb and moved toward her. "Smells good."

She glanced over her shoulder at him, smiled. "Wait till you taste it."

He came up behind her, brushed her hair aside and kissed her neck. "I can't wait."

"I'm busy here, buster." But she leaned back against him with a sigh.

"I'm busy, too." He nipped her neck with his teeth, felt the shiver move through her. "Don't mind me, you just keep doing whatever it is you're doing."

"I'm washing the bowls and utensils I used." She'd tried to sound impatient, but her tone was more seductive than clipped.

"Used for what?" he asked, but he was much more interested in that little spot behind her ear that made her breath catch.

"I felt like baking." She wasn't even pretending to wash dishes anymore. Eyes closed, she'd tilted her head back and laid it on his shoulder.

"What do you feel like now?" He nibbled on her

earlobe, then slid his hands under the hem of her shirt, traced the curve of her hips with his palms.

The steady, high-pitched *beep, beep, beep* of a timer rudely interrupted.

Damn.

Straightening, Kiera shook her arms free of bubbles, grabbed a towel sitting on the counter and moved to the oven. He watched her open the door and pull out a tray holding two coffee mugs.

His irritation at being interrupted shifted to amazement. A steaming dome of chocolate bubbled around the rim of the coffee mugs.

"I hope you like soufflé," she said, setting the tray on the stove top.

Soufflé? He furrowed his brow. She'd made *soufflé?*

"You don't have much in your cupboards or refrigerator." She bit her lip. "But I found a few eggs, some sugar packets and pats of butter. I had the chocolate bar in my purse."

He stared at the coffee cups in disbelief, still trying to absorb the fact that she'd actually made soufflé.

"It's better hot." She picked up a spoon from the counter and handed it to him. He scooped out a bite of the dessert and tried it, felt an explosion of chocolate pleasure on his tongue.

Good Lord. Too stunned to speak, he simply stared at her.

"I realize I should have left," she rushed on, twisting the towel in her hands. "But it's still a little early and I was worried someone might see me."

"You baked this," he finally managed. "In my kitchen."

She shifted uneasily. "I hope you don't mind."

"Mind?" He stepped closer to her, tugged the towel from her hands and tossed it on the counter. "A half-naked, sexy woman makes me the best damn chocolate soufflé I've had in my entire life and you think I would mind?"

He pulled her into his arms, caught her small gasp with his mouth and kissed her. Not with the desperate hunger clawing unexpectedly in his gut, but softly, so softly he surprised himself. Her lips parted, warm and willing, her eyes fluttered closed.

"This is how much I mind," he murmured against her mouth, felt her smile. "Miss Daniels, you are the damnedest woman."

She stilled, then laid her palms on his chest and eased back, kept her gaze lowered. "Sam—" she paused "—Daniels isn't exactly my last name."

He could have told her he already knew she'd lied about that. He'd looked at her file the first day she'd been hired, and he'd also ran a search on her name. He'd found nothing that came close to matching any information she'd given on her application or even anything she'd told him. Except that Rainville, Texas, was famous for its bee festival.

He could have—*should* have—had her fired. Still wasn't sure why he hadn't. But he'd simply trusted his gut and looked the other way.

Standing in his kitchen, holding her, he could feel her internal struggle with revealing even this small piece of truth. As badly as he wanted to, he knew if he pushed her she might disappear as quickly as she'd shown up.

And if he knew anything at all, he knew he wanted her to stay.

"I'm sorry I lied," she said quietly. "But I needed this job."

He felt the cool slide of cotton when he ran his palms up her arms. "You're rehired."

"I can't stay, Sam." With a sigh, she dropped her hands to her sides. "Chef Phillipe—"

"I'll handle Phillipe."

Shaking her head, she stepped away. "It's better this way."

"Better?" He narrowed his eyes. "Better for whom?"

"For everyone," she insisted. "The restaurant, the staff, the hotel. For you."

He reached out and snagged her arms, pulled her close again. "Don't tell me what's better for me. What the hell were we doing here today?"

Blue fire sparked in her eyes. "What are you saying, that you think I slept with you so I could keep my job?"

"Of course not." Hell, he didn't know what he was saying. His hands tightened on her arms, but he could feel her slipping away. "Dammit, Kiera, if you run away every time there's a problem—"

"Let go of me." The fire in her eyes turned to ice. "Now."

Swearing, he let go of her, watched her chin lift as she stepped back.

"You don't know anything about me," she said, shaking her head. "Nothing."

"That's the understatement of the century." He hadn't intended to sound sarcastic, but that damn stubborn streak of hers had put a crack in his hard-won patience.

Narrowing her eyes, she turned and walked toward the bedroom.

"Dammit, Kiera," he yelled after her. "Where do you think you're going?"

"I'm leaving." She shot him a cool glance over her shoulder. "Don't worry, I'll take the suite elevator down so no one will see me."

"Did I say I was worried?" he snapped, clenching his jaw when she disappeared into the bedroom.

He started after her, swore, then stopped, raked a hand through his hair. Swore again.

No woman had ever made him feel helpless like this before. Made him feel out of control or cut off at the knees. He didn't like it.

Not one damn bit.

He wouldn't chase after her. If she wanted to leave, he told himself, then fine. She could leave. If she wanted to be so damn secretive, then that was fine, too.

He couldn't keep her here against her will—well, actually, he probably could—but he didn't want her that way. He wanted her to trust him. He wanted her honesty. She wasn't willing to give him either one.

So when she came back out of the bedroom, her head high and shoulders squared, he let her leave, made no attempt to stop her.

Long after she was gone, the taste of her, a sweet mix of chocolate and woman, lingered in his mouth. He drowned it with a bottle of scotch and cursed the day she'd walked into his hotel.

Eight

Kiera yanked open the dresser drawer, grabbed a pair of jeans and threw them in her suitcase. Three tank tops followed, along with an assortment of bras and panties. She stormed across the bedroom into the bathroom, picked up her pink-striped toiletry case, then stomped back and tossed that in the suitcase, as well.

Sam Prescott had to be the most impossible, difficult she'd ever met. To think that she'd actually *slept* with the man infuriated her. She'd heard every warning bell, spotted every Off Limits sign, and yet she'd completely ignored every one of them. She'd let muscles, a smooth tongue and a pretty face override logic and sweep her off her feet.

She paused and stared at herself in the mirror, then sighed in disgust. Given the chance, she knew she'd do it all over again.

In a heartbeat, dammit.

She'd spent half of last night berating herself for sleeping with Sam, the other half wishing she was still in his bed. It grated on her pride that she'd so easily, and eagerly, gone to his bed.

She picked up a brush and pointed it at her reflection. "Couldn't you have shown even a little hesitation?" she said with exasperation. "Did you have to throw yourself at him?"

Turning away, she dropped the brush into the hanging travel bag on the back of the bathroom door, then closed the zipper. When she looked back in the mirror, it wasn't her own face she saw, but Sam's.

Dammit, Kiera, if you run away every time there's a problem…

"I'm not running away from anything," she snapped at the mirror, then spun on her heels and walked back into the bedroom. Her packed suitcase laying open on the bed screamed that she was a liar.

Okay, so maybe this time she *was* running away. But sleeping with Sam had exacerbated an already complicated situation. If she stayed, the situation could only get worse.

If she stayed, she'd fall in love.

Oh, who are you kidding? she thought, then sank down on the edge of the bed. What was the use in denying it?

She'd already fallen in love.

Hard.

She cursed herself, then Sam. She didn't want to be in love. Not this kind of love; the ache-in-the-chest, weak-kneed, I-want-to-have-your-babies-can't-live-without-you kind of love. She'd seen what that kind of love had done to her mother, how it had destroyed her. Until Sam, she hadn't understood feelings like that, hadn't understood how a man could have the power to take away a woman's self-respect, her identity. But last night, when she'd left Sam's suite the overwhelming urge to run back to him, to give him anything in the world he asked for, scared the hell out of her.

That was why she had to leave Wolf River. To prove to herself she wasn't so far gone that she couldn't walk away. So far gone that she couldn't, in time, forget about him and love someone else.

She'd hadn't come here to fall in love. She'd come for answers to questions. She'd come to find out the truth behind the lie. But here she was, questions still unanswered, the truth still beyond her reach, her heart aching.

Part of her wanted to go home to Stone Ridge Ranch. She knew she'd find comfort there, knew that Alaina would soothe her pain, that Alexis would call from New York and give her a pep talk and tell her there were dozens of good-looking men, why fuss over one? Even Trey, who would undoubtedly yell for an hour or two, would soften when he saw she was hurting. Then he'd probably go and beat Sam up.

The thought actually lightened her mood for a moment, but she knew, of course, that she couldn't go home. Not now. Not for a long time.

So Paris it was, she'd decided, even though the initial excitement over her trip was now nonexistent. Paris would give her a chance to regroup, to refocus and let her heart mend.

She jolted at the sound of the knock from the other room. *Sam!* She quickly tamped down the urge to jump up and sprint across the room. Instead, she slowly drew in a deep, calming breath and waited for a second knock. *Let him stew,* she thought, pleased with herself that she strolled, not ran, across the living room.

But it wasn't Sam standing there, Kiera discovered when she opened the door.

It was Clair.

The spark of cool indifference she'd worked up to greet Sam fizzled, then sputtered out. "Clair, hello."

Clair, dressed neatly in a chic, navy-blue pantsuit, had more color in her face today, and a firm sense of purpose that made Kiera uneasy.

"May I come in?" she asked.

"Of course." Kiera stepped aside, couldn't help but notice the somber tone in Clair's voice. "Is something wrong?"

"Yes, actually, something is wrong." Clair moved inside and glanced toward the sofa. "May I sit down?"

"Of course." Worried, Kiera closed the door behind her and followed her into the living room. *The baby,* was her first thought, and she felt the panic twist in her stomach. *Or Sam.* Something had happened to Sam!

No, that didn't make any sense. Even if something had happened to Sam, Clair wouldn't have come here. She didn't know about yesterday, Kiera thought. No one knew that she and Sam, well, that they'd been together. In his suite. Intimately.

Or did they?

Her stomach clenched even tighter at the thought,

and she searched her brain for some kind of explanation. Not that there was one, she realized. She and Sam had slept together. That hardly required an explanation. Biting her lip, she watched Clair sit on the sofa, her back straight as a pin, her gaze no-nonsense.

"I understand you quit yesterday."

Speechless, Kiera stared at Clair in amazement. *That's* why she'd come here? Kiera realized that Clair was a hands-on owner, but still, one waitress quitting hardly warranted a personal visit.

"I—I'm sorry." Her brain still stumbling over Clair's statement, Kiera had to clear her throat before she could speak again. "I assure you, normally I would have given two weeks' notice, but under the circumstances it seemed like the best thing to do."

"The circumstances," Clair repeated thoughtfully. Her dark hair brushed one shoulder when she tilted her head. "Are you referring to Phillipe's temper tantrum or your relationship with Sam?"

Kiera's breath caught. *Sam had told Clair?* Anger slowly seeped through her shock. How *could* he!

"I can see what you're thinking." Clair shook her head. "And you can relax. Sam didn't say a word to me, about you quitting or anything else. He's hardly the type of man to kiss and tell."

Relief swept through Kiera, along with a blush. "But—"

"I'm not blind, Kiera," Clair said with a soft smile. "I saw the way he looked at you that afternoon in my office. In all the time I've known him, I've never seen him look at any woman like that. Do you know he handed me a letter of resignation this morning?"

Kiera sank down on the sofa beside Clair. "He did *what?*"

"I told him I wouldn't accept it unless he'd murdered a guest, and even then I might take into consideration whom he'd killed. There's an oafish brute on the fourth floor driving the entire staff crazy."

It took Kiera a moment to realize Clair was making a joke. "He—Sam—" She could feel her pulse throbbing in her temple. "Did he say why?"

"Just that his contract was up and he thought it was time for him to leave," Clair said. "Then I heard you called in this morning and quit, so I knew something was going on. It didn't take long for me to find out about the fracas in the kitchen yesterday with Phillipe, then put together the pieces from there."

This isn't happening, Kiera thought desperately, wishing she would just wake up from this bad dream. She'd intentionally antagonized Phillipe, slept with her boss, then quit her job and Clair knew everything. And if that wasn't bad enough, Sam had quit, too.

Kiera couldn't imagine what this woman thought of her. Wasn't even certain what she thought of herself, for that matter. "Clair, I'm sorry," Kiera said hoarsely. "I—"

"Stop right there." Clair shook her head. "I did not come here for an apology. Whatever did or didn't happen between you and Sam yesterday doesn't concern me. What does concern me is the prosperity of the Four Winds. Sam has increased business thirty percent since he came to work for me and I don't want to lose him. But even more important to me…" she added, her voice softening "…he's my friend, a good friend. I don't want to lose that, either."

"But you refused his resignation." If she was the reason that Sam left the Four Winds, Kiera could never forgive herself. "He's going to stay, isn't he?"

"I hope so," Clair said, then covered Kiera's hand with her own. "But it's not just Sam I don't want to lose, Kiera. I don't want to lose you, either. If you're worried about Phillipe, you needn't be. He'll be gone in two weeks."

"Gone?" Kiera swallowed hard. "Surely not because of anything that I—"

"No, no, no." Clair laughed softly. "There have been problems from the first day we hired him, and we overlooked them because he had the credentials and a six-month contract. I'd hoped we could weather it out until Chef Bartollini returned, but we found out he's not coming back. Sam and I agreed it wasn't a good idea to tell Phillipe we've hired a replacement."

"You've hired a new chef?" Just the thought improved Kiera's dark mood, but then she realized that Sam had known yesterday. She'd ranted and raved about Phillipe and what an idiot the man was, and Sam hadn't said a word about a new chef!

"As much as I want Phillipe gone," Clair continued, "if he quits before the new chef can start, I may have to close the restaurant. Between the Cattlemen's conference this next week and the Central Texas Retailer's Association coming the week after, we'll be in big trouble. One little coffee shop couldn't possibly handle the needs of that many guests."

It would be a nightmare if they had to close Adagio's even for a day, Kiera realized. Between the complaints and the lost revenue, the Four Winds would feel the bite big-time.

"Tell me what I can do to convince you to stay at Adagio's," Clair said, squeezing Kiera's hand. "More money? Better hours? A promotion? Just name it."

Clair's generosity, and her kindness, only increased Kiera's guilt. *Tell her,* her conscience whispered. *Tell her who you are, why you came. You owe her the truth. Tell her now...*

But she couldn't. Coward that she was, she couldn't bear to lose Clair's trust.

"I'm flattered, truly I am." She slipped her hand from Clair's. "But I'm not just leaving the restaurant, I'm leaving Wolf River."

"You're leaving Wolf River?" Disappointment and surprise lined Clair's brow. "Because of Sam?"

"It's more complicated than that." More than she could ever explain. "Thank you, but I'm sorry, I can't stay."

Clair shook her head and sighed. "And I was so hoping you could be there."

Kiera frowned. "Be where?"

"At my cousin Dillon's Fourth of July barbecue. Jacob and I are going to announce we're pregnant." Her eyes sparkling, Clair grabbed both of Kiera's hands. "It's only a week away. I can see you're determined to leave, but please, just stay a little longer and come to Dillon's. I'd love for you to meet my family, be there when we tell everyone the good news."

"You want me—" Kiera swallowed hard "—to meet your family?"

"You'll love them," Clair said enthusiastically. "And the Blackhawk Ranch is absolutely amazing."

The Blackhawk Ranch? Kiera's heart raced, and she had to pull her hands away from Clair before she could see how badly they were shaking. "But, but, I couldn't—"

Unswayed, and obviously delighted with her plan, Clair scooped up her purse from the sofa and slipped it over her shoulder. "Of course you can. Now promise me you'll come and I promise I won't make you feel guilty over quitting, which was my last ace to play, by the way." The Blackhawk Ranch, Kiera thought dimly. The Blackhawk family. *Dillon Blackhawk.* Panic ripped through her, took her breath away. Dear God. She couldn't. She *couldn't.*

But she had to, she realized. It was her one opportunity, her last opportunity to find out who these people were. To find out who *she* was.

"Practically half the town is coming," Clair said, then, as if to sweeten the deal, added, "Sam will be there, too."

Kiera wasn't certain if that was a good thing or not, but the thought of seeing him again, even if just one last time, made her heart beat all the faster.

"All right." Kiera sucked in a deep breath, prayed she wasn't making a mistake. "I'll come."

The reservations desk and lobby of the Four Winds was crowded with early check-ins for the upcoming Cattlemen's conference. The event was scheduled to open July fifth, but quite a few of the attendees came in before the first day for the "Shoot the Bull" sessions where the ranchers talked shop in a less structured environment that included plenty of alcohol, cigars, food and more than one friendly game of late night cards. Ranchers worked hard and played hard, and the Four Winds welcomed their business.

Sam stood on the sidelines, watched closely to ensure that each guest was greeted with a smile, offered drinks and cookies while they waited in line to register and reminded them that the hotel spa was taking reservations for massage and facial packages. Like a well-oiled machine, every employee did their job smoothly and efficiently—exactly as they'd been trained.

He studied the flow of cars being valeted, the stream of people moving through the double glass doors, and it gave him satisfaction to know that even in the flurry of activity surrounding him, there was a controlled system operating. Order in chaos, he thought.

Which pretty much summed up his own life, he decided. Only without the order part.

It irritated the hell out of him that Kiera had actually quit, that she wouldn't even discuss letting him handle the situation with Phillipe. If she'd have given him a chance, he might have even told her that Phillipe would be gone in two weeks.

But she hadn't given him a chance, he thought, clenching his jaw. She'd simply walked out without so much as a backward glance.

The damn woman made him crazy.

No woman had ever driven him crazy before. No woman had ever got under his skin the way Kiera had.

He hadn't even been able to sleep in his own bed last night. He'd smelled the scent of her shampoo on his pillow, seen her lying there on his bed, her hair flowing like a black river, her eyes glazed with passion, heard her whispering his name.

He'd had to sleep on the sofa, though he'd hardly call lying there most of the night, angry one minute, worried the next, sleeping. But somewhere during the night, just before the sky began to lighten with the new day, he'd decided he wasn't giving her the easy way out. That he wasn't letting her walk away. If she wanted a fight, fine.

He'd give her a fight.

He decided he'd give her a day or two to calm down and think things over before he had it out with her. He'd also decided that it was probably best that she had quit. He couldn't, in good conscience, have a personal relationship with her if she worked here, and he sure as hell had no intention of sneaking around. As it was, he'd already destroyed his integrity as general manager.

Even though Kiera had quit, he still felt he'd had no choice but to hand Clair his resignation. His blatant breach of policy had demanded he resign. He would have expected nothing less from any other employee in a management position. As general manager, he had a duty to the hotel, to Clair and to all the employees.

But Clair had firmly refused his resignation, had insisted he couldn't possibly leave with two conferences coming in back to back, and who else could handle Phillipe when he was given his walking papers? Though he'd been determined when he walked into her office, Clair had served a sufficient dose of guilt to change his mind.

For the time being, at least, he'd stay.

"Excuse me, mister, but can you tell me where I might find the manager of this joint?"

Sam glanced over his shoulder. Clair stood beside him, a worried look in her eyes. "Is there a problem, miss?"

"A big problem. See, there's this scary guy hanging around the lobby who looks like he wants to hurt someone, and I thought maybe you could ask him to leave."

Concerned, Sam quickly scanned the room, then realized he'd been had. Lifting an eyebrow, he looked back at Clair. "What does this guy look like?"

"Well, I'll be darned." She leaned in close and squinted her eyes. "He looks just like you."

"All right, all right," he said with a sigh, then relaxed his shoulders and even managed a grin. Given his state of mind, he supposed he might have looked less than approachable. "I get your point."

"Can't have you frightening small children and faint-hearted women," Clair said cheerfully, then added, "Come have lunch with me."

"I should probably keep an eye on check-ins." He glanced back at the crowd, happily sipping water and champagne and munching on chocolate cookies.

"You know perfectly well our staff can handle check-ins." Clair slipped an arm though his. "I'm starving. Have lunch with me and I'll tell you about my visit with Kiera this morning."

He froze, then looked down at Clair. "What about Kiera?"

"I figured that would get your attention," she said, looking much too pleased with herself. "Come on,

I'm starving. Jacob's gone to pick Evan and Marcy up from the airport and I don't want to eat alone. We'll talk over lunch."

"We're here, Miss Daniels."

Busy chewing on the ragged edge of a fingernail—a bad habit she'd determinedly kicked twelve years ago—Kiera hadn't realized the car had stopped. She'd held her paper-thin nerves together by reciting recipes and converting ingredient measurements in her head, a practice she'd picked up from her childhood days spent with Cookie in the kitchen. But all the measurement conversions and nail biting in the world couldn't stop the sudden nausea rolling through her stomach.

She was at the Blackhawk Ranch.

"Are you all right?" The limousine driver glanced at her in his rearview mirror. He had friendly eyes, a thick, salt-and-pepper mustache and eyebrows to match.

"Thank you, I'm fine." Kiera smiled weakly at the man. Clair had called three minutes before the car and chauffeur had shown up, and though Kiera had insisted she could drive herself, Clair had refused to take no for an answer. The driver, Martin, had entertained her with stories of Wolf River residents, including the three teenagers who'd thrown a firecracker down what they thought was a gopher hole, but was really an air vent for their daddy's underground moonshine shed. "Blew a hole in the backyard the size of a tractor," Martin had told her. "Fortunately for the boys, their daddy hadn't been in there at the time."

The driver handed her a card with his cell phone

number. "I'll be going back and forth from town until midnight. Just call me when you're ready to go home."

How about right now? she thought, but simply thanked him and took the card, then took a deep breath and stepped out of the shiny white limousine. Groups of people streamed past her while trucks and cars maneuvered for parking spots. Children, boys and girls, ran in circles around two small barking balls of fur. Music floated on the air, along with the enticing scent of grilling meat.

Kiera stood amid the flurry of activity, felt the breeze lift the hem of her long denim dress. When the limousine drove away, gravel crunching under its tires, it took a will of iron not to turn and run after it.

I don't belong here, she told herself. She could call Martin right now, before he even made it back to the highway, and she could leave.

And then she saw the house.

It towered two stories high, redbrick with white trim and two sets of wide bay windows. Dormers winked grandly across the slate-gray roof, and tall, double oak entry doors flanked by bouncing red, white and blue balloons greeted guests. Beyond the house stretched acre after acre of low rolling hills and thick-branched oak trees.

The house drew her, and she moved with the flow of people, down a flagstone walkway past a tidy bed of yellow daisies and white petunias, up the porch steps, then through the gleaming double doors. Inside, the house was even more magnificent. White marbled entry and sweeping staircase. White walls with a high ceiling and crystal chandelier.

Certainly not like any ranch house she'd ever seen before. And definitely not like the one she'd been raised in.

The interior of the house might have been considered cold if not for the festive red, white and blue streamers and balloons decorating the staircase and the three-foot floral display on an entry table. When the children who'd been playing outside streaked through the front door, shrieking and screaming like little banshees, Kiera stepped out of the way into a narrow hallway under the stairs. She watched them, couldn't help but wonder how her life might have been different if she'd been raised here instead of Stone Ridge. Would she think differently? Act differently? Want different things?

From the corner of her eye, she spotted the framed photographs on the wall. Family photos, she realized, including the same one that Clair had in her office with herself and her brothers. There were several more, but one that caught her eye and made her pulse jump—a man with his arms around a pretty redhead. The distant sound of a band tuning up and the din of voices faded away. Breath held, she leaned in closer, saw the unmistakable Blackhawk features. She knew in her heart this was Dillon Blackhawk, which made him William Blackhawk's son.

The thought sent a chill up her spine. She searched frantically for a photo of the man, but strangely, there were none. When her mother had lived at Stone Ridge, she'd enshrined William Blackhawk's image with candles and crucifixes. Here, there was nothing.

"Hey."

Kiera jumped at the sound of the man's voice and spun around, hand clutching her throat.

Sam.

The black cowboy hat surprised her, but it suited him, she decided. She drank in the sight of him, appreciated the way his navy-blue Western shirt accentuated his broad shoulders. His jeans, slightly worn and low on his hips, showed off his long, powerful legs. It was all she could do not to slip a finger under his silver embossed belt buckle and pull him closer. "You scared me."

"I know." Unsmiling, his eyes burned into hers. "Sorry 'bout that. I'll be more careful."

She had the distinct feeling he wasn't talking about now, but the other night. She hadn't seen him since they'd made love, and she'd missed him, had struggled with wishing he would call and hoping he wouldn't.

But now, looking into his dark brown eyes, breathing in the now familiar scent of his skin, the past week and her irritation melted away. She couldn't even remember why she'd walked out, why she'd wasted one precious minute of the short time they would have together. Desperately she wanted to throw herself in his arms, might have if the procession of guests moving through the house hadn't suddenly seemed to increase. But here, standing in this hallway under the stairs, it seemed as if she and Sam were the only two people in the world.

"You hiding out here?" he asked.

"Maybe a little," she admitted. "I thought maybe if I looked at some of the photos, I'd at least recognize a few people here today, even if I don't know their names."

Sam glanced at the wall, studied the pictures for a

moment. "You saw this one with Clair and her brothers, Rand and Seth, and this one—" he pointed at a large group picture "—looks like the entire Blackhawk family."

Not the entire Blackhawk family, Kiera thought, clutching the strap of her purse. "There are so many of them."

"Growing bigger every day," he said with a nod. "I could name them, or just take you outside and introduce you. Everyone's here."

Everyone's here. Her heart beat faster at the thought. Was she walking into quicksand? She was certain if Sam weren't here, she would call the limo driver right now and ask him to come get her.

But Sam was here, and his presence gave her the courage she needed to see this through. "I think I just need a minute."

"Okay." He leaned back against the wall, and slowly swept his eyes over her. "Nice dress."

Her blood warmed under his perusal; her skin tingled. When his gaze reached her feet, he lifted a surprised brow and glanced back up.

"Nice boots, too."

"Thanks." She'd bought the brown leather cowboy boots in town yesterday, even though she already had a closet full at her family's ranch. She glanced at Sam's polished black boots and smiled. "I like yours, too."

"They're required wear at Texas barbecues." He pushed away from the wall and closed the space between them. "Especially for a two-step."

She arched an eyebrow. "The boss man dances?"

"With you, I do." He ran a fingertip along her shoulder. "And I'm not your boss, anymore. Remember?"

"I remember." She shivered at his touch. She remembered everything. "So, are you any good?"

He lifted one corner of his mouth in a slow grin.

"At dancing," she added, held her breath when his fingertip moved to her collarbone.

"Damn good," he said with a nod. "So is that a yes?"

What woman could say no to this man? she wondered. *Obviously, not me.* The light touch of his fingertip tracing the edge of her neckline curled her toes. "It's a maybe."

"I'll accept that for now." He slid his hand down her arm. "I missed you, Kiera."

She dropped her gaze, watched him lace his fingers with hers, felt her heart swell. "I missed you, too."

"I've been worried about you, had to call Mattie every day to make sure you were all right."

Surprised, she looked up. "You called Mattie? At the Shangri-La?"

"I didn't think you wanted to talk to me," he said, squeezing her hand. "Mattie always wants to talk."

Wasn't that the truth? Kiera thought with a soft laugh. She told herself she should be mad at Sam for checking up on her, or maybe just because he hadn't called her himself. And maybe later she would be mad at him. But not now, she decided. Not today.

Today she wanted to simply enjoy being with him. To enjoy dancing with him. Today she wouldn't worry about tomorrow. Today she would live for the moment.

And tonight...

"Excuse me."

A man's voice from behind Sam had Kiera pulling

her hand away. When she looked up, all thoughts of enjoying herself shattered.

Dillon Blackhawk stood in the hallway. He smiled hesitantly when her gaze met his.

"Sorry to interrupt," Dillon said, then turned his attention to Sam. "But I've been sent to find you."

Nine

If Sam hadn't been touching Kiera when Dillon spoke, he might not have noticed anything strange except for the brief widening of her eyes and terse intake of breath. A normal reaction for anyone who'd been surprised.

But in that brief second before she'd pulled her hand from his, he'd felt something ripple through Kiera when she'd looked into Dillon's eyes. Panic, he thought, and recognition—an awareness, of sorts, that went far beyond the ordinary.

"Just got here." Sam turned to Dillon and shook the man's hand. "How's it going?"

"Can't complain." Dillon shifted his gaze back to Kiera and touched the brim of his cowboy hat. "You must be Kiera."

"I—" She swallowed, then held her hand out. "Yes. Nice to meet you."

"Likewise. Clair's told me a lot of nice things about you." Dillon took Kiera's hand, held it, then narrowed his eyes. "Have we met before?"

"No." Shaking her head, she pulled her hand away. "I think I just have one of those faces."

"Hardly." Grinning, Dillon looked at Sam. "Better keep an eye on her. I'm a happily married man, but there's more than one randy rancher out there who'll try and steal her away."

"They can try," Sam said evenly, but with enough heat behind his words to make Kiera blush. Just the thought of another man sniffing around her made him want to skip the party altogether and drag her back to the hotel where they could be alone.

"I appreciate you having me here today." Kiera's obvious change of conversation wasn't lost on Sam. "Clair told me your ranch was amazing, but that doesn't begin to describe it."

"Thanks." Dillon shrugged off the compliment. "I'd take you on a tour, but if I don't deliver you both to Clair pronto, I'll be in the doghouse with her. Sam's been to the ranch a couple of times. I'm sure he wouldn't mind showing you around."

Sam nodded, remembered a private little spot behind the barn where he and Kiera could be alone for a few minutes. "I can manage that."

"Great." Dillon gestured to the entryway. "After you, m'lady."

It wasn't just the house and grounds that were amazing, Kiera thought when they stepped outside. Clair had told her that half the town would be here, but it looked more like the *entire* town. Clusters of people packed the large stone patio and spilled over onto an expanse of lawn the size of a baseball field, where the band, a dance floor and long wooden tables had been set up. The conversation and laughter pulsing from the crowd was almost as loud as the live music.

"Looks like Clair got waylaid by Madge," Dillon said when he spotted her on the other side of the crowded dance floor. "Let me get you drinks, then I'll go save her."

"I've got it." Sam waved Dillon on. "Clair needs you more than we do."

"Isn't that the woman from the diner?" Kiera asked after Dillon had left, leaning in close so she could be heard over the band's fast-paced rendition of "Norma Jean Riley." "The one with six sons?"

"That's Madge." Grinning, Sam nodded at the food tables. "And that's her husband, Pete, standing by the ribs with their three youngest boys."

They were all tall and lanky, Kiera noted, recognizing the teenager who'd waited on her. He was a cute kid, but at the risk of staining her dress, she decided she'd wait to say hello when he didn't have a drink or food in his hands.

Sam lowered his head. "What's your pleasure?"

She shivered at his question and the warmth of his breath on her neck. The rise of heat in her blood had nothing to do with the late afternoon temperature. She angled her head so her lips were close to his ear and whispered, "Whatever you're having."

She watched his jaw tighten and his eyes darken, felt the air crackle between them. She'd never been so bold before, but there'd never been anyone like Sam before, either.

"Don't move," he demanded. "And don't talk to any strange men when I'm gone."

"What if someone says hello to me?" she teased, enjoyed the sudden tic in the corner of Sam's eye. "I wouldn't want to be rude."

"Manners are highly overrated. But just in case anyone's watching—"

He shocked her by slipping an arm around her shoulders and kissing her on the mouth. Not hard enough or long enough to be scandalous, but enough to brand her as his. And then, just as abruptly, he dropped his arm away and hurried off.

Still in a daze, her lips still tingling, Kiera wandered to the edge of the crowd and watched the flow of people. The spread of food that had been laid out to the left of the patio could feed a small country, she noted. Six barbecues made from large, round oil drums grilled a continuous procession of steaks, ribs and chicken, and vats of sweet corn on the cob and baked beans were refilled every few minutes. There were at least four different salads, three different breads and a table of pies, cakes and cookies that would tempt the taste buds of the most determined dieter.

She was still trying to absorb the fact that she was actually here, at the Blackhawk Ranch, when a little boy suddenly bumped into her, yanking her from her thoughts.

"Sorry!" the child yelled, then chased after three other boys.

Kiera watched the youngster run off, remembered playing with her sisters and brother when she was that age. She missed them, she realized. If she'd learned nothing else coming here to Wolf River, it was how desperately important her family was to her. How much she needed them.

Her gaze shifted to Sam, who was currently making his way toward her with two bottles of beer. He winked at her when their eyes met, and her heart skipped. As she watched him approach, she realized it wasn't only her family she needed.

Now that she'd met Sam and fallen in love with him, she needed so much more.

"Nathaniel Joseph, you apologize to this woman right now."

Kiera looked over at the blonde who'd come up behind her. The woman's blouse was fireball-red, her jeans Versace, and she had a complexion that belonged in a skin-care advertisement. Beside her, Kiera recognized the little dark-haired boy who'd bumped into her a moment ago.

"Aw, Mom, I said I was sorry," he mumbled, his eyes downcast.

"It's really not necessary—"

"Oh, yes, it is." The woman pursed her lips and looked at her son. "Nathan?"

"I'm sorry I bumped into you," the child said, lifting his gaze.

"And?" the blonde prompted.

The little boy scratched his head and thought, then grinned. "And it won't happen again?"

The woman nodded in approval. "Now introduce yourself."

Proud of himself now, the child stuck out his hand. "How do you do," he said with practiced politeness. "My name is Nathan Blackhawk."

Blackhawk? Breath held, Kiera took the child's small hand. "How do you do, Nathan. My name is Kiera Daniels."

"You're Kiera Daniels?" Smiling, the woman held out her hand, too. "I'm Julianna Blackhawk. My husband, Lucas, is Clair's cousin. We've heard so much about you."

Kiera glanced nervously toward Sam, saw that he'd been stopped by an older couple wearing patriotic T-shirts and cowboy boots to match. "About me?"

"Can I go now?" Nathan whined.

"No more running into people," Julianna admonished, then shook her head with a sigh when he dashed off. "The Blackhawk children certainly aren't making a good first impression."

"It really was an accident." Kiera watched the boy join up with the other children and jump around like a little monkey. "He's adorable."

"You wouldn't have said that yesterday when he and his two sisters thought it would be neat to turn our cat into a sparkle kitty." But there was a hint of laughter in Julianna's eyes. "I suspect I'll be combing glue out of the cat's fur and vacuuming up glitter for the next year."

In spite of the nerves rattling up and down her spine, Kiera couldn't help but laugh. Children had always been a complete mystery to her. She'd been so busy with school and working that she'd never even thought about having a family of her own. But as she glanced at Sam, watched him break free from the people he'd been talking to, she thought about it now. Wondered what kind of father he'd make. What their children might look like…

"Clair is quite impressed with you," Julianna said. "She says employees like you are rare. 'One in a million,' I think were her exact words."

If only Julianna knew how accurate that statement was, Kiera thought. The guilt seeped in again, as did the overwhelming need to tell these people who she really was. But she couldn't. Not here, not today.

Not ever.

"I've never worked for anyone like Clair before." Kiera was glad she could finally be truthful about something. "It's unusual for the owner of a large hotel or restaurant to know the names of the staff, let alone invite them to parties."

"We all agree she's pretty special." A smile lit Julianna's eyes. "Rand and Seth are certainly happy she's settling here in Wolf River. It's so wonderful to see them all together again. And now with Dillon moving back here, too, it feels complete."

"Why did they all leave?" Kiera hoped her question sounded casual when, in fact, her hands were trembling.

"Long story." Julianna flicked a glance toward her son, watched him tumble on the lawn with the other children. "And complicated. Damn, grass stains are a bitch."

Complicated. Exactly the word Sam had used that day in Clair's office. Obviously, something had happened in this family's past they didn't discuss.

Kiera knew exactly what that was like.

"I understand she's working on you to stay here, as well." Julianna turned her attention back to Kiera. "Any chance you might?"

"I'm afraid not." Kiera shook her head. "But I enjoyed working at the Four Winds."

"There are definite advantages." Julianna smiled at Sam when he successfully made it past a throng of boot-scooting dancers. "Hello, Sam. I was just talking about you."

"Is that so?" He leaned over to kiss Julianna's cheek, then handed a longneck to Kiera. "Should I ask?"

"Much more fun to keep you guessing." Julianna slid one arm through Sam's and the other through Kiera's. "Come on, let's go join the others. I want Kiera to meet the whole motley crew."

Heart racing, her nerves stretched razor thin, Kiera let Julianna escort her across the patio toward a table where the Blackhawk family had gathered. One by one, she shook their hands. Rand, with his reserved gaze and black eyes. Seth, with his quick smile and slash of dark brow. And then Lucas, Julianna's husband, a cousin, Kiera remembered. The resemblance between them all was remarkable, she thought. A testament to the strength and power of the Blackhawk blood.

With Sam by her side, she met the wives and some of the children, and when Clair and Dillon joined the group, it felt as if a circle had been completed.

A circle she didn't belong in, she knew, easing back while they all teased each other and laughed among themselves. They'd welcomed her warmly and openly, been nothing but kind and generous. It no longer mattered to her who William Blackhawk had been, or what he'd done. Kiera knew in her heart that these were good people. People she could not intrude upon, or bring her troubles to.

When Sam brushed the small of her back with his hand, she glanced up at him, saw him watching her with a curious expression. Her entire life she'd always been good at getting what she wanted, had learned to be strong and work hard to accomplish any goal she set her mind and heart on.

For the first time, she realized she couldn't have everything she wanted. Couldn't have the one thing she wanted more than her next breath.

She would leave, but not without telling Sam the truth. Not the whole truth but hopefully enough so that he would at least understand why she'd deceived him.

"Sounds like a two-step," he said when the band struck up John Michael Montgomery's, "Be My Baby Tonight." "Think you can keep up with me?"

Smiling, she put her hand on his shoulder. "Mister, I'll leave you panting in the dust."

"Darlin'—" he dragged her against him "—you'll be begging for mercy after one round."

"A little less talk," she said, quoting the song, then laughed when he swung her around, certain that her heart had wings.

Somehow, she kept up with him, and he with her, on the dance floor and later, much later, in bed, until they were both panting, both begging for mercy.

And in the wee hours of the morning, lying in his arms, Kiera couldn't help but think how they'd both lost.

Ten

"You've got a fine hotel here, Sammy, a damn fine hotel. Growing faster than a cat with its tail on fire."

Sam didn't mind the slap on the back from Tyke Madden, especially considering he was the president of the Cattlemen's Association that currently filled the Four Winds Hotel. Still, Sam couldn't help but wince inwardly at the man's use of the name, "Sammy."

"The Four Winds is at your complete disposal, Tyke."

"Hell, I ain't gonna be disposing of nothing." Tyke chewed on an unlit cigar, then hitched up his suit pants. "You keep feedin' us boys grub like you did this morning, and I'll be wearing my expand-os to meals."

Tyke Madden was one of the "good-ol-boys" from way back. The barrel-chested, cigar-chewing cattleman was wealthy, outspoken and influential. If Tyke came away from the conference happy, then everyone would be happy. Which meant more business for the Four Winds.

Smiling, Sam turned to Mrs. Tyke Madden, a platinum blonde who'd been a stripper thirty years ago and damn proud of it. "Have you booked your massage and facial yet, Amanda?"

"Sweetcheeks, I got me a two-hour appointment with Michael in twenty minutes." Too many years of cigarettes gave her voice a throaty growl. "I expect to be naked and on the table in ten."

The woman was in her fifties, but talk was she'd kept her great figure by installing a pole in the Madden master bedroom.

"I'll call the spa and make sure he's ready for you," Sam offered.

"Hell," Tyke guffawed and gave his wife a hug. "Ain't nobody ever ready for my little sugarbug. Better make sure that Michael has health insurance."

Sam thought it best not to comment on that.

"Honeybear." Amanda squinted her eyes. "Don't we know that girl over there?"

Sam looked in the direction Amanda's gaze had taken and spotted Kiera coming in through the hotel's double glass doors. When he'd left her motel room at three this morning, he'd made her promise to have lunch with him at two o'clock today. *Right on time,* he thought, glancing at his watch. Most women would have made him wait, but he'd learned from the beginning that Kiera was not most women.

"Sugarbug, you know I never look at other women," Tyke said, though everyone knew he had a roving eye.

"I never forget a face or a name, which was quite handy in my previous line of work," Amanda said with a wink, then slipped on the glasses she kept attached to a sequined lanyard around her neck. "I swear I've seen that girl somewhere before, though it's been a long while."

Was it possible? Sam watched Kiera smile at the doorman as she walked past, then glanced back at Amanda, who was tapping her chin.

"A…b…c…" She paused, narrowing her eyes in thought. "No, not *c*, it's *K*. Karen…Kate…Kirsten…"

Sam stiffened. "Kiera?"

"That's it." Amanda snapped her fingers. "Now let's see, her last name—"

"Daniels," Sam supplied.

Amanda stared at Kiera, who was heading toward Adagio's. "I don't think so," she said, then glanced at her watch. "Oh, hell, gotta go. Don't wanna be late for Mike. Come on, honeybear, walk me to the spa."

Dammit! Sam watched the couple walk away and it was all he could do not to grab the woman by the arms and stop her, beg her to remember.

Later, he decided, and started toward the restaurant. It would be easy enough to invite Amanda and Tyke for drinks in the bar. Maybe a nice glass of Glenlivet would help the woman's memory.

He imagined that Kiera wouldn't appreciate his inquiries, but after spending yesterday afternoon with Kiera at the barbecue, then making love with her again last night, he knew he couldn't just let her walk out of his life. Not now.

Not ever.

The thought staggered him. He'd never felt that way about any woman before. Had never considered…

God, he couldn't even say it in his mind.

"Sammy—"

Sam turned at the sound of Amanda's call and her heels clicking as she ran across the marbled floor toward him. "Sweetcheeks," she said brightly, "I just remembered her last name."

Kiera sipped a glass of ice water, thinking how strange it felt to be sitting in Adagio's among the other patrons rather than waiting on their tables. The hostess, a college student named Ginger, had given her a big hug when she'd walked in, but the restaurant was so busy there'd been no time for anything more than a quick hello before she'd been escorted to a booth in the back of the restaurant. Kiera knew she wouldn't have had a table at all if Sam hadn't reserved it for them.

It seemed odd how familiar Adagio's felt to her considering the short time she'd worked here. The scent of the rosemary and olive bread, the feel of the crisp linen napkins, the classical music that softly drifted across the room, repeating itself every hour. More than familiar, she thought, watching the waiters balance trays of food and the diners enjoying themselves. It was comfortable. As if she'd been here all her life.

She glanced across the restaurant, watching for Sam to walk in. He was easy to spot, not only because he was taller than most men, and disturbingly handsome, but because she'd developed an internal radar system when he was close. The closer he got, the more her system jangled its alarm.

No sign of him.

She sipped her water again, then dropped her hands into her lap to twist her napkin. He was obviously running a little late. On the first day of a conference, it made sense he'd be tied up taking care of a hundred little problems. But he'd be here. She was certain of that. As each second passed, her stomach knotted just a little bit tighter.

Truth time.

She'd spent the morning carefully wording her speech, had paced the living room while she recited it out loud. She would tell him why she'd come here. Why she couldn't stay. But she couldn't, wouldn't, tell him who she was.

He'd press her on the point, of course. Which was why she'd decided to tell him here, while they were at lunch. She knew he couldn't yell or try to intimidate her or even show his irritation. There were too many hotel guests watching, not to mention employees. He'd pretend that everything was fine, figuring that when they were alone later, she'd break under his badgering, or maybe even his kisses, and tell him her name.

What he wouldn't know is that she wouldn't be here later. She'd already checked out of the motel. Her bags were in her car she'd valeted. When lunch was over, she was going to drive away from Wolf River. From the Blackhawk family and from the man she loved.

"Kiera?"

She jumped at the sound of Ginger's whispered voice, saw the hostess standing by the table. Her brow was furrowed tightly; her gaze darted back nervously toward the kitchen.

"What's wrong?" Kiera reached out and touched the hostess on the arm, could feel her trembling.

"Chef Phillipe," she said, keeping her voice low. "He's on a rampage, much worse than usual."

"Ginger, I don't work here anymore."

"I know." The hostess bit her lip. "But you're the only one here who's ever stood up to him and I thought that maybe, at least until Sam could get here, that you could do something?"

"Where's Christine?" Kiera glanced around the busy restaurant, looking for the manager.

"That's the problem," Ginger said, her voice shaking. "He's got her cornered in the kitchen, yelling at her. Something about getting fired."

Oh, God, Kiera groaned inwardly. Obviously the man had found out about that he was about to get canned and he was taking it out on the manager.

A pregnant woman.

Kiera threw her napkin on the table, then slid out of the booth and hurried through the restaurant, but not enough to draw attention. *Why today?*

But when she stepped into the kitchen, every thought of Sam and their lunch date flew out of her mind.

Christina, her face pale and her eyes wide, was pressed between a work counter and a sink while Chef Phillipe berated her. Tyler and two other servers and Robert were staring wide-eyed and dazed, too stunned to move.

The bastard!

"This restaurant will be nothing without me, I will

sue you all, every last one of you, you are all *bon pour rien,* incompetent—"

"Get away from her right now, *imbécile!*"

The chef whirled around, then froze when he saw who had dared call him a stupid baboon—and in French, nonetheless!

"You!" Eyes bulging, he moved away from Christina. "*Que faites-vous ici?* And who are *you* to tell *me* what to do?"

"You're a coward and a bully." Kiera egged him on so he would move farther away from the manager. "You shame your profession and you shame yourself."

"You do not speak to Chef Phillipe this way!" His face bright red, Phillipe moved menacingly toward Kiera. "You *idiot sans valeur,* worthless idiot. You will leave my kitchen immediately."

"Funny," Kiera said as if she were bored. "I heard it wasn't your kitchen anymore."

When Phillipe's eyes bulged, Christina stepped forward. "Kiera, don't—"

"Get out of here, Christina," Kiera said calmly without taking her eyes off the chef. "Now."

Christina glanced from Phillipe to Kiera. "But—"

"Now," Kiera repeated firmly and the manager quickly backed out of the kitchen.

"You *dare* to come in here and speak to me with such impertinence," Phillipe hissed, moving closer to Kiera, his hands clenched into tight fists. "Who do you think you are?"

Kiera reached for a cast-iron frying pan sitting on the counter beside her, then held it up. "I'm the one who's going to bean that fat head of yours if you take one more step toward me."

Phillipe hesitated, then made a choking sound and charged at her like a mad bull. Adrenaline running, poised for battle, she raised the pan, knew she could easily duck out of the stocky man's way and give him a rap on the back of his head that would send him spinning.

She wasn't certain what happened next; it happened too quickly. But suddenly she was staring at Sam's broad back, and the chef was laid out on the floor.

Sam had punched Phillipe!

"Thanks," she mumbled, "but I really didn't—"

Sam spun and grabbed her shoulders. Anger flared in his eyes and nostrils. "What the hell were you thinking?"

"He had Christine backed into a corner." Her blood was still pumping fast, and she had a death grip on the frying pan in her hand. "She's seven months pregnant, for God's sake. What was I supposed to do?"

His hands tightened painfully on her arms, then with an oath he released her and turned back to Phillipe, who lay wailing on the floor that his nose was broken and he was going to sue.

"Shut up or I'll break something else," Sam threatened.

Rage, blood-red, white-hot, raced through Sam's veins. He stared at Phillipe, wished to God that the man would say something, *anything,* to give him an excuse to hit him again. But other than some quiet whimpering in French, the chef had stilled.

Sam glared at the waiters and sous-chef, who stood huddled by a stove. "What the hell happened here?"

It was Robert who took a cautious step forward. "He

was ranting about calling a lawyer and how he had a contract so nobody could fire him, and when Christine came into the kitchen, he started yelling at her."

Sam grabbed Phillipe by the scruff of his neck and hauled him up, struggled with the urge to punch him again, just for good measure. "How did you find out you were going to be let go?"

"I saw the letter on Clair's desk this afternoon." His voice was a nasally whine.

"Clair wasn't in her office this afternoon." Sam tightened his grip on the man. "And she sure as hell wouldn't leave a letter of termination lying on her desk."

Phillipe's pain-filled eyes widened when Sam brought his thumb and forefinger toward the chef's nose. "I was looking in a drawer for a pencil, that's all," the chef said in a rush. "I just happened to see a file with my name on it."

"You're as bad a liar as you are a chef." As much as he wanted to inflict further pain on the man, Sam simply shoved him away. Phillipe stumbled backward but managed to stay on his feet.

"Not that it matters." Sam shook his head in disgust. "You won't be able to get a job at a hot dog stand when this gets out."

"I am Chef Phillipe!" The wounded man straightened indignantly. Blood dripped from his nose onto his white apron. "I have prepared meals for royalty, been awarded culinary honors. Working in this kitchen, with your inept staff, has been beneath me. I will own this miserable hotel by the time my lawyers are through. I will—"

When Sam took a step toward the chef, he shrank back and his hands instantly shot up to protect his nose. "Tell it to the judge," Sam said. "Maybe if you're nice, he'll let you prepare meals for the other inmates in your cell. Now let's go and have a nice chat with the sheriff. He's waiting for us out back."

Sam looked at Kiera and shook off the image of Phillipe coming at her. "We'll talk after I deal with this," he said tightly, saw her eyes narrow with irritation. "Not *one* word, Kiera. Not now. Just be here when I get back."

She wanted to argue, he could see the fire in her eyes and that signature lift of her pretty little chin. He breathed a sigh of relief when she nodded. At least there was *one* less problem to deal with, he thought, then glanced around the kitchen at all the stunned staff who'd filed in to watch the action.

"Get the orders out that you can and stall until I get back," he barked. "We'll have to shut down hot foods for now and see if we can squeak by with salads and sandwiches."

He heard the grumbles and moans and ignored them all as he escorted a protesting Phillipe through the back door of the kitchen to the waiting squad car.

"I'll come down and make a statement as soon as I can break away." Sam handed the irate chef to Rafe Duncan, Wolf River's sheriff. "But you can start with two charges of assault, the first one being Christine Desmond."

The sheriff's face turned hard as a rock. "Is she all right?"

"Just scared. She's with Clair."

The sheriff pulled his handcuffs off his belt. "I have a sister named Christine Desmond. Brunette, pregnant, manages the restaurant. Wouldn't happen to be the same one, would it?"

Already knowing the answer, Chef Phillipe groaned. "I have my rights—"

"We'll get around to your rights soon enough." The sheriff clamped the handcuffs on Phillipe and gave them a tug that made the chef yelp. "You said there were two assaults."

"I'll get back to you on the second one," Sam said. "I've got to handle damage control right now."

"I'll be waitin' for you." The sheriff shoved the distraught chef into the back seat of the squad car. Phillipe was sweating profusely.

Heading back to the kitchen, Sam swore viciously with every step. *Of all the damn times for this to happen.* The hotel would be all right in catering, they had a full staff there because of the conference. But an entire week without a chef in their fine dining restaurant would greatly upset the guests looking for a meal away from the banquet food. *Dammit!*

And if that weren't enough, not even ten minutes ago he'd found out about Kiera. Who she really was and why she'd come to Wolf River.

His mind was still reeling from it. But as much as he wanted to drag her out of that kitchen and up to his office to hash it out, he couldn't deal with that now.

He stood outside the kitchen entrance, resisted the urge to kick the door open. The kitchen staff would look to him now for direction. He had to set the tone, keep everyone calm. He combed his fingers through his hair, then straightened his jacket.

Kiera better damn well be where he'd left her, he thought irritably. If he had to chase her down, there'd be hell to pay.

Calmly, quietly, he pushed open the door, narrowed his eyes when he saw she wasn't standing by the salad station where he'd left her. He gritted his teeth, prepared himself to go after her. But then he saw her. Wearing an apron, her hair clipped on top of her head, she stood at the grill.

Cooking.

"Salmon up in two," she yelled out, sprinkling herbs on the fish with her right hand while she dumped pasta into boiling water with her left.

"I need plates," she yelled over her shoulder at one of the busboys. "*Platos, por favor.* Tyler, what's your ticket?"

"Picatta, no capers." Tyler called out the order while he assembled a salad. "Table fifteen wants a side of marinara."

"Robert, you take it," Kiera shouted to the sous-chef. "Watch your basil and add a kiss of red wine. I need those plates now!"

Arms loaded with plates, a busboy hurried from the dishwasher to the grill station while two of the servers scurried about.

"Hot plate." One server zigged while the other zagged.

"Order up, six." Kiera slipped the salmon onto a plate and drizzled it with a sauce she'd had simmering in a pan. "Filet's in oven."

Dumbfounded, Sam stared. He'd obviously been in kitchens before, many times, but as he watched Kiera work with the staff, he felt a rhythm like never before. Like a choreographed dance, he thought.

"Split order ready in one," she called out and scooped up an order of penne onto two plates. "Rico, cut me more tomatoes, pronto, pronto. Robert, if you add a little cream to that sauce, that pretty girl at table six will want to have sex with you. *I'll* want to have sex with you," she added, which made Robert laugh and turn bright red.

Sam raised an eyebrow but stayed back, watching the show. The orders flew at her, but she never faltered, never hesitated, somehow managed to do six things at once and keep track of the rest of the kitchen, too.

Apparently she'd done this before.

There'd been clues all along, he thought. Her expertise in the front of the restaurant, her observations of Phillipe. He'd watched her cook before, once at her motel, then the soufflé in his suite. She'd told him she *liked* to cook, and when he'd been eavesdropping the day she'd been hired, he remembered she'd told Janet that she'd had *some* kitchen training.

Obviously, she'd had a great deal more than *some* training.

How obtuse could he be? Just when he thought he knew who she was, he realized he didn't have a clue.

Amazement, admiration and annoyance all meshed inside of him, then settled in his gut like a lump of concrete.

He stepped back out of the kitchen before she saw him. Obviously she had the kitchen under control, and for now he'd let her work.

Turning, he headed for Clair's office.

* * *

"Kiera, that was amazing." Two glasses of red wine in his hands, Robert followed Kiera out of the kitchen. "*You* are amazing."

"Thanks, partner." She sank down in the same corner booth where she'd sat almost eight hours ago, waiting for Sam. It felt like a lifetime had passed since then. "You're pretty amazing yourself."

She took the wine Robert offered her and they clinked glasses.

The dimly lit restaurant was quiet now, with only a few diners still straggling over desserts and drinks. As of ten minutes ago, the kitchen was officially closed for the night.

It was the first time today she'd had a chance to sit down. Her feet were throbbing, her shoulders were aching and marsala sauce stained the front of her tan slacks.

She couldn't remember when she'd been happier.

"You were so right about cutting back on the thyme and adding the cumin in the house chicken." Robert leaned forward, his face bright. "And you still have to show me how you made your rémoulade, that was awesome. And your marsala, I would kill for that recipe."

While Robert went on, Kiera simply smiled and sipped her wine. Robert had been bullied by Phillipe for so long, he'd lost his love of cooking. It warmed her heart to see the passion in his eyes and hear the exhilaration in his voice.

"You're going to make a wonderful chef, Robert." She raised her glass to him. "Don't ever let anyone tell you that you won't."

Robert lowered his gaze and stared at his glass of wine. "I—I'm sorry about earlier today. When Phillipe was yelling at Christine and then he came at you, I just froze."

"Don't even think about it." She reached across the table and laid her hand on Robert's. "Believe me when I tell you I've dealt with bigger, tougher men than Phillipe Girard."

"Actually," Robert said awkwardly, "I, well, none of the staff here know exactly *what* to believe about you. There was all kinds of talk before, but after today, well…you can imagine."

"I certainly can." But the fact was, she didn't care. She had a much bigger, much more immediate problem to deal with than what the staff at Adagio's thought of her.

Sam was waiting to speak to her.

Tyler had given her the message ten minutes ago. It was short and to the point: *Meet me in my office.*

He hadn't even said pretty please.

She'd seen him when he'd come back to the kitchen after hauling Phillipe outside, had been surprised that he hadn't said one word to her. She'd worried that he might even close the restaurant until another chef could be brought in. But he hadn't. He watched her, then backed away and let her work.

He'd trusted her. And the fact that he had made her load of guilt twice as heavy.

"I've got to go now, Robert." She drew her hand away and stood. "Just don't forget what I said. You're going to make one hell of a chef."

She left him sitting there, left Adagio's, and couldn't

bear to look back. She knew this would be the last time she'd be here.

To avoid the crowds of rambunctious cattlemen milling around the hotel, she took the service elevator to the sixth floor and stepped out when the doors *swished* open. The hallway was empty and deathly quiet.

Sucking in a deep breath of courage, she opened the outer door to Sam's office and stepped inside. It was dark, but the inner office door was ajar and a soft sliver of light shimmered through the crack. She moved toward it. *You can do this.*

When she pushed the door open, then stepped inside the dimly lit office, she saw him standing at the window, arms folded as he stared out into the darkness.

"Sam."

He turned, moved out of the shadows toward her.

"Please, just stay over there. I'll never get through this if you don't." She had to say what she needed to say all at once, or she was certain she'd fall apart. She kept her gaze locked with Sam's, refused to let herself look away. "You know I haven't been completely honest with you, that I've kept things from you."

"Kiera—"

"Sam, *please.*" She held up a hand to stop him. "Let me talk."

He clamped his jaw shut.

"I wasn't running from an abusive relationship, which I let you believe," she began, "but I told you the truth about the black eye. I did fall off a horse, which is actually quite embarrassing, considering I was raised on a horse ranch in East Texas."

Hoping that she could hold herself together, she folded her arms. "I have two older sisters, twins, and a brother who's bossy and over-protective and—"

When Sam started to speak again, she shook her head. "And in spite of the fact that I found out they, and my own mother, have been deceiving me my entire life, I love them all very much."

It felt good to say it, she realized. She'd been so angry, mostly with Trey, and she didn't want to be angry anymore. She was too tired, too weary from all the lies.

"I went to culinary school in New York straight from high school," she said. "After I graduated I travelled and worked around the country before I went back to New York. For the past two years I've been a chef at a popular new restaurant—" she almost said the name, but caught herself in time. Even now, there were things she couldn't, didn't dare, tell him. "Four months ago, on a whim, I applied for an assistant's position with a world-renowned chef in Paris. I was shocked when they actually hired me, but it was the opportunity of a lifetime, so of course I accepted. I quit my job, spent two weeks on my family's ranch and scheduled in three weeks' vacation time to spend in Paris before I started my new job."

She pressed her fingers to her temple, rubbed at the threatening headache, then went on, "The night before I was ready to leave, I overheard my brother and one of my sisters arguing in the kitchen. They thought I'd already gone to bed, but I was too wound up to sleep and I'd come back downstairs. When I heard my name mentioned, I listened."

It seemed like a hundred years ago, but she could still hear the whispered quarrel, Alaina's frustration and Trey's unbending resolve.

You have to tell her the truth, Trey. You've already waited too long. If she finds out on her own—

She won't find out. We'll let her get settled in Paris, have a good time. I'll tell her in a few months.

You've been saying that for the past four years. Dammit, she's not a child anymore. She has a right to know the truth. Will you stop being so bullheaded and just tell her?

Kiera pushed the memory from her mind, forced herself to concentrate on the present, on this moment. *You're almost there,* she told herself.

"When I finally stepped into the kitchen and confronted them, my brother refused to talk to me, so my sister told me." Kiera could still see worry in Alaina's eyes, hear the pain in her voice. "She told me that my father had never married my mother. That he had abandoned us all when I was three. All those years I thought he was dead, he was living here, in Wolf River. Married, with a family."

"Kiera, please." Sam's mouth pressed into a hard line. "You don't need to tell me this."

"But I do." She opened her eyes, prayed he could see into her heart. "Don't you see? I was lying, too. Just like my mother had lied, just like my sisters and brother. I don't want to lie anymore. Not to you, Sam. You've been the most wonderful thing that's ever happened to me."

She stepped toward him. "Being with you—"

"Kiera, stop—"

"Making love with you," she whispered.

"God, Kiera, *stop!*"

She did stop, the urgency in his voice, the fierce expression on his face, confusing her. From the corner of her eye, she spotted movement in the far, darkened corner of the room. Breath held, she turned.

Oh dear God.

She watched in horror as her brother stepped out of the shadows.

Eleven

Violence glinted in Trey Blackhawk's dark eyes; Sam recognized the look only too well. But the violence wasn't directed at Kiera, Sam knew. It was directed at him.

No question about it, he thought, accepting, and bracing himself for, the inevitable. After what Kiera's brother had just heard, there was going to be hell to pay.

"Trey." Kiera's voice was barely audible in the wire-tight silence. "What are you, how did you—"

"I called him this afternoon." Sam stepped closer to Trey and Kiera. "Just before Phillipe's tirade in the kitchen."

Brow furrowed, Kiera shook her head as she glanced from Trey back to Sam. "I—I don't understand."

"One of the guests at the Four Winds spotted you coming into the hotel today and recognized you."

Amanda had been extremely accommodating once she'd remembered Kiera's name. "She met you a few years ago when they bought a couple of yearlings from your family's ranch."

"Amanda and Tyke Madden." Shades of light and dark cut across the sharp angles of Trey's face as he spoke. "You were home from school at the time. I'm sure you remember them. 'Honeybear and Sugarbug'?"

"Oh. Right." Slowly, Kiera's gaze swiveled back to Sam; her eyes narrowed to slits. "Wait. Did you say you *called* my brother?"

"I thought he should know where you were."

"You *thought?*" Hands thrust on her hips, Kiera rounded on him. "What gives you the right to interfere in my family business? Just because we slept together—"

The low growl rumbled from Trey's throat just before his arm swung out and clipped Sam's jaw. If Sam hadn't been expecting the blow, he might have gone down.

Kiera squeaked, then jumped between the two men, but Sam brushed her away in case the "discussion" escalated. Dammit! He didn't want to fight over a man's right to defend his sister's honor.

"I'll give you that one, Blackhawk." Damn, but the man packed a punch. "The next one I'll have to take payment."

"Go for it." Trey stepped close again, locked eyes with Sam. "What the hell kind of man takes advantage of a vulnerable woman?"

"Trey Blackhawk!" Kiera squirmed in between the two men, who stood nose to nose. "That's none of your business! I'm a grown woman, for God's sake. Stop this right now."

A muscle jumped in Trey's jaw, but slowly, reluctantly, he eased back, then turned to Kiera.

"What were you thinking?" Trey admonished. "What could you possibly hope to gain from coming to Wolf River?"

"You wouldn't talk to me, even Alaina shut me out, told me to wait. Wait for what?" She threw out her hands. "The truth fairy to appear in my bedroom one night and slip a note under my pillow? Yes, I wanted to know who William Blackhawk was, I wanted to see where he lived. I wanted to understand why he destroyed our mother and how he could leave all of us, his own children, without so much as an it's-been-great-but-go-to-hell."

Eyes glistening, Kiera reached out and took hold of her brother's arms. The desperation in her voice, the raw pain, almost had Sam reaching for her. But he couldn't. However this unfolded between sister and brother, he knew he couldn't step between them.

"*Why,* Trey?" Kiera's knuckles turned white on Trey's arms. "Why won't you tell me the truth about our father? The whole truth. What are you still holding back from me?"

"William Blackhawk was a bastard." Trey's lip curled. "That's all you need to know."

"That *isn't* all I need to know," she said on a low sob. "I have a right to know, dammit, *tell me.*"

"I'll tell you."

Sam whipped his head around and saw Clair standing in the doorway.

* * *

This isn't happening, Kiera thought wildly. *None of this is real.*

Her heart jumped into her throat when Clair stepped into the room. The look in her eyes, distant and cold, shimmered in the dim light of Sam's office.

Kiera's hands slipped from Trey's arms and she turned on knees that threatened to buckle.

"Clair, I'm sorry." Kiera swallowed the lump in her throat. "I'm so sorry. I never wanted you to know about me, about my father."

"Sam—" Clair moved closer to Kiera "—would you turn up the light please?"

A chill shivered up Kiera's spine as Clair's eyes met hers. When the light filled the room, Clair studied Kiera's face, looked at her as if she'd never seen her before.

"There'd always been something I couldn't put my finger on," Clair said quietly. "A connection I didn't understand. It's subtle, but I can see it now. The shape of your eyes." Clair's gaze shifted to Trey. "You could almost be Rand's twin, you look so much alike. Your name is Trey, I believe I heard Kiera say?"

Trey nodded. Neither offered a hand.

"You knew my father?" Kiera asked, ignoring the hand that Trey put on her arm.

Clair shook her head. "I was born in Wolf River, but I wasn't raised here. I grew up in South Carolina, lived there until I met Jacob and moved back here a few months ago."

"South Carolina?" Confused, Kiera glanced at Sam, but he'd retreated from this family drama playing out, and she couldn't blame him. Kiera had brought this on herself, but now that she had, she'd see it through.

"After my parents died in a car accident, I was adopted. So were Rand and Seth. Rand was raised on a small ranch in West Texas and Seth in New Mexico."

"But you had other family here," Kiera said. "Why were you separated and adopted?"

"I'll tell her."

It was Trey who spoke. His iron-hard expression frightened Kiera, and suddenly she wasn't feeling like a grown woman at all. She felt like a child. Helpless and scared and alone.

"There were three Blackhawk brothers, full-blood Cherokee." Trey's tone was void of all emotion. "Thomas, who was Lucas's father. Jonathan, who was Rand, Seth and Clair's father. Then there was William, Dillon's father."

"And our father," Kiera added, digging her fingernails into her fisted palms.

"William alienated himself from his brothers after they married white women." Disgust edged Trey's words. "He considered their children impure."

"But that makes no sense." Kiera could barely hear over the buzzing in her head. "Our mother is white."

"She was the forbidden fruit," Trey said. "Which made her all the more tempting. She was a pretty young widow when he met her, living on a ranch in a tiny border town almost four hundred miles from Wolf River. Who would ever know? He told her up front how it would be, paid off her bills and visited often, let her tell the town they had gotten married, even let her have his children. But he never intended to marry her."

Kiera wanted to hate her mother for being so weak, for letting a man use her like that. But she could only pity her.

"After a few years," Trey went on, "she became a burden to him, *we* became a burden. He gave her a choice, accept one big check and never say anything, or he'd leave her with nothing. She had four children, what could she do? She took the money, then concocted a story of how he drowned saving a little boy's life, told the story so many times that, in her mind, it became a reality. Now, in her confused mind, she actually believes that story."

Growing up, Kiera had learned not to ask too many questions about her father. She'd understood that the wrong word or comment could send her mother into her darkened bedroom for weeks on end, heavily sedated. Kiera had heard the doctor whisper "mental break-down," but it was years before she really understood what it meant.

From the time he was a teenager, Trey had always been the patriarch of their family. He'd taken care of everyone and run the ranch, too, but with an iron fist. Kiera had swung from hating him one minute, to adoring him the next. She looked at him now, under-stood why he'd been so angry his entire life, why he'd tried to protect them all. He'd known their father hadn't died, but he'd let everyone, including their mother, believe the lie.

The truth hung in the air, ice-cold; Kiera felt it shiver in her bones. And she knew there was more. "Our father's the reason Clair and her brothers were separated and adopted out, isn't he?"

"He told everyone we'd died in the accident." Clair wrapped her arms around her waist, as if she might protect the child growing inside her from the ugliness of her words. "William Blackhawk was wealthy and influential. He knew how to manipulate people, pay them off to make things happen. Rand and Seth were just little boys, they thought their family was dead. I was a toddler, too little to remember anything more than images and feelings. We all found each other a few months ago and we're making up for lost time."

Lost time? Kiera thought. How could you make up for that much lost time? Bile rose in her throat and she closed her eyes, could only imagine what Clair and her brothers had endured at William Blackhawk's hands.

Kiera turned and looked up at her brother. "How do you know about Clair and her brothers, what our father did to them? How *could* you know?"

"I hired a private investigator two months ago," he said. "Alexis and Alaina had been content to let the past be, as I was, but I figured when you finally learned the truth, you'd probably do something rash. I wanted to at least have an idea of who these people are, what they might do if you suddenly showed up."

"They're wonderful people," she said quietly. "They treated me with warmth and kindness and I responded with lies." She looked at Sam, then Clair. "I'm sorry. I'm so sorry."

"Kiera." Trey took her arm. "We should go now."

Sam moved forward, but before he could speak Clair

held out a hand to stop everyone. "No, please. Just stay the night here, at the Four Winds. We'll talk again, in the morning, when we've all had some rest."

"I appreciate the offer." Trey nodded stiffly at Clair. "But it's not necessary."

"For God's sake, Trey," Sam said through clenched teeth. "Can't you see Kiera's exhausted?"

"I don't need you telling me what my sister is." But he looked at her, saw the truth in her pale cheeks, and Trey's resolve took a hit. "Fine, we'll go back to your motel."

"I already checked out." She rubbed at the increasing pain in her head. "My bags are in my car."

"We'll find another place, then."

"Not at this hour you won't." Sam stepped in front of Trey. "Dammit, stop being an ass and think about Kiera."

Murder threatened in Trey's narrowed eyes. "Get the hell out of my way, Prescott, or we'll take this outside."

"I'll take it anywhere you want, Blackhawk." Sam stiffened, obviously preparing himself for another blow. "You want to go a few rounds, I'll be happy to oblige. Just let Kiera get some rest before she falls over."

"Stop it!" Kiera couldn't bear to see the two men she loved taking shots at each other. She laid a hand on her brother's chest, though it might as well have been a brick wall. "He's right, Trey," she said, lowering her voice. "It's too late to find a place to stay, and I am tired. Clair, if you're sure it's all right…"

"I'll call Housekeeping." Clair glanced at everyone in the room, then shook her head in disbelief. "We'll have breakfast in the morning and talk again, after we've all had a chance to sleep on this. Trey, if you come with me, I'll get you a key and have your luggage brought up."

"I can get my own luggage, thank you." Trey's jaw tightened when he looked at Sam. "Come on, Kiera—"

Kiera shook her head. "Go with Clair, Trey. Please."

He hesitated, then reluctantly followed Clair out of the room, but not before curling a lip at Sam. Unblinking, Sam didn't budge.

With a soft click, Clair closed the door behind her and Trey. The quiet of the room pounded in her skull, and she wished they were in the dark again. She steadied herself, tightly gripped the last thread of control and faced Sam.

He stood no more than three feet away, and she felt as if he might as well be on the other side of the world.

"I didn't want you to find out this way," she said softly.

"You didn't want me to find out at all."

Anger gripped his voice. After the lies and the deception, it was no less than she deserved. "I thought I could come here, find out about my father, who he was, why he'd left us. I was so certain that once I knew, I could let it go and move on with my life."

"Is that what you're going to do now?" Sarcasm laced with the anger. "Move on?"

"My job in Paris starts in three days. If I can get a flight tomorrow, I'll have just enough time to get settled in."

"So that's it, then?" he said through clenched teeth. "Now that you found out what you came here for, you can just walk away?"

She wanted to reach out to him, needed him to understand what she was feeling. But she couldn't, didn't dare touch him. Knew if she did, she would never want to let go. In spite of the cold shame sweeping through her, she held her voice even. "My father was a racist and maliciously ripped a family apart. He brought Clair and Rand and Seth nothing but pain. How could they ever look at me and not be reminded of that?"

"You don't give the Blackhawks enough credit." He bit the words out. "They've rebuilt their lives and each one of them is stronger because of it, more determined to make each and every day count."

"All the more reason for me to leave them alone." *To leave you alone,* she thought, and felt the pain squeeze her heart. "I'm sorry I came here, sorry I brought more heartache, but I'm not sorry about you, Sam. I know how you must feel, how you—"

He moved so fast she never saw it coming, and his hands were gripping her arms.

"You don't know a damn thing." He nearly lifted her off the floor. "You blow through here, deceive everyone, then think you can just blow out again and everything will be fine?"

"I—I'm sorry." The crazed look in his eyes caught her off guard. She struggled to breathe, to even think. "That's not what I meant."

"You come here, jump into my bed—"

"I did *not* jump." The anger felt good, so much better than the pain.

"The hell you didn't. You made me want you, dammit, and I didn't *want* to want you. All along, I knew you were hiding something, and still I wanted you." He let go of her so quickly, she stumbled back. "You want to run again, fine, then run. You do it so well."

Numb, she stared at him, felt the ice slowly form around her heart. How had it come to this? she thought dimly, closing her hands into fists so she wouldn't reach out to him, beg him to forgive her.

She loved him, and that would be her punishment, she realized. Because she would always love him, would always remember every minute of every day they'd spent together.

Somehow she managed to lift her chin and meet his angry gaze. Somehow she even managed to say goodbye.

And somehow she managed to turn and walk out the door.

Twelve

Standing at his office window, Sam watched the dawn slowly lift the darkness of the night. The courtyard and pool below were empty, the surrounding walkways damp from the early morning sprinklers. Overhead lights flickered off, and the distant roll of thunder promised a summer storm.

Just another day, he thought, watching the sun rise higher through the gathering clouds. Just another god-damned day.

He'd have to shower before he made rounds and greeted guests, of course. He rubbed a hand over his face, felt the stubble of his beard against his palm. He couldn't very well greet guests looking as if someone had just died.

Looking as if his heart was bleeding right out of his chest.

He'd stayed in his office after Kiera had walked out last night. He'd contemplated a visit to the bar, but chose to lick his wounds in private, rather than wash them down with an audience. He assumed everyone would know soon enough about Kiera. Who she was, who her father was. Tongues would be wagging from one end of Wolf River all the way to the next county, and the name William Blackhawk would once again be whispered in grocery store aisles and beauty salon chairs.

Who didn't love a good scandal?

He'd stood here all night, wondering how the hell he'd missed it so completely. He ran the past two weeks through his mind, over and over, then over again. There'd been clues, he could see that now, and Clair was right, there'd been something familiar about Kiera. But he'd been blind from the first moment he'd laid eyes on her.

Blind and stupid.

He glanced at his watch, considered a quick visit to the gym, thought maybe he could sweat off some of his frustration. But he wouldn't be alone. Even at this early hour there would be at least two or three guests and maybe a couple of employees in there. And with the mood he was in, he didn't trust himself to even be in the same room with another person without biting their head off.

For good measure, and just because he couldn't stop himself, he kicked his desk chair, watched it fly across the room and crash into a tall ficus tree. Dirt spilled from the heavy pot and a few loose leaves drifted to the floor.

Sure, he thought, *take it out on office furniture and potted plants.*

He should be thanking Kiera for leaving, he told

himself. If she'd stayed, he might have considered something exclusive with her, maybe something long-term.

Something permanent.

The thought turned his throat to dust. He'd spent a lifetime avoiding these kind of complications. He'd flown free as an eagle, not a damn care in the world. And then she'd walked into his life, and like a sparrow, he'd flown smack dab into a plate-glass window.

He was still dazed, still dusting himself off, and the bitter taste of her goodbye lodged tightly in his throat. He'd get over her, he told himself, gritting his teeth. Like her, he'd move on.

"You look like hell."

He glanced up sharply, saw Clair standing in the doorway. Dressed in a freshly pressed blue work suit, she looked crisp and new as the morning sun. He sighed heavily when he saw Dillon and Jacob were with her.

"Reinforcements?" he asked.

"Friends." She moved into the room, glanced at the chair tipped on its side and the spilled dirt. "You look like you could use a couple."

"Looks are deceiving, Clair." He frowned at the two men. "But we already know that, don't we? How's it feel to learn you have a sister, Dillon? Three actually, according to Kiera, and of course, there's Trey. With his dazzling charm, I'm sure you'll both be buds in no time."

With a sigh, Clair looked at Dillon and Jacob. "What did I tell you?"

"He's got it pretty bad, all right," Dillon said with a nod. "Don't you think so, Jacob?"

"Big-time." Jacob slipped an arm around his wife's shoulders. "I was there myself a few months ago, wasn't I, darlin'?"

"Me, too." Dillon nodded, his expression etched with pity. "Not a pretty sight, is it?"

"What the hell are you all talking about?" Sam barely kept his voice in check. He'd always liked these two men, but he was quickly changing his mind. "So maybe I had a thing for Kiera, but dammit I don't like being lied to. And why the hell are you all in such a damn good mood? She lied to you, too."

"I suppose she did," Clair said. "For all the right reasons, though. I know what it feels like, Sam. I was one of William's innocent victims, just like Kiera. Don't be angry with her. She needed the truth, but she's still reeling from it. Give her some time."

"We haven't *got* any time, dammit." He did yell now, felt the insanity explode inside him. "She's moving on, going to Paris. What the hell am I supposed to do about that?"

"Well, I'm not sure." Clair glanced from Dillon to Jacob. "You boys got any suggestions?"

"Far from me to interfere," Dillon said with a shrug.

"Wouldn't dream of it." Jacob shook his head and scratched the back of his neck. "But we did see her step into the elevator with her brother a few minutes ago. Looked like they had their luggage with them."

The smell of daylilies and roses filled the lobby of the Four Winds Hotel. The bouquet, a lush, five-foot-tall spray of fresh flowers on a wide, round glass table, brightened up the room and welcomed guests as they entered the hotel.

And as they left.

Her chest aching, Kiera stood by the arrangement, hoping it might somehow shield her from the pain of leaving. How strange it was that she'd lived in six different states, worked in eight large, cosmopolitan cities, but here, in Wolf River, was the one place where she'd felt as if she belonged. Bittersweet, she thought, which made her think of chocolate, which made her think of the soufflé she'd made for Sam.

But then, everything made her think of Sam.

A roll of thunder rattled the hotel windows.

She'd tried not to think about him. Even as she called a few minutes ago and left a message for Clair that they wouldn't be able to join her for breakfast, she'd been thinking of Sam, about how much she'd miss him. She told herself that once she got to Paris she would be so busy she wouldn't have time to think about him. She had a wonderful adventure ahead of her, living in Paris, working with a famous chef. It was a dream come true.

Surely the pain would ease with time, she told herself. Time and distance, and a demanding, busy work schedule.

She watched a couple walk off the elevator, holding hands and smiling, and the crack in her heart widened.

Oh, hell. Who was she lying to now? Time and distance wouldn't make one bit of difference. She would always love him, and somehow she'd simply have to learn to live with the pain of losing him.

She blinked back the moisture in her eyes, remembered the first time she'd seen him, watching her in that elevator, and she'd known at some instinctive level that they would be together. He'd been right about one thing, she thought dismally. She *had* jumped into his bed. And she'd do it again in a heartbeat. She loved him, maybe she'd loved him from that first moment, before she'd even seen his face. Maybe even before, if she believed in that sort of thing.

Which, unfortunately, she did.

So now here she stood, her overnight bag at her feet, waiting while her brother flustered the pretty blond desk clerk, who'd been told that the room Trey wanted to pay for had been comped. Trey, stubborn creature that he was, insisted he be given a bill. The poor girl had no idea what to do but had been on the phone for five minutes, obviously trying to locate the reservations manager.

He'd let her have her space last night after they'd got to their suite. As much as her brother loved a good fight, for once, thank God, he'd backed off. Even this morning, the only thing he'd said to her was, "I called the car rental company and made arrangements for them to pick your car up here at the hotel. I'll drive you to the airport."

Any other time, she might have argued with him. But she was coherent enough, barely, to know that he was right. If she got behind the wheel of a car in her current state of mind, there was no doubt she'd end up in a ditch somewhere. She understood that was how Trey showed his love—by taking control. They'd had a lifetime battle over the issue. She supposed they always would.

But just before they'd walked out of the suite, he'd stopped, then pulled her into his arms and held her tightly. Displays of tenderness were rare with her brother, and the unexpected hug threatened to unravel the loose threads barely holding her together. And yet, as the same time, she drew strength from his closeness.

She'd been angry with Trey for hiding the truth from her, but, in his own way, she understood that he'd only wanted to protect her. She'd forgive him for that—eventually. But could she forgive herself for all the grief she'd brought to Clair and the other Blackhawks?

And would they ever be able to forgive her?

Would Sam ever forgive her?

"You ready?"

She turned, saw Trey standing beside her. His dark eyes skimmed over her face.

"Yes."

"Why don't you wait here while I go get the truck?" He took her bag. "It's starting to rain."

She watched him walk through the glass double doors and head for the front parking lot. Lightning flashed, then thunder rumbled, stronger this time, and the sky suddenly opened. How appropriate, she thought with a sigh, and spotted Trey's truck behind two other cars pulling in to valet. Her pulse quickened, knowing he'd be here any minute and she'd really be leaving.

She glanced around the hotel lobby one more time. Everything looked so perfect here, so in sync. Felt so right. Knees wobbling, she headed for the doors.

The doorman smiled and stepped forward. "Good morning, Miss Kiera. Going to brave the storm?"

Kiera stopped and looked at the man, knew his name

was Joseph. *Going to brave the storm?* She glanced at the pouring rain and black sky outside, thought that it was nothing compared to the storm inside her.

Going to brave the storm?

Was she?

Or, like Sam had said, was she going to run away?

"Are you all right?" Joseph asked, frowning.

"No," she whispered. "I—I don't think I am."

A blast of air from outside swept around her. She stared at Trey's truck, pulling up out front, then back at Joseph.

"Is there anything I can do for you?" the doorman asked.

"No," she said, staring at the man. "I think I need to do it myself."

Lightning flashed when she spun on her heels; she felt the electricity rushing over her skin. She ran to the elevators, pushed the button several times and jumped inside when the doors finally opened. A tiny, gray-haired lady stepped inside with her. Kiera pushed the sixth-floor button at least three times.

"Com' on, com' on," she murmured, dancing from one foot to the other. *Isn't this just like me?* she thought. Impulsive and impatient? *Won't I ever learn?* She gave the door close button a solid smack. "Hurry."

"Bladder?" the woman asked politely.

Laughter bubbled in Kiera's throat and she shook her head. "A man."

"Oh." The old woman gave a knowing nod, then smacked the button herself. Biting her lip, Kiera watched the doors close.

A hand slipped in between the last sliver of space,

stopping the doors from closing. *No,* Kiera wanted to yell, almost did.

Until Sam stepped inside.

Breath held, she stared at him. He stared back, his eyes glassy and narrowed with determination.

The doors closed behind them.

His suit and tie were wrinkled, his hair messy and he definitely needed a shave. She thought he'd never looked better.

"You're not leaving." He worked a muscle in his jaw. "I won't let you."

"Sam—"

"Don't say a word, dammit." He pushed a button to stop the elevator. "Now it's your turn to be quiet and listen."

She bit her cheek, willed every muscle in her body to be still.

"I watched my mother marry and divorce half a dozen times," he began. "She kept shoes longer than she kept husbands. By the time I was twelve, I didn't even bother to remember their names, I just assigned them a number."

Sam dragged a hand through his already tousled hair. "They were all decent enough guys, except for Number Five. He turned mean after he lost a job, started drinking and one night he took out his frustration and anger on my mother. I walked in right after he'd used his fist on her. I was sixteen at the time, big for my age. They took him away in an ambulance that night and he became ex–Number Five."

She thought about the black eye she'd had when he'd first seen her. What he must have thought, what he would have felt. Shame filled her. "And I let you believe that about me, that I'd been in that kind of relationship."

"You told me the truth about that, but I still made an assumption. I shouldn't have. Now will you just let me talk?"

She pressed her lips firmly together, wished he would hurry.

"I joined the Army when I was eighteen," he continued. "Right after she married Number Six. I was in for four years, decided to get an education when I got out and put myself through college moonlighting at hotels. I liked living in different places, liked not having roots. Liked being able to move on whenever I felt like it."

When he paused, she started to speak again, but he put his fingertips on her mouth. "I never wanted to get married, never wanted a family, didn't think I'd make a good father, considering my lack of role models. I figured my brothers and sisters could give my mom grandkids."

"Brothers and sisters?" She could barely stop herself from kissing the fingers he still held to her lips.

"I have three sisters and two brothers," he said. "I'm the oldest."

She raised an eyebrow. "*That's* why you're so bossy."

He traced her lips with his index finger. "I don't care about your father. What he did or who he was. I don't care you hid your past from me. The only thing that matters, the only thing I care about, is you, Kiera Blackhawk."

It was the first time she'd ever heard him say her name, her real name, and the sound of it, the thrill, swam through her. She gazed up at him, wanted to tell him how she felt, that she loved him, but she couldn't find the words.

A hard glint narrowed his eyes. "You want to go to Paris, fine. We'll go together. They have hotels in Paris. Lots of them. I'll go to China, if you want, dammit. But don't leave." He grabbed hold of her shoulders. "Don't leave me."

He dropped his mouth on hers, kissed her urgently, then barely lifted his lips from hers. "Marry me."

Her heart stuttered. She stared at him, the emotion, her love for him, overwhelming her. "You—you want me to marry you?"

"Now." He tightened his grip on her arms. "Today. Tomorrow. Whenever you want, as long as it's soon. I'm not letting you go, not again. Dammit, Kiera, will you say something?"

She tried, she really did, but her throat had swelled with tears of joy.

"Might help if you tell her you love her," a tiny voice echoed in the elevator.

Sam turned his head sharply, saw the elderly woman watching them. Surprise clearly registered on his face, but he was a man on a mission and refused to be distracted, even by an audience. He glanced back at Kiera.

"I love you." He leveled his gaze with hers. "God help me, I love you."

"I love you, too." She reached out, touched his cheek, felt the stubble of his beard tingle up her arm. "I was coming back to tell you."

"You weren't leaving?"

She shook her head. "Not without telling you how I feel, without giving us a chance. Even if you turned me away, I had to know. If I decided to stay in Wolf

River, I knew I could face anything as long as you were by my side."

"I'd like to see you get rid of me." He kissed her again, with a tenderness that made tears flow. "Say yes, Kiera. Say you'll marry me. That you'll love me and have my babies."

Babies, she thought, as in *plural,* and her head spun. Until this minute, she hadn't realized how much she wanted babies. *Sam's* babies.

"Yes," she whispered, sliding her arms around his neck. "Yes to all of the above. *Yes.*"

This time when he kissed her, neither one of them heard the elevator doors open, or noticed that their audience had grown.

"This family keeps getting bigger by the minute," Dillon said to Clair.

With a wistful smile, Clair looped an arm through Dillon's, then leaned back against Jacob's broad chest. "Isn't it wonderful?"

"Best damn elevator ride I ever took." Clutching her purse to her heart, the gray-haired woman walked off the elevator.

"What the hell—"

At the sound of Trey's angry voice, Sam lifted his mouth from Kiera's and frowned. "We're getting married, Blackhawk. Deal with it."

Trey frowned back and stepped to the elevator, stared hard at Sam. "You break her heart, I'll break your legs." He stuck out his hand. "Welcome to the family."

The two men shook hands, then Sam punched the close doors button again. "Tell me you love me again," he murmured, pulling her into his arms after the doors closed.

"I love you, Sam Prescott." Smiling, she pushed the button for the sixth floor, then slid her hands up his arms. "I love you, I love you."

"Tell me you'll marry me." He brushed his lips over hers.

"There you go again, bossing me around." But she tightened her arms around his neck and pressed her lips to his. "I'll marry you, Sam Prescott. Today, tomorrow. Any day you say."

He kissed her, lingered over her soft, sweet lips while the elevator steadily climbed to the top floor. He figured that Clair and Jacob could handle any hotel problems for at least an hour. Maybe even two. "Tell me you'll make chocolate soufflé every day for the rest of our lives."

Laughing, she tossed her head back and looked into his eyes. "That would be boring."

The elevator doors opened and he scooped her into his arms, nibbled on her ear while he carried her down the hallway. "Darlin'—" he murmured, kissing her again when they were inside his suite "—of all the things I can be sure of, nothing about our life together will ever be boring."

* * * * *

BLACKHAWK'S
BOND

To Caroline Cross, for keeping me sane, and to Jan Stockton, a real-life horsewoman and heroine. Thanks for sharing your time, your knowledge and your friendship.

One

The wolf paced.

Her wrists bound and staked firmly to the ground, she lay on her back and watched the animal tread back and forth, its large black paws moving smoothly and silently over the crisp leaves carpeting the forest floor. The scent of damp, fertile earth hung heavy in the still night air, filling her nostrils and lungs. Fear slithered up her spine and seeped into her blood. She opened her mouth to call out for help, but the words remained lodged in her throat.

Escape! her mind screamed at her, and she struggled to free herself from the thick ropes holding her arms above her head. Her limbs, heavy and leaden, refused to move.

Her pulse quickened, and she glanced back at the wolf. Its eyes glinting yellow, the animal paused and lifted its massive head, sniffed the air. A growl rumbled deep in its throat.

Dressed in ceremonial leathers, the Elders moved forth from the shadows of the trees that framed the inky sky. Their faces, tattered and worn, turned toward the wolf, and they nodded with solemn approval. A circle of fire burst forth, surrounding her, and the Elders vanished in the flames of brilliant red and gold. She called out to them, begged them to return, to set her free.

An eerie howl answered her.

She watched the wolf—no, a man—step through the flames. Her breath caught in her throat at the sight of his powerful warrior's body, naked, except for the loin-cloth slung low across his lean hips. Firelight danced in his long black hair, his sun-bronzed skin gleamed. Fierce, angry stripes of red and black war paint hid his face. Smoke clouded her vision, and the sound of distant drums beat in her head, through her rushing blood.

Panic swam through her when he approached, and once again she wrestled with the ropes at her wrist, but they held fast. He stood over her, gazed down with eyes the color of the sky.

"Submit to me," he demanded.

She shook her head.

He knelt beside her. "You belong to me."

"I belong to no man."

His smile flashed white through the haze of smoke. He slid his hand over her shoulder, down her arm. His palm was rough against her smooth skin. The ropes

*holding her, coarse and tight only a moment ago, turned
to velvet.*

She shivered at his touch.

"Submit to me," he repeated.

*"No." Her breath caught when his fingers loosened
the straps of the white sheath she wore. He peeled the
fabric back, baring her breasts. An arrow of heat shot
through her body; through her veins. Lightly he stroked
his fingertips down her throat.*

*Her chest rose and fell in short, air-gulping breaths.
Fear and anticipation consumed her. When he fisted his
hand and brushed his knuckles lightly over her breast,
the flames rose higher, hotter. He lowered his head, and
she felt the burn of his breath on her neck—*

Gasping for breath, her body shaking, Alaina Blackhawk bolted upright in bed. Eyes wide, she stared into the
darkness of her bedroom, then clasped a hand to her throat,
felt the pounding beat of her pulse against her fingers.

A dream, she told herself. *Just a dream.*

But it had felt so real, so incredibly real. She could
still smell the damp earth, the smoke. Could feel the bite
of the ropes on her wrists, the coarse texture of callused
hands skimming up her arms.

Her skin still tingled, her body throbbed with unful-
filled desire.

She hugged the bedclothes to her, waited for her
pulse to slow and the shivering to ease.

Pale streaks of moonlight slanted across the walls, into
the darkened corners. She drew in a deep, shuddering
breath, then dragged her trembling hands through her hair.

A sense of dread hovered over her like a great bird of prey, its large talons stretched wide, ready to swoop. She felt the breeze of its wings on her heated skin, looked up and realized it was her ceiling fan, nothing more.

She laughed dryly, then lay back down and pulled the sheets up to her chin. It was silly to be afraid of a dream. If anything, she told herself, she should have *enjoyed* it, even with all that "submit to me" nonsense.

The only thing she intended to submit to, she thought with determination, was a few more hours of sleep.

But even as her eyes closed and her skin cooled, even as she finally dozed off, she heard the distant sound of drums, and the lonely howl of a wolf….

No one looked twice at the dusty black pickup that turned off Highway 96 and headed east. This was Texas, after all. Trucks were as common in these parts as air, and there was nothing noteworthy about this one, anyway. No shiny paint job, no fancy rims, not one Don't Mess With Texas decal. When the pickup drove through the small town of Stone Ridge, the good folks simply nodded and gave a friendly wave, same as they would have done for anybody passing through.

But the driver of *this* truck, however, wasn't just "anybody," it was D. J. Bradshaw. *The D. J. Bradshaw.* And if folks had known *that,* jaws would have dropped faster than the Honorable Judge Pockerpine's oak-carved gavel.

It wasn't every day that the Lone Star state's most elusive—not to mention wealthiest—rancher showed his face in public.

And what a face it was.

D. J. Bradshaw personified the word *rugged*. With his large hands and powerful, six-foot-five frame, men said he'd been born to work the land he'd inherited from his daddy. Women, well, they thought those callused hands and muscled body had been born for something *much* more private.

And much more interesting.

Then there was that thick, devil-black hair and cobalt-blue eyes, that slash of dark brow and square-cut jaw, that hard set mouth and sun-bronzed skin. One look at D. J. Bradshaw and every woman—from the most refined female to the most demure maiden—was ready to slap on a cowboy hat and go for a ride.

Those lucky few who'd taken that ride still smiled at the mere mention of his name.

Once outside Stone Ridge town limits, D.J. slid a Bob Seger CD into the truck's player, cranked up "Against the Wind" then revved the engine and cut through the thick August heat rippling off the asphalt. No place better than a back country road to put pedal to metal, D.J. had always thought, taking the one-ton, 486 engine to full throttle. Gravel and dirt blasted off the back tires, leaving a generous layer of rubber on the road and dust in the heavy air.

"Bob" was singing about old-time rock and roll when the sign appeared twenty miles from the Louisiana border. D.J. slowed, then pulled off the main road onto a two mile, cedar-lined stretch of driveway leading to Stone Ridge Ranch. Golden ragwort splashed yellow across the lush green landscape, a sharp contrast to the prickly pear and rocky canyons he'd left only six hours ago.

D.J. drove under a tall iron archway with the SRR insignia, took note of the cattle and horses grazing beside a thick grove of fern-choked pines. When he rounded a grassy bend, a bridge stretched across a swiftly running stream and the truck tires clattered over the wooden planks.

He saw the stables first—red brick, with gray-shingled roof—and parked in front of them. He'd read a full report on Stone Ridge Stables weeks ago. Five thousand acres of prime timber and grazing land. Four ranch hands, one foreman, one housekeeper, a small herd of cattle and a stable full of prize winning quarter-horses. Though the ranch was legally owned by a woman named Helena Blackhawk, it was her son, Trey, and a daughter, Alaina, who ran the operation. There were two other daughters, as well. Alexis, who lived in New York, and the youngest, Kiera, who was a chef, and currently living in Wolf River.

D.J. liked to know the people he intended to do business with.

He'd also seen a detailed list of Stone Ridge Stables' profit and loss statements, bank accounts, a record of sellers and buyers they'd dealt with for the past five years. Information he'd need when he made the Black-hawks an offer to buy their ranch.

Stepping out of his truck, he caught sight of the main house and thought Southern antebellum. Thick vines of honeysuckle clamored up the white columns of the wraparound porch and a lush green lawn stretched across the front yard. To the west of the house, a stand of poplars shaded a rock and fern garden bordered with chunks of flat stone.

The scent of honeysuckle and the tinkling of wind chimes drifted on the hot, humid breeze, along with the amiable chatter of men working a horse from a nearby corral. He looked at his wristwatch, then glanced at the black underbelly of the clouds gathering on the horizon, hoped like hell he'd be back on the road before the storm blew in.

He started toward the house, stopped at the sound of a woman singing from inside the stables. He couldn't make out the words, but the melody was soft and sweet and vaguely familiar. It drew him into the stables, past several occupied stalls, until he came to the last open stall on the right.

Tall and slender, the woman stood with her back to him, brushing the muscular neck of a black stallion that had to be at least two hands above her head. Her hair, chestnut-brown, flowed in a thick ponytail down the back of her white sleeveless blouse. Her legs were long, her boots well worn. A bright red bandana peeked out from the back pocket of her snug faded jeans.

"Blue Bayou," he thought, recognizing the song.

He supposed he should say something. At the very least, clear his throat or shuffle a boot. Something to make her aware of his presence. But he was still curious, not to mention captivated by her voice and the slow caress of her delicate fingers sliding over the horse's sleek coat. The animal seemed captivated as well, D.J. noted. Except for a slight twitch in his left shoulder, the stallion stood motionless and calm.

When the woman stepped away from the horse and reached for a blanket hanging on a hook in the stall, D.J. allowed himself one last moment to appreciate her slender curves, then cleared his throat as he took a step forward.

Big mistake.

Startled, the stallion charged the open stall door. D.J. reached out and grabbed the lead line, but not in time to avoid the slash of a hoof across his forearm when the horse reared.

"Whoa!" D.J. held on when the horse reared up again. *"Whoa!"*

Nostrils flaring, black eyes wide, the horse dropped back down onto its front hooves, then jerked its massive head upward. The woman rushed forward and grabbed the animal's halter.

"Easy," she said firmly, then slid a hand down the stallion's neck. "Easy, boy."

Snorting, the horse pawed at the dirt and tossed its head. The woman grabbed the lead line and moved between D.J. and the animal. "I've got him now."

He let go of the line and stepped back, studied the woman's face as she led the horse back into the stall. Her features had an exotic appearance, but with a softer, smoother edge. High cheekbones, pale gold skin. A sweeping, narrow arch of dark brow over thickly lashed eyes as pale blue as an early morning sky. And her mouth. Damn. He let his gaze linger a moment on her upturned, lush, wide lips, and decided that his business here had suddenly become much more interesting.

"You're bleeding," she said.

He lifted his gaze to hers, saw the concern in her eyes. "What?"

"Your arm." She stepped away from the horse and glanced at him. "It's bleeding."

D.J. looked down. He'd been so distracted, he hadn't even noticed the gash on his arm or the blood dripping down his hand. *Damn.*

Her long legs closed the distance between them quickly. "Let me look at it."

"That's not—"

She reached for his arm. When he tried to shrug her off, she tightened her hold. "Be still," she said, using the same tone with him as she had with the horse. "It's deep."

Frowning, he watched her pull the bandana from her pocket and wrap it around his arm. When she applied pressure, he felt the warmth of her hand through the fabric. A tingling sensation, like tiny sparks of electricity, rippled over his skin, then shot up his arm.

What the hell?

Alaina Blackhawk glanced up sharply and met the man's narrowed gaze. Heart pounding, she stared at him, then jerked her hand from his arm.

"I'll get something to put on that," she said, backing away on knees that suddenly felt weak. "I, uh, have antiseptic, some bandages, in the tack room."

"Don't bother." Shaking his head, he removed the bandana. "It's barely a scratch."

Breath held, she looked down at his arm, saw that the bleeding had stopped and the cut was, indeed, barely more than a scratch.

It can't be.

Slowly, she lifted her gaze back to his. Even though heat still lingered in her fingertips, a chill shivered up her spine. "So it is," she said. "Just a scratch."

She heard the harsh, deep tone of his voice, knew that he had asked her something, but she was still too confused, her mind too muddled to understand. He'd tipped his black Stetson back and she could see his hair was the color of coal, his eyes a sharp, deep blue. A jagged scar ran beside the dark slash of his left eyebrow, and a bend at the bridge of his nose only added to the rough appeal of a man who clearly met life head-on.

She suddenly realized he'd asked her a question. "Excuse me?"

"I said—" he tilted his head, studied her "—are you all right?"

She fought her way through the cobwebs in her brain. "Yes, of course. You just startled me."

"Sorry." He looked at the stallion, watched the animal pace nervously in his stall, then glanced back at her. "I was looking for Trey Blackhawk."

She knew she should stop staring at him, that she should say or do *something*—at the very least, introduce herself. Even if she had practically been raised in a barn, she'd also been raised to be well-mannered, lest anyone think that the Blackhawk children were "heathens," so her mother had repeatedly said.

But she wasn't the only one staring. When his gaze swept down her neck, then her shoulders, and lingered for a moment on her breasts, Alaina's breath caught. She was twenty-seven years old, for God's sake. Men had looked at her before; for that matter, they'd looked a lot. It was only natural a woman who lived and worked predominantly with men was going to be stared at. But she'd gotten used to it, and most of the time, she didn't give it a thought.

This wasn't one of those times.

This time her body, with a will of its own, responded. Her pulse raced, her skin tingled, her breasts tightened. She watched his eyes darken, then slowly lift to meet hers. When he raised a questioning brow, it was all she could do not to turn and run.

"Alaina."

At the sound of Trey's voice, the force surrounding her vanished abruptly. Startled, she turned and saw him walking toward her. *Thank God.* She looked at her brother, his dark hair, his rock-hard features, that typical frown on his handsome face—and her world shifted back to normal.

Trey's gaze moved from his sister to the man standing a few feet away. "Mr. Bradshaw?"

"D.J." The man stepped forward to accept the hand Trey held out. "You must be Trey."

Bradshaw? Alaina watched the men shake hands. It took a moment to sink into her muddled brain, another moment to connect the dots. D.J., as in D. J. Bradshaw? The has-more-money-than-God, most-eligible-bachelor-in-Texas, D. J. Bradshaw?

"I see you've already met my sister," Trey said.

D.J. slid a glance in her direction. "Actually we hadn't gotten around to names. Alaina, is it?"

Because she couldn't risk touching him again—not just yet, anyway—she simply shoved her hands into her back pockets and nodded. "Mr. Bradshaw."

"D.J." He touched the brim of his hat.

"D.J.'s here to look at Santana," Trey said.

"Santana?" Alaina glanced at her brother. "Why?"

"There's been quite a buzz about the horse since you bought him from Charley Cooper last month." D.J. tipped his hat back. "Talk was two vets diagnosed him with navicular and he was going to be put down."

"Navicular is often misdiagnosed." It had been a stroke of good luck that she'd happen to hear about Santana and had managed to make a deal with the horse breeder. "Cooper should have gotten a third opinion."

"I agree." D.J. nodded. "Which is why my vet was out here two days ago."

Alaina narrowed her eyes in confusion. "Excuse me?"

"D.J.'s made an offer on Santana," Trey said. "Contingent on his own vet's report. You must have been in town when he stopped by."

Setting her teeth, she glanced back at her brother. "Yes, I must have been."

How convenient, she thought. Two days ago Trey had sent her into town to pick up a prescription for their mother. Somehow she managed to keep her tone casual. "Trey, could I have a word with you, please?"

Trey shook his head. "Later, Al."

"Now would be better."

"Alaina—"

"Go on ahead." D.J. slipped his thumbs into his belt and shrugged one broad shoulder. "I can wait."

"Thank you." Turning on her boot heels, Alaina walked out of the stables. A hot, northeast wind whipped up the loose strands of hair around her face and the oppressive humidity sucked the breath out of her lungs. If she had to commit murder, it was going to be a difficult day to drag the body out of sight.

When they were out of earshot, she whirled on her brother. "Why didn't you tell me?"

"About Bradshaw or Santana?"

"Dammit, Trey, don't patronize me," she said through gritted teeth. "You knew how I'd react."

"Exactly why I didn't tell you." Folding his arms, he stared down at her. "We're running a business here, Alaina. I haven't got time for this."

Alaina jammed her hands on her hips and met her brother's dismissive gaze. "You know perfectly well I'm still working with Santana."

"You told me his leg is healed." One of the ranch hands called to Trey, but he waved the man off. "If Bradshaw's vet agrees, then we've sold a horse. In case you've forgotten, Al, that's what we do here. Sell horses."

"In case *you've* forgotten—" frustration tightened her hands into fists "—I'm the one who makes sure our horses are ready to sell. And yes, his leg is healed, but I'm telling you he's still not ready."

"He's not ready?" Trey asked. "Or *you're* not ready?"

She opened her mouth to argue, then closed it again. "That's not fair, Trey."

"This isn't about fair." He wiped at the sweat beading his brow. "This is business. If Bradshaw wants the horse now, he gets the horse now."

"I just need a couple more weeks before—"

"If he makes an offer, it's a done deal." The distant rumble of thunder darkened Trey's frown. "So you and I can stand here and waste time locking horns about it, or you can accept it and move on."

"You're good at that, aren't you—moving on?" The sarcasm slipped out before she could stop it, and she bit her tongue, wished she could yank the words back.

A muscle jumped in his jaw. "Someone in this family has to be. We've got a ranch to run, Alaina. Bills don't get paid by sticking our heads in the clouds."

She sucked in a breath, let the sting of his words ripple through her. "Is that what you think I do around here? Stick my head in the clouds?"

Trey's mouth hardened, but he hadn't time to respond before another rumble of thunder sounded, louder and closer. They'd been so intent on their argument, neither one of them had noticed the dark clouds quickly sweeping in.

With a sigh, Trey lifted his hat and raked a hand through his hair. "No one works harder than you around here, sis," he said quietly. "And I know why Santana is special to you, but sometimes, even when you don't want to, you just gotta let it go."

Trey slipped his hat back on his head and walked away. Alaina opened her mouth to call him back, until she saw that D.J. stood just outside the stable entrance. Arms resting on the corral fence, he appeared to be watching two of the ranch hands saddle training a sorrel mare.

Horse breeders were a tight-knit community with loose tongues. When word got out—and it would—that Stone Ridge Stables had sold the stallion to Bradshaw, it would attract recognition and buyers from around the world.

D. J. Bradshaw had that kind of prestige and power.

And while none of that mattered to Alaina, she knew it mattered to Trey. And Trey mattered to her. No matter how much they argued and disagreed, no matter how many hurtful words might be said between them, she loved him.

Let it go, Trey had said.

Could she?

She watched him join Bradshaw at the corral and the men walked back into the stables. Closing her eyes, she drew in a slow breath, and knew she couldn't stop the sale of the horse any more than she could stop the rain that started to fall.

Two

The storm blew in fast and hard, bringing with it pitchforks of lightning and rolling claps of thunder. Rain fell in sheets, bounced off the dust dry dirt and formed pond-size puddles outside the stables. While ranch hands scurried about calming nervous horses and securing equipment, D.J. followed Trey up the wooden steps of the front porch.

"He's not easy to get in or out of a trailer." Stomping his boots on a thick door mat, Trey had to yell to be heard over the pounding rain. "If you decide to buy him, we'll deliver him to you."

D.J. shook the rain off and scraped the mud from his own boots, slipped off his hat when they stepped into the spacious front entry. The floors were glossy hardwood, and a fringed, burgundy and forest-green Oriental runner stretched toward a living room to the left. Walls the color of whipped butter displayed a collage of family photos that continued up a wide, oak paneled stairway and at the base of that stairway, a seven-foot mahogany grandfather clock loudly *tick-tocked,* drawing D.J.'s attention to the time. *Damn.* He'd hoped to be heading back home already.

A simultaneous bolt of lightning and slap of thunder struck close enough to make the house shake and the lights flicker.

"You might want to reconsider staying for dinner." Trey tossed his hat on a wall hook beside the front door. "At least wait for a break in the storm."

"Thanks." Though he was tempted by the tantalizing scent that filled the air, D.J. shook his head. "I'd like to get back on the road as soon as possible."

"You won't be gettin' nowhere tonight, not in this gully washer."

A man no taller—or wider—than a fence post came around the corner, wiping his hands on a green-striped kitchen towel. His eyebrows and moustache were as gray and wiry as the long hair he'd secured into a ponytail at the base of his skinny neck, and his eyes were nearly lost in a craggy sea of wrinkles.

"D.J., this is Cookie," Trey said with a wave of his hand. "Cookie, this is D. J. Bradshaw."

"Heard you was here." The elderly man skipped the dark slits of his eyes down D.J., then back up again. "You look like your pa."

D.J. noticed the old man's limp when he moved into the room. "You knew my father?"

"Can't say I knew him." Cookie shook his head. "Met him once, and your ma. She bought one of my apple pies at a county fair, more'n twenty years ago now. Said it was the best apple pie she'd ever had."

D.J. raised a brow. "Was that the Crowley County Fair?"

"That's the one." The elderly man shoved one corner of the towel into his belt buckle and held out a hand. "Won me a slew of blue ribbons that year."

"You were a celebrity in my house," D.J. said, shaking the man's hand. He'd only been thirteen at the time, but his mother hadn't stopped talking about that apple pie. "My mother told my father she was going to run away with you."

Cookie shrugged one bony shoulder and blushed. "Damn shame, what happened to your folks. A damn shame."

D.J. nodded. "Thanks."

Thunder grabbed hold of the house again and gave it another shake. Trey frowned at the flickering lights and looked at Cookie. "You were saying something about the storm when we walked in?"

"Big rig jackknifed out at the highway. Couldn't get out if you wanted," Cookie said. "Or git in. Jimmy called and said he was stuck ten cars deep and the sheriff is rerouting everyone back to town. Won't git a tow truck out till the morning, very least."

D.J. mentally echoed Trey's single swear word. Even

though he was obviously aware of the fact he couldn't do a damn thing about the situation, he still couldn't stop the knot of frustration tightening his gut. *So much for being home by midnight.*

"Was anyone hurt?"

D.J. glanced up at the dusky sound of the woman's voice and watched Alaina move down the stairs, couldn't stop the tug low in his belly. Her dark, thick braid hung over one shoulder of the red flannel shirt she'd changed into, and her jeans, a softer blue than she'd worn earlier, stretched across her slender hips and down her long legs.

"Hard to tell," Cookie replied. "Jimmy said three or four cars were smashed up and Drew Gibson's truck had flipped, but he was standing on the side of the road, kicking one of his tires, so I guess he's all right."

"Knowing that fool Drew, he probably caused the whole damn thing." Despite the sarcasm, there was concern in Trey's voice. "I'm going to call the sheriff and make sure Jimmy's not just looking for a night in town with Lucinda."

"I don't suppose you have another way out?" D.J. asked. "Maybe a back road?"

"Nothing that's even remotely passable in this weather." Trey shook his head. "Cookie set another place at the table, and Alaina, show D.J. to my office. I'll be right there."

D.J. watched Alaina open her mouth to protest, then quickly shut it again. Clearly she was not happy about having company. *That makes two of us, darlin',* he thought.

She led him down a wide hallway to a room rich with oak paneling and a wall of floor-to-ceiling glass that provided an ample view of the rolling hills surrounding the ranch. An impressive display of trophies, blue ribbons and silver buckles lined bookshelves, along with several framed certifications.

"I'm sure Trey won't be long." She gestured to a black leather armchair beside a large oak desk. "Have a seat, Mr. Bradshaw."

"D.J."

"Right." She turned and opened a leaded glass liquor cabinet. "What would you like?"

He slid his gaze down the smooth column of the woman's neck while he considered her question, decided it was best not to say the first thing that came to his mind. "Whiskey."

Might as well cut the edge off, he thought, watching the rain pour off the eaves outside the office. Even if the roads had been open, he knew he'd never make it home tonight in this kind of weather. With a little luck, that tow truck would get the highway cleared bright and early.

And based on the starch in Alaina Blackhawk's voice and shoulders, that was about as lucky as he'd get tonight.

"How's your arm?" she asked, opening a bottle of Jack Daniel's.

"Fine."

He came up behind her while she poured his drink, noticed the strands of hair that had escaped from the braid she'd knotted down her back. A strange urge to tuck them back into place took hold of him, but he resisted, and instead, leaned in and satisfied himself by drawing in the faint scent of jasmine drifting from her skin.

Her breath caught when she turned and found him standing so close. He had the distinct feeling she would have stepped away if her back hadn't been to the wall, but she recovered quickly and offered the glass to him.

"Thanks." When he took the glass, a spark snapped where their fingers touched. Raising a brow, he met her startled gaze.

"Static in the air," she said, her voice a bit breathless and snatched her hand away. "From the storm."

As if to punctuate her words, a flash of lightning illuminated the room, highlighted the red and gold in her dark hair and danced in her soft blue eyes. Her face seemed to glow and he had the urge to slide his fingers over her cheek, had to remind himself where he was and why he was here. Not to mention the woman's brother would be walking in at any moment. It didn't take a genius to figure out that making a pass at Alaina, as tempting as it was, wouldn't go over well with her brother.

Pity, he thought, then lifted his glass and sipped, enjoyed the spicy rip of flavor in his mouth. "You didn't come back to the barn."

"There was no reason to." She moved a shoulder. "Trey knows Santana. Once your vet comes back with a clean report—and he will—you'd have to be blind or stupid not to buy him. Obviously you're neither of those things."

"Careful, Alaina." He watched her over the rim of his glass. "That was almost a compliment."

Dropping her gaze, she turned to cap the bottle. "I apologize if I've been rude."

"I didn't say you were rude." He shifted his gaze to a far corner of the room. "But I am glad there's a lock on that gun cabinet over there."

When she turned back, there was a hint of a smile on her lips. "I know where the key is."

"I'll keep that in mind," he said, stepping back. "So you want to tell me why you don't want me to buy Santana?"

His question clearly caught her off guard and she turned, busied her hands adjusting bottles in the cabinet. "What makes you say that?"

"Like you said—" he sipped his drink "—I'm not blind or stupid."

She hesitated, then turned and met his gaze. "I'm still working with him."

"Trey told me." And obviously she wasn't ready to turn the job over to anyone else, he thought. It wasn't uncommon for trainers to be possessive and more than a little protective with their horses. "I assure you, my trainers are top-notch."

Thunder rumbled through the walls again, and a wind slashed rain against the windows. "I don't doubt that they are, but switching trainers, no matter how good they might be, can be difficult on some horses. Santana is used to me. He trusts me." Passion flared in her eyes, raced through her voice. "He knows that I—"

She bit her lip and glanced away.

Lord, don't stop now, he thought, fascinated by her swift and fervent outburst of emotion. "That you what?"

"Oh, Alaina, I'm sorry. I didn't realize you had company."

D.J. straightened and backed away, saw the woman standing in the doorway. An older, blond version of Alaina, he thought. Same pale blue eyes and face structure, same sweeping arch of brow. The linen blouse she wore was beige, her slacks brown. Her eyes darted nervously to the storm outside, then back again.

"Are you all right, Mom?" Alaina's voice softened. "Is something wrong?"

"I can't find Trey," Helena Blackhawk said, her words shaking slightly. "The storm—"

"Trey is fine." Alaina moved across the room. "He's just checking on the roads."

"Are you sure?" The woman placed a trembling hand to the rope of earth-tone beads at her throat. "He's been gone so long."

"He'll be right back." Alaina slipped an arm around her mother's shoulders. "This is D. J. Bradshaw. He's come to buy one of our horses."

"Mrs. Blackhawk." D.J. nodded at the woman. "A pleasure."

"Have you seen my son, Mr. Bradshaw?"

D.J. glanced at Alaina, saw the silent plea in her eyes, then glanced back at Helena and smiled. "Yes, ma'am. He was here just a minute ago."

"Oh, thank God." The woman sighed with relief. "My William died in a storm just like this one," she said. "Right after he saved a little boy from drowning. Did you know my husband, Mr. Bradshaw?"

"No, ma'am, but I am sorry for your—"

"Everything all right here?"

Trey stepped into the room and looked at Alaina, who nodded. "Mom was worried about you."

"I'm fine, Mom," Trey reassured his mother.

"You shouldn't be out in this storm." Helena reached out and touched her son's cheek, then glanced back at D.J. "No one should be. I'll have Cookie set another place at the table and prepare the guest room."

Rain fell steadily for the next few hours, and though an occasional rumble could be heard in the distance, the thunder and lightning had moved on. A typical summer storm, Alaina thought, standing at her bedroom window. She stared out into the black night, listened to the rain rushing through the gutters overhead. Weather like this blew in all the time.

What wasn't typical was what the weather had blown in with it.

She thought about the man sleeping in the guest room at the end of the hall, pressed a hand to her stomach and felt the flutter under the cotton nightshirt she wore. *So I'm not immune to D. J. Bradshaw's good looks and charm,* she thought irritably. A man who looked like that, with that kind of money and power, she'd have to be half-dead or in a coma not to respond, for crying out loud. It didn't mean a damn thing.

So then why can't you sleep?

Because of Santana, she told herself and turned away from the window. The horse had been stressed even before she'd brought him to the ranch, but the storm today had made him more tense. Knowing that he would be sold before she had the time she needed with the animal frustrated her, though not nearly as much as the fact that Trey hadn't even discussed the horse's sale with her, and that he'd intentionally sent her on an errand so she wouldn't find out. She knew that the ranch finances were strained because of their mother's medical and living expenses, just as she knew that those expenses were only going to increase over time. She'd tried to discuss the money situation with Trey, but he kept telling her that she needed to concern herself more with the horses and less with the money.

Lord, he made her want to spit nails.

Too keyed up to go to bed, she reached for her jeans and boots and pulled them on, then slipped into the hallway. The third step on the stairway creaked, as it always did, and at the same time she hit the last step, the grandfather clock started to bong out the midnight hour. Before it finished, she had her rain slicker on and was out the front door.

The aroma of Trey's Cuban cigars lingered on the front porch where, after dinner, he and D.J. had smoked. It was a scent she enjoyed, even though she thought it a nasty habit. Slipping the hood of her slicker over her head, she dashed across the yard to the stables, felt the pull of the mud under her boots every step of the way. In the distance to the north, silent lightning ripped through the sky and the energy of the storm exhilarated her.

With her mood lighter and her blood pumping, Alaina reached for the battery operated lantern hanging on a wall hook beside the stable doors. She flipped it on, filling the stables with a soft, golden glow. Pulling her slicker off, she threw it on a bale of hay, grabbed a fistful of oats, then made her way to Santana's stall.

"Hey, boy," she called to the stallion, who'd been pacing in his stall. The horse tossed his head and approached, then stretched his long neck and chomped on the oats she offered.

She stroked the animal's jaw while he ate, cleared her mind of the stress she'd been carrying all day. The smell of leather and hay and horse surrounded her and she closed her eyes, breathed the familiar scents in. The stables had always been her haven, a place where she could relax. There were so many memories here. Her first horse—a buckskin pony her mother had given her when she'd turned eight. The first time she'd seen a mare give birth. The first time Trey had let her help in the birthing.

There were other firsts, though with more mixed emotions. Her first kiss from Jeff Porter, a ranch hand's son. She'd been thirteen, in braces, and she'd had a painful crush on the lanky fourteen-year-old. The kiss had been sweet, but strangely disappointing. There had been other boys later, more kisses, equally disappointing.

"Must be me, huh, Santana?" Alaina smoothed her hand over the stallion's soft muzzle, frowned when the animal tossed its head. "Well, you needn't be rude," she said with annoyance. "So maybe I am different. Not much I can do about it."

Here in the stables was where she'd first learned just *how* different she was. Talk about mixed emotions.

"Can't sleep?"

She jumped back at the sound of D.J.'s voice, watched him move out of the shadows. "Good God," she snapped through clenched teeth and pressed a hand to her thumping heart. "You scared me."

"Sorry." Rain dripped from the brim of his hat. "I saw someone run out the front door to the stables and I thought there might be a problem."

"What do you mean, you saw me?"

"I was on the front porch."

He moved slowly into the circle of light surrounding her, approached her with the same caution one might use with a skittish horse. It amazed her how quietly such a large man could move. She suddenly felt awkward, and very much alone out here, two things she never felt in the stables.

She moved back to Santana's stall door, did her best to keep her tone matter-of-fact. "I thought you'd gone to bed."

"Going to bed and sleeping are two different things."

Her cheeks warmed at his comment, though she was certain he hadn't intended anything suggestive. At least, she didn't *think* he did. She glanced at him, watched him casually lean one broad shoulder against the stall frame and decided it was simply her own awareness of the man that made her think about sex.

She put her hand out for Santana, and the stallion snorted softly against her palm. "I hope there wasn't a problem with the accommodations."

"The accommodations—" he repeated the formal word with amusement in his voice "—were excellent, as was the dinner and the company. I appreciate the hospitality, especially considering the fact you and your family were stuck with me."

"I'd say it was the other way around." She doubted very many people—especially women—would consider themselves "stuck" with D. J. Bradshaw. "And my mother enjoys company, especially when she's staying at the ranch."

"She doesn't live here?"

"Not for the past couple of years. Her doctor in Austin thought—" Alaina hesitated, had no idea why she was discussing her mother's state of health with a complete stranger. "It's just better for her to be in the city, so she only comes out to the ranch for short visits. We don't have very many guests here, other than an occasional friend one of my sisters might bring home."

"Alexis and Kiera."

It surprised her that he knew their names, but then she remembered her mother had talked about them during dinner. Thankfully her mother had done most of the talking, telling story after story that may or may not have happened. But if D.J. had been uncomfortable with Helena Blackhawk's obvious obsession with the past, he hadn't shown it. He'd been a perfect gentleman and listened attentively, said all the right things at all the right times.

Which is what he seemed to be doing now, she thought and decided there was a very fine line between manipulation and control.

"When my sisters were in college they always thought it was funny to bring their city pals to the ranch and give them a taste of the country life. We used to place bets on how long the different friends would last." Alaina smiled at the memory. "After a couple of days without their lattes and sushi, most of those friends were chomping frantically at the bit to escape from here."

"And you?" D.J. reached out a hand to Santana, but the horse tossed his head and backed away. "Were you ever chomping at the bit to escape?"

"Me?" She laughed at the idea, remembered her one trip to New York and how overwhelmed she'd felt. All the cars packed in, the horns honking, the herds of people. She hadn't been able to breathe. "No, I missed my sisters, and I understood their decisions to leave here, but the ranch was my life. Is my life. Simple as that."

"Something tells me there's not one thing about you that's simple," D.J. said quietly.

The brim of his hat and the darkness hid his face from her, and somehow it seemed not as if he was looking at her, but as if he was looking *through* her. The thought sent shivers up her spine. She felt the heat of his body, smelled the masculine scent of his skin, knew if she touched his chin, the dark stubble of his beard would vibrate through her fingertips. Her awareness of him, of his closeness, made her wary and more than a little anxious.

"What about you?" Somehow, she managed to keep

her voice conversational. "You ever want to escape? Be someone or someplace other than where you are?"

"Not at the moment."

His response made her pulse quicken. This time, there was no question there was a suggestive tone in his voice. "That's not an answer."

He leaned in, lowered his head close enough she could feel his breath on her cheek. "I forgot the question," he said.

So had she.

She knew she should tell him to back off, or back away herself, but she seemed incapable of either. The rain drummed softly on the roof and the darkness closed in, heightened her already overloaded senses, until she swore she could hear the beat of his heart and taste the passion.

Smell the danger.

His mouth was within an inch of hers, then closer. Anticipation shivered through her and she waited, breath held, but didn't move.

Neither did he.

Frustrated, she nearly closed the whisper of space between their lips, until she realized that was exactly what he wanted her to do. *Not gonna happen, Bradshaw,* she thought and eased back.

He watched her for a moment, then slowly raised a brow. "You're not curious?"

His question rippled over her like a warm wave. *Hell, yes.* But she'd be damned if she'd let him know that.

"I'm curious about D. J. Bradshaw," she said, managing to find a thread of calm and hold onto it.

"Curious why a man with your kind of money and status took up so much of his valuable time to drive so far and look at one horse."

"I'm a hands-on kind of guy."

She imagined that was quite an understatement, and the image of those hands on her made her take a step back. "Or maybe you're just bored and looking for a little diversion."

"If I was just bored and looking for a diversion," he said with a slow smile, "I assure you, I wouldn't need to drive eight hours."

Whether they were talking about horses or women, if D. J. Bradshaw wanted either one, Alaina had no doubt that he wouldn't have to move even one of those big, strong muscles of his. All he'd have to do was crook one finger.

"No, I don't suppose you would." Turning, she reached for the lamp. "I should be getting back in."

"My vet called about an hour ago."

Her hand jerked, then closed around the handle and she turned back. "Oh?"

"He gave Santana a clean bill of health." He paused a moment, as if to measure her response, then said, "His leg is good as new."

She'd known what the vet's report would be, and even though she'd had all evening to prepare herself, she still couldn't stop the sharp little slice of pain in her heart. She hated that Trey was right, that she'd become too emotionally attached.

How could she not?

"Congratulations," she said, though the word felt hollow. "You've bought yourself a magnificent horse."

"Actually—" D.J. straightened "—I haven't made my decision yet."

"I don't understand." She furrowed her brow. "Trey said your decision was based on the vet's report."

"It was. Now it's based on you."

"Me?"

"I'd still like to buy Santana," he said, "but only if you'll come along and finish his training at the Rocking B."

"What?" Certain she hadn't heard him right, she simply stared.

"You said you needed more time with the horse, so I'm offering it to you."

"At your ranch?"

"At my ranch."

"You're kidding, right?" She locked her knees into place so they wouldn't buckle on her. "Why would you do that?"

"Several reasons." Tipping his hat back, he folded his arms. "One, like you said earlier, changing trainers could result in a setback."

"Still—"

"Two," he went on. "I have a brood mare arriving in two weeks and I think she's perfect for Santana. I need the stallion ready for her, or we'll miss her season. And worst case scenario, we lose control during the breeding and Santana reinjuries his back leg."

Alaina was well aware of the fact that when a stallion covered a mare, there were always potential problems and injuries, to both horses. The breeding process needed to be kept as controlled as possible.

"Three, I'd like to watch you."

Her spine stiffened and she lifted a chin. "Excuse me?"

"Watch you work." He emphasized the last word. "I'm impressed with your style."

"My style?" Now she *knew* he was kidding. "You know nothing about me."

"I know what I see. It's obvious you've had phenomenal success with Santana in a short period of time. I've seen you with him, how he responds to you. I'm not so shortsighted not to realize there's always something to be learned, Alaina."

She raised the lamp and looked into his eyes, but was unable to read his expression. "What did Trey say about this?"

"I figured I should talk to you first." D.J. met her gaze straight-on. "But I understand if you'd rather discuss it with him before you give me an answer."

Alaina knew perfectly well what Trey would say if she took this deal to him. It didn't matter that she was twenty-seven years old and more than capable of taking care of herself, Trey's overly protective side would have instantly said no. And if D.J. hadn't asked her first, Alaina had no doubt that Trey would never have even told her. He simply would have said that the deal had fallen through.

And D.J. knew it, too.

She'd spent her entire life sheltered, stayed within the safety net of family and the ranch. While Alexis and

Kiera had fought for their freedom and won it, Alaina had chosen to let Trey make all the decisions in her life, business and personal. It had been easier that way.

Safer.

But now, suddenly, she had an opportunity to make a decision for herself, for the ranch, and though the thought of it turned her stomach inside out, it also thrilled her. She would not only have the extra time she so badly needed with Santana, but an opportunity to actually work on one of the largest and most famous horse ranches in the entire state of Texas.

How could she say no?

She stared at D.J., considered the possibility he might have a fourth reason for her to come work at his ranch, but then she dismissed the idea. He'd been toying with her tonight, playing head games, but D. J. Bradshaw was a businessman. His decision would have been based solely on facts, not a frivolous, passing moment between two strangers. She doubted that a man like D.J. would give the moment, or her, a second thought.

She stared at D.J., knew he was giving her time to think, but she also knew he wanted an answer now. In the quiet of the barn, she was certain he could hear the hammering of her heart.

Two weeks, at the Rocking B with D.J. As much as the man unsettled her, surely she could handle two weeks.

She ran through several scenarios as to how she might approach Trey on the subject. Calm and logical was the first one. Determined and steadfast was the second. Angry and in his face was the third. But no matter how they started, they all ended the same. He'd yell, then forbid it, then they'd fight about it and he'd yell some more. She'd never won an argument with her brother, not over something as big as this, and she had no reason to think this time was going to be any different.

But for her, this time was different. This time it really mattered. This time it was something *she* wanted.

So the question was, did she want to do this the hard way, or the easy way?

It didn't take two seconds to come up with an answer to *that* question.

Drawing in a slow breath, she straightened her shoulders and met D.J.'s dark gaze. "All right," she said and nodded slowly. "I'll do it. But on one condition…"

Three

"So you're telling me that Trey Blackhawk doesn't know?"

D.J. looked over his shoulder at Judd Mitchell, his ranch foreman. They'd just ridden in from looking over the yearlings in the north pasture and had one of their weekly "business meetings," which covered everything from animals to equipment to staff. There wasn't anything that happened on the Rocking B that Judd didn't know about, and more than one ranch hand had grumbled that the man must have eyes in the back of his head.

D.J. had considered not telling his foreman about the arrangement he'd made with Alaina two days ago, but decided the man would figure it out anyway. And since she was expected to arrive within the hour, D.J. figured now was better than later.

"That's the way she wanted it." D.J.'s horse, a roan gelding named Sergeant's Duty, blazed his way through a thick patch of devil's grass. "No skin off my nose."

"Might be," Judd said.

The edge of accusation in Judd's tone had D.J. pulling up the reins on his horse. "What's that supposed to mean?"

Judd reined Roxie, his dapple gray, next to Sergeant. "Means he might take exception to you failing to mention that you made a side deal with his sister."

D.J. shrugged, knew that whether he wanted it or not, there was advice coming. "She offered up the terms, I accepted."

When Judd snorted, D.J. lifted a brow and met his foreman's steady brown gaze. At forty-six, Judd had a face that resembled the bark of a pine tree, and a long, straight, solid body that looked like the trunk. He was the only man on the Rocking B who D.J. would tolerate giving him a lecture, and even with Judd, there were limits.

"She might have set the terms." Judd glanced overhead at the soft blue, late afternoon sky, watched a Cooper's hawk glide, then dive into a grove of cypress. "But you set her up."

"What the hell is that supposed to mean?"

"She didn't have to come here to finish the horse's training." There was no judgment in Judd's statement, only question. "She could have worked at her own place for the next two weeks, then delivered the stallion in time for breeding."

"Santana's high strung," D.J. said, his irritation mounting. Sergeant, sensing his rider's mood, stomped a hoof and flicked his tail. "The horse is used to her, and I want the transition to go smooth."

Judd's saddle creaked when he pushed up the brim of his white hat and leaned back. "You talking about the transition of the horse, or the transition of you buying Stone Ridge Stables?"

"I haven't even made an offer yet."

"But you will."

He already had a lawyer drawing up the paper-work. "I will."

"Don't expect she'd take kindly to you withholding that little piece of information," Judd said dryly.

"Don't expect she will."

Judd nodded, let the silence pass between them for a moment. "So is she pretty?"

"What the hell difference does that make?" D.J. snapped. "I'm running a business here, dammit. Her looks have nothing to do with my decision."

The amusement in Judd's eyes had D.J. clenching his jaw. His foreman had gone fishing and D.J., idiot that he was, had just swallowed the bait whole.

"She's good with horses," D.J. said flatly. "The men might learn something watching her work."

"You want her working with the men?"

"That's her decision." But D.J. thought about a few of the younger, randy men whose brains weren't in their heads, but located much farther south. "You just make sure no one steps out of line."

Judd smiled slowly. "You included?"

D.J.'s reply comment was short and rude and when he nudged Sergeant into a trot, Judd's laughter followed.

Alaina turned off the highway and drove another thirty miles into a pretty valley with rolling hills and large outcroppings of rock. The summer heat had browned the mesquite and low growing shrubs, but groves of cypress and oaks stood tall alongside a slow moving river. This was Rocking B land, as far as the eye could see and way beyond. Acre after acre, mile after mile of picturesque land in the Texas sun belt. Late afternoon sun glistened off the water and glowed in the treetops, dappled the pastures and meadows.

When she passed the first outbuilding and paddock, her hands tightened around the steering wheel and she drew in a slow breath. It wasn't the first time today she'd questioned her sanity. She doubted it would be her last.

You're a grown woman, she told herself. *You have a right to make your own choices.*

Still, the deception—or omission of truth—depending on how she looked at it, did not sit well with her. Guilt was a useless emotion, as tough to shake as a burr on wool. But she'd made her decision, shook hands on the agreement and she wouldn't back down now.

The knot of nerves in her stomach tightened as she passed more paddocks and outbuildings, and when she rounded a bend and spotted the main house, her jaw went slack. She'd seen large ranch houses before, had delivered more than one horse to wealthy clients who lived in mansion-size homes. But this was something else altogether and Alaina eased up on the gas pedal to gawk.

The two-story house towered upward from the surrounding oak trees, a blend of split granite stone and river rock with a diversity of peaked roof lines, stone chimneys and leaded paned windows. The structure blended well with the landscaping, a stark use of native shrubs and grasses and rock.

She decided the house fit the man. Solid, big and more than a little foreboding.

As if her thought had conjured him up, she saw him then, dismounting a roan by one of the corrals. Two big dogs, one black, one gold, danced at his heels. His back was to her, but she recognized the black Stetson and those broad shoulders. He'd rolled the sleeves of his white shirt to his elbows, and his faded jeans rode low on his lean hips.

When he turned at the sound of her truck and lifted his gaze to hers, her heart jumped. Once again she questioned the sanity of her coming here, then once again thought about the horse in the trailer behind her.

Slowing the truck to a crawl, she watched a young, sandy-haired man run over to D.J. and take the reins of his mount. When D.J. glanced over his shoulder at another man riding up on a dapple gray and spoke to him, she resisted the urge to look in the mirror and straighten the hair she'd clipped on top of her head, settled for a quick hand comb to sweep back the loose strands. *As if it matters,* she thought, annoyed at her feminine impulse to primp for a good-looking man. She was wearing a faded pink T-shirt, old jeans and cowboy boots, for crying out loud. Not exactly the kind of outfit that gave a man ideas.

And not that she *wanted* to give him any ideas, either. She didn't. She just wanted to look presentable, that's all.

She pulled in front of the barn and watched him walk toward the truck, his long strides slow and easy. She placed a hand over her stomach when it started to tap dance, then flipped her air conditioner on high to cool the heat on her cheeks.

She rolled her window down when he reached the truck door. "This okay here?"

"Fine." He reached for the door and opened it. "Leave the keys in it. One of the men will move it later."

Nodding, she cut the engine and slid out of the truck, wished she could stretch the kinks out of her shoulders and legs, but decided against it. Based on the curious stares coming from the men working in the corrals, she thought it best not to draw any more attention to herself than necessary.

But then she looked back at D.J., felt the heat of his gaze slide over her, her throat turned dry as the dirt under her boots.

And then suddenly the dogs were racing across the yard toward her, barking a friendly and excited greeting. Alaina braced herself for the incoming missiles and the impending impact.

"Baxter! Taffy!" D.J. yelled at the dogs, who just managed to stop short of launching themselves. "Sit!"

The animals braked to a halt mere inches from her and sat, their bodies quivering with tightly coiled energy.

"Any problems?" D.J. asked.

"Hit a little traffic in Houston." She rubbed a hand over the black dog's head, then the gold one. Tongues rolling, they both pressed against her palm for more. "Smooth sailing from there on."

"Any other problems?"

"If you mean my brother, he wasn't too fond of me delivering Santana by myself." To say that Trey had been adamantly opposed was an understatement. They'd argued about it for twelve hours straight yesterday. Well, actually, *she'd* argued. He just kept saying no and walking away. "He wanted to come with me."

"And you convinced him otherwise," D.J. said, stating the obvious.

"I told him that I need some time off and since the Rocking B is practically on the way, I'm going to visit my sister when I leave here."

"The sister in Wolf River?" D.J. tilted his hat back. "Kiera, right?"

"Yes, Kiera." The man had a hell of a memory, Alaina thought, and reached into the cab of her truck for her leather gloves. "I doubt he would have bought it if I'd told him I was driving to New York."

"I suppose not," he replied with a grin. "So are you?"

D.J.'s smile stirred up the butterflies in her stomach. "Am I what?"

"Going to see your sister?"

"Well, of course I am," she said, with a touch of indignance. "I wouldn't lie to my brother. I just didn't give him a time frame between my leaving here and going there."

"I see." D.J. lifted a brow.

"He was still going to come with me." She'd had to think fast when Trey had made that announcement. "Until I told him that Kiera and I were going to be planning her upcoming wedding. He backed off so fast, he nearly tripped over himself."

She'd watched her brother face angry bulls and growling bears, but the only time she'd seen the man flinch was at the mention of marriage. She looked at D.J., could have sworn he'd leaned back himself when she'd mentioned the "w" word.

Men, she thought, shaking her head.

"Long as I call or leave him a text message every couple of days, he won't bother me." *Or you,* she thought, pulling her gloves on. "You've got me for two weeks, Mr. Bradshaw," she said and gestured to the trailer. "Let's go take a look at your horse, shall we?"

It took an hour before Alaina managed to persuade the anxious stallion out of the trailer. Several of the hands had circled in as well. A couple had offered to help—obviously hoping to make a good impression on the pretty woman—and Alaina had politely allowed them to try. One of the men had hobbled off in embarrassment after a hoof made contact with his knee, and another bowlegged cowboy had slunk back after the horse had managed to nip him hard enough on the arm to draw blood.

With Judd at his shoulder, D.J. had stood back and

quietly watched, decided to let the men see for themselves that Alaina knew what she was doing. When she finally coaxed the animal out of the trailer, without bodily harm to her or the horse, the men clapped.

"Show's over," D.J. barked when the men hovered. "Bobby, show Miss Blackhawk to Santana's stall. I'll be there in a minute."

Bobby, a baby-faced kid from Montana with curly blond hair, tripped over his feet, then blushed when Alaina smiled at him. D.J. rolled his eyes when they walked away with Santana.

"Good choice," Judd commented. "Pair her up with the youngest, shyest pup. Especially her being so homely and all."

"I'm not pairing her up with anyone." The hands had slowly strolled back to the corrals, but not without casting furtive glances over their shoulders at Alaina and mumbling to each other. "And I never said she was homely."

"Never said she wasn't, neither."

D.J. frowned at his foreman. "You wanna sharpen whatever point it is you're trying to make?"

"Production's gonna seriously drop with a woman around," he said simply and shrugged. "Especially one who looks like that."

D.J. watched Alaina lead Santana into the barn, couldn't stop his eyes from drifting down and watching the sway of feminine hips. Judd had a point, dammit, D.J. realized. If he couldn't keep his eyes and thoughts under control, how the hell did he expect his men to?

Only one way, he figured.

"Tell them she's with me," D.J. said tightly.

Judd lifted one bushy brow. "You sure about that?"

Hell, yes, he was sure. He didn't want his hands standing around drooling over a woman when there was work to be done. What they did on their own time was their business. But then he realized he didn't want them drooling over Alaina on their own time, either.

"Just imply it." He looked over at the men, saw them grinning at each other and laughing, figured they were already taking bets on who would score with the pretty brunette first. The thought settled in his gut like a shard of green glass. "That ought to keep them out of trouble."

"Sounds like it's going to get you *into* trouble." Judd pushed his hat back and cocked his head. "Somehow, I don't think Alaina's going to appreciate your effort to protect her virtue."

"She's only here for two weeks," D.J said with a shrug. "It's for her own good."

"Whatever you say, boss."

"Just remember that." D.J. frowned as his foreman then headed for the barn where Bobby, was busily pitching fresh straw into Santana's stall while Alaina filled a trough with water. The stallion flattened his ears and jerked his head back when D.J. leaned against the stall door.

D.J. frowned at the horse. "I'm beginning to take this personal."

Smiling, Alaina closed the spigot, then reached out to stroke the stallion's nose. "He just needs a little time to adjust. Don't you, boy?"

The horse snorted, then tossed his head, as if to say no, which made Bobby laugh. When D.J. turned his frown on the ranch hand, he sobered up and put his back into pitching more straw.

"You must be tired after your drive," D.J. said. "Bobby can take care of things here."

"I'm fine." She led the horse to the trough and put her hand in the water, enticing the horse to drink. "I'm sure Bobby has other things to do."

"No, ma'am," Bobby said, eager to please. "I can feed him and brush him, too, if he'll let me."

Alaina glanced at Santana, and D.J. wasn't sure if she hesitated because she didn't want to leave the horse, or she was nervous about going with him.

"I don't mind, really," Bobby added. "You go on."

Got to give that kid a raise, D.J. thought when Alaina reluctantly nodded. She quietly murmured something to the horse and smoothed a hand down its neck. "Just a handful of oats and some hay, and if you really want to make friends, he's a sucker for a slice of apple."

"I'll find one," Bobby said with such enthusiasm that D.J. knew he'd drive all the way to town and buy one if he couldn't. Hell, he'd probably drive to the next county, D.J. thought, and wondered if he'd made a mistake choosing Bobby to help Alaina. She'd barely been here an hour and the boy was already smitten. In two weeks, he'd be a complete goner. Poor kid was about to get his heart broke and he didn't even know it.

Alaina handed the lead line to Bobby, then wiped her hands on the front of her jeans. "All right, then," she said, glancing over. "I'll just get my bag out of the truck."

"I think I can manage that." D.J. opened the stall door for her and closed it after she passed through. "Dottie sees you carry your own suitcase and I'll be in a world of hurt."

"Dottie?"

"My housekeeper." They walked to the truck and D.J. plucked the suitcase from the back seat of the crew cab. "She's been jumping out of her skin since she heard you were coming. We don't get much female company and she's looking forward to having another woman in the house."

Alaina's heart stumbled at D.J.'s words. *His house?* She hesitated, watched him stride ahead of her. "I'm staying in your house?"

D.J.'s boots clunked across the slate stone walkway. "Of course. Where did you think you would stay?"

"Well, I—I don't know. I guess I just assumed I'd be in the bunkhouse."

D.J. paused, narrowed a look at her over his shoulder. "With the men?"

She glanced at the ranch hands, saw a couple of them watching her. No, she supposed that wasn't a good idea. But then she looked back at D.J. and didn't think sleeping in his house was such a good idea, either. She considered getting a room in town, but then she'd not only be on the road a couple of hours a day back and forth, she wouldn't be close to Santana.

The lesser of two evils? she wondered, then hurried after D.J. when he continued on toward the house.

She caught up with him as he was reaching for the front doorknob

"What will your men think?" she asked.

D.J. stilled, then looked down at her and frowned. "I don't give a damn what my men think."

She realized she was acting like a child. She was an adult, a grown woman, not the odd, shy little girl who'd endured the giggles in school and the whispers in town. What did it matter what his ranch hands—or *anyone,* for that matter—thought about her? She'd spent too much of life worrying about that sort of thing. No more, she told herself.

But before she could respond, the front door flew open.

"You're here! Oh, come in, come in! I'm Dottie."

She was a short woman, big-boned, with tightly trimmed silver hair that swept back from her face like the fins of a 1955 Falcon. Glittering green eyes nearly disappeared beneath the deep lines of her smile and matched the color of her short-sleeved blouse.

"I saw your truck drive up over an hour ago and been waitin' on pins and needles." Still pumping Alaina's hand, Dottie looked at D.J. and clucked her tongue. "Shame on you, Dillan Joseph, making this poor girl work her first day here."

Alaina glanced at D.J., who gave her an I-told-you-so-look.

"I am here to work," Alaina said, overwhelmed and amused at the same time and wondering when the woman was going to let go of her hand.

"Not your first day, you're not." Dottie pulled her into

the house. "I made my special roast for supper and a dessert that makes a grown man reach for a hankie."

D.J.'s eyes lit up as he closed the door. "You made chocolate cake?"

"Don't you be sneaking a piece." Dottie finally let go of Alaina's hand and shook a finger at D.J. "And don't think I won't know if you stick a finger in the frosting, either."

At the sound of a buzzer from the other room, Dottie swung around. "That's my potato casserole," she said, then shot D.J. a look. "I'm sure Alaina wants to freshen up before dinner. You show her to her room and I'll get her something wet and cold."

"Please don't go to any trouble on my account," Alaina said, but the woman had already hurried off.

"There's no stopping her when she's like this." D.J. moved toward a sweeping staircase. "Best thing to do is just ride it out. She'll calm down in a few days."

A few days? Alaina turned to follow D.J., then stopped in her tracks. If it wasn't enough that Dottie had been overwhelming, D.J.'s house was simply staggering. Cathedral ceilings that had to be over twenty feet high. Hardwood floors so smooth you could slide in your socks from one room to the next, windows so tall a giraffe could see in. And though it was a masculine house, the layers of bright rugs, pine moldings and antique furniture softened the harsh edges.

"This is beautiful." Wanting to take it all in, she looked up and turned slowly, watched the rays of the late afternoon sun stream in through an overhead skylight.

A smile on her face, she glanced at D.J. He stood on the stairs, watching her and when her gaze met his, her pulse leaped. The look in his eyes, hungry and intense, made her breath catch.

"Land sakes, what are you still doing here?" A glass of lemonade in her hand, Dottie came back into the entry. "You sure didn't get very far."

"I was just admiring the house," Alaina said, struggling to compose herself.

"Mr. B built it for D.J.'s mama. Such a shame they never got to live here." Dottie shook her head and sighed, then frowned at the sound of a muffled meow. "That fool cat. She had kittens three weeks ago and she won't stay put with them. Keeps moving them all over the house."

"Keep her out of my bedroom," D.J. grumbled.

"Esmeralda—that's the cat—" Dottie lowered her voice "—she moved her babies to his bed for a couple of days and poor D.J. slept on the sofa till she moved them again. He'll deny it if you ask him, though. Says he doesn't like cats."

"Dammit, Dottie, I told you I just fell asleep on the sofa, that's all," D.J. barked and started back up the stairs. "And I *don't* like cats."

Dottie's grin said she knew better and she handed the glass of lemonade to Alaina. "Here you go, honey, this should take the dust out of your throat. I best go see where Essie has moved her family to this time."

"Thank you." Alaina watched the woman disappear around a corner, then she looked back at D.J., who'd nearly reached the landing. She took a long gulp of the lemonade and followed after him, certain that the ice-cold drink, or even ten ice-cold drinks, wouldn't be enough to wash away the dryness in her throat.

Four

The last time that the dining room in D.J.'s house had seen a guest was three years ago, when Dottie's sister, June, had visited the ranch. Dottie had gone through the same rigmarole then as she had tonight. The china came out of the cabinet, the silver had been polished, the cloth napkins ironed. And in the center of the eight-foot-long table, a crystal vase filled with flowers cut fresh from her garden just that morning.

D.J. thought it was silly for three people to eat at a table that seated twelve, especially when the kitchen table was smaller and more comfortable than the formal setting of the dining room. But he knew women liked the hubbub of entertaining, so he figured he could manage to indulge Dottie's overblown display of social pleasantries for at least one night.

Not that he really had a choice. He might own the place, but everyone knew who the real boss in this house was.

"My Velma's first baby, Bridget Ann, she popped out like a piece of toast," Dottie was telling Alaina. "But the next one, little Timmy, he hung on tight as a tick, till they finally did a C-section. Velma swore no more children after that, but now here she is, eight months pregnant and looks like she's ready to pop."

Oh, for God's sake. D.J.'s fingers tightened on the fork in his hand. It was one thing to sit through Dottie's endless tales of her own three grown children, but stories about childbirth and babies popping out was just going too far.

D.J. pushed his plate away and cleared his throat.

Dottie didn't pause. Instead she moved on to the next daughter, Marlene, and her first pregnancy. And since Marlene had four kids, D.J. knew that this line of conversation was going to take a while.

He cleared his throat again, a little louder this time, and Dottie glanced over at him.

"Coffee?" he asked.

"We'd love some," Dottie said, but when D.J. frowned, she lifted her brow and rose from her chair. "Oh, right. All this carrying on when I've got cake in the kitchen. Silly me. I'll be right back."

Alaina reached for her plate and started to rise. "I'll help."

"Absolutely not." Dottie snatched the plate from her

and flapped a hand in protest. "Don't you dare move a muscle. You're a guest in this house."

"Thank you, but—"

"No buts." Dottie shook her head. "I insist."

Alaina looked at D.J., as if imploring him to change the woman's mind, but he simply shrugged.

"Now, I have coffee, regular or decaf," Dottie offered while she collected silverware and plates. "Or maybe you'd like some tea? I have peppermint, orange pekoe or Earl Grey. Then, of course, there's milk, whole or skim, or a bottle of brandy that's just screaming to be opened."

"Coffee is fine," Alaina answered, her eyes a bit wide. "Regular, please. Black."

When Dottie scurried away, D.J. watched Alaina shift in her chair. The meal had been easy while Dottie was there, chattering away like a squirrel with a bag of acorns. But now it was just the two of them and Alaina was clearly uncomfortable. She folded her napkin, folded it again.

"I'm sorry for any inconvenience I've caused," she said when she finally looked up. "I'm sure you have better things to do than sit here and listen to all this woman talk."

During the meal, D.J. had thought of at least a dozen things he'd rather be doing. Mucking out stalls, scrubbing down troughs. Jumping off a cliff. But at the moment, he couldn't think of anything but the way Alaina had looked this afternoon when she'd stood under that shaft of light streaming down through the entry skylight. Shades of red and gold had danced in her thick, dark hair and her entire body had seemed to glow silver-white. The smile on her wide lips and pleasure in her soft blue eyes had felt like a fist to his gut.

He'd taken a long shower after he'd showed Alaina to her room. A cold one.

"I'm just here for the cake." He sat back in his chair. "And trust me, Dottie is having a great time."

"The way she cooks, I'm surprised you aren't bigger." Her cheeks turned pink and she bit her lip. "I mean, that you're in such good shape."

Her cheeks turned even pinker.

"Thanks." He grinned at her. "You're in pretty good shape yourself."

He hadn't seen a woman blush in a long time, and it looked damn pretty, he decided. She mumbled a thank you, then fiddled with her napkin again. He watched her long, slender fingers sliding over the fabric, smoothing and folding. He remembered what her hands had felt like the first time she'd touched him in her barn. And though the sensation had been extraordinary, it had also been invigorating somehow and he hadn't been able to get it out of his. Hadn't been able to stop wondering what her hands would feel like moving over more than his arm.

The thought sent an arrow of heat straight to his groin and he decided they needed to talk about something other than what kind of shape they were both in.

"I know a Blackhawk," D.J. said casually and stretched his legs out under the table.

Alaina's hands stilled on the napkin. "It's a common name."

"Rand Blackhawk." Based on the stiffness in her shoulders and voice, he'd obviously pushed a button. "He was a horse trainer just outside of San Antonio, but he's got a ranch in Wolf River now. Didn't you say your sister lives there?"

"She's only been there a month." Alaina reached for her water glass. "She's a chef at the Four Winds Hotel. Have you heard of it?"

He had the distinct feeling she was trying to change the subject, which only made him more curious. "That's quite a coincidence," he said as he watched her take a long sip of water. "Rand's sister, Clair, owns the Four Winds."

"I've never met them."

Again, an answer that wasn't an answer. If the Blackhawks in Wolf River were related to Alaina, she clearly preferred not to say so. He hadn't talked to Rand since he'd gotten married a few months ago. D.J. considered giving his friend a call, maybe ask a couple of questions.

Alaina rose from her chair. "I should see if Dottie needs any help in the—"

"There we are, now." Dottie bounded in from the kitchen carrying a wooden tray loaded with mugs of coffee, giant wedges of chocolate cake and a glass bowl of whipped cream. She set the tray on the table, then scooped a fluffy cloud of cream on each slice. Smiling, she placed a plate in front of Alaina, then D.J. "I've turned down three marriage proposals after serving this."

"I was one of them," D.J. said and dug into his slice, was savoring that first delicious taste of chocolate when he made the mistake of looking at Alaina. He watched her take a delicate bite, then slowly slide the fork out of her mouth. A look of sheer pleasure lit her soft blue eyes just before she closed them and moaned softly.

Damn if his heart didn't thump against his rib cage.

While she heaped praise on Dottie, D.J. slouched his shoulders and hunkered down over his plate, careful not to look at Alaina again. He'd be damned if he'd let a woman interfere with his appetite.

"It's all in the chocolate," Dottie explained to Alaina. "I have to order it special from this little town in—oh, Esmerelda! There you are."

D.J. glanced over and saw the black and white cat sitting in the dining room doorway, looking as if she owned the whole damn world. She'd always been a barn cat, but somehow she'd managed to slip into the house to have her kittens and Dottie adamantly refused to put her back outside until they were older.

He *didn't* like cats, blast it. Only thing they were good for was mousing, he figured, and since the animal had moved into the house, she wasn't even good for that. She'd not only taken over his bedroom for two days with those kittens of hers, but to add insult to injury, the ungrateful feline barely gave him the time of day.

At the moment, Queen Esmeralda was staring with interest at Alaina.

"Aren't you a pretty lady?" Alaina said sweetly and held out her hand.

The cat stood and stretched, as if to say, "Yes, aren't

I?" then strolled slowly over and rubbed her head against Alaina's fingers. D.J. could hear the cat purring all the way across the table.

He watched Alaina stroke her hand over Esmeralda's arched back, and there it was again. The need to feel her touching him. Frowning, he stood, tossed his napkin on the table and grabbed his coffee.

"I've got work in my office," he said and looked at Alaina. "You need anything, just ask Dottie."

The dream found her, reeled her into the forest mists and laid her gently on a bed of soft leaves. The stillness soothed her and she breathed in the quiet, then sighed with contentment. She belonged here, in this place where the spirit of her ancestors shimmered on the cool night air. From the thick shadows, she felt their eyes on her, watching…waiting.

The wolf howled.

A sudden wind whipped through the trees and she shivered at the icy chill that snaked through her veins. She tried to stand, to run, but her arms and legs were so heavy. A bolt of fire shot upward from the ground, then another, and another, until a circle of crackling flames surrounded her. A ribbon of smoke curled toward her, wrapped around her wrists and bound them together. She struggled, but could not break free.

She watched the man emerge from the flames, and she fought to stay calm. She'd known he would come, had waited for him. He was The One.

But the wavering shadows and smoke hid his face

and uncertain, she shrank back. What if she was wrong? Would she lose her power?

He moved closer to her, all sinewy muscle and glistening skin. The chill in her blood heated, spread through her body. I am weak, she thought, biting her lip against the throbbing need. So weak.

He lowered his body, moved over her, slid his hands up her arms to her bound wrists.

"Submit to me," he whispered, his voice husky.

If only she could see his face. If only she could touch him, as he touched her. Then they would both know the truth. When his mouth dropped to her neck and nipped, she trembled. No! she thought. I can't—

Alaina bolted upright in bed. *Where am I?* Frightened, she glanced around the strange room, for a moment thought she was still dreaming, then the haze cleared from her brain and she remembered where she was.

D.J.'s house.

The air she'd sucked into her lungs shuddered out. *That dream!* she thought, clutching the soft cotton sheets to her breasts. *That damn dream!* It was bad enough she'd had it in her own bed three nights ago, but now it had followed her here, to the Rocking B. Her heart was still clamoring in her chest when she dropped back onto the bed.

"It doesn't mean anything," she whispered and curled up tightly. "It *doesn't.*"

Like a mantra, she repeated the words over and over, until she almost believed them. Alaina flipped from her side to her back, stared at the ceiling for a full two minutes, tapped her fingertips together for another minute, then flipped to her other side.

After the long day of driving, then the huge meal that Dottie had prepared, she should have slept like a baby all night. Instead—she glanced at the bedside clock—she was lying here wide-awake at 4:00 a.m.

Still, Alaina reasoned, she was in a strange bed, a strange house. It was understandable that she was a little tense. She flipped to her back again. Okay, so she was a *lot* tense. That was understandable, too.

She was sleeping in D. J. Bradshaw's house, for heaven's sake. Or, at least, *trying* to sleep, she thought with a sigh. Dottie had given her a tour of the house after dinner, and she knew that his bedroom was at the end of the hall. She could still see his king-size bed clearly in her mind. The massive oak headboard, the Navajo print bedspread, a pair of black boots dropped casually on the hardwood floor at the foot of the bed.

It had all felt so…intimate.

At least with another woman in the house, Alaina wasn't quite so tense. She knew Dottie was downstairs, in the bedroom off the living room, and the thought comforted her. The housekeeper would be the buffer that Alaina needed between herself and D.J. She wouldn't deny that the man made her nervous. And it wasn't just D.J. she didn't trust, either.

It was herself.

He made her think things, made her feel things, she'd never thought or felt before. And though she might be naïve when it came to the opposite sex, she wasn't so completely inexperienced not to recognize that look in a man's eye. D.J. had made it clear he was attracted to her, and there was no doubt in her mind that he knew she was attracted to him, as well. If they'd been alone here in this house for two weeks, there was no telling what might have happened.

Bless you, Dottie.

As long as the woman was under the same roof with them, Alaina was certain she had nothing to worry about.

Stop acting like a child and go to sleep, she told herself sharply, then closed her eyes. She listened to the quiet, heard the house settling around her, the slow, deep sound of her breathing…and then the faint, steady beat of a drum…

Her eyes popped open again and she swore, threw the covers off, then got up and dressed.

Five

It was his favorite time of the morning. Just before the sun skimmed the horizon and turned the sky pale gray, just before the men clomped out of the bunkhouses, slurping coffee and jangling spurs. The air was cool and still, heavy with the scent of dew. If you listened carefully, very carefully, you could hear... nothing.

Dropping his hat onto his head, he made his way toward the barn, paused at the end of the walkway and glanced back at the second-story bedroom window where Alaina, like the rest of the ranch, was sleeping.

An image crept into his head, the same image he'd kicked out of his mind probably a hundred times last night. Those long legs of hers stretched out on her bed, her dark hair fanned out around her pillow, her lips softly parted with sleep,

A hell of an image.

Females were a distraction on the ranch, especially females who looked like Alaina. It was the main reason he'd never brought any of the women he'd dated to the Rocking B. Not only because women got ideas when you brought them home, but because he preferred to keep work and women separate.

Alaina was the first woman who had fallen into both categories. He'd asked her here for business reasons, but he desired her physically, as well. An interesting dilemma. He hadn't decided yet if he would just let nature take its course and see what happened, or if he'd give it a nudge. Either way, he thought a nice long ride out across his valley to check on the water pumps in the south pasture would not only cool his blood, but give his mind time to clear. Dottie wouldn't have breakfast on the table for two hours, anyway. Might as well get a jump on the day.

He was halfway across the yard when the sound of boots and the clunk of hooves on hard dirt pulled him up short. Narrowing his eyes, he watched Alaina walk out of the darkness, leading Santana behind her. He blinked to make sure she wasn't an illusion he'd conjured up by simply thinking about her.

"Mornin'," she greeted him and moved closer, her braid draped over the shoulder of her denim jacket.

Her voice had a throaty, still half-asleep tone, and the sound was like warm silk sliding over his skin. She was real all right. "You're up early."

"Thought I'd take Santana for a walk around the corrals before things got busy around here, let him get used to the smells and feel of the place without any distractions." She reached up and patted the horse's neck, then glanced back. "You're up pretty early yourself."

"I've got some pumps to check out in one of the pastures." He held his hand out to the horse and the stallion tossed his head up, but didn't back away. "Why don't you ride along, get the lay of the land? I'll show you some trails you can take Santana on when he's ready."

"I don't know." She looked at the dark house. "I told Dottie I'd see her—"

"Dottie won't be up for an hour and she puts breakfast out an hour after that." When she still hesitated, he started toward the stables. "Come on, I'll saddle up Gypsy Belle for you. We'll be back before the food hits the table."

"Gypsy Belle?" Alaina hurried after him. "Isn't she the mare that won the national futurity last year?"

He thought that might get her attention. "Yep."

"And you'd let me ride her?"

"Sure." He flipped the light on in the barn, watched a few sleepy horses stick their heads over their stall doors. "If you want to."

"If I *want* to?" Her eyes lit up like it was Christmas morning. "You're kidding, right?"

"Nope." He opened Gypsy's stall door, and the pretty chestnut mare nuzzled his shirt pocket, hoping for a treat. "She's a little spirited. Think you can handle her?"

"Gosh, I don't know." She shook her head as if she doubted herself, but there was a smile in her eyes. "I'm just a girl."

Hardly, he thought and grinned. "I'll saddle her up while you put Santana away."

"D.J."

He'd already started to open Gypsy's stall when she called his name. He glanced over his shoulder, saw the uncertainty on her face. "Yeah?"

"Last night—" She hesitated, then drew in a breath. "Last night you asked me about Rand Blackhawk."

"Just making conversation." The smile had disappeared from his eyes, and he realized he missed it.

"If I'm going to be here for two weeks," she said firmly. "I'd just like to say it now and get it out of the way."

Folding his arms, he leaned back against the stall door, watched the play of emotions move across her face and the tight press of her lips. Whatever it was she wanted to say, it obviously wasn't easy.

"Rand is my cousin, my father's nephew." She stared into one of the dark stalls, drew in a breath and met his gaze. "You've probably heard of William Blackhawk. He owned the Circle B in Wolf River."

"William Blackhawk is your father?" Of course D.J. had heard of him. He'd never actually had any dealings with the man, but the Circle B was one of the largest cattle ranches in the state.

"I don't really remember him," she continued. "I was only five when he left."

D.J. remembered what Helena Blackhawk had said

about her husband drowning, realized the pieces weren't quite fitting together. "He left?"

Absently Alaina stroked Santana's neck. "I know what my mother told you, and she truly does believe that's what happened to my father. We don't know where she came up with the story, but over the years she's convinced herself, her children, even the people in Stone Ridge, that her husband had died trying to save a little boy who'd fallen into a river. It was easier than accepting the fact that she'd had a ten-year affair with a married man, then been paid off when he was done with her and his illegitimate children."

An affair. Now it was beginning to make sense. D.J. bit back the swear word on the tip of his tongue. While he'd thought there might be a connection between Alaina's family and the Blackhawks in Wolf River, he'd certainly never considered it would be quite so close.

"Alaina," he said quietly, "you don't have to tell me any of this."

"I know I don't have to, but if you know Rand, you'd hear this sooner or later, and I'd just as soon you heard it from me." She used her fingers to comb back the loose strands of hair falling across her cheeks. "Trey and Alexis and I have all known the truth about our father for years—we even knew three years ago when he was killed in a plane crash."

D.J. realized she hadn't mentioned the youngest sister. "And Kiera?"

Alaina shook her head. "We kept the truth from her. She's our baby sister and we all thought we were protecting her. A few weeks ago, Alexis and I decided it was time for her to know, but Trey wanted to wait until she got settled into a chef's position she'd accepted in Europe. She overheard us arguing about it, then went to Wolf River herself, without telling us. She can be very impulsive."

D.J. lifted a brow and grinned at her. "Like you coming here?"

"That was practical," she insisted, but there was a smile in her eyes. "Anyway, when Trey found out, he went there to rescue her, so he thought. But it turned out she didn't want, or need, to be rescued. She's engaged now, to the manager of the Four Winds, and is building a relationship with our father's family, including Rand, and his wife, Grace."

D.J. had been at Rand and Grace's wedding a few months back, had never seen two people more in love, or happy. "They're good people."

"Yes," she said softly, glanced down at the lead line in her hand and sighed. "Did Rand ever tell you he was adopted?"

D.J. shook his head. "He worked here as a trainer for me a few years back and we stayed friends after he left, but we never talked much about family."

Santana gave an impatient snort and Alaina laid a hand on the horse's cheek to calm him. "His parents were killed in a car accident when he was a little boy. He was in the car, too, but he survived, along with his brother, Seth, and his sister, Clair."

Alaina paused, as if she needed to compose herself,

then met D.J.'s eyes. "My father was the only living relative, and when he was called to the scene of the accident, he separated the children, then paid a man, a lawyer, to adopt them out, letting Rand and Seth think their siblings had died. Clair, whose birth name was Elizabeth, was too little to remember."

It took D.J. a moment to wrap his brain around the enormity of Alaina's words. William Blackhawk had sold off his orphaned nephews and niece? Not even knowing what the hell to say, he just shook his head on one simple, earthy swear word.

"They've all found each other again," Alaina said, and there was relief in her voice. "I'll be meeting them for the first time when I leave here. But knowing what my father did to them…"

She dropped her gaze, but not before he saw the shame there. "Like I said—" D.J. pushed away from the stall "—they're good people, smart enough to know you aren't your father."

Nodding, she drew in a deep breath and lifted her eyes. "Thank you."

"No thanks necessary." He tamped down the unexpected need to touch her, to comfort, and instead, shrugged one shoulder and turned to open Gypsy's stall door. "Now how 'bout we take that ride?"

They rode south across the valley, through a thick grove of cypress and dogwoods. Along the eastern skyline, a silent trumpet of pale blue blared across the horizon, while in the branches overhead, birds greeted the new day with loud chirps and fluttering wings. The air was cool, heavy with the scent of wild sage and peppergrass, and somewhere to the left of her, though she couldn't see it, Alaina could hear the sound of tumbling water.

Gypsy Belle pranced under her, and Alaina knew that the chestnut mare wanted to take the lead, rather than follow. And while she might respect the horse for that, Alaina was perfectly happy to keep her distance behind D.J. Not only because he knew the way, but because it gave her an opportunity to study the man without him knowing it.

He looked good in the saddle, she thought. He sat tall, his broad shoulders completely at ease, his long legs the right fit for the large roan gelding he sat astride. Of course, since she'd been raised on a ranch, she'd seen a lot of men who looked good in the saddle. Some who'd even looked better than good.

But never one who made her mouth water.

When he glanced back at her, she quickly looked away, pretended to be studying the trail. It was bad enough she'd snatched at the carrot he'd dangled by offering to let her ride Gypsy Belle, the last thing she wanted was for him to know she was staring at him, too.

She'd surprised herself by dragging her family skeletons out of the closet. She'd carefully guarded those demons, had kept them under lock and key in a basement of shame and disgrace. But for some reason, she couldn't bear the thought of D.J. hearing about her father and the horrible things he'd done from anyone else. She'd needed to tell him for herself. Needed to see his eyes. Needed to know if he would look at her differently, treat her differently.

He hadn't. He simply listened, without judgment, without turning away, and for the first time in her life, if only a little, her shame had lightened.

"Up here," he said, and pulled her out of her thoughts. She glanced in the direction he pointed, toward a narrow path leading upward through a patch of boulders and brush. Though it seemed odd to be riding uphill when they were headed for a pasture, Alaina gave Gypsy Belle her head, knowing the horse could see much better in the dim light than she could.

The trail turned steeper and narrower, and they picked their way through a rock and dirt trail edged with prickly pear and shrubs of mesquite. She watched a rabbit peek out from a bush, its nose twitching anxiously, and she prepared herself, just in case that cute little bunny or one of his friends decided to dart across the trail. They continued upward, maybe for another thirty yards or so, until the trail widened and finally leveled out to a large, flat summit.

They were on a mesa, she realized and followed D.J. to a large oak. "I thought you were going to check on the pasture pumps."

"We will." He dismounted and walked over to her. "I want to show you something."

Suspicious, she glanced around, suddenly felt way too alone. "Graves of all the other women you've enticed up here?"

He laughed softly. "You're the first."

She wasn't sure if that was a comforting statement or not, but she could just make out his face in the gray light and saw the amusement shine in his eyes.

"Hurry up. We haven't got much time."

"Time for what?" she asked, watched him turn and walk away. He didn't reply, just gestured for her to follow. She bit her lip and looked around. She was on an isolated mesa, and absolutely no one in the world— other than D.J.—knew where she was. Call her crazy, but she was just a little nervous.

Or maybe excited.

"Hurry," he called back to her.

"What do you think, girl?" Alaina patted Gypsy Belle's neck. "Should I follow him?"

The animal pawed the ground and snorted. Not much of an answer, Alaina thought with a frown, then drew in a deep breath and dismounted.

He stood on the edge of the mesa, his back to her, and she moved closer. The air was cooler up here, lighter, the only sound a rustling of the leaves through the low brush.

Inching her way toward him, she was no more than a few feet away when he lifted an arm and pointed at the horizon. "There."

She turned her eyes to the skyline, watched the first brilliant slit of sun emerge from the rugged hilltops. Silver-white, the rays streamed upward, transforming the dull gray sky to baby-blue. Below them the valley, bisected by a river, stretched out like a carpet of soft browns and pretty greens. Specks of cattle and horses dotted the pasture and hillsides, and windmills, at least ten that she could see, towered above the landscape, swirling in the dawn's breeze.

Awestruck, she watched the sunrise, could feel the beauty of it shimmering through her.

"Pretty, isn't it?" D.J. said and turned to look at Alaina. He'd brought her here on an impulse, and seeing the wonder and amazement on her face, he was glad that he had.

"Beautiful," she murmured.

He moved beside her, pointed to a stand of tall cypress. "There's an eagle living in those trees, and if you look close, on the other side of the river, that's where the deer gather to drink."

She squinted, then whispered breathlessly, "Oh, I see them. There's so many."

He watched her gaze dance over the valley, taking it all in, couldn't help the swell of pride in his chest.

"I don't know how my sister does it," she said softly.

"Kiera?"

She shook her head. "Alexis. It amazes me that we're identical twins."

D.J. tried to picture Alaina's twin, but couldn't imagine another woman who looked like the one standing in front of him. "You don't know how she does what?"

"Lives in New York." Alaina looked back at him. "All that concrete and steel blocking out the sun. Noisy, crowded streets, jammed with people rushing about. Why would anybody choose to live like that?"

He'd wondered that himself, especially on the days

he'd come up here. "Guess that what makes life interesting. Different people, different choices."

She scanned the valley again, and drew in a sharp breath. "Oh, look, the eagle!"

D.J. watched the bird lift out of the trees and soar across the sunrise. When he looked back at Alaina, he saw the moisture in her eyes and frowned. "You okay?"

"I think I'm just a little overwhelmed by it all." Laughing, she wiped at her eyes with the back of her hands. "Sorry."

"Don't be." He pulled her hands from her face, and with his thumb, wiped away a tear sliding down her cheek.

And then it was there again, he thought. That... feeling. It was nothing he could exactly put his finger on, sort of a vibration he sensed whenever he touched her. Or whenever she touched him. Something stirred inside him and he looked down at her, watched the sunrise bloom over her face and sparkle in her eyes.

He watched those eyes widen when he tugged her close to him.

"You know," he said, circling her small waist with his hands, "there will never be another sunrise like this one."

Wary, she eased her head back and met his gaze. "Is that so?"

"That's so." When she started to pull away, he tightened his hold. "I've been up here dozens of times and every one was different."

She arched a dubious brow. "Different how?"

"Sometimes the sun jumps up like a giant mirror, so bright you can barely look at it." He angled his body against hers, tucked all those soft curves firmly against the hard length of his own. "Other times, it just sorta creeps up, slow and easy."

"Like a snake?"

"Maybe more like a storm," he said, grinning. "Some days up here you can even smell the clouds coming long before you see them." He lowered his head and breathed in the sweet scent of her. "Other days, all you can smell are the spring flowers."

He could see her pulse jumping at the base of her long neck, felt her tense in his arms. But still she didn't pull away.

"What—what kind of flowers?" she asked.

Lord, he wanted to kiss her, but she kept stalling. "Lupine, bluebonnets, primrose." He dropped his lips within a whisper of hers, until he felt her breath meet his. Damn, he was running out of flowers. "Flax, baby-blue eyes, fireweed…"

Oh, to hell with it.

He stopped trying to think and covered her mouth with his. Her lips were soft and warm and sweet as honey, and he traced them lightly with his tongue until she sighed and opened up to him. Sliding his hands up her back, he deepened the kiss, felt her tremble in his arms. He could lose himself in the incredible taste of her, and the thought almost had him pulling away. But need overrode reason and all he could do was pull her closer still.

It almost felt surreal, Alaina thought dimly. As if she were standing on top of the tallest mountain, in a warm cloud of desire. No one had ever kissed her like this before, made her mind go blank, until there was nothing but sensation after sensation rippling through her. Even though she'd known he would kiss her, maybe from the very first time she'd laid eyes on him, nothing could have prepared her for this rush of heat, for the sparks of sheer, intense pleasure. She could feel the sun on her face, hear the whisper of the breeze through the grass, the distant stomp of a horse's hoof. She melted into the kiss, into D.J., and afraid that her legs might give out, she slid her arms around his neck and held on.

He pulled her closer, fitted his body intimately with hers. She felt the hard press of his arousal between her legs, her breasts crushing against his broad, muscular chest. She met every hungry thrust of his tongue with her own, made a small sound deep in her throat, and he answered, then tightened his arms around her and crushed his mouth to hers. Excitement coursed through her veins, and she squirmed against him, needing to be closer still. Fire raced over her skin, and the rapid beat of her heart sounded like a drum in her head…

A drum?

What was happening to her? Why was her dream intruding? This was just a kiss, she told herself. An amazing kiss, but just a kiss. Her dream had no place here. Not with this man. It *couldn't*. But the fact that it had frightened her, brought her back to reality and had her jerking her head away.

"Wait." She struggled to get that simple word out. "I—I can't."

His arms tightened around her, and she was certain if he kissed her again, she would be completely lost. When he looked down at her, his eyes burning deep blue, it was all she could do not to drag his lips back to hers.

They were both still breathing hard as he stared at her, then his mouth flattened and he slowly loosened his hold. She stumbled back, pressed her fingertips to her lips, shocked at what she might have done. "I'm sorry."

His eyes narrowed. "For what?"

"I didn't mean to, I wasn't trying to—" Lord, she could barely say it. "Lead you on."

He raised a brow, studied her for what felt like hours, though it was only seconds, then he shook his head. "You're the damnedest woman, Alaina Blackhawk."

She had no idea what he meant by that, and she might have asked him, but he'd already turned and headed back to his horse. *Better to just leave it be,* she thought and followed after him.

The sun had been up at least an hour by the time D.J. and Alaina arrived back at the ranch. Baxter and Taffy greeted them with tongues rolling and excited barks. Though D.J. would have much preferred a quiet entrance, he knew there was no stopping those blasted dogs once they were riled up.

Several of the men were already in the corrals, and heads turned when they rode past. A few nodded, but they all knew better than to openly stare. For the short time she would be here, it would keep the hounds at bay, if they thought Alaina was his.

There was something about her, an innocence of sorts, that had both surprised and frustrated. There'd been a naïve sweetness about her, maybe in the way she'd trusted him, or that subtle shimmer of inexperience when his lips had first touched hers.

He wanted her, but she was a complicated woman, D.J. thought, and if there was one thing he didn't want, it was complications.

"Baxter!" D.J. shouted at the dog when he barked at Sergeant's back hooves. Damn dog was too stupid to realize that one kick from a twelve hundred pound horse could snap him like a twig. "Back off!"

Waving his hat, Bobby climbed over the corral fence and whistled for the dogs. They both ran toward the hand, yapping loudly and wagging their tails.

"Morning, boss." Bobby dropped his hat back on his head and smiled at Alaina. "I fed Santana for you and brushed him. Tried to check his hooves, but he got cross about it so I let it be."

"Thanks, Bobby." Alaina slid off Gypsy Belle. "But you really don't need to."

"I don't mind. I can walk him for you, too." Bobby looked at D.J. eagerly. "If that's okay with you, boss."

"Fine," D.J. said through gritted teeth, not sure what was more irritating, Bobby's sloppy grin or the dogs running circles around Alaina. "Take care of Sergeant and Gypsy first. And shut these damn mutts up."

"Yes, sir." Bobby grabbed both horses' reins and called the dogs, but when they spotted one of the hands driving into the yard, they raced to greet the newcomer.

Shaking his head, D.J. watched the dogs run in one direction while Alaina headed for the house and wondered how the hell, in less than twenty-four hours, he felt as if he'd lost complete control.

Six

"That's my sweetheart," Alaina crooned to Santana. "Come on now, you can do it. You know you can."

A saddle in her hands, she moved slowly toward the stallion. Head high and eyes wide, the horse watched her approach.

"I'm not going to hurt you, baby." She inched closer. "I would never hurt you."

Santana pricked his ears and tossed his head, but for the first time since she'd been working with him, the animal didn't try to back away.

"That's my big, brave boy," she murmured and positioned herself next to the horse. "Here we go now."

With one quick, smooth move, she swung the saddle onto the horse's back. He whinnied and pranced, but didn't rear. Elated, Alaina stroked the stallion's neck. She could feel the tension and energy coursing through Santana's muscles and she continued to murmur sweet nothings while she caressed his sleek coat.

"See, that's not so bad, now, is it?"

After two frustrating days of the animal immediately bucking the saddle off, this was a huge breakthrough. She waited for the horse to settle down again, then moved to the cinch and buckled it. Of course, she knew that while she may have won this particular battle, she was far from winning the war.

Which was exactly how she felt about her relationship with D.J.

Not that she had a *relationship* with the man. He'd kissed her, she'd kissed him back. End of story. She supposed they'd both simply been caught up in the moment of being alone, watching that amazing sunrise. No point in making a big deal about it, she told herself. It was just a kiss.

She hoped by the end of her two weeks here, she could convince herself of that.

No man had ever turned her inside out like that. Made her ache to be touched, to be loved. She'd tried to reason it was simply the magic of the moment, that she hadn't had enough sleep the night before, that she'd been vulnerable after the erotic dream that had been haunting her, then telling D.J. about her father.

But then she'd remember the feel of his lips on hers, the press of his hard body, and she knew it was so much more.

With a sigh, she smoothed a hand down the stallion's head. She'd managed to keep her distance from D.J. since that kiss, had kept busy working with Santana, and in the evening, with Dottie around, there wasn't much chance for a conversation, or for them to be alone, thank goodness. Being alone with D.J. was a dangerous thing. He was a man used to getting what he wanted, and he'd made it clear he wanted her. She'd seen him watching her for the past three days, had felt his gaze burn through her. Like the wolf, she thought. Waiting.

"All right, Al. You got a saddle on him."

She turned at the sound of Bobby's voice, saw the hand leaning over the stall door. He had a tendency to pop up several times during the day, whenever he wasn't busy with his regular ranch duties. "You doubted me?"

"Shoot, no." He grinned at her. "That stallion's an ornery one, but I knew he'd come around. You could sweet talk the thorns off a cactus."

"Thanks, I think." She smiled at the kid, knew that he had a little crush on her, though she'd been careful not to encourage him. It was nice that someone other than Dottie was talking to her, though, especially since the other men had kept their distance. Alaina knew she was the first woman to ever work on the Rocking B and more than likely the hands didn't approve of a female moving into their territory. It really didn't matter, whatever the reason was. She'd be gone by the end of next week, anyway.

"Dottie sent me to fetch you up to the house," Bobby said. "Wants you to come right away, if you can."

Alaina glanced at her wristwatch and frowned. It was already past five and she would have been going in soon, anyway, so it seemed odd that Dottie would ask for her. "Is there a problem?"

"Didn't say, but she tell me not to let D.J. know she was asking for you."

Not tell D.J.? Now that *was* odd, Alaina thought, and reached for the cinch on the stallion's saddle.

"You go on ahead." Bobby stepped into the stall. "I'll take care of Santana. We're buds now."

Alaina might have refused his offer if she didn't sense that something was wrong. Dottie wasn't the type to ask for help, so whatever it was, it must be important. "Thanks, Bobby. Ah, do you know where D.J. is?"

"Last I saw him, he was in the barn tack room with Judd."

Outside the stables, Alaina paused and glanced around. A couple of the men were working with a yearling in one of the corrals, and a couple more were unloading hay from a flatbed, but no sign of D.J. She headed for the utility room on the side of the house, scanned the yard before she ducked inside, pulled her boots and socks off, then opened the door and stuck her head inside the kitchen.

"Dottie?"

The room was empty, which was strange because the housekeeper was always cooking by this time. Alaina checked the downstairs, then called up from the bottom of the stairs.

"Up here," came a faint reply.

Worried, Alaina hurried up the stairs. "Where are you?"

"Here." Dottie's voice sounded out of breath. "In D.J.'s bedroom."

Alaina found the housekeeper in D.J.'s huge walk-in closet, sitting on the floor in the corner.

"What's wrong?" Alaina rushed to Dottie's side and knelt beside her. "Are you hurt?"

"No, no, no. I'm fine. It's the kittens." The woman picked up a flashlight, turned it on, then shined it into a small hole near the baseboards. "Three of them are inside the wall."

"What?" Alaina knelt down on the floor and peeked into the hole, saw two pairs of eyes shining back at her. "How did they get in there?"

"Esmeralda sneaked them into the closet, but they obviously found the hole on their own. She was cater-wauling so loud, I came up to see what happened."

"Where is she now?" Alaina asked.

"She wouldn't stay out of my way so I put her in my bathroom downstairs with the other two." Dottie sat back and swiped a hand across the beads of sweat on her brow. "My hand is too big to fit inside and I've been trying to entice them out for two hours, with no luck. I was hoping to get them out of here before D.J. comes in."

"Let me try."

When Dottie moved out of the way, Alaina lay down on the shiny hardwood floor and called to the kittens, but they didn't budge. Alaina slipped her hand into the hole up to her wrist, felt whiskers brushing against her fingertips, then reached her arm deeper into the wall and felt a paw. "Almost…"

She wiggled in farther and managed to wrap her hand around a tiny ball of soft fur. Smiling, she tried to pull it out.

And couldn't.

She struggled to free herself, but only seemed to make it worse. "I'm stuck."

"Oh, dear." Dottie looked at the hole, then shook her head and sighed. "No way around it, then. I'll go get a hammer."

"Wait—"

But Dottie had already hurried out and there was nothing Alaina could do but wait.

D.J. dropped his boots on the porch and limped in through the front door. Getting tossed off, stepped on, or kicked by a horse was pretty much a day in the life, but all three on the same day bruised more than a man's body.

Unbuttoning his shirt, he headed up the stairs. He'd intentionally bypassed the kitchen, was in no mood for Dottie fussing over him. He was hot and sweaty. All he wanted was a long, hot shower and an ice cold beer.

And a soft woman.

He frowned at the last thought. Thinking about a woman was what had caused him so much grief already. If he'd been paying more attention to his work instead of drifting off into lustful fantasies about Alaina, he wouldn't have an imprint of a hoof on his thigh. And if that hoof had been five inches to the left, he doubted he'd be thinking about *any* woman, let alone do anything else, for quite some time.

He shrugged his shirt off and tossed it on the bed, then pulled off his belt and unsnapped his jeans, was heading for the bathroom when he passed by the open door on his closet, stopped when he thought he heard a muffled voice coming from inside.

He stuck his head inside the closet, noticed several of his boots had been tossed into a pile, then noticed a pair of long, denim-clad, legs and bare feet stretched out on the floor.

Alaina?

He couldn't see beyond the pile of boots, but he could hear her whispering in a reassuring, calm tone, something about help on the way and don't worry.

What the hell…?

Moving into the closet, he could see her head was in the corner, her left arm folded against the wall, her right arm—past her elbow—inside a hole.

He knelt beside her, watched her body stiffen as her head slowly turned toward him.

"Hey, Alaina."

"Hey, D.J."

Unable to resist, he took a minute and scanned the length of her body. Her white tank top had risen and her jeans, cut low across her hips, revealed the bare skin on her lower back. He caught a hint of hot-pink underwear and something else that made his eyebrows lift.

"Never took you for the tattoo type," he said casually, could only see what looked like the tip of colorful butterfly wings, resisted the strong urge to tug her jeans lower and take a good look. Instead he allowed his gaze the pleasure of following the curve of her round bottom.

She wiggled and managed to turn on her side, pulling her tank top down. Which, of course, only drew D.J.'s attention to her breasts.

"I can explain—"

"The tattoo?" he asked. "Or why you're lying in my closet with your arm stuck in my wall?"

"The latter, or course." Her face was as pink as the polish on her toenails. "There's a kitten in your wall. Three, actually."

His bad mood and sore leg forgotten, he rocked back on one foot. "Is that what you say to all the men whose closets you sneak into?"

"I did *not* sneak in here," she protested. "Dottie—"

When she bit her lip, then pressed her lips firmly together, D.J. figured he had a pretty good idea of what had happened. "And where is Dottie?"

"She went to get a hammer."

He winced at the thought of his housekeeper with a hammer and started to rise.

"Where are you going?" she asked.

"To get my camera, of course."

Her hand reached out and grabbed his arm, latched on like a vise. "Don't you *dare!* Get back here and do something."

"Well, now, there's an invitation I can't refuse." Grinning, he lay down on his side and faced Alaina. "What would you like me to do?"

"Wipe that smile off your face for starters," she said tightly. "Then get my arm out of this damn hole."

"It's not every day a pretty girl gets her arm stuck in a hole in my closet." He propped his head on his bent arm, watched blue sparks fly out of her eyes. "I'm just savoring the moment."

"Dammit, Bradshaw, this isn't funny."

"You're kidding, right?"

"All right, so maybe it is," she said with a sigh. "But if you were a gentleman, you'd control yourself."

"Darlin', no one ever said I was a gentleman." He reached for a long strand of her hair that had fallen across her cheek and rubbed it between his forefinger and thumb. It felt like silk. "And at this moment, you can't even imagine the control I'm managing to exercise."

It seemed impossible to Alaina that—given the situation—she found herself responding to D.J.'s closeness. The fact that he was half-naked certainly contributed to the overwhelming presence of his body less than six inches from her own, not to mention that broad, muscled chest she couldn't seem to tear her eyes away from. Even the earthy scent of his bare skin, a mix of sweat and dust and horse, wasn't unappealing. If anything, she was...turned on.

"D.J., be serious." She considered pushing him away, but then she'd have to touch him and she wasn't certain she trusted herself. "Dottie will be back any minute."

"Remind you of high school?" he asked, lowering his voice. "Necking in the cab of your boyfriend's truck, worrying you'll get caught?"

"I wouldn't know," she admitted, then wished she hadn't.

"You don't?" He lifted a surprised brow, then lowered his head closer to hers. "Well, there's a lot of kissing going on, the we're-in-a-hurry kind."

When his lips nearly touched hers, Alaina held her breath. "D.J.—"

"Then there's some definite groping," he went on, and slid a fingertip along the waistband of her jeans. "Racing hormones. Hands all over the place."

How easy it was to imagine. The urgency, the thrill of danger, of excitement. Heavy breathing, steamed up windows, the struggle to maneuver steering wheel and cramped space. When D.J. lightly drew his finger back and forth over the tip of her butterfly wings, his touch burned through the fabric of her jeans, made her skin hot and tight. "Stop that," she whispered, but made no effort to brush his hand away.

"You gotta make me believe you," he murmured and circled the snap of her jeans with his finger. "I wouldn't make you do anything you didn't want to."

There was no doubt in Alaina's mind that D.J. never *had* to make a girl—or woman—do anything they didn't want to. Here she was, stuck in a wall, with Dottie about to walk in any minute, and all she could think about was D.J.'s lips almost touching hers and his finger one tiny tug away from opening her jeans.

Lord, I must be sick.

When the tip of his callused finger slipped under the hem of her tank top and slid—just barely—over her stomach, her pulse raced and her breath came in short, shallow gulps. She wanted his mouth on hers and she closed her eyes, parted her lips…

When D.J. rolled away, her eyes flew open. Disappointment and frustration coursed through her. She felt like kicking him, but without her boots on, she doubted the blow would have much impact. She watched him stand and pull a white T-shirt from a shelf.

"Dottie's coming." He slipped the T-shirt over his head and knelt down beside her again. "Put your head on the floor and don't move."

"What?" She stared at him, couldn't decide if he was kidding.

"Put your head on the floor," he repeated.

He wasn't kidding. "Why would I—"

She squeaked when he dropped one hand on her head and pressed her cheek to the floor, then raised his other hand. She squeezed her eyes shut when his fist came down over her head and punched a hole in the drywall.

"Why didn't you do that five minutes ago?" she said irritably and wiggled her arm loose.

"And miss all that fun?" He gave her a cocky smile and broke out another chunk of drywall. "Not a chance."

"You're right, Bradshaw." She frowned at him and scooted out of his way. "You are no gentleman."

Chuckling, he widened the hole and looked inside the wall as Dottie rushed into the closet, a hammer in one hand and a saw in the other. The housekeeper's eyes shifted from D.J. to the large, jagged hole in the wall, then set the tools on a shelf. "I, ah, guess we don't need those anymore."

D.J. threw Dottie a look over his shoulder, then reached into the hole, pulled out kitten number one, a calico.

Alaina took the kitten and stared into its tiny face. It squeaked out a mew. "Oh, you poor baby," Alaina cooed and laid the kitten in her lap. Kitten number two, black and white like its mama, came out next, blinking its big green eyes. Alaina laid the kittens in an empty shoe box and squeezed in closer to watch over D.J.'s shoulder.

"I'll go get Esmeralda." Dottie turned, then paused at the closet doorway, tears in her eyes. "You wonderful, wonderful man."

"So what do you think?" D.J. grinned at Alaina while he reached deeper into the wall for kitten number three. "Do you think I'm a—"

"What?" Alaina watched D.J.'s grin suddenly fade. "What's wrong?"

D.J.'s mouth hardened and he reached deeper into the wall. "This one's not moving."

Seven

D.J.'s gut tightened at the kitten's closed eyes and limp body. It was the pure white, long-haired runt of the litter and he knew it was Dottie's favorite. There were strands of fibers on the kitten's mouth. "He must have been sucking on the insulation."

Alaina reached for the kitten. "Let me have it."

D.J. shook his head. "I should take it before Dottie gets back."

"Just give it to me, D.J." she said urgently. Gently she removed the kitten from his hand and held it up to her ear. "There's a heartbeat, but it's faint."

"Alaina—"

"He'll be fine." She closed her eyes. "He'll be fine."

"The fiber glass—"

"Shh."

He watched her stroke the kitten, wanted to tell her to stop, to just let him handle it, but her determined expression held him at bay.

"Alaina, don't."

She didn't respond, and he narrowed his eyes, wasn't even certain that she heard him. Her fierce expression softened, her breathing slowed, and a calm smoothed her face. Gently she cradled the kitten in her hands, held it against her cheek. And still the kitten didn't move.

"Alaina," he whispered, but she didn't even seem to hear him. He dragged a hand through his hair, cursing his own feeling of helplessness and her stubborn refusal to face the obvious.

He reached to take the kitten from her, stopped at the sound of its tiny, screechy mew. The kitten's eyes slitted open, and it mewed again, this time a little stronger.

Son of a gun.

"Alaina." He touched her cheek with his thumb. Her eyelashes fluttered open and she looked around as if she didn't know where she was. "Are you all right?"

She stared at him for a long moment, blinked several times. Her lips slowly curved up. "He might be little, but he's a fighter."

Her smile lit her entire face and glowed in her eyes. He felt the warmth of it seep through him and lodge in his chest. "Yeah, I guess he is."

Esmeralda ran into the closet, sniffed her babies in the shoebox, then meowed loudly until Alaina placed the littlest ball of white fur into the shoebox beside its siblings.

Out of breath from running up the stairs, Dottie came into the closet, carrying the other two kittens. "Everything all right?"

"Fine." D.J. looked at Esmeralda. The cat was busy licking her kittens and she purred as loud as a motorboat. Grinning, he glanced back at Alaina. "It's just fine."

Alaina fell asleep after she took a shower and dressed. One minute she'd been sitting on the edge of her bed, getting ready to go downstairs for dinner, the next thing she knew it was dark. Confused, she glanced at the bedside clock, moaned when she saw it was eight-thirty.

Dammit, she should have known this would happen.

She sat on the side of the bed, pressed her fingers to her temple and waited for the room to stop spinning. Her mind was still groggy and thick, her vision blurred, but she knew that would pass shortly. It always did.

Dragging her hands over her hair, she stood slowly and tested her legs. When they held her, she made her way to the door and stepped out into the hallway, was heading for the stairs when the light from D.J.'s open office door caught her attention. If he was anything like Trey—and he was—she assumed he didn't like to be bothered when he was in his "cave." But she was embarrassed she'd fallen asleep, not just through dinner, but for the past three hours. She at least owed him—and Dottie—an apology.

Biting her lip, she moved closer to the open door and looked inside.

He sat behind a large mahogany desk, his tall frame

hunkered down in a high-back, brown leather chair while he stared intently at a computer screen. His hair looked wet and uncombed, as if he'd just showered and pulled a T-shirt over his head. Her heart thumped and she looked away, needed a minute to gather her wits.

The room was floor-to-ceiling bookshelves, she noted, every shelf filled to overflowing. A football trophy had been carelessly squeezed into a corner and a cow skull stared blindly from its place on top of a pile of ranching periodicals. But it was the telescope sitting on a tripod in front of a pair of wide windows that had her lifting a brow.

"I wouldn't have taken you for a man who liked to look at the stars."

He glanced up, pressed a button to clear his monitor, then dropped his head back against his chair and met her gaze. "Sleeping beauty awakes."

Blushing, she stayed in the doorway. "Sorry to bother you."

"You're saving me. If I have to balance one more column on one more account, I think I might shoot myself." He stretched his legs out, crossed one booted ankle over the other. "You okay?"

"I'm fine. It was just a headache." She couldn't really explain it any other way. "I'm sorry I didn't come down for dinner."

"Dottie checked in on you before she left, but you were sleeping so soundly she didn't want to wake you."

Alaina frowned. "Dottie left?"

"Her daughter, Velma, called a little while ago." D.J.

picked up a mug of coffee on his desk and sipped. "She went into labor early."

"Oh." Alaina chewed on her lower lip. She and D.J. were alone, she realized, truly alone, and the thought made her shoulders tense. "I hope she and the baby are all right."

"She would have called if there were any problems." He sipped on the coffee again. "She left a plate of food for you in the fridge. You hungry?"

She looked at D.J., the long stretch of legs, his damp, mussed hair, those broad shoulders, and she had to swallow before she could speak. "Maybe later. I thought I'd check on the kittens."

"I've banished them to the laundry room," he said. "Hopefully they can stay out of trouble in there."

"Did you check for holes?" Alaina asked, smiling.

"Oh, yeah. Here, sit." He rose from his chair, sat on the edge of his desk. "How'd you do with Santana today?"

Santana. Between all the commotion this afternoon, then falling asleep, she'd nearly forgotten. Needing to keep some distance between herself and D.J., she bypassed the chair he'd offered, shoved her hands into the front pockets of her jeans and wandered the room. "I got a saddle on him today."

D.J. nodded. "That's progress."

"He's still a little unhappy with the situation, but I think he might let me ride him tomorrow." She glanced over the books on D.J.'s shelves. He had everything from land management to horse training to veterinarian medicine, not to mention several shelves of classics and current, bestselling novels. So the man liked to read, she thought with interest and spotted an older Dick Francis novel. She pulled it from the bookshelf and opened it, noted the tattered book cover and dog-eared pages. "I loved this one."

"I haven't read it." He stared at his coffee, then set the cup on his desk. "It was my mother's."

"Oh." He'd never once mentioned his parents, though she'd heard both Cookie and Dottie say their death had been a shame. "What happened?" she asked softly. "To her and your dad?"

He was quiet for a long moment, stared out the window into the dark night, and she was certain she'd stepped into territory he simply didn't want to discuss.

She closed the book and slipped it back on the shelf. "I'll just go check on the—"

"A fire," he said, his voice distant. "We lived in a smaller house where the front pasture is now. It was already here when my parents moved here forty years ago, but my dad had always wanted something bigger for my mom, so he built this one for her. Since she'd never been able to have more children after me, she entertained instead. I hated those parties we had at the old house and all the ones she dragged me to. My mom loved them."

Alaina watched D.J.'s eyes soften, then he dragged his fingers through his hair and sighed. "Took them five years to build this one, another year to decorate and furnish. When it was finally done, we packed up the rest of our things and moved everything over to the new house, but my mom wanted to stay one last night in the old one. She talked about the past, made my dad and me go through her old photo albums after dinner, said she didn't want me to forget where I'd come from. My dad talked about the future, how we were going to build the biggest and the best horse ranch in the state."

Alaina had no memories of both her parents, only her mother lighting candles every night under a photo of the man who'd abandoned her and her children. "That sounds like a wonderful evening."

A muscle jumped in D.J.'s jaw. and he slowly shook his head. "I was sixteen, bored and annoyed because school had just let out and there was this cute little redhead who liked to hang out at the pool hall in town. Last thing I wanted to do was sit at home with my parents. I kept grumbling about it, so my mom finally told me to go have some fun. She didn't need to tell me twice. I was out of there and on my way to town like a bullet. It was just past midnight when I got back and saw the flames and everyone running around. The hands had managed to drag my parents out before the roof went up, but the smoke had already overtaken them. They died in their bed."

He blamed himself, Alaina realized. She could see it in his eyes, could *feel* it. She wanted to tell him not to, but she knew it wouldn't matter, knew that he'd made the decision to accept fault. No one could change that decision but himself.

"Cleaning rags," he said, leveling a gaze at Alaina. "A big pile of goddammed cleaning rags."

"I'm so sorry." She knew the words would sound

empty to D.J., but she said them anyway. She wanted to go to him and put her head on his shoulder, but she could see the stiffness in his shoulders, the tight set of his face and knew that her comfort would not be welcomed.

The silence stretched around them, long and dark, heavy, and when the shrill ring of the phone finally broke that quiet, Alaina jumped.

"Hey, Dottie." D.J. looked up, met Alaina's worried gaze while he listened. "Uh, huh…no kidding…you don't say…all right…sure."

Chewing on a fingernail, she moved closer to D.J., grateful for Dottie's timing. She could hear the buzz of the housekeeper's voice, though, and Alaina craned her neck to listen, hoping to catch a few words.

"Here, tell her yourself."

Without warning, D.J.'s arm reached out and slid around her waist. Alaina squeaked when he pulled her between his legs and held the phone up to her ear.

"You all right?" Dottie asked.

Lord, she couldn't breathe, let alone think straight with D.J.'s thighs pressing against hers. He held onto the phone, forcing her head close to his if she wanted to hear. "I—yes, I'm fine," she choked out, laid a hand on D.J.'s chest to prevent him from pulling her against him. "How—how's your daughter?"

Between the roar of the blood pumping in her head and Dottie talking so fast, Alaina could barely hear, but she managed to pick up enough words to know that mother and daughter—Alyssa Anne, six pounds, seven ounces—were doing very well.

"That's wonderful." Alaina struggled to keep her voice even, sucked in a breath when D.J. slowly, but insistently, drew her closer. She could feel the rapid beat of his heart under her palm, smell the fresh scent of soap on his skin. She knew Dottie was saying something about the birthing process, but Alaina couldn't have kept the words straight if her life depended on it. How could she possibly think, or breathe, standing between D.J.'s legs, his hand moving over the small of her back, his mouth so close to hers she'd barely have to lean forward for their lips to touch?

She couldn't, she realized, but even more frightening, was the fact that she didn't want to think or breathe or move away.

Lifting her eyes to D.J.'s, Alaina saw the need burning there, knew that it mirrored her own. His gaze sharpened, then lowered to her mouth. Anticipation trembled through her, buzzed in her head.

She looked at the phone, realized the buzzing she heard was the dial tone.

"She hung up."

"Yeah." Keeping his eyes on her mouth, D.J. took the phone and replaced it on the cradle. "She did."

"Oh." He had both hands around her waist now and that single word was the best she could manage.

"I should tell you." His thumbs stroked the small of her back. "I lied to you."

"You did?" *Two words.* Better, she thought.

He dropped his mouth closer to hers. "I wasn't really working tonight."

"No?" Damn. Back to one word.

He shook his head. "I was thinking about you."

"Me?"

"Pretty hard to keep my mind on work, when I'm thinking about what you look like when you're sleeping." His arms tightened around her, drew her closer. "All I could see was you, lying on your back, with that incredible hair of yours streaming across your pillow."

Heat flooded her veins, ran like a molten river through her body. She felt a moment of panic, as if she'd been caught in a trap. But the moment passed, and she knew that if she truly wanted to stop this, she could.

God help her, she didn't want to.

Breath held, she waited, watched his head lower to hers, felt the warmth of his breath, smelled the clean scent of his soap. When his lips finally touched hers, her eyes fluttered closed.

He tasted like rich, dark coffee, with all the potent kick that had her nerves jangling and sprinting at the same time. She heard a sound, an animal-like moan, and realized it came from deep in her throat. His mouth was hard and firm, familiar to her now, but more demanding than the kiss on the mesa, more impatient. But she was impatient, too, and she strained against him, wanting more.

She'd been so cautious her entire life, afraid to truly let herself go, to let herself *feel* without restraint. There were risks involved. Her dream had warned her of that. But at this moment, the only thing that mattered was being here, with D.J. She melted into him, felt her knees grow weak. Afraid she might slip through his arms, she held onto him, shivering with pleasure.

Hurry, she thought, but didn't want to take her mouth away from his to tell him. So she told him with her hands, raced her fingers down his neck, over the hard muscles of his shoulders. She'd felt that broad chest earlier, without his shirt, and she wanted her hands on his skin again, this time unfettered. Uninterrupted.

Blood pumped like a fist through D.J.'s body, hot and hard and fast. He'd known there was heat simmering under Alaina's carefully controlled surface, but he'd never expected it to slam into him like a two-by-four. He feasted on her mouth, tasted the honey sweetness of her, and the little sounds she made in her throat drained all the blood from his brain and sent it south. He dragged his mouth from hers, fisted his hands in her silky hair and tugged her head back, blazing kisses down the smooth column of her neck. He felt her pulse skip under his tongue and he savored the heat of her soft skin, nipped at the intoxicating taste. Her moan vibrated through him, and the urgency, the need, tightened inside him like a coiled spring.

He was close to losing it, dangerously, foolishly close, and the soft sounds she made, her whispered pleas, nearly pushed him over the edge. He could take her here, he realized. Right here, right now. The floor, the desk—hell, he didn't care. But he'd never prepared for anything like this, not even in his wildest fantasies, and while he could still hold himself together, he needed to get her to his bed.

When she moved her hips against him, sweat beaded on his forehead.

On an oath, he wrapped his arms around her and crushed her to him as he stood, lifting her off the floor.

"Bed," he choked out.

"Yes," she murmured, then locked her mouth on his again.

He carried her to his bedroom, worried more than once they might not make that short distance. Her soft breasts pressed against his chest and he had to remind himself to breathe. He needed to touch her, needed her naked and underneath him, needed her legs wrapped around him.

Like a beacon, moonlight slanted through the windows, casting a silver glow across his bed. Together they tumbled across the bedspread, and he rose above her, slid his hand down her throat, felt her pulse jumping under his fingers. Her face glowed in the pale light; her eyelids, heavy with desire, fluttered open. She met his gaze, held it when she reached for the hem of her tank top and pulled it off. He caught her arms before she could lower them again, circled her wrists with his hands and pinned them over her head. Her breasts, full and round, enclosed in white satin, rose and fell with her labored breathing. The glorious sight of her, her lips swollen with his kisses, her body writhing under him, aroused him to the point of pain.

"I've wanted my hands on you from the first moment I saw you," he said, his lungs nearly bursting. "Thought about you here, like this."

"Like this?" she whispered, lifting her hips against his.

He swore his heart stopped just before it slammed against his ribs. Lightning quick, he rolled to his back, caught her gasp with his mouth, kissed her until she melted over him. "Just like that," he murmured. "And like this."

The thrill of his hands on her breasts ignited sparks of white-hot pleasure through her body. She couldn't think, could only feel. Sensation after sensation spiraled through her, tightened like a fist. Every hurried brush of lips, every caress, was filled with brilliant, swirling colors. Wanting, needing more, she rushed her hands under his T-shirt, and the heat of his hard, muscled stomach vibrated through her fingertips like an electrical current.

"Your shirt," she gasped, sliding her hands up his broad chest. "Off."

And then they were rolling again, arms and legs tangling. Satin shimmered to the floor, boots dropped. She reeled from the intensity of the force driving her, and when his mouth dropped to her bare breast, when his tongue swept hot and moist over her beaded nipple, she arched upward on a moan. He teased with his teeth and lips, and when he drew her into his mouth and suckled, an arrow of fire shot straight from her breast to the throbbing ache between her thighs.

His mouth trailed hot kisses down her stomach at the same time he reached for the snap of her jeans and flicked it open. She heard the hiss of her zipper, felt the denim slide down her hips while his mouth moved lower still. He trailed kisses along the hollow of her hip while he tugged her jeans off and tossed them aside. She clutched at his shoulders and shivered when he slid a fingertip along the elastic band of her panties, then slipped underneath and stroked the most intimate part of her.

She moved against him, was certain she couldn't stand anymore, that she might die from pleasure this intense. "Please," she moaned. "D.J., please…I need you…"

He slid her panties off in one swift move, and when he moved away from her, she moaned in protest and opened her eyes, watched him unsnap his jeans and tug them off. He kept his eyes on her and the look on his face, fierce and primal, made her heart jump wildly. The sight of him standing over her, his broad shoulders and lean waist, his arousal, took her breath away. Excitement and fear and need coursed through her blood.

It took him but a moment to protect himself and when he turned back to her, his eyes glinting, his muscles taut, her breath shuddered from her lungs. He lowered his body to hers, slid his hands down her thighs and spread her legs, then drove himself inside her. And froze.

Eyes wide, he lifted his head, stared at her. "What…?"

"Don't stop." Afraid he might pull away, she wound her arms around his neck and held him tight.

"Alaina—"

"Don't stop," she pleaded, lifting her hips up, taking him deeper inside her. "Please."

"But you—" When she moved her hips again, he swore. "God, why didn't you—"

She dragged his mouth to hers and wrapped her legs

around him, letting instinct drive her. Need pounded through her, consumed her, and she heard him swear again, then grasp hold of her hips and move inside her, slowly at first, then faster, deeper. She met him thrust for thrust, gasping, frantic, until the need burst into flames and exploded inside her, showering sparks of red and gold. She floated with the embers, held on tight when D.J. groaned deep in his throat, then shuddered violently. Smiling, she sank back into the warm waves still rippling through her and let them carry her away.

At thirty-four, D.J. had thought nothing would shock him. Had thought nothing would surprise, or catch him off guard. He'd seen a lot, experienced a lot, considered himself well prepared to handle anything that came along.

Until now.

He held Alaina in his arms, too stunned to speak, wouldn't even know what to say if he could find his voice. The woman had quite simply devastated him, and the fact that she was a virgin—that utterly confused him. No woman had ever done that to him before—devastated or confused.

He pressed his lips to her forehead, then rolled to his side and pulled her with him. "Are you—did I—"

She stopped him with a kiss. "You were wonderful," she whispered. "That was wonderful."

"Yeah?" In spite of the guilt nipping away at him, he couldn't stop the swell of smug satisfaction. "Well, for a beginner, you were pretty damn wonderful yourself."

"Was I? Really?" She looked up at him, a mixture of

hope and uncertainty in her eyes. "'Cause you don't have to say that, I mean, I appreciate the gesture, but—"

He flipped her onto her back so quickly, she hadn't time to utter a squeak before his mouth was on hers. He kissed her, hard and long, until her arms came around his neck and he could feel her body humming under his.

"I assure you, Miss Blackhawk," he said against her mouth. "That was no gesture. You were incredible."

Her lips curved into a smile. "Thank you," she murmured, sliding her hands down his back. "You made it…special."

He'd made it special? Good God, he thought about what had just happened, what she'd given him—and done to him—and knew there were no words. He lifted his head and gazed down at her. "You could have told me."

"I could have." Her eyes slowly opened. "And maybe if the circumstances were different, if we'd been dating, or I'd known this was going to happen, I might have."

"But tonight—"

She put her fingers on his mouth. "What if I had told you? Would it have changed anything?"

Would it? he asked himself. Maybe he would have resisted her, backed off. Done the right thing. Oh, hell. Who was he kidding?

"No." He sighed and pressed his lips to her fingertips. "But I would have been more careful."

"If I wanted careful, I would have gone back to my bedroom, alone." Shyly she dropped her gaze, ran her fingers over his jaw and down his neck. "I'm glad I didn't."

"That makes two of us." But he was still reeling from

what had just happened between them, still trying to understand. "I look at you and see a beautiful, exciting woman, and I'm seriously wondering what's wrong with all the men in your town."

"There's nothing wrong with the men," she said quietly. "I'm the one who—"

When she stopped, he tucked a finger under her chin and lifted her head until she met his gaze. "Who what?"

She hesitated, then shrugged one shoulder. "Let's just say it was my choice."

"Alaina—"

"Bradshaw, stop." She frowned at him. "Just stop right there and get rid of the I-just-ran-over-a-puppy look. I'm twenty-seven, and maybe that's old by most people's standards, but dammit, I waited because I wanted my first time to be right, to *feel* right. It did, and it does. I have no expectations, and you have no accountability. We are two mature, consenting adults, and don't you go and ruin this with some misguided sense of guilt."

Surprised by her outburst, he stared down at the firm press of her mouth and the indignant glint in her eyes. Would this woman never cease to amaze him? he wondered. When she pushed at his shoulders to move him off her, he stayed put.

"Did anybody ever tell you that you're sexy when you're naked and mad?" he asked.

She stilled at his words, then looked up at him with surprise. "You think I'm sexy?"

He dropped a kiss to her lips. "Lady, if you were any sexier, I'd be in the hospital."

She arched a brow. "The hospital, huh?"

"ICU."

"You don't say." Her smile was angelic, but he saw the devil in her eyes when she slid her hands slowly up his arms. "So how far is the hospital from here?"

She raised up and moved her lips over his, a slow, thorough kiss that sucked the breath from his lungs and every thought from his brain. When she arched her hips upward, the heat, and the urgency, surged once again and the force of it staggered him. Unsettled him.

But the soft feel of her body under his, the silky slide of her arms over his shoulders, swooped over him and gripped hold with talonlike claws. He wrapped his arms tightly around her, felt the need overtake him, and he brought her with him.

Eight

The sun stretched hot and hard across the late morning blue sky, laid down heavy with the scent of horse, baked dirt and sweat. From the barn, the persistent clang of hammer on anvil rang out on the thick summer air, while Baxter and Taffy barked lazily at men riding in from the outer pastures.

His arms draped over a fence post, D.J. watched Alaina trot Santana around the inside of the corral. It was the third day she'd ridden the stallion, the first day the horse hadn't been determined to pitch her off. But as stubborn and cantankerous as Santana could be, Alaina had refused to back down even once. She'd been patient and calm, unfaltering, always seemed to know when to be firm, or when to back off and give the horse his head.

She was one hell of a woman. And for the moment, she was his.

He liked waking up with Alaina in his arms. Liked the way her lashes fluttered just before she opened them, the way she stretched that long, curvy body. The way her soft blue eyes would meet his, then darken with desire when he pulled her underneath him. *Damn,* he liked that.

He'd taken her to his bed every night since that first time, and every night, she continued to surprise him, not only with her eagerness, but with her fiery sensuality. When she'd told him she was making up for lost time, he told her he had to be the luckiest man in the world.

During the day they kept their distance from each other, barely even spoke to each other, but the minute they were in the house, well, they didn't talk a whole lot then, either, he thought with a smile.

"She's a hot one."

D.J.'s smile turned to a frown when Judd leaned against the fence beside him. "What the hell did you say?"

"Easy there, boy, I was talking about the weather." Judd tipped his hat back and looked at Alaina. "But since you mentioned it—"

"Shut up," D.J. snapped.

Well, now." Grinning, Judd glanced back at D.J. and lifted a brow. "Isn't this interesting? D.J. Bradshaw, riled up over a woman."

"Like hell I am." To prove it, D.J. kept his fist at his side. "Haven't you got something to do?"

"Nope." Enjoying himself now, Judd touched the

brim of his hat when Alaina cantered past. "Looks as good coming as going."

D.J.'s lip curled. "You trying to provoke me?"

"I'm talking about Santana," Judd said innocently. "Damn, you're sensitive. So it's serious, then, is it?"

"I don't know what you're talking about."

"Sure you do."

Because he knew that Judd was like a dog with a bone when something was on his mind, D.J. just shrugged. "No, it's not serious."

"So it's just sex?"

Because Judd had prepared himself for it, he managed to stop the fist that D.J. threw at his jaw. "Simmer down, son. Just wanted to know if your intentions are honorable."

Eyes narrowed, D.J. jerked his arm from Judd's grasp. "None of your damn business."

"Something wrong?"

D.J. looked up, had been too focused on Judd to realize that Alaina had reined in Santana a few feet away. *Dammit, anyway.* He hoped like hell she hadn't heard any of the exchange between himself and his foreman. "Nothing's wrong."

"Heat makes some men downright surly." Judd winked at Alaina. "Lookin' good, darlin'."

D.J. swore silently and gritted his teeth. In spite of the irritation clenching his jaw, D.J. watched Alaina slide her hand over Santana's neck and couldn't stop the raw hunger that surged through his blood. And just thinking about what those fingers felt like on his skin sent all that blood south.

"He is, isn't he?" Alaina smiled. "He's still got quite a temper, but we're working on it."

"He'll settle down." Judd cocked a grin at D.J., which earned him a dark scowl. "Soon as he figures out he can't have everything his way."

"Well, he better hurry up about it." Alaina held tight on the reins when the horse tossed his head and pawed a hoof. "We haven't got much time."

D.J. saw the amusement in his foreman's eyes, vowed to seriously hurt the other man when they were alone. *Were his intentions honorable?* He thought about Stone Ridge Stables, about the offer to buy the ranch that was sitting on his desk, told himself that sleeping with Alaina had no influences on his business deals.

"I thought I'd ride into town this afternoon." Alaina glanced at D.J. "Santana could use a break and Bobby tells me you have a good livery in Bridle Peak."

His first reaction was to tell her she sure as hell *wasn't* going to Bridle Peak on a Saturday, when more than half the local cowboys came into town looking for a cold brew and female companionship.

"I can send one of the men," he offered casually. "Just tell me what you need."

"Not necessary," Alaina said. "I'd like to check it out myself, and I thought I'd walk around town a bit."

When the stupid grin on Judd's face widened, it was all D.J. could do not to knock it off. Dammit, he'd had enough of the man's nonsense. He could think whatever he damn well pleased.

"Fine," D.J. said through gritted teeth and pushed away from the fence. "I'll go with you."

D.J. was quiet on the hour long ride into Bridle Peak, and Alaina sensed that he wasn't exactly excited to be going to town. Still, with the air-conditioning on high, Shania Twain singing "I Feel Like a Woman" on the radio and the seemingly endless, but majestic landscape stretching out from the highway, she was enjoying the change of pace and scenery too much to let his terse silence spoil her good mood.

It wasn't as if she hadn't done her best to discourage him from going with her. Before she'd gone into the house to shower she'd told him straight out she'd *rather* go by herself, that she wanted to do some shopping. She'd figured that would have placed almost as high on the eight-letter-words-to-send-men-running scale as weddings and marriage.

But it hadn't, and he'd come into the house just as she was strapping on her sandals, taken one look at her dressed in her white blouse and pink skirt, then given her a look that scorched her from the tips of her bare toes to the top of her still damp hair. Because she'd known that all he'd have to do was reach for her and they'd end up in the bedroom instead of going to town, she'd quickly retreated to the laundry room to play with the kittens.

That's all it took to make her knees weak or her pulse race—a heated look or a subtle brush of his fingers. It still shocked her how uninhibited she'd become when making love with D.J., how wanton.

She'd wondered if all women felt so completely over-whelmed by the experience, so absolutely consumed. Except for Alexis, she'd never discussed the subject of sex with another woman, and even then, Alaina had listened more than she'd actually talked. Alexis had made it sound exciting, but she'd never said that it turned you inside out and shook you apart. That it made you ache and it made you yearn.

She'd gone willingly into D.J.'s arms—and to his bed—that first night. And she'd gone willingly every night since. She refused to allow herself to consider the possibility of any kind of future relationship with him, just as she refused to think about any kind of future without him. She'd let that pain come later. Now, it was so much simpler not to think at all, but to simply be in the moment and let herself feel.

The sound of a horn honking snapped her out of her thoughts and she realized the truck had slowed and they'd already turned off the highway and were entering into town. She glanced back at the truck that had passed them and saw a friendly arm waving out of the driver's window.

Bridle Peak looked pretty much like any other small Texas town, she thought, noting the two-story brick buildings with the usual mix of quaint mom and pop businesses, the slow stroll of Saturday afternoon shoppers, the dusty pickup trucks and weathered cowboys. Still, as similar as so many of the towns were, they each had their own individual charm, their own culture and history, and it was always fun to explore a new place. She noticed a gallery of local artists and a wildlife museum, then a cute little gift store with a jewel-toned shawl in the window that would look nice on her mother. "You can just drop me off here."

D.J.'s hands tightened on the steering wheel, and he pulled sharply into a parking space and practically slammed on the brake. "You trying to get rid of me?"

The irritation in his tone, not to mention his erratic driving, startled her. "What are you talking about?"

"First you tried to talk me out of coming with you, now you want me to drop you off." Jaw set, he frowned. "I'd say that's trying to get rid of me."

"You're the one who's been pawing sod since I said I was going to town." Good Lord, and they said *women* were moody. "You obviously didn't want to come, so why did you?"

"Why did you get all dressed up to come look at a livery?"

"What?" She glanced down at her simple white blouse and plain pink skirt, then looked back at him, stunned. "You came to town with me because of the way I'm dressed?"

A muscle jumped at the corner of his eye. "I didn't say that."

"So what are you saying?"

"Not a damn thing." He pulled his hat lower on his head, got out of the truck and came around to open the passenger door. "I'll be at Sawyer's. Be there at six."

He slammed the door shut after she slid out, then walked away without so much as a backward glance. She stared after him, bewildered by his strange behavior. And then the thought struck her, had her furrowing her brow.

Was he *jealous?*

No, she shook her head and laughed at herself. He couldn't be. Certainly not because she'd wanted to come to town, or because she'd put on a skirt. It wasn't even a short skirt, for heaven's sake—if anything, it covered more than it showed.

Frowning, she watched those broad shoulders of his disappear into the barber shop. What was he thinking, that she'd come to town "dressed up" so she could flirt with other men? She was torn between being insulted and being thrilled.

She decided to go with the thrilled.

Glancing at her wristwatch, she realized she didn't have much time. She didn't know who or what Sawyer's was, but she'd find out. In the meantime, she'd come to town with a plan, and she had no intention of allowing D.J.'s bad mood deter her.

"So this fool here is so plowed, he's singing Be My Baby Tonight to a cow."

From his corner booth, D.J. glanced over at Tommy Hunt, a local ranch hand who'd been loudly telling the story to the other men gathered around Sawyer's new pool table. Tommy dug a cell phone out of the front pocket of his jeans.

"God bless the man who invented cell phones with cameras," Tommy said and held the picture up, eliciting cheers and laughter from the other men.

"How do you know it wasn't a woman who invented it?" Missy, Tommy's girlfriend said, thrusting one curvy hip out.

"Too many buttons to push." Tommy pointed the camera at Missy's abundant breasts and took a picture, which brought forth a new round of laughter.

"Yeah, well, I certainly knew which buttons to push last night, didn't I, Tommy, baby?" Missy shot back, and all the men howled and clinked their beer bottles.

D.J. had done his best to ignore the rambunctious group since he'd walked in almost an hour ago, had politely shrugged off the ranch hands attempts to draw him in. He knew most of them, knew they were pretty harmless and any other time, he might have joined them for a quick beer. But he wasn't in the mood for their foolishness today, and if he'd had any idea that Sawyer's had recently added a pool table and two pinball machines, giving the restaurant more of a tavern environment, he never would have told Alaina to meet him here.

And where the hell was she? he wondered, taking a pull on the bottle of beer he'd ordered. It was nearly six-thirty, dammit. She should have been here thirty minutes ago.

While he tapped his fingers on the wooden tabletop and waited for her, he glanced at the bull riding event on the TV over the bar, watched a rider hang on to one big, mean looking bull for six seconds before he got tossed, then stomped on until the rodeo clowns drew the furious animal away.

He stared at the front entrance to the restaurant and frowned. So she was late. So what? It wasn't as if Bridle

Peak was exactly a hot spot for crime, for crying out loud. It was perfectly safe to walk around town by yourself, day or night, and the place wasn't big enough to get lost for long. He had no reason to be worried. Alaina was a big girl, and he was sure she was capable of taking care of herself. D.J. took another sip of beer as a new round of rowdy laughter from Tommy and his friends burst forth, making him wonder how many randy cowboys were walking around town right now, no doubt salivating over that pretty little lady in the pretty pink skirt.

The thought had his hand tightening on his beer. What the hell was wrong with him? He'd never been this bothered over a woman before, never had his insides knot up on him wondering where she was, what she was doing. He knew he'd overreacted when he'd stomped off earlier and left her standing by the truck, but when she'd asked him to drop her off, something had just snapped.

He'd never snapped before, dammit.

He tried to tell himself that he just felt responsible for her, that's all. He'd asked her to come to his ranch, he'd agreed not to tell her brother that she was staying at the Rocking B. If he felt unusually protective, it was because he'd taken her virginity, and he couldn't help but feel accountable for her safekeeping while she was at his ranch.

But every excuse had fallen as hard and as flat as that bull rider on the TV, and he felt as if he was getting stomped on by his own damn ignorance. It was more than that, and he knew it was more than that.

He cared for her—he cared *about* her. The feelings he had were unfamiliar to him, and he'd tried to explain them away because they made him nervous. He didn't like being nervous, he thought irritably. And he sure as hell didn't like caring this much.

The beer he'd lifted stopped halfway to his mouth when she walked in the door. And so did his heart.

Her cheeks were flushed from the heat outside and she'd clipped her thick mane of hair onto her head, exposing the long, delicate column of her neck. Her eyes had a smoky look to them, her lips were glossy pink. The light behind her created a silhouette of her slender body and his throat turned to sawdust at the sight.

He watched her glance around the room until she spotted him, then she moved toward him, several shopping bags in her hands and a smile on her face.

Except for the low volume on the TV, the room had quieted and D.J. quickly looked over at the group of young ranch hands. Eyes wide, slack-jawed, they all stared openly at Alaina, watched her stroll across the restaurant and slide into the booth across from D.J. When the men saw who she was sitting with, every pair of eyes met D.J.'s. The fiery look he narrowed back had the men quickly looking away.

"Sorry I'm late." She settled her bags on the seat beside her. "I lost track of time."

D.J. set his teeth. He'd been sitting here staring at the clock and she'd lost track of time? He swore silently and tossed back the rest of his beer, then smacked the bottle down on the table. "Let's go."

"Go?" Her brow furrowed. "I thought we were eating here."

"It's not that good." He threw a couple of dollars on the table and started to rise. "There's another place you'll like better."

"This place is fine, and it smells wonderful." She picked up a menu and settled back in the booth. "Everyone I talked to said this was the best barbecue in the entire county and their tri-tip is to die for."

Reluctantly D.J. sat back down and glanced at the ranch hands again, caught of couple of them sneaking looks at Alaina. Someone just *might* die, he thought, glaring at the men until they looked away.

He was trying to come up with another excuse to leave when Stacy, the waitress appeared and slid two glasses of water on the table. He had dated the pretty blonde in high school a couple of times when she'd been on the cheerleading squad. She was married now with two kids and quite obviously another on the way. Curiosity all but dripped when she glanced quickly at Alaina, then turned her attention back to him.

"Long time no see, D.J.," Stacy said. "How's it going?"

"Fine." Any other time, he would have shot the bull with Stacy. Today, all he wanted to do was order, eat and get the hell out. Stacy, on the other hand, appeared to be in no hurry at all. Because he knew that the woman would keep the chitchat going at least until she got an introduction, D.J. nodded at Alaina. "This is Alaina Blackhawk."

"Stacy." The waitress offered a hand and smiled. "I heard a woman trainer hired on at D.J.'s ranch. That you?"

"I'm just here for a few days." Smiling back, Alaina took the woman's hand. "When is your baby due?"

"Eight weeks." Stacy smoothed a hand over her protruding stomach. "He's kicking so darn much we've already nicknamed him Bronco."

Oh God, no. D.J. gritted his teeth and tamped down the threatening groan. No baby talk, *please* no baby talk.

But he might as well have tried to stop the sun from rising or setting, and while Stacy went on to describe her last two deliveries and then pulled out pictures of the little darlings, D.J. gritted his teeth and made an effort to be polite. He decided if he'd been given a choice, he'd take the ranch hands lascivious staring over Stacy's chatter about diapers and teething.

But since he didn't have a choice, D.J. mentally sighed and settled back in the booth, listened to the clack of pool balls and clinking beer glasses while he watched another bull rider on the TV get thrown, then pop back up and run before the bull could crush him.

After what felt like ten hours instead of ten minutes, Stacy finally pulled her order pad out of the pocket of her black skirt. "So what are you two having?"

"I heard your tri-tip is good." Alaina looked at the menu. "But the barbecued chicken sounds good, too."

"Bring her both." Before she could change her mind or the women took another ten minutes to discuss chicken versus tri-tip, D.J. took the menu and handed it to the waitress. "I'll have the same."

"You want four dinners?" Stacy asked, raising a brow.

Alaina frowned at him. "D.J.—"

"I'm hungry," he said evenly. "We'll take home what's left,"

"You're the boss." But Stacy shook her head as she wrote the order. "Drinks?"

Alaina ordered a margarita with salt and he ordered another bottle of beer. When Stacy walked away, Alaina leaned back in her seat and folded her arms, then arrowed a look of utter exasperation at him.

"What?"

"Don't give me that," she said coolly. "You're jumping around in your seat like a three-legged grasshopper."

He frowned at her analogy, reached casually for the beer he'd been nursing the past hour and finished off the last warm swallow. "I don't know what you're talking about."

"Tell you what," she said and started to scoot out of the booth. "You see if you can figure out what's eating you while I go play a game of pinball."

He reached out and grabbed her arm with lightning speed. "Dammit, Alaina, sit down."

She glanced down at the hand he'd wrapped around her wrist, then looked back up and arched one brow.

"Please." He eased his grip, but didn't release her, let loose of the breath he'd been holding when she settled back in her seat.

"All right." He pressed his mouth into a hard line. "Maybe I have been a little tense."

"Maybe?" She tilted her head. "A little?"

"Okay," he said through his teeth. "I admit it. I didn't want you coming to town by yourself. You're a beautiful woman, Alaina, and on Saturdays this town is full of horny ranch hands looking for a little fun."

"And you think because I fell into your bed so easy, I'd come to town and—"

"Goddammit, no." Anger flared in his eyes. "I didn't think that."

"I'm sorry," she said quietly, then sighed. "I know you didn't. But, D.J., I work on a ranch, for heaven's sake. I work with men day in and day out. You might not believe it, but I really do know how to block a pass."

"Maybe so." Shaking his head slowly, he brushed his thumb over her hand, and her softness rippled up his arm in a slow river of electricity. "But I don't want them looking at you like that. I don't want them thinking what I know they're thinking."

When Alaina stared at him in stunned silence, he felt like a fool, wanted to kick himself for all but beating his chest. Dammit, what the hell was he thinking? He'd never said anything like that to a woman before, and he had no right to say it now, not when he wasn't offering her anything in return.

But what if he did? He wanted her, he wanted her ranch. What was to say he couldn't have both?

When Stacy suddenly appeared with their drinks, D.J. actually blessed the waitress for her timing, and for continuing her in-depth child rearing discussion with Alaina until their food order was ready. It gave Alaina, and him, time to pretend he hadn't almost complicated their relationship.

They kept their conversation superficial over dinner.

She told him how much she'd enjoyed Bridle Peak and the people, that she'd bought her mother and sisters gifts, a shawl for her mother, some spices for Kiera and a polished rock paperweight for Alexis. She'd also picked up a frame for Dottie that said I Love My Grandma.

It was dark by the time they drove home, and he kept the radio just loud enough to discourage any more talk. He figured he'd said too much already, and what he really wanted wasn't conversation, anyway. The tension of the day had wound him up and the best way to unwind was in his bed, with Alaina naked and underneath him.

With that image in his mind most of the way home, he was already hard by the time he pulled into the driveway at the Rocking B and parked the truck. He came around to open Alaina's door, but she beat him to it, and with her shopping bags in her hands, hurried ahead of him into the house. Frowning, he followed after her, moved up the stairs to find that she'd already gone into her bedroom and closed the door. His frown darkened and he raised a fist to knock, swore instead and went to his own bedroom. He sat on the edge of the bed, tugged his shirt from his jeans, then dragged off one of his boots. He threw it across the room, felt a small bit of satisfaction when it landed against the closet door with a solid thud.

He'd scared her off, dammit. Without meaning to, he'd implied that he wanted an exclusive relationship with her. Considering she was leaving in a week, he didn't know why he'd done that. He dragged off his second boot, started to throw that one, too, then stopped, when a movement in the doorway caught his attention. He turned, stopped breathing when he saw her standing there, wearing a black lace babydoll.

The boot slipped from his hand and dropped to the floor, along with his jaw.

"I bought you something today, too," she said, and moved into the room toward him.

Nine

Alaina had never seduced a man before. Before this morning, she'd never even considered it. She hoped like hell that the shocked look on D.J.'s face and the drop of his jaw meant that she was doing it right.

When his boot had slipped from his fingers and fallen to the floor, she took that as a good sign. In spite of the nerves rattling upward from the tips of her bare toes, she managed to slink toward D.J. without her knees knocking.

"Would you like to unwrap it?" she purred and held out the pencil-box-size package.

"What?" His voice broke, and he swallowed hard.

"Your gift." She took her time closing the distance between them, watched his eyes darken as he took in the plunging V-line of the garment she wore. "Would you like to open it?"

His gaze slid to the satin bow that tied the front of the babydoll together. When he reached for her, she backed away and held out the wrapped box that he obviously hadn't even noticed. It took a moment for his eyes to focus on the package, then he glanced up at her and lifted a brow, clearly debating if he was going for the smaller package, or the bigger one. She held her breath, prepared herself if he made any sudden movements.

But he didn't, just kept his gaze locked with hers and held out his hand until she placed the box in his palm.

He didn't bother to be neat, just tore open the white paper and lifted the lid, then looked inside.

"It's a monocular," she said. "Small enough to fit into a saddlebag. I thought you might like it when you go up to the mesa."

He stared at the gift and his gaze softened for a moment—until he looked back up at her.

"Alaina," he said tightly and set the present aside. "Come here."

The fierce expression in his eyes and the hard set of his jaw made it difficult to breathe. She didn't know what the rules of seduction were, if a true femme fatale would play hard to get or tease a little longer. But her skin was already tingling in anticipation of his touch, her breasts tight and aching for the feel of his hands and mouth. If there *were* rules, she thought, moving closer to him, to hell with them.

She stood in front of him, her heart racing, placed her

palms on his broad shoulders and straddled him. His hands slid down her hips and he cupped her bottom, realized that she wore a thong. His oath could have inspired a gospel. His grip tightened, and the tension shuddered from his body into hers.

Her chest rose and fell rapidly, and the texture of his callused palms on her soft skin sent fire racing through her veins. Slowly she brought her mouth to his and swept her tongue along his bottom lip, took her time tasting and nibbling, until she trembled with need. Wrapping her arms around his neck and her legs around his waist, she deepened the kiss, moaned when he pulled her closer, until his arousal pressed intimately against the V of her thighs. She squirmed against him, wanting him inside her, but black lace and denim kept them apart.

Emotions overwhelmed her, feelings she couldn't tell him, but would show him, instead. Her mind had warned her not to hope for more than this, but her heart hadn't listened. She loved him, and he was part of her now, would always be part of her, no matter what happened.

Her fingers rushed over the buttons of his shirt, then rushed inside to hot, bare skin. His muscles rippled under her fingertips, tightened when she moved her hands lower and unsnapped his jeans. Desire swam through her, clouded her vision, and the urgency, along with the need, grew.

They fell backward onto the bed and her hair tumbled down, spilling over her shoulders onto D.J.'s. She rose over him, felt a power shudder through her unlike anything she'd ever experienced before. *Love,* she thought dimly. Love had made her strong. Made her complete.

She held his gaze, reached for the satin bow at the front of her babydoll, then slowly pulled one end of the ribbon. She stared down at him, watched his dark gaze shift downward to her breasts. When the black lace parted and she splayed her hands low on her stomach, she heard his intake of breath, felt the coiled restraint in his body. He didn't move, just watched her, and the raw, fierce need in his eyes gave her courage. She slid her hands up her belly, her rib cage, lingered on her breasts, then upward, until lace shimmered down her arms and fell away.

He reached for her, and she closed her eyes when his hands covered her breasts and caressed her. She felt as if she were floating on a wave of heat, and when his mouth replaced his hands, she rose higher, where the air was hotter, thinner. She was certain she called his name, heard the distant sound of a moan, hers, his, and then they were tumbling again and he was inside her, where she wanted him, where she needed him.

Pleasure shuddered, dark and wild, then broke, slamming through her again and again as she fell off the edge. Holding tight, she brought him with her.

It was a long time before he could breathe, even longer until he could move. Beside him, Alaina laid motionless, except for the rapid rise and fall of her chest. Somehow he found the strength to reach for her and drag her into his arms.

"Wow," he said hoarsely.

He felt her smile against his shoulder.

Their bodies were slick with sweat, still humming from the intensity of their lovemaking. They were both naked, though with his mind still reeling, it took him a moment to remember exactly how they'd achieved that state. Damn.

He owed her a new thong.

He didn't know what to say. He'd never experienced anything like this before, wasn't even certain he knew what—other than the obvious—had happened. He was completely off balance here, but why should that surprise him. He'd been off balance since the moment he'd met her.

The question was, what was he going to do about it?

When she pressed her lips to his chest, he decided he didn't need an answer right now. "You all right?"

She nipped at his skin. "You tell me."

Chuckling he pulled her closer. "Better than all right, I'd say."

"Good answer." She settled into the crook of his arms, but her fingers, restless and warm, moved in a circle on his chest. "You were better than all right, too."

"That so?"

She gasped when he rolled her underneath him. He kissed her deeply, tenderly, until he could feel her melting again, then lifted his head and gazed down at her. "Thank you."

Her eyes fluttered open. "For what?"

"My present."

A smile curved her kiss-swollen lips. "Which one?"

"Both." He touched her cheek, then traced her mouth with his fingertip. He wanted to tell her what both of her gifts meant to him, but he didn't have the words. "Anytime you want to go shopping again, just let me know."

"I'll do that."

When she pulled his mouth back to hers, he felt the heat flood through his veins again and before he couldn't think at all, wondered how the hell he was going to let this woman go.

Moonlight shimmered over the treetops, sprinkled silver through the tall branches. The scent of jasmine drifted on the cool night, carried with it the sound of a nightingale. Peace settled over the forest, soft as a lover's whisper, smooth as a silken scarf.

She sat beside the fire, warmed her chilled hands over the dancing flames. Contentment vibrated through her fingertips; she belonged here, with the night, with the fire. From the shadows, the Elders watched, and she felt their approval.

Her lover would be here soon, she was certain. She'd never seen his face, but she'd always known he was The One. She'd waited for him a lifetime and excitement raced through her; she longed for his welcoming embrace.

A breeze shuddered through the branches overhead, then rustled the bushes. She heard the crunch of leaves and smiled, then turned, eager to be in her lover's arms.

No one was there.

The air turned icy, and she shivered, then stiffened when the wolf stepped out of the darkness. Barring his teeth, he moved closer, blood dripping from his fangs. Afraid, she shrank back, one hand clutching her throat, the other her heart. Desperately she wanted to run, but fear held her in place, strong and cold as steel shackles.

"No," she cried when the wolf leaned back on its haunches, then sprang. "No!"

"Alaina, easy." D.J. held the arms she'd clutched to her chest. "It's just a dream, baby. Just a bad dream."

She blinked, watched the darkened bedroom come into focus, then remembered where she was. In D.J.'s bedroom, in his bed. *A dream,* she thought, closing her eyes again in relief. *Thank God.*

"You're shaking." He pulled her close, pressed his lips to her forehead. "It's fine, now. I'm here."

"I'm sorry." She buried her head in his shoulder, embarrassed, but moved by the tenderness in his touch. "I didn't mean to wake you."

"I don't mind." Gently he stroked her back. "Wanna talk about it?"

Talk about it? She'd never told anyone her dreams, she realized, good or bad. She heard the beat of his heart against her ear, felt the warmth of his skin, the strength of his muscles. His closeness soothed her frazzled nerves and she relaxed against him.

Maybe if it had just been a dream, a simple nightmare, she could have shared it with him. But it wasn't; she knew in her heart it wasn't, and that frightened her more than the dream.

From the beginning, she'd known that the drums had been a warning. A warning she had foolishly ignored.

"I'm fine now." She didn't want to think about the dreams anymore. This moment, right now, was all that mattered. Pressing her mouth to D.J.'s strong chest, she tasted the salt on his skin, and her own desire. "I don't really feel like talking."

"Okay." D.J.'s heart jumped when she slid her hand down. "So you just want to go back to sleep, then?"

She shook her head while her mouth began to follow the path her hand had taken. "I have all this energy all of a sudden."

"Yeah?" He sucked in a sharp breath. "So what do you want to do?"

Smiling, she kissed the edge of his rib cage, then moved lower. "Why don't I show you?"

Experience had taught Alaina that horses—especially stallions—could be highly unpredictable creatures. No element of training was more important than trust, and until that bond was complete, she knew she had to be on her guard at all times, to never take the animals for granted.

It seemed to her that men weren't so different.

She smiled at the thought, tightened the cinch on Santana's saddle, then gave the horse a friendly pat before she put her boot in the stirrup and swung herself onto the animal's back.

"Easy now." She felt Santana's muscles tense and quiver under her, knew he was anxious to run. "That's my boy."

Gathering the reins, she gave the stallion time to settle down while she glanced around the yard. In the roundpen, one of the hands worked with a bay, and in the corral next to the barn, Bobby exercised a bay gelding. She heard the hum of a tractor behind the barn, a distant radio wailing Brooks and Dunn, the screech of a hawk overhead.

Two days, she thought. Two more days and she'd be gone.

She knew it was a mistake to allow herself to believe they might have a future. But she'd seen something in his eyes the past few days, felt something in his touch, and fool that she was, she'd let herself dream, had dared to hope that he might ask her to stay. It frightened her that he wouldn't ask her almost as much as it frightened her that he would. Because if he did, she would have to tell him the truth about herself.

She'd never told anyone outside her family. Had never wanted to before now. Before D.J.

At the sound of the dogs barking excitedly, she turned and saw him riding in from one of the pastures with Judd and two other hands. As always, her stomach fluttered at the sight of him and her pulse quickened. She watched him, etched his image in her mind, prayed that she would be able to recall every detail. The lines at the corner of his eyes when he frowned, the tight set of his jaw when he was angry, the groves beside his mouth that deepened when he smiled. There were other details, of course, more intimate. The touch of his lips, the taste of his skin, the feel of his hands. She'd locked them all into her mind, into her heart.

When Santana pranced underneath her, Alaina pulled her attention back to the horse. Though he was still a little skittish, the stallion had healed completely, inside and out. She rubbed a hand down his long neck, certain there would be ribbons in his future and lots of wonderful babies. She hoped she'd be able to see them one day.

"What do you say, boy?" With a light press of her knee, she turned the horse toward the trail leading to the river. "Let's go for a ride."

Easing Santana into a canter, Alaina guided him through the stand of trees behind D.J.'s house, decided they could both use a good run. When they moved into an open, flat meadow dotted with Indian Blanket, she let the horse have his head. He shot forward, hooves pounding, dirt flying, and flew across the land, streaked past an oak, circled an outcropping of boulders, then raced toward the river.

Exhilarated, Alaina gave a whoop. She'd ridden hundreds of horses, but none that were more magnificent than this one. She leaned forward in the saddle, ignored the strands of hair that had broken from her braid and whipped across her face. They raced on, the scent of flowering snakeweed heavy in the warm afternoon air, and white, wispy clouds spotting the deep blue sky. A perfect day, she thought, reining the stallion in as they approached the bank of the river. The sun sparkled like diamonds off the rushing water and fat cattle grazed the hillsides, the peacefulness broken only by the distant sound of Taffy's and Baxter's barking, then D.J.'s shrill whistle.

One more moment to cherish and hold close, to always remember.

They ground to a halt at the water's edge, where the river was narrow and shallow, edged with thick shrub and a small grove of cypress. Three days ago, the first time she'd taken Santana out of the corral, D.J. had ridden here with her. They'd sat under the shade of a tree while their horses cropped grass, and he'd told her that his father had brought him fishing here when he was a boy, that sometimes his mother would join them and sit on the bank, a book in her hand and a thermos of iced lemonade at her feet.

Alaina looked down at the riverbank, pictured the woman sitting here, reading her Dick Francis novel, glancing up every so often to smile encouragement at her husband and son. Alaina felt the love that still lingered here, and then the image blurred, and Alaina suddenly saw her own face instead of D.J.'s mother, saw herself watching a grown-up D.J. and a young boy laughing as they reeled in a wiggling, silver fish. His son, she thought.

Their son.

Wishful thinking, she realized. Dangerous thinking.

Cursing her foolishness, she turned Santana toward the shade of the trees. She felt as if she'd always known this place, the ranch, the land. Every tree, every crop of grass, every stone. Her chest ached at the thought of leaving, and she couldn't stop the thickening in her throat, couldn't stop the moisture gathering in her eyes.

Tell him you love him, a tiny voice whispered in her

mind, but she shook her head. She wasn't brave enough, was certain she would die if he couldn't say the words back.

She brushed her tears away, realized the left rein had slipped from her hand. With a sigh, she stood in the stirrups, braced her hand on the saddle horn as she leaned down.

Her fingers were inches away from the rein when Baxter and Taffy burst from the underbrush on the heels of a zigzagging rabbit.

Santana lunged upward, and the stallion's neck slammed into Alaina's shoulder, knocking her from the saddle. Because she knew she couldn't stop herself from falling, instinct took over and she went with it, watched the ground rise up to meet her at the same time Santana kicked out his back hooves, making contact with a sickening, bone-cracking thud.

Not with Alaina, but with Baxter.

The dog yelped as he flew in the air, then dropped with a thud, his body limp and still. Blood, bright red, seeped from his head, and he lay motionless, his eyes closed.

No, please God, no.

"Baxter," she called to the dog as she pushed up on her elbow, ignored the pain that shot through her shoulder and the stars that burst in front of her eyes. She would have grabbed onto Santana's saddle to pull herself up, but the horse had danced nervously several feet away.

Struggling to her feet, Alaina staggered toward the wounded animal, calling to him, prayed he would at least open his eyes, that she could reach him before it was too late. Whimpering, Taffy crawled on her belly toward Baxter, her head low and ears back, her nose twitching with the smell of blood.

"Alaina!"

She heard the sound of D.J.'s voice, the thunder of hooves as he rode up, but she didn't even raise her head. She dropped onto the ground beside Baxter, laid her hands over the animal's chest, felt a fleeting shimmer of life there through the fur and skin.

Don't you die, she thought, splaying her fingers. *Don't you dare die.*

Closing her eyes, she knew she would have to go deep inside herself if she was going to help this animal. She let the calm settle over her, warm and soothing, felt it gather force under her rib cage and pulse and spread through her veins. The vibration increased, and as it always had, took on a life of its own. She did not attempt to control it, knew that she couldn't even if she wanted to. She was simply a conduit for the energy that coursed through her, a channel for a power she'd never asked for or understood.

A heartbeat sounded in her ears, grew stronger, louder. *Baxter's heartbeat.* Her mind filled with an explosion of white, and in the distance, D.J. calling her name. She felt him beside her, touching her, but she kept her eyes closed, didn't move. Dimly she knew she would have to deal with the cost of him witnessing this. But that would be later. Now, she could only stay the course.

When she heard the whimper, she wasn't certain if

it was Taffy or Baxter, but then she felt the movement under her hands, a deep, life-giving breath, then a quiver of flesh. The light dimmed, and her mind slowly cleared. A warm, rough tongue licked at her hand, and then her arms were filled with dog.

Her eyes fluttered open and Baxter greeted her with a wet, sloppy kiss on the cheek. Joy surged through her, made her heart leap. Smiling, she hugged the animal, then felt Taffy nudging in closer to lick Baxter's face.

But her elation was short lived. When she turned to D.J., she saw the disbelief in his shocked gaze. He stared at her without speaking, without moving. She wanted to explain, knew she didn't have much time. But even as she said his name, even as she struggled to find the words, she knew it was too late.

The blackness reached up and grabbed her, squeezed tighter, then tighter still, until it completely closed around her.

She woke slowly to the sound of a steady beep and the scent of antiseptic. A fog had settled over her brain, where a tiny little man with a great big hammer worked furiously to drive nails into her skull. The headache would pass quickly, she knew, as would the roll of nausea. She rode the unpleasant sensations as she would a wave, and when it finally crashed, she opened her eyes.

Where on earth…?

The dimly lit room was empty, void of pictures on the walls. A television hung on the wall, its screen black. She heard the distant sound of a man's voice, a woman answering, then the ring of a bell. Dammit, dammit, *dammit*.

She was in the hospital.

Baxter. It came back to her in a rush, and she bit back the groan deep in her throat, then blinked to clear the last mists of her fog away. She'd passed out before she'd been able to tell D.J. what would happen. That he shouldn't worry, and she would be fine after she slept.

Of course, she doubted he would have believed her, anyway. She would have simply sounded like a crazy woman.

She saw him then, standing by the window, staring out into the night, his shoulders stiff and his jaw tight. How was she ever going to explain? She searched frantically for words, was still searching when he glanced over his shoulder at her. His gaze met hers, hardened and he slowly turned.

"You okay?"

"Yes." Her throat was dry, her voice hoarse. "D.J.—"

"I'll go get the doctor."

"No." She sat, but a little too quickly and the room started to spin. "No, please. Just give me a minute. That's all I need. Just a minute."

She touched her fingertips to her temple, waited a moment for her balance to come back. "How long have I been out?"

"Five hours." He stayed by the window. "I brought you into town straight after—" He stopped, and a muscle twitched when he narrowed his eyes. "I got your sister's number off your cell phone and called her."

Alaina nodded, said a prayer of thanks that he'd called Kiera, not Trey. "What did she tell you?"

"Not enough." He snapped the words out. "Just that I should let you sleep and you'd be fine when you woke up in a few hours."

"I am fine." Even her headache was gone now, she thought, pushing the sheets away. "Where are my clothes?"

"Where are your clothes?" His voice was raspy and tight. He took a step toward her, stopped. "You give me the scare of a lifetime, then ask me where your clothes are?"

"D.J., I'm fine now." But the distance he kept between them frightened her. "Can we just leave now?"

He shook his head. "Not until you tell me what the hell happened out there this afternoon."

"Is Baxter all right?" she asked, wanting to avoid his question almost as much as she wanted to know about the dog.

"That's what I'm talking about, Alaina." He stared at her, a mixture of confusion and disbelief. "Baxter is great, barely a scratch. Santana kicked that dog in the head and threw him fifteen feet. An animal doesn't just get up and dance around after a blow like that."

"Maybe it was just a graze," she said weakly.

"I want to know what you did."

"I don't know how to tell you." She drew in a breath, released it slowly. "How do I explain something I don't understand myself?"

"Try."

She laid back on the bed, stared at the ceiling. "It's just part of me. Who I am. When an animal is hurt, I have to help them, to touch them, and then it just happens."

"It." He narrowed his eyes. "What the hell is *it?*"

"It just is," she whispered. "Like an energy, of sorts, that moves through me, a sensation that transforms and restores balance."

"You're telling me you're a healer?"

She winced at the word as much as the cold glint in his eyes. "If you need to give it a label, then fine." She lifted her chin, met his gaze. "Yes, that's what I am."

He stared at her for a long moment, then turned away and moved to the window again.

"Did you use it on me?"

She had to swallow the thickness in her throat before she could answer. "No, I didn't *use* it on you."

"That first day I met you, when Santana's hoof caught my arm. Something happened then, didn't it?"

"That had never happened to me before, D.J.," she said quietly. "Not with a person. But when I touched you, yes, something happened."

"So you know what I'm thinking, too? What I'm feeling? If I'm going to take a trip or win the lottery?"

"Of course not. I'm not psychic, D.J."

"Santana." He dragged a hand through his hair. "The kitten. Baxter. You—"

"Helped them," she finished for him when he hesitated. "Yes, I did. I can't always help an animal that's hurt, especially if it's too late, but when I can, I do."

"I don't believe it. I saw it, but I don't believe it." Like a caged animal he started to pace. "How have you and your family managed to keep this quiet?"

"We have to." She sighed, thought about how many times she'd had to explain away an animal's incredible recovery. How many animals she hadn't been able to help because someone was watching. "The cloud of scandal we live under because of my father is bad enough. The last thing my family needs is attention like this."

She closed her eyes, rubbed at the nagging throb in her temple. "You think I like being different from other women—hell, from other people? But I didn't choose this, D.J., it chose me. I accept it. I'm sorry I never told you, D.J.," she said quietly. "I should have trusted you."

"No, Alaina—" a deep, familiar voice came from the doorway "—you shouldn't have."

"Trey?" Stunned, Alaina watched her brother move into the room, then glanced at D.J. and narrowed her eyes. "Did you—"

D.J. shook his head.

"Are you all right?" Trey asked tightly.

"Yes, of course, I am." She saw the concern in Trey's eyes, and the controlled anger, prayed he wasn't going to make a scene. "But what are you doing here, how did you—"

"I haven't heard from you for a couple of days, so I called Kiera. It didn't take me long to figure out something was wrong and get the truth out of her."

"Trey—"

"We'll talk about it later," Trey said, then looked at D.J. "You gonna tell her, Bradshaw, or shall I?"

D.J.'s mouth pressed into a hard line. "What the hell are you talking about?"

"Trey, please." The tension in the room was fist tight. She had to stop this before it got out of hand between the two men. "If you'll just let me—"

"I'll tell her then." Trey kept his cold gaze leveled at D.J. "This man you think you should trust didn't just want to buy a horse from us, Alaina. He wants our ranch, too."

Alaina looked at D.J. That was absurd. He'd never said anything to her about buying Stone Ridge Stables. Trey had to be wrong.

"Where did you hear that?" D.J. asked tightly.

"I know a few people," Trey said. "They know a few people. Things leak out. Seems that you've been quietly buying up smaller ranches all over South Texas."

"D.J.?" Breath held, Alaina waited for D.J. to deny it, wondered why he hadn't already. When he didn't, she knew it was true. Dear God, it was true.

What an idiot she was. Hadn't she questioned why a man with D.J.'s money and man power would personally come to Stone ridge Stables to buy a horse? Why he'd want her to come finish Santana's training at his ranch? When she'd asked him not to tell Trey, she'd played right into his hands.

Right into his arms.

The thought ripped through her heart. "Trey, could you give me a moment alone with D.J., please?"

When Trey hesitated, she looked at him, implored him with her eyes. He shot a warning glance at D.J., then turned and left the room.

"All this time," she said quietly, "it was Stone Ridge Stables you wanted."

"I had an offer drawn up to buy your ranch, yes." There was no apology in his voice.

"Did you really think that bringing be to the Rocking B and sleeping with me would influence our decision to sell?"

"Dammit, Alaina," he said through clenched teeth. "One has nothing to do with the other."

The fact that he might actually believe that only ripped the hole in her heart wider. "Strange, but for me, it does. But then, what do I know about these things? I don't get out much."

He swore again, took a step toward her, but she put up a hand to stop him. "I'm going to leave now, with Trey. I'd appreciate it if you'd give me a head start to get back to your ranch and get my things. It will be easier that way, for all of us."

"We're not leaving it like this, Alaina," he said tightly.

"Yes, D.J., I am." She slid out of bed, straightened when her bare feet touched the cool tile floor. "Now if you don't mind, I'd like to get dressed and leave."

A muscle jumped in his jaw, and her heart stopped when she thought he might reach out to her, was certain she'd fall apart if he did.

But the moment passed and he simply turned and walked out. When he knees nearly buckled, she laid a hand on the bed to steady herself. Don't think, she told herself. Don't feel.

She felt the river of ice move through her, welcomed the numbness to the pain she knew would come later.

Ten

There was always work to be done on a ranch and over the next two days, D.J. made it his own personal mission to do it all himself.

Today, he'd left long before the sun had come up, spent his morning in the northeast boundary of the Rocking B checking fence, then headed for the north pasture where he'd looked in on his yearlings. His afternoon had consisted of moving a small herd of cattle to higher ground, then rounding up strays, but one stubborn longhorn had persistently given him grief. After a long, drawn out battle of wills and a stinging rope burn, D.J. had finally emerged the victor.

Not that the stupid cow gave a damn.

He rode in now from the river's bend where he'd

spent the afternoon repairing a jammed windmill pump. Work was the one thing, the only thing that seemed to block out thoughts of Alaina, though more often than not, she crept in anyway, usually at the worst possible time. His distraction had resulted in a bruised ankle, a deep scratch from a line of barbed wire and a lump on his shin the size of a walnut—the outcome of dropping an anvil he'd been moving in the tack room.

He welcomed the physical pain, knew how to deal with it much better than the twist in his gut and the ache in his chest.

He'd told himself he was glad she'd left like she had. No tearful goodbye, no angry accusation. She'd simply left.

And if he'd stayed in town that night and had a few too many beers, so what? She'd wanted to leave without letting him explain, so fine. He'd never explained himself or his business to any woman before and he wasn't about to start now. And if he'd felt a twinge in his chest when he'd driven back into the yard the next morning and seen her truck gone, that didn't mean anything, either, dammit.

He slowed his horse when they reached the outcropping of rocks by the river. He could almost see the tips of cypress from this spot, and once again, for the hundredth time, the image of her kneeling beside Baxter jumped into his head. Her hands on the dog's chest, her eyes closed, her face intent, but peaceful. He thought she'd been hurt, too, and he'd never known that kind of cold fear before. When she passed out, he'd checked her for injuries, but he'd seen nothing. He'd driven her to the hospital like a bat out of hell, had already checked her in before he had the presence of mind to track down her sister.

He'd wanted to yell at Kiera when she'd told him to wait it out, and that Alaina would be fine. How could she be fine? She'd passed out. And after what she'd done—

Oh hell, he just couldn't seem to wrap his brain around it.

She'd left two sealed notes on the kitchen table. One for Dottie, one for Bobby. Nothing for him.

He hadn't lied to her, dammit. So he'd wanted to buy her ranch. That was business, that's all.

Renewed frustration had him urging Sergeant to run again. D.J. managed, just barely, not to think about Alaina until he reached the edge of the ranch, but when Baxter and Taffy came barking up to greet him, there she was again, in Baxter's happy bark and Taffy's goofy gallop.

She was everywhere, and it was making him crazy.

The dogs followed him into the barn and Baxter, noticeably more cautious now, kept a respectable distance from Sergeant's hooves. At least the *dog* had learned something from getting kicked, D.J. thought with a sigh.

D.J. looked around the stalls for Bobby, then slid off his horse. When Alaina had been here, the hand had never been far away. Since she'd been gone, D.J. barely saw the kid.

He started to yell for the hand again, but then he heard singing from Santana's stall, and he froze.

Blue Bayou.

It wasn't Alaina's voice. It was Bobby's, off-key, and most of the words wrong. Furrowing his brow, D.J. stepped to the stall, watched the ranch hand brush the stallion while he quietly sang.

D.J. stood at the open stall door and frowned. Wasn't it bad enough he couldn't get the woman out of his mind? Did he have to hear that damn song, too?

"You singing, or is that horse just stepping on your toe?" D.J. said with more irritation than he intended.

Good-natured kid that he was, Bobby just smiled. "Santana likes it."

"Says who?" D.J. watched Baxter and Taffy stick their noses into the stall and sniff, but he held them back with a command and the dogs sat.

"Alaina." Bobby moved to the horse's hind quarters. "She told me in her note that if Santana got tense or nervous to sing 'Blue Bayou.' Calms him right down every time."

"What makes you think that 'Row, Row, Row Your Boat,' wouldn't work just as well?" D.J. argued, when the question he really wanted to ask was what else Alaina had said in her note.

"I tried a bunch of different ones, but this one's the one." Bobby looked over, a hopeful look in his eyes. "You heard from her?"

D.J. pressed his mouth into a hard line. Bobby was the only hand who didn't have the sense not to ask a question like that. "Go see to Sergeant," he snapped and moved into the stall. "I'll finish here."

"Sure, boss." Somewhat reluctantly, Bobby handed

him the brush, then shoved his hands into his front pockets. "So if you do talk to her, will you tell her I said hi?"

"Sure," D.J. said through gritted teeth, waited for the hand to leave before he swore, then muttered under his breath, "She's gone. Deal with it."

When Santana snorted, D.J. frowned, noticed that Baxter and Taffy were still sitting at the stall door, intently watching him. "Stop looking at me like I'm the bad guy here, all of you. I didn't ask her to leave—it was her decision."

When the dogs lowered their heads and Santana stomped a hoof, D.J. swore again. "I didn't ask her to leave, dammit. I didn't *want* her to leave!"

His hand tightened on the brush and he felt three pairs of eyes boring into him. He could hear the question inside his head as loudly as if he'd shouted it with a bullhorn.

So why did you let her?

"Alaina, for heaven's sake, we're taking you to have dinner, not a root canal. Will you please relax?"

Sitting in the back seat of the hotel Town Car, Alaina stared out at the passing landscape and prayed she wouldn't lose what little lunch she'd had earlier at the Four Winds. "I am relaxed."

"Right." Rolling her eyes, Kiera glanced over her shoulder from the front seat. "That's why you've got a death grip on the armrest."

Alaina shot her sister a cool look, then turned her attention to the man driving the car. "Sam, will you please tell your fiancée that she should be more respectful of her elders, and that I'd appreciate a little quiet time before I meet the people whose lives our father nearly destroyed."

"Be happy to." Grinning, Sam looked at his bride-to-be. "Your sister says—"

"Never mind." Kiera sighed and turned around, folding her arms. "You've got about ten minutes before we get there. I'll zip it until then."

In spite of her nerves and the knots twisting her stomach, Alaina couldn't help but smile. Kiera had been clucking over her like a mother hen for the past three days, cooking her special meals in the hotel suite that Sam had reserved for her, bringing her flowers from the hotel florist, handing her tissues to dry her eyes and blow her nose.

It was humiliating, crying over a man.

Amazingly, she'd managed to convince Trey not to follow her to Wolf River and she'd been grateful she'd had the time alone to pull herself together on the four hour drive.

She'd finally walked into the Four Winds, had greatly appreciated that Kiera hadn't questioned her middle of the night arrival, she'd simply hugged her, then led her to her room and insisted she sleep. Not one question had been asked about D.J., or what had happened.

She stared blankly down at the deep, dry river creek that ran along the two lane road. The land was rocky here, with oak trees and coyote bush, pretty in its isolation, craggy hills, and spots of pink wildflowers. It was the first time in three days she'd been outside the hotel.

It had taken her that long to find her balance again, to finally put her feet on the ground and stand straight. The past two days she hadn't been so sure, but today she knew that she'd be a little stronger every day, and that slowly, day by day, the pain would ease. D.J. had lied to her, even used her and even though her heart might be broken, she'd have her life back, and eventually she'd even find joy again. In her work, with her family.

With another man.

She closed her eyes at the thought, let the pain ripple through her, and willed herself to believe that. She had to believe it. How else could she move on?

She heard the crunch of gravel under the tires and the bark of a dog, looked up and saw Rand and Grace Blackhawk's brand new one story ranch house. It was a beautiful Cape Cod blue with white trim, lots of windows and gabled roof lines. A riot of yellow and white daisies spilled from flower beds and pots on the wide, brick entry.

"Are you sure I'm dressed all right?" Alaina glanced down at her jeans and blue blouse, had wanted to wear something nicer, but Kiera had insisted they were all going for a ride to see Rand's ranch, and riding clothes were a requirement.

"You look great." Kiera smiled, then tilted her head. "You ready?"

Biting her lip, Alaina nodded.

Sam parked the car in front of a three-car garage, then stepped out and opened the door for her. She took the hand he offered and managed a smile, even though her heart was pumping like a steel bellow.

She hardly knew her sister's fiancé, but she'd liked him the moment she'd met him. Not just the tall, handsome exterior, but the inner man, as well. He was good for Kiera—perfect, she thought. It was obvious he loved her, and she loved him. As happy as that made her, she still couldn't stop the twist of pain in her chest for the love she'd lost.

"They won't bite." Kiera slipped her arm through Alaina's. "I promise you'll love them."

When the front door opened, Alaina's eyes widened. Kiera had told her how much Rand Blackhawk looked like Trey, and it was true. Before she could hold her hand out, Rand had wrapped his big arms around her and hugged.

There were more hugs from other cousins, Lucas, Seth, Dillon. Even Clair, who'd been battling morning sickness in her second month of pregnancy, had shown up for the casual family gathering. The wives all hugged her next and she tried to keep the names and couples straight: Grace with Rand; Julianna with Lucas; Jacob with Clair; Hannah with Seth. Dillon with Rebecca. And the children! There were so many of the little munchkins, all of them except the babies currently chasing several large balls around the backyard. Alaina knew it would take her some time to get to know who went with whom, but time was the one thing she had.

There was love here, Alaina thought as she stood in the middle of everyone talking at once and the children running in and out with a golden retriever pup jumping at their heels. She could see the love. Could feel it.

And strangely, it felt like home.

Alaina wished that Trey were here, that he could be a part of this. She knew it would be hard for him to let these people into his life, to trust them. Trey had been the one to keep their family together after their father had abandoned them and their mother had drifted into another reality. Growing up, they'd only had each other and that had been all they needed. But they were grown now, lives of their own. It was a difficult concept for Trey, but in time, he'd come to accept it.

"Kiera tells me you've been at the Rocking B," Rand said, handing Alaina an iced tea after they'd all moved into the backyard and broken into smaller groups.

Even though she'd known that sooner or later D.J.'s name would come up, even though she'd told herself she wouldn't blink when it did, she still stiffened. "I was working with a stallion D.J. bought from our stables."

"Santana." Rand took a pull on the bottle of beer in his hands. "Kiera mentioned the horse to me. Sounds like D.J. got a great animal."

"He's a champion." She couldn't help the pride that swelled in her, or the ache. "Kiera tells me you're just getting your ranch started up again. You might want to look at some of our stock."

"I'll do that," Rand said with a nod, then glanced at Kiera. "There's something Kiera and I would like to talk to you about, privately."

Alaina stiffened, glanced at Kiera, who was standing with Sam and Lucas. Her sister never would have told Rand about her relationship with D.J., especially considering the two men were good friends. But when Kiera suddenly looked over, then excused herself from her conversation, and moved across the lawn, Alaina suddenly wasn't so certain. "Oh?"

"Why don't we step inside?" Rand suggested, and moved to a pair of French doors off the patio that led into an airy office with built in desks and shelves. When Kiera joined them and Rand closed the doors, Alaina felt her pulse quicken.

She stood there, her fingers tightening on the glass in her hand, glanced from Kiera to Rand, but couldn't read their expressions. Why were they both staring at her so strangely? Alaina swore she'd seriously hurt her sister if she'd even mentioned—

"You should probably give me that glass and sit down," Kiera said, reaching for the tea.

"What's wrong?" Alaina furrowed her brow, but because her knees were starting to weaken, she did as Kiera asked.

"Nothing at all." Kiera smiled and looked at Rand. "You tell her. Just give her the short version for now."

Somebody tell me, for God's sake, Alaina wanted to scream.

"Your grandfather left you five million dollars."

Alaina stared at Rand, certain she hadn't heard him right. "What?"

"He knew about your mother," Rand said quietly. "About all of you. Before he died, he left trust funds, with instructions for each of you to be contacted when you turned twenty-five and the money released. When your father found out, he managed to gain control of the funds and transferred them to an offshore account. Two weeks ago, Dillon found the original documents in a safe-deposit box and just three days ago gained posses-sion of the accounts."

Alaina opened her mouth, but no sound came out. She looked at Kiera, who knelt beside her and grinned.

"Five million dollars in a trust bearing account for twenty-five years," Kiera said, and there was disbelief in her eyes, too. "Sister, that's a lot of money."

She couldn't even fathom how much. Alaina blinked several times. This wasn't real. It couldn't be.

"It took me a couple of days to absorb it," Kiera said softly. "I wanted you to be here, with everyone, when we told you."

She lifted a shaky hand to her temple. "Does Alexis know? And Trey?"

"I thought we'd tell them together, in person." Kiera squeezed Alaina's fingers. "It'll be more fun, don't you think?"

Good Lord, she didn't know what to think. All that money? She couldn't stop shaking her head. "What will we do with it all?"

"Oh, we'll think of something," Kiera said, laughing. "Let's go for a ride, sis. Just you and me. Talk about it."

"But everyone is here," Alaina protested. "We can't just—"

"I've got two horses saddled for you." Grinning, Rand pulled Alaina to her feet. "Think you can manage to stay in the saddle?"

"I—I think so."

Kiera grabbed Alaina's hand, dragged her across the lawn while the rest of the family looked on, laughing and smiling. Numb, Alaina stumbled behind her sister. When they reached the barn, Kiera jumped onto the saddle of a pretty calico mare tied to a post, and Alaina swung up on a buckskin gelding. She hadn't ridden with her sister for a long time and Alaina let her lead, galloped after her down a shrub lined dirt trail, then through a meadow dotted with oak trees.

She tried to process the enormity of the money, and what it meant, but strangely, it didn't mean nearly as much as she thought it should. If it did, why would she be thinking about D.J., why would the hole in her heart feel just as deep and empty as it had before? There were things she could do with the money, things she could buy, but nothing came to her mind that she wanted.

Nothing except D.J.

"I'll race you to that tree over there," Kiera yelled over her shoulder, pointing to a large oak on the other side of the meadow.

Maybe this would ease some of the heartache, Alaina thought, and let her horse have its head. She raced past her sister, felt the wind whip her hair and stream over her face. When she got back to Stone Ridge, she would start working with that palomino yearling they'd picked up at auction, then there was Reinhold's Light, the two-year-old bay who hadn't learned his manners yet. She also had a fall garden to plant and she'd been trying to learn to knit, though the one scarf she made looked more like a stretched out dishrag.

In time, work would heal her. And Kiera's upcoming wedding, she thought. It hurt, and she knew it would for a long time.

I'm not my mother, she told herself firmly. She'd survive without D.J. She'd always love him, but she'd survive.

Glancing over her shoulder, she saw that Kiera had fallen way behind. Culinary school and all that cooking had turned her little sister into a tenderfoot. Smiling, she turned back and when she looked at the oak tree, her smile faded.

A lone rider sat under the shade of the wide branches.

Heart pounding, she reined her horse in, had to blink to make sure she wasn't hallucinating.

D.J. And Santana. Just sitting under that oak tree as if it were the most natural thing in the world.

Alaina looked back at her sister, saw that she'd ridden back in the direction of the house. *The little sneak.*

She'd deal with Kiera later, she told herself and eased her horse back into a walk, gauged the halfway mark between her and D.J. and stopped. Her pulse was racing so hard and fast, she could barely hear over the roar in her ears.

He moved toward her, but his face was shaded under his black Stetson. It took every ounce of strength she possessed to keep herself from jumping off her horse and running to him.

Though it was only seconds, it felt like hours before he finally reached her, before she could see his face.

He looked tired, she thought, and decided that was a good thing.

"Hello, D.J."

"Hello, Alaina."

She felt his gaze on her, intense and longing, and it sucked what little breath she had right out of her lungs. "What are you doing here?"

"Just taking a ride."

"That's one hell of a long ride."

"You have no idea." He slid off Santana, patted the horse's neck. "Santana missed you."

"Is that so?" Alaina's fingers tightened on the reins.

D.J. nodded, came to her side and glanced up at her. "I missed you."

She said nothing, just watched him, her breath held. Whatever it was he'd come here to say, she wouldn't make it easy for him.

"We want you to come back," D.J. said, lacing his fingers with hers. The smile faded from his lips as he met her gaze. "I want you to come back."

His touch weakened her, and she struggled against the need and want threatening to make a fool out of her for a second time. "You lied to me."

A muscle twitched in his hard jaw and he looked away for a long moment, swallowed hard, then looked back. "I'm sorry. I should have told you I was making an offer to buy your ranch. The truth is, I was afraid you'd leave if I did."

His apology and admission surprised her. But it wasn't enough. It simply wasn't enough. "I can't come back," she whispered. "No more than I can change who I am."

In his entire life, nothing had ever scared D.J. as much as the resolve shining in Alaina's blue eyes. If he'd lost her, really lost her, then he'd lost everything.

"I don't want you to change, baby. Not one tiny bit. I want you exactly the way you are." He tightened his hand on hers, afraid to let go. "I *love* you exactly the way you are."

Her eyes widened and she stared down at him, her lips parted in shock. "You—you love me?"

He reached up, wrapped his arms around her waist, dragged her off her horse and pulled her against him. "I've spent a lifetime being alone, found every excuse I could to keep it that way, nice and safe. But then you came along, shooting sparks and electricity, and I ran out of excuses. I fell in love with you the moment I laid eyes on you."

She felt good in his arms, soft and warm and the touch of her hands on his chest gave him strength. "This thing of yours, sweetheart, whatever it is, I love that, too. It's good and pure and I figure you have it for a reason, so who the hell am I to question that? God, please forgive me for being an idiot and tell me you'll come back."

Alaina felt herself weaken, was still reeling with the shock, and the joy, of his admission. She wanted to say yes, that she'd come to him on any terms, but she couldn't.

She touched his face with her fingertips, pressed her lips softly to his and sighed. "I can't come back, D.J.," she whispered. "I saw what that did to my mother, to my family—"

"Stop. Stop right there." D.J.'s eyes narrowed fiercely. "Is that what you think? That I'm asking you to live with me?"

She suddenly felt foolish, didn't know what to think. He'd told her he'd loved her. Asked her to come back—

"Alaina—" he gripped her arms tighter when she tried to pull away "—I'm not asking you to live with me. I'm asking you to marry me."

"You want me to marry you?" she repeated, prayed that she'd heard him right.

She stumbled back when he released her, watched as he reached into the front pocket of his shirt and pulled out a gold band with a simple, but elegant diamond. "This was my mother's," he said quietly, holding the ring out to her. "Will you wear it, at least until I can buy you something bigger?"

Stunned, she stared at the ring, felt the tears burn her eyes and thicken her throat. She wanted to tell him she didn't want anything bigger, that all she wanted was him, but she couldn't find her voice.

"Marry me." He looked into her eyes. "Love me. Have my children."

Marriage. Children. D.J. Everything she'd ever wanted and more. She pressed a hand to her heart, was certain it would beat right out of her chest. "I do love you," she whispered, then jumped into his arms with a laugh. "I do. Yes. Yes."

He swung her, then pulled her close and kissed her, a long, deep kiss that poured his love into her. Joy swelled in her heart. She heard the birds chattering in the oak tree, the call of a hawk overhead, felt the breeze shimmer over her skin. When he set her back down, she held on, afraid her knees wouldn't hold her.

"I love you." He kissed her again and reached for her hand. When their fingers touched, sparks crackled in the dry air. Breath held, she watched him lift his gaze to hers and smile, then slip the ring onto her finger.

"It's beautiful." She stepped back from her, watched the sun sparkle off the diamond. "It's perfect."

A sudden nudge from behind pushed her into D.J.'s arms again. She turned and looked at Santana, then broke into laughter.

"Shall we go back to the house?" D.J. asked after another long, deep kiss.

"Not yet." She rubbed her lips over his, felt the vibrations move from her body into his, then back again. She'd never felt more whole, more loved. She glanced up, realized she hadn't told him about the trust fund, but when he brought his mouth back to her, she knew it didn't matter. They had time to talk later, she thought, kissing him back and smiling.

A lifetime.

* * * * *

BLACKHAWK'S
AFFAIR

One

Jordan Alastair Grant had built an empire keeping one step ahead of the competition and two steps ahead of his past. He'd been rich, he'd been poor, he'd been rich again. Money itself meant little to him. The exclusive cars, the custom built houses, the private company jet— as far as he was concerned, they were all just props. A means to an end. It was winning that truly made his blood rush. That sharp kick of pleasure deep in his gut when an opponent either threw in the towel or went down for the count.

Business was just a game, he'd always thought. Stocks, oil, investments—each transaction, every endeavor, just another roll of the dice, one more playing piece on the board.

He had the look of power. Six-foot-four, precision-cut, thick, dark hair, the solid, muscled body of an athlete he kept well-toned with daily workouts into his gym. His face, roughly chiseled and hard-edged, had the ability to intimidate with one razor-sharp glance from his bottle-green eyes, or charm with a simple tilt of his firm, wide mouth. His dark slash of brows, depending on his mood, or his need, could cut an adversary at his knees or make a woman swoon.

And if some people might think he was cold and calculating, what did it matter to him? As long as he got what he wanted, he didn't much give a damn what anyone thought.

He heard the landing gear lower on the jet and glanced at his Rolex. Right on schedule.

"We'll be landing in ten minutes, Mr. Grant."

Denise, the stewardess, moved toward him from the galley. An attractive redhead with a dimpled, beauty pageant smile and hazel eyes, she was a temporary replacement for Jordan's permanent flight staff.

The past few years he'd traveled more often than he liked, but with offices in Dallas, Lubbock and Houston, not to mention the West Coast affiliate, there hadn't been much choice. At thirty-four, he'd had enough of the daily grind of twelve hour days, seven days a week, most of it spent in board meetings or on a plane. Jordan had put the hours and sweat into his companies and other ventures, made his fortune. He'd enjoyed the challenge of it all when he was younger, but he was ready to move on now—or to be more accurate, he was ready to go back.

Back to his roots.

Jordan had been raised on Five Corners— twenty thousand acres of prime East Texas land that included cattle, lumber and oil. Richard Grant, Jordan's father, had been a genteel, socialite Bostonian with connections, but no money. Enter Kitty Turner, Jordan's mother, the daughter of a wealthy rancher with truckloads of money, but no connections.

It was a match—merger—made in heaven.

But while Richard may have appreciated and enjoyed the money that came with his marriage to Kitty, he detested everything about ranching and living in East Texas. The isolation, the physical labor, the camaraderie of the "good old boys." Richard had considered Five Corners beneath him.

Lost in his thoughts, Jordan hadn't realized Denise was still standing beside him, asking him something. He glanced up at the flight attendant, realized she'd asked him if he'd like more coffee.

"Thank you, no."

She leaned over him to collect his empty cup. "Shall I have the pilot notify your driver?"

"Not necessary." The subtle brush of the woman's hand across his arm did not go unnoticed—or the lingering eye contact. "I have a friend picking me up."

"Is there anything else I can do for you, sir?"

He shook his head, watched her turn and slowly saunter away to prepare for landing. He was certain the woman could do many things, but today, he only had one woman on his mind.

One with raven hair, sapphire eyes, endless legs.

He still remembered the feel of those legs wrapped around his waist.

He shrugged off the memory, and the pinch

to his pride when those legs had walked out on him. Okay, so maybe it was more than a pinch, he admitted reluctantly. Maybe it was more like the swing of a wrecking ball straight to his gut.

But that was eight years ago. He thought he'd been in love. Worse, he'd thought she'd been in love. It was a mistake he hadn't repeated.

The wheels of the small jet touched down smoothly on the small, private air strip, bumped a bit, then taxied to a stop at the end of the asphalt runway. He glanced out the window, saw the familiar green of the surrounding East Texas forest, ablaze now with fall colors. He'd grown up in those woods, played army and built forts there when he was a boy, broke his arm jumping off a rock into the lake when he was fourteen, and when he was sixteen, crashed his first truck—a brand-new, V-8, 486 silver Ford with black leather interior—straight into a hickory pine. He still had the thin, jagged scar over his left eyebrow where he'd hit the steering wheel with his forehead.

Jordan stared deeper into the thick trees, thought of other experiences in those woods, experiences of a more intense, sexual nature. Memories that would make a schoolgirl blush

She wouldn't like him being here, he knew,

but it didn't matter. After eight years, it was just
too damn bad what she liked or didn't like.

It was time.

October had always been Alexis Blackhawk's
favorite time of year. When the cloying heat of
humid summer days began to soften, the nights
turned long and cool, the air crisp. As a child,
she'd loved the soft yellows of the cottonwoods,
the earthy russets of oak, the vibrant orange of
roadside pumpkin stands.

At the moment, however, what she especially
loved was the shiny red convertible she'd just
shifted into fourth gear. With the open road
ahead of her, Mary J. Blige on the radio and the
whip of the night wind through her brand-new,
chic-salon, chin-length haircut, Alexis couldn't
help but think, *Life is good.*

She took the turn off the highway a smidgen
too fast, held tight to the wheel as the car
skidded sideways. Smiling, she flattened the
sole of her Jimmy Choo high heel against the ac-
celerator, spitting dust and gravel off the car's
rear tires as she raced down the familiar dirt
road leading to Stone Ridge Stables. In spite of
the bumps and dips, the sports car handled like

a dream, and the power of the engine hummed in her head and sang in her blood. *I just might have to buy me one of these when I get home,* she thought, though living in New York, it would be frivolous, especially since she wouldn't have much opportunity to drive it, anyway.

Still, she could certainly afford to be frivolous, she knew, and her smile widened. Inheriting millions from a grandfather she'd never known had given her the ability—and the freedom—to be as absurdly frivolous as she wanted. Overnight, she'd gone from two maxed out credit cards, an overdrawn checking account and less than two weeks away from having her electricity turned off, to having more money than she knew what to do with.

Not that she hadn't figured it out quickly, of course. After a three day clothes shopping marathon on Fifth Avenue, she'd found and bought the apartment of her dreams on the West Side. It was as perfect as perfect gets. After she moved in, she intended to do her part to support the Gross National Product by tastefully furnishing every big, beautiful, high-ceilinged room, not to mention filling the walk-in closet in her master suite.

So many shoes, she thought, so little time.

Her headlights flashed across a pasture where sleepy cows barely lifted their heads to acknowledge their midnight visitor. At the edge of the stables, she flipped off the radio, then cut the lights as she rolled to a stop in front of the house where she'd been born.

She hadn't been home for a while—over a year—but nothing had changed. For that matter, nothing had changed on her family's ranch in her entire twenty-seven years. Same clapboard white, same black antebellum shutters, same honeysuckle climbing voraciously up the two-story porch columns. She breathed in the scent of it, felt the stillness, heard the nightsong of a mockingbird and the deep croak of a bullfrog.

There were memories here. Some she took comfort in. Others she preferred to forget.

She cut the engine and stepped out of the car, stared at the dark house while she rolled her tired shoulders. Since her sisters and brother weren't expecting her until tomorrow afternoon, they would all be asleep. The excitement of living on a ranch, she thought, shaking her head and smiling. She wasn't sure which was worse—going to bed before 1:00 a.m., or getting up at six.

With a sigh, she left her suitcases in the trunk, then grabbed her overnight bag from the front seat and crept into the house. Living in the city for the past nine years, she'd almost forgotten the blackness of a night without a moon. When her heels clicked on hardwood entry, she slipped her shoes off and felt her way across the floor, remembered her days as a teenager, sneaking in past her curfew, praying that Big Brother Trey wouldn't hear her.

He always did, of course, and their ensuing argument would not only wake the rest of the house, but the bunkhouse and next county, as well. She'd tell him to stop treating her like a baby, he'd tell her to stop acting like one. She'd tell him she didn't have to do what he said, he'd tell her until someone bigger and meaner came along, yes she did.

Since there weren't too many men in Stone Ridge bigger than Trey—and in her opinion, no one meaner—he'd always win. Kiera and Alaina would always sympathize with her, behind closed doors, but they never interceded or questioned Trey's authority. He was the man of the house, the one who had stepped up and taken charge after their father had left.

And her mother, Alexis remembered those days with a flash of sadness, her mother simply hadn't the ability to deal with an unruly teenager. Most days her mother could barely make it out of bed, let alone run a ranch or be a parent. So Trey had done it all, taken on all the responsibilities, ran the family with the same iron fist he ran the ranch. Not once could she remember hearing him complain.

There were things Alexis was sorry for, things she'd said, things she'd done to make her brother's life more difficult. But the past was the past, she knew, and regret was a useless emotion. She'd managed to get grants and work enough side jobs so she could go to college, had gotten her degree in fashion, and somewhere along the way, she'd like to think that she'd grown up. She had a dream job as an editor with *Impression* magazine, a terrific man she'd just started dating and now, all that money. Every day when she woke up, she had to pinch herself.

The fact that Kiera and Alaina were both suddenly in love with terrific men, and both engaged, was icing on the cake—the wedding cake, she thought with a smile.

Kiera's wedding was less than a week away, Alaina's following closely behind. They'd all planned this time together at the ranch as a last hurrah—a chance to reconnect before husbands and babies took over their lives.

Everything would be different now, of course, Alexis thought with a mixture of sadness and pleasure. But still, it was good, all good, and she knew it wouldn't be long before the sound of tiny feet would be pattering across these glossy hardwood floors. She decided she'd make one hell of an aunt.

Stubbing her toe on the leg of an entry table, Alexis bit back the curse, waited for the pain to subside, then slowly made her way to the stairs. She knew exactly where to step to avoid all the creaks, a little trick she'd learned in high school. At the top of the stairs, she felt her way to the guest bedroom, stepped inside and flipped on the light.

The bed and the surrounding floor were covered with cardboard boxes, some marked *Alaina*, some *Kiera*, and Alexis knew she wouldn't be sleeping in here tonight. With a sigh, she flipped off the light again, made her way across the hall, then slipped into Alaina's bedroom. Though she couldn't see a thing in the darkness, Alexis heard the sound of Alaina's steady breathing and she crept toward the big, four poster bed. The mattress dipped when she sat on the edge, but Alaina didn't stir. Quietly, Alexis pulled off her beige blazer and crepe slacks, left her camisole on, then slid under the cool, crisp sheets.

If only for a few days, it felt good to be home.

Growing up, she and Alaina had shared a bedroom, laid awake many a night talking about boys and school, or complaining about Trey. If there was anything they had agreed on—Kiera included—it was that their big brother was a heartless bully.

A heartless bully they loved beyond life itself.

She thought of another man, one whom she'd also thought was a heartless bully, one whom she'd also loved deeply. But thoughts of that man only brought hurt, so she pushed him out of her mind. This was no time for shattered dreams, Alexis chastised herself. This was a time to celebrate, to be happy.

She laid on her side and snuggled under the sheets, stared into the darkness, until she finally gave in to the exhaustion of a long, busy day of work and travel. Closing her eyes, she slowly drifted off to sleep, with the strangest feeling that somewhere, something wasn't quite right....

* * *

There was a woman in his bed.

Jordan blinked a few times, just to make sure he wasn't still dreaming, then rubbed the sleep from his eyes.

Nope. No dream. There really *was* a woman in the bed next to him.

Hell of a way to wake up.

Her back was turned to him, and she hugged her pillow and the edge of the bed. He raised up on his elbow and in the pale gray of the early morning light, studied the outline of her long, slender body stretched out beside him. The ends of her thick, dark hair skimmed her graceful neck, and the lacy edge of a white camisole peeked out from under the sheets. Jordan lifted the sheet and lowered his gaze.

After all, someone had set a present in front of him, the least he could do was look at it.

White thong, he noted, and sucked in a breath through gritted teeth. Nice—make that *very* nice—rear end. On her hip, a small unicorn reared, its white mane flowing. She stirred, rolled to her back.

Well, well, well. Jordan raised a brow. His present just kept getting better.

She'd cut her hair, he noted, and decided that the shorter, tousled look fit her heart-shaped face extremely well. Though it was subtle, the angles of her high cheekbones had sharpened, as had the delicate line of her jaw. Her mouth hadn't changed, though. It was still just as wide and lush, tipped up at the corners. Still just as tempting.

She sighed softly, lifted one hand to rest beside her head. Her long fingers curled toward her smooth palm, her nails were perfectly manicured with pretty white, French tips. Remembering the feel of those hands on his skin, his pulse jumped.

If he was a gentleman, he supposed he could slip out of bed, at least pull on a pair of jeans before she woke up. He supposed he might even be able to leave the room without disturbing her, save her a bucket load of embarrassment when she opened her eyes and realized it wasn't her sister she'd crawled into bed with during the night.

But he wasn't feeling very gentlemanly at the moment, and besides—he settled his head into the palm of his hand and stared down at her— it wouldn't be nearly as much fun.

She smelled as good as she looked, he thought. Like a warm breeze on an exotic beach. He breathed the scent in, let his gaze travel down the slender column of her graceful neck, watched the peaceful rise and fall of her full breasts. This time, his pulse didn't just jump, it sprinted.

He slid a fingertip along her jaw and whispered her name. "Alexis."

When she didn't respond, he threw caution to the wind—hell, he was only human—and he let his finger glide smoothly down her neck, over the pulse at the base of her throat, her collarbone. Her skin was warm and soft as rose petals.

"Alexis."

He moved lower, skimmed his fingertips over the swell of her breast, watched her nipple harden under the thin cotton camisole. Lust shot like an arrow straight to his groin and he felt himself harden. Damn, but she tempted him, and his palm ached to cup her in his hand, his mouth ached to taste her.

He might have, but when her eyelashes, thick and dark against her smooth, golden skin, fluttered softly, he reluctantly reconsidered. She stirred, stretched one arm over her head as she drew in a deep breath, then sighed. When her lids slitted open, her sleepy, ocean-blue gaze met his.

"Mornin'," he murmured.

"Morning," she breathed and closed her eyes again.

He waited a beat, then two.

Her eyes flew open, focused now.

She squeaked at the same time she pushed away from him, her long legs caught in the sheets and she flopped over the edge of the mattress onto the floor.

Two

Please, please, *please* let this be a nightmare, Alexis thought frantically and squeezed her eyes shut. *Just let me wake up now, still in bed, my sister sleeping beside me….*

But based on the cold, hardwood floor pressing against her backside, the sting of pain vibrating up her elbow, and the lingering burn of his fingertip on her jaw, she had the horrible, awful feeling that she was, in fact, very much awake.

Which didn't make it any less of a nightmare.

She opened her eyes, groaned when she saw

him staring down at her, his gaze wickedly amused.

The urge to scramble away from him overwhelmed her, but with her legs still wrapped up in the sheets, she couldn't move, and realized if she tried, she'd pull loose the last little bit of sheet covering Jordan from the waist down.

"Was it something I said?" he asked, raising one brow.

She watched his gaze slide from her face down to her breasts, and she snagged a pillow from the bed, hugged it close. "What are you doing here?"

"Sleeping." He scrubbed a hand over his morning beard, then raked his fingers through his hair. "At least I was, until your snoring woke me up. You should see a doctor about that."

"I do not—" She stopped, frowned darkly. He'd always been able to ruffle her feathers, dammit. "You know perfectly well what I mean. What are you doing in Alaina's bed?"

"Come back up here with me—" he patted the bed beside him "—and I'll tell you."

"I most certainly will not." Struggling not to yell, she glanced at the bedside clock—5:30 a.m.—prayed no one else in the house was up yet. Even if she was an adult, even if nothing had happened—or was *going* to happen—in this bedroom, the mere thought of Trey walking into the room and seeing her with Jordan like this made Alexis's stomach clench.

"Okay, be that way." He sighed, shook his head. "I'll come down there with you, then."

When he moved toward the edge of the four poster bed, her breath caught. She grabbed one of her high heels and pointed it at him. "Jordan Grant, don't you dare."

"You used to say that to me when you wanted me to kiss you."

She opened her mouth to deny it, but because she couldn't, frustration took over and she tossed the shoe at his head instead. Unfortunately, he managed to duck the missile, which sailed across the bed and landed with a thud against the wall.

Stupid, stupid. Biting her lip, Alexis held her breath, listened several seconds for the sound of footsteps from the hall outside. When she heard nothing, she slowly exhaled.

"Dammit, Jordan—" she whispered sharply "—what are you doing here?"

"Trey invited me."

"We agreed you wouldn't come to the ranch at the same time I was here." She tensed at the sound of water running through the pipes, knew that someone was up in the house, and it was most likely Trey.

"We never agreed on anything, sweetheart," Jordan said. "Which, I seem to recall, is the reason you walked out on me."

She wouldn't let him bait her into an argument, Alexis told herself. Especially not right now.

"I didn't *walk* out on you, *sweetheart,*" she said, tilting her chin up. "I ran."

"Ouch." Wincing, he rubbed at his chest. "Touché, Allie."

Her satisfaction at wounding him was short-lived when her eyes followed the path of his hand. It was impossible not to notice that his broad chest was even broader and more muscled, more cut, than it had been eight years ago. It was also impossible not to remember what those hard muscles had felt like rippling under her fingers.

Instinctively she scooted back, and the sheet slid farther down his lean waist, revealing an arrow of dark masculine hair. Her pulse did a pole vault and she gasped, snapped her gaze up.

"You're in my sister's bed, naked?"

"Jealous?"

She refrained—barely—from hurling herself at him. She was going to kill him. Quietly, so Trey wouldn't hear. All she had to figure out was how to get his six-foot-four, two-hundred-twenty-pound body down the stairs and out of the house without anyone seeing. "Jordan, so help me—"

"You always were high-strung," he said, shaking his head. "But if it makes you feel any better, your sister isn't even here. Neither one of them are, for that matter. You're the only female in the house."

"What do you mean, my sisters aren't here?" She blew a thick strand of hair from her eyes, decided to let the high-strung comment go for the moment. "Where are they?"

"Don't know exactly." He yawned, scratched at his neck. "But Trey said something about them spending an extra day shopping in Houston since you weren't coming in until today."

They were shopping? Without her? They could have at least called, Alexis thought, mildly miffed she'd been left out, then froze when she heard bootsteps in the hall and realized she had a much bigger problem at the moment.

The steps stopped outside the bedroom door. She had visions of her brother walking in, his eyes narrowing at the sight of her sitting on the floor, half-naked, and Jordan in the bed, naked as the day he was born. Afraid to move, afraid to breathe, she stared at the door handle, waited for it to turn….

When the bootsteps moved away and she heard the familiar creak on the stairs, relief flooded through her. She closed her eyes and exhaled.

"Just like old times," Jordan said.

"No, it is not." She opened her eyes and clenched her teeth. "I'm not nineteen and impulsive, or so easily impressed by a handsome face and broad chest. I look for a little more depth in a relationship now, qualities beyond the physical."

"So I take it the sex hasn't been so good since we were together."

"I didn't say—" She caught herself, annoyed that he'd nearly sucked her right back into his little game of macho superiority. "My sex life, my *life*, for that matter, is none of your business. Now if you wouldn't mind turning around so I can get dressed and get out of here before Trey sees my car…"

He made no move to turn away or even avert his gaze. "You never used to be shy, Allie."

"You never used to be such a lech," she tossed back.

"If appreciating a beautiful woman's body makes me a lech, then fine, guilty as charged."

With a sigh, he rolled over, dragging the sheets with him and leaving Alexis without any covers. She scrambled for the slacks she'd pulled off before getting into bed and shimmied into them, but didn't bother with the blazer. All she wanted was to get out of this room, and hopefully sneak into Kiera's old bedroom before Trey realized that she'd come home last night. Even eight years ago, her brother hadn't known about her whirlwind relationship with his best friend—nor had anyone else, for that matter. She certainly didn't want them finding out now.

As far as she was concerned, she and Jordan never happened.

She stuffed her blazer and high heel into her bag, collected her shoe's mate, then hurried for the door and quietly turned the knob.

"Hey, Allie."

Frowning, she glanced over her shoulder, saw him lying on his back, arms behind his head. She cursed at the little jump in her pulse at the sight of him in the bed, shot him an impatient look.

"Nice tattoo."

She nearly choked on the swear word she had to swallow back, somehow managed to gently close the door—rather than slam it the way she really wanted to—and crept across the hall into her sister's bedroom.

Inside, she ran for the bed, dropped her face into a pillow and screamed.

The smell of coffee, bacon and pancakes finally enticed Alexis out of the bedroom. She hadn't been able to sleep after her early morning encounter with Jordan, anyway, and since she had no intention of hiding out from the man in her own brother's house, she'd decided she might as well face the dragon head on. She'd showered, pulled on the only change of clothes in her overnight bag—a simple indigo, V-neck sweater and a pair of Blue Snake jeans, then, out of habit, swiped on a dab of mascara. If she'd fussed with her hair a few moments longer than necessary, it was only because the cut was new and she hadn't gotten used to it yet.

Her primping had nothing to do with Jordan,

she told herself when she hit the bottom stair. Absolutely nothing at all.

He'd never actually told her why he was here, though she assumed it was because of the wedding, though now that she thought about it, Jordan had an office in Dallas, which was much closer to Wolf River than Stone Ridge. He had no reason to be here, staying at the ranch, though he'd said Trey had invited him, which still didn't make any sense.

She'd known that sooner or later their paths would cross, and she'd carefully orchestrated her life to make it later. Eight years' worth of later. She'd expected he'd be at Kiera's wedding, had even prepared herself for it. It obviously would have been easier to see him with a hundred other people around—much easier than waking up and finding him in bed with her.

But she was calm now, composed.

Dressed.

She heard the sound of male voices, the scrape of a chair across the wooden floor, the clatter of plates and silverware. Familiar sounds. The kitchen had always been the heart of this house, the one place the family had gathered, where they'd laughed, where they'd cried, where they'd screamed at each other. Where they'd comforted.

The first time she'd met Jordan had been in this kitchen. He'd been seventeen, she'd been ten, hiding from a manic mother determined to crush her rebellious daughter's wild ways. Under cross examination, Jordan hadn't given her up, even though he'd watched her duck behind the door in the mud room. She'd had a crush on him from that moment on—out of gratitude, she realized now. Misplaced appreciation for a simple gesture of compassion. It had taken her nine years to get his attention.

She'd spent the last eight years wishing she hadn't.

Squaring her shoulders, she breezed into the kitchen, forced a smile when Jordan and Trey both glanced up at her over their coffee cups.

"Mornin'." She moved toward her brother and kissed his cheek. "You need a shave, cowboy."

"You need some meat on your bones. Cookie—" Trey looked at the gray-haired man who'd been keeping their house and preparing their meals for more than twenty-five years "—give my sister a tall stack with extra butter."

"Just coffee for me, thanks." She smoothed a hand over the braid Cookie wore halfway down his back and gave him a peck on his weathered cheek. He grumbled that she was too skinny and she needed to eat, but the man was usually grumbling about something.

"I'll eat something later," she promised and glanced at Jordan. "My stomach's been off since I woke up. Hey, Jordan."

"Hey, Allie." Jordan nodded. "Long time no see."

"Well, you know what they say about time." Alexis took the mug of steaming coffee Cookie poured for her and leaned back against the white tiled kitchen counter. The amusement she'd seen in his green eyes earlier was gone. Now, she saw only the hard-edged businessman who commanded a room just by walking into it. Even in worn jeans and a denim shirt, Jordan Grant was a man who radiated power.

"It flies when you're having fun?" Jordan replied.

She lifted her cup and sipped. "That a long time is determined by which side of the bathroom door you're on."

"Some things never change." Shaking his

head, Trey plucked another pancake from a platter on the table. "I never understood why you two were always at each other's throats."

The expression stirred an image in Alexis's mind—of Jordan's mouth on her throat, her mouth on his. When his gaze met hers, she knew he was thinking exactly the same thing. Her cheeks warmed and she quickly looked away.

When she was younger, she had intentionally picked at Jordan or started fights so no one would know her true feelings. But that first summer she'd come home from college, the first time Jordan had looked at her like a woman and not a child, everything had changed between them. Everything except the fact that she still hadn't wanted Trey to know how she felt about his best friend, was certain that if he, or anyone, found out, it would end in disaster.

As it turned out, her and Jordan's relationship had ended in disaster without the help of anyone but themselves.

"Trey told me he was picking you up at the airport this afternoon," Jordan said conversationally.

She knew he was trying to unnerve her. Dammit if it wasn't working.

She speared a glance at him. "I caught a late flight last night and rented a car at the airport. I was hoping to surprise my family."

"Nothing you do surprises us, sis." Trey forked up a bite of pancake smothered in syrup. "But I would have moved the boxes off your bed if I'd known. Where'd you sleep?"

"I'm in Kiera's room," she said, which was true for the moment, but hadn't really answered the question of where she'd slept. "If I'd realized you had company, I wouldn't have come in early."

"Jordan's not company, and you know it." Trey washed the last of his pancake down with a swallow of coffee, then scraped his chair back from the table and stood. "I don't know what the feud is between you two, but I don't have the time or the inclination to referee. Why don't you both just kiss and make up and be done with it?"

"All right," Jordan said, offered his cheek.

Alexis frowned at him, was thankful when the phone rang and distracted the conversation. Cookie answered it, then signaled it was for him and limped out of the room. Her frown darkened and she looked back at her brother. "What's wrong with Cookie's leg?"

"Needs a hip replacement." Trey plucked his hat off a hook beside the back door. "Surgery's scheduled for next month."

She furrowed her brow. "What's he doing in here, standing on his feet?"

"Stubborn fool won't listen to me," Trey said. "Maybe you and your sisters can talk some sense into him."

Her history with stubborn men wasn't the best, Alexis thought, glancing at Jordan and Trey, but she'd do what she could. Cookie was more family than hired help, and she couldn't stand the thought of him being in pain. He'd been there with them through the darkest times, made them soup when they were sick, cocoa when it was cold and rainy. Baked their birthday cakes and holiday dinners. He'd always been here, she'd never considered there would be a time when he wouldn't be. Couldn't imagine the ranch without him.

"I'll be in the stables." Trey settled his hat on his head and looked at Jordan. "You might want to take a look at a few of my mares, since you're in the market again. We're going to auction in a couple of weeks, but I'll give you first pick."

Jordan nodded. "I'll be out shortly."

Alexis waited for Trey to leave, then narrowed a look at Jordan. "What does he mean, you're in the market again?"

"I'm moving back to Five Corners."

"What do you mean, you're moving back?" Coffee sloshed over the sides of her cup. "Your parents sold Five Corners seven years ago, right after their divorce."

"True." Jordan finished off the slice of bacon he'd picked up, then pushed his plate away. "They sold it to me."

"They what?" She stared at him, mouth open, eyes wide, didn't even try to hide the shock of his announcement.

"I was sick of their arguing over who got what and how much." He moved a shoulder. "I had my trust fund, so I bought it myself and until last month leased it out through one of my corporations."

Alexis felt as if her head was going to explode. Why didn't she know this? Why hadn't Trey ever mentioned that Jordan had bought Five Corners? Between her sisters not being here, Cookie's surgery and Jordan staying at the ranch, Alexis was beginning to feel as if no one bothered to tell her anything.

"Does that bother you, Allie?" Jordan asked quietly. "Me moving back to Stone Ridge?"

Did it bother her? Hell, yes. But she'd be damned if she'd let him know just how much. She wrapped her hands tightly around her coffee cup so he wouldn't see them shake and shrugged. "Just surprises me, that's all. West Texas property is much more popular with rich oil barons."

"True enough. But I'm not here for oil."

"Why are you here?"

He leaned back in his chair, leveled his gaze with hers. "I'm here for you."

Three

For the next three hours, Alexis fumed.

For you.

From her upstairs bedroom, she stared down at Jordan, who leaned against the corral fence, his long, sinewy arms draped over a metal rail while he watched one of the hands working with a big roan. She remembered all the times she'd stood in this very spot and secretly watched Jordan, all those years she'd pined for her brother's best friend and he hadn't given her a second glance.

For you.

He'd only said that to rattle her cage, she knew, and the fact that he'd succeeded annoyed her more than the comment itself. That, and Cookie walking back into the kitchen before she'd been able to respond.

Before Jordan had gone out the back door and headed for the corral, he'd actually had the nerve—right in front of Cookie!—to brush his lips over her cheek and say, "Nice seeing you this morning."

Fortunately, Cookie had been so busy complaining about doctors and hospitals, he hadn't paid any attention to Jordan's nonsense—which was more than she could say for herself. It had taken a will of iron not to follow Jordan outside, but she'd managed to stop herself, refusing to give him the satisfaction.

And what would she have said, anyway? It wasn't as if she had any say in what the man did or didn't do with his life. If he wanted to move back to Five Corners and run a ranch, fine. When she got back to New York, she'd send him a plant, she decided. Something big and gawdy.

With thorns.

So she'd stayed in the kitchen, put Jordan out of her mind and visited with Cookie. Drank coffee and nibbled on pancakes and bacon, listened while the cook filled her in on the latest news. Doyle, one of the newest ranch hands, Cookie said, fancied himself a ladies' man and she should stay away from him. Elton, who'd been with Stone Ridge Stables for four years, was working on his third marriage and she should stay away from him, too. The town had hired a new sheriff after Neil Harbor, the old sheriff, got drunk on duty and shot his toe off, and talk was that Jody Sherman, who owned the hair salon, had offered the new sheriff free haircuts. Cookie had raised one thick, salt and pepper brow on the word "free," implying that the woman had been offering more than a haircut. He'd then told her to stay away from the sheriff, too.

And they said women were gossips.

But Alexis had only been half-listening to Cookie. As hard as she'd tried to stay focused, her mind had kept drifting to Jordan's comment, and her fingers had continually strayed to the spot where his mouth had touched her cheek.

For you.

When he turned and glanced up at her window, her pulse jumped and she ducked back. Dammit, the man had eyes in the back of his head! Frowning, she folded her arms and paced around the boxes she'd moved off her bed. Why was she hiding up here, anyway? She'd already brought her suitcase in and unpacked, she should be outside, enjoying the beautiful autumn weather instead of fussing over Jordan.

For you.

She moved back to the window, watched Trey and Jordan walk into the stables. He wasn't here for her, she told herself. He was simply messing with her mind. After eight years, surely he'd moved on. She certainly had. And if she thought about him on occasion, that was normal. After all, she'd had a crush on him most of her life, then a brief, though incredibly intense relationship. It stood to reason she'd think about him, have certain feelings for him, even if things hadn't worked out between them. Thankfully, she'd been smart enough to get out before she fell any harder for him. Before he consumed her.

She wouldn't give control like that to any man. She'd seen firsthand what that kind of love had done to her mother. It had obsessed her, and eventually driven her crazy. *I'm stronger than that,* Alexis thought. *I have to be.*

Eight years ago, she'd shed tears over Jordan, felt a pain like nothing she'd ever known. But she'd put those feelings, and Jordan, behind her, and she'd never cried over any man since.

"Allie!"

Alexis jumped at the sound of her sister's shout, then turned and rushed down the stairs. Kiera and Alaina were coming through the front door, their arms loaded with shopping bags.

Kiera dropped the packages on the hardwood floor and ran at Alexis, laughing as she threw her arms around her. Alaina joined them a moment later and they all hugged as one.

"You cut your hair!" Kiera pulled back. "I love it!"

"So do I." Alaina touched the ends brushing her twin's chin. "It's perfect for you."

"Trey didn't even notice," Alexis complained, dragging a hand over her scalp. She realized that Jordan hadn't commented on her new style, either. Not that it mattered, she thought quickly. Because it didn't. Not one little bit.

"And you." Alexis took Kiera's face in her hands. "My baby sister. Getting married."

"I can't believe it myself." Kiera blinked back her tears. "In five days I'll be Mrs. Sam Prescott."

"*Chef* Mrs. Sam Prescott," Alaina added proudly. "Our little sister is now officially executive chef at the famous Four Winds Hotel five star restaurant in Wolf River."

"Executive chef?" It was Alexis's turn to blink back tears. "When did this happen?"

"Three days ago," Kiera said, grinning. "And now that Alaina and D.J. have decided to have their wedding at the Four Winds, too, I'm going to design an entire menu just for them."

Alexis looked at her twin. "You didn't tell me you set a date."

"I'm sorry, we just decided on the second weekend in December." Alaina bit her lip. "But it's not set in stone, so if it's not good for you—"

"Don't be silly, of course it's good for me. Any time at all is wonderful." Shaking her head, she hugged both her sisters again. "Come on, the champagne's already on ice. And speaking of ice, let's have a look at your rings."

Two hands came up simultaneously and Alexis sucked in an admiring breath at the sparkling diamonds. Kiera's was an elegant emerald cut, Alaina's a more delicate oval. Both were at least a stunning two carats each. "Now that's what I'm talkin' about, girls. I haven't even met these men and I like them already."

Laughing, they all tumbled into the kitchen. Alexis popped open one of the two bottles of Cristal she'd brought from New York, filled three flutes she'd found in the back of a cupboard, and raised her glass. "To sisters."

They clinked glasses and sipped, then they were all talking at once.

"Please tell me my bridesmaid dress won't make me look like a poodle."

"It won't. Allie, I love your jeans."

"They haven't hit the stores yet. I'll get you both a pair."

"Get us that sweater while you're at it. It's gorgeous."

"A honeymoon in Paris. How romantic."

"Wait till you see the hotel chapel. It's beautiful."

When the conversation finally settled down and they all stopped trying to talk over each other, Alexis opened the second bottle of champagne and refilled their glasses.

"So what's it like, Allie?" Alaina brought her knees up and wrapped her arms around them. "Being an editor with a fancy New York magazine and having your own fashion column?"

"Such a bore." As if she were annoyed, Alexis tossed her head back. "Parties, fashion shows, endless shopping. Free clothes."

"So how much do you pay them to work there?" Kiera asked.

"Don't tell them, but I would," Alexis said. "Especially now that I can afford to."

"It's still surreal, isn't it?" Alaina shook her head solemnly. "Our whole lives, never having enough money, barely scraping by, then each of us suddenly inheriting all this money from a grandfather we never knew."

"Do we even know exactly how much it is?" Alexis asked. Last she'd heard, the accountant was still adding up the different accounts that had been earning interest for the past twenty-two years.

"Not yet," Alaina replied. "But it's probably enough to start your own magazine, if you wanted to."

A possibility to consider, Alexis thought, then

lifted her glass and looked at Kiera. "Or your own restaurant."

"Maybe one day," Kiera said, shaking her head. "But right now I've got everything I want. I'm just glad Trey will be able to expand the ranch the way he's always wanted to and we don't have to worry about Mom getting the best care."

A quiet settled over the room. They'd celebrated their good fortunes, avoided mentioning their mother, but they all knew it needed to be discussed. It was just so damn painful.

With a sigh, Alexis set her champagne glass down. "How is she?"

"Kiera and I went to the hospital yesterday to see her," Alaina said quietly. "She thought we were on our way to watch Trey play football and told us not to be out too late."

Helena Blackhawk had always lived in the past, Alexis thought sadly. One that she'd created in her mind. A fantasy world where the man she'd loved—the married man—hadn't abandoned her and her children. "I take it you haven't told her that you're both engaged and getting married?"

Kiera shook her head. "Her psychiatrist discouraged it. She has such a difficult time with any kind of change, and lately she'd been even worse. The doctor is experimenting with some new medications, though, so we're hoping they might help. I was even thinking I could postpone the wedding for a few weeks, wait and see if maybe she—"

"Don't even think about it." Alexis wagged at finger at Kiera, then Alaina, who had the same guilty look in her eyes. "Or you. You've both found wonderful men who obviously adore you and would do anything for you. If I'm half as lucky as you two, maybe we'll be celebrating for me in a few months."

Damn. Alexis quickly bit the inside of her lip and wished she could take that last part back. Obviously, the champagne had loosened her tongue, and she could only hope the comment would slip by unnoticed.

No such luck.

"You're dating someone?" Kiera asked.

"Alexis is always dating someone," Alaina said, but she'd leaned forward with interest.

"But she never mentions it." Kiera arched a brow. "Especially in the same sentence as the M word."

"I did not say the M word." Alexis did her best to casually backtrack. Lord, she wasn't ready for this conversation. "I simply said maybe, that's all. You two just have weddings on the brain."

"What's his name?" Alaina asked.

"Where did you meet him?" Kiera piped in.

Alexis sighed and shook her head. Her sisters would be like she-wolves circling in on prey. Women in love thought everyone else should be in love, too—or at least want to be in love. She wasn't, and didn't want to be.

When Trey and Jordan came stomping in from the mudroom off the kitchen, Alexis could have kissed them. Well, Trey, anyway, she amended silently.

Trey looked at the champagne bottles and glasses, then frowned at Jordan. "Looks like they're celebrating without us."

"Jordan!" Kiera jumped up and kissed him. "You made it! Please tell me this means you're coming to the wedding."

"Would I miss seeing my favorite girl get married?" Jordan pulled Kiera into a warm hug.

"Two-timer." Alaina kissed Jordan's cheek, then wrapped her arms around him, too. "I thought I was your favorite girl."

Jordan grinned at Alaina. "Your turn's in two months."

Alexis resisted rolling her eyes and downed the last of her champagne, though it seemed to have lost its bubble. She knew her sisters had always thought of Jordan as a second big brother and she knew that they assumed she'd felt the same way, though nothing could have been further from the truth.

If there was one thing she'd never had for Jordan, it was brotherly feelings.

"Sounds like it might be Alexis's turn coming up pretty soon, too." Kiera rooted in the cupboard for more glasses. "She was just starting to tell us about her new boyfriend."

When Jordan's glance swiveled toward her, Alexis gritted her teeth. Terrific. Just what she wanted. To discuss her new boyfriend with Jordan.

"Is that so?" Jordan lifted an interested brow. "She didn't mention him this morning."

Alexis tightened her fingers on the stem of her glass. She knew perfectly well his "this morning" comment was a reminder she'd been in bed with him earlier. "I don't believe the subject came up."

"Come on, sis, give." Kiera handed a glass

of champagne to Jordan and Trey. "At least tell us his name."

Dammit. With everyone looking at her, waiting for an answer, what choice did she have? "Matthew," she said evenly. "Matthew Langley."

"Matthew Langley?" Kiera's eyes narrowed in thought, then widened. "As in Matthew Langley, the entertainment reporter on channel ten?"

Unimpressed, Trey took a sip of his champagne and made a face. "Never heard of him."

"He's on channel six here." Alaina's voice was laced with awe. "Wasn't he voted one of the top ten best looking news men on television?"

Stunned, Alexis might have asked her sister how she knew that, but she didn't want to encourage the discussion. "We're here to talk about your weddings, not my love life."

"It must be serious," Kiera said, and looked at Alaina knowingly. "She's avoiding our questions."

Alaina nodded. "And she used the L word."

"It's an expression." Alexis pressed her lips tightly together and met Jordan's fixed gaze. "I'll let you know when it's serious."

"Do me a favor if you decide to get married, okay?" Trey set the champagne down and rooted inside the refrigerator for a beer. "Unlike your sisters here, spare me the torture of wearing a monkey suit. Just go to Vegas."

While Kiera and Alaina responded fervently to their brother's complaint, Alexis glanced at Jordan. His gaze met hers, and he lifted his champagne glass to her, then sipped.

With Trey under fire, Alexis saw her chance. She frowned at Jordan, then smoothly rose from her chair and escaped the kitchen without her sisters even noticing. With both Kiera and Alaina riled up, she figured she probably wouldn't even be missed for at least fifteen minutes, maybe longer. Plenty of time for her to put some distance between herself and Jordan and all that talk about boyfriends and weddings.

Quietly, she opened the front door, closed it behind her, then headed for her car. A drive would clear her head, she thought and slid behind the wheel, then remembered she'd had two glasses of champagne. She dropped her head back against the headrest, closed her eyes on a heavy sigh.

So much for her escape.

"Move over."

She jerked her head up as Jordan opened the driver's door, glared at him. "I will not."

"We need to talk, Alexis. Move over."

With him practically sitting on top of her, she hadn't much choice, and she scrambled over the center console with all the grace of a ballerina wearing flippers.

"Hey—" she complained when he started the engine, but he wasn't listening. He backed out smoothly, turned the car around and drove toward the highway. "Stop this car."

"No."

When the car tire hit a dip in the dirt road, Alexis fell against Jordan's shoulder, then quickly pushed herself away. "Jordan Grant, turn this car around right now."

"Not gonna happen. Whether you want to or not, we're going to talk." He spared her a sideways glance. "Put your seatbelt on."

She recognized that look in his eyes—the intense determination—and knew that outside of jumping from a moving car, she was trapped. She might be annoyed, but she wasn't stupid. Snapping her seatbelt on tight, she settled back in her seat and folded her arms, as if to dismiss him.

It didn't surprise her that he handled the sports car well. Jordan had always liked fast cars. In their senior year of high school, he and

Trey had spent most of their evenings tinkering on one engine or another. She'd never understood the fascination, but she'd hung around and watched anyway, and she'd learned the difference between a carburetor and a piston. When she'd turned fifteen, Jordan had taken her out driving once. All she could think about was how handsome he was, how close he was sitting to her. She'd been so nervous she'd ran his truck off the road into a ravine.

He hadn't let her drive again.

Now here they were, twelve years later, and dammit if she still wasn't thinking how handsome he was, how close he was sitting to her.

Dammit if he still wouldn't let her drive.

He turned east onto the highway, away from town. Other than woods and a neighboring ranch, there wasn't much in the direction he was heading. Except the lake, she thought and sat a little straighter. He wouldn't take her to the lake. The lake was their place. Where they'd gone to be alone. Where they'd talked and shared their dreams. Where they'd first made love.

"Do you have a destination in mind?" she asked with as much boredom as she could muster. "Or are you driving aimlessly?"

"I always know where I'm going, Allie," he said evenly. "You know that."

She did know. The problem had been she'd always known where she was going, too, and their paths had been in opposite directions.

Pretty much like now.

When he turned off the highway, there was no longer any doubt where he was driving to. Even for Jordan, this was callous. He knew perfectly well what the memories here were, knew that even eight years later, it would hurt her to come here.

"Why are you doing this?" she asked, angry with herself that he still had the ability to unearth emotions she'd buried long ago.

"I told you." He drove down the single lane dirt road lined with cypress. "We need to talk."

There was something in his tone, in the hard set of his jaw, that worried her. "About what?"

"This guy you're seeing—what's his name, Michael?"

"Matthew." She narrowed her eyes, knew that Jordan had intentionally gotten the name wrong. "Matthew Langley. Why do you want to know?"

"How serious are you?"

"None of your business," she said coolly. Still, in spite of her irritation that he'd abducted her and was now grilling her about Matthew, she had to admit she was curious. Curious why he would go to all this trouble, especially after all this time.

Not that Jordan needed a reason, she thought, other than he felt like it. That would be good enough reason for him. Or maybe in his caveman brain, after seeing her half-naked this morning, he thought he could bring her out here on the pretense of "talking," then conjure up a few old memories and see if he might get lucky.

Was he ever in for a surprise.

He pulled off the dirt road and the tires crunched over rock and leaves until he stopped in front of an outcropping of rocks where they used to climb. The lake was still today, and the warm, afternoon sun glistened off the calm surface. They'd skinny-dipped here under a full moon, made love on the shore, or sometimes they'd climb to the top of the rocks and lay out blankets, watch for shooting stars and make wishes.

When she was nineteen, for three months, she'd thought this place was heaven.

She looked at Jordan, and in spite of the warmth of the sun, a chill shivered over her skin and dread began to creep through her veins. "You have something to say, Jordan, just say it."

He stared at her for a moment, then nodded. "I never signed the annulment papers."

Four

She went still. So still, Jordan doubted she was even breathing. He'd brought her out here because he'd been certain she would scream when he gave her the news. But then, when had Alexis ever done what he'd expected?

"What?" The single word was barely a whisper.

"I meant to sign them, of course." He was still waiting for her to take a breath. Or a swing. "I guess it just got away from me."

"It…got—" she did take a breath now, a deep, shuddering intake of air "—*away*…from…you?"

"I was in the middle of a merger and changing offices when the papers came and somehow they got lost in the shuffle."

Eyes wide, she swallowed. "You're telling me we're still married?"

"Technically?" He rubbed at the back of his neck. "Yes."

She stopped breathing again, kept her gaze on his as she fumbled for the door handle. He could have stopped her when she stepped out of the car, but he figured she needed a little space and a few minutes to absorb what he'd just told her. He watched her walk toward the lake, moving one foot woodenly in front of the other until she stood at the edge.

Overall, he thought that went rather well.

At the ranch, when Trey had teased her about getting married in Vegas, Jordan had seen her reaction. No one else but him would have noticed, or understood, the subtle stiffening of her shoulders, the slight tightening of her eyes. He knew exactly where her thoughts had flashed.

Vegas. Chapel of Cupid's Heart. Honeymoon suite.

Of course, the honeymoon hadn't lasted much longer than the ceremony, but that had been her decision, not his.

He looked at her now, standing on the shore of the lake, arms at her sides as she stared out over the glassy blue water. With a sigh, he stepped out of the car and approached cautiously.

If there was one thing he could predict about Alexis, it was that she was unpredictable.

He supposed her fiery temperament is what had caught his attention in the first place. If it had simply been those big blue eyes and dynamite figure, he could just as easily have fallen for Alaina. They were, after all, nearly identical in the looks department. When they were growing up, he'd always thought of them as the sisters he'd never had.

But that summer Alexis had come home from college, something happened. He suddenly couldn't look at her and think little sister anymore. All he could see was a woman. A grown, sensual female who'd made it clear she was just as interested in him as he was in her. He'd fought the feeling, made a point to stay away from the ranch, even skipped the Friday night poker game with Trey and some of the ranch hands.

But skipping that game had ended up being

his downfall. He'd gone into town that night instead, thinking he'd play some pool at the tavern, have a couple of beers, see if one of the waitresses there could take his mind off Alexis.

The tavern door hadn't even closed behind him when he saw Alexis leaning over a pool table, setting up her shot. He might have turned around and walked out if Jimmy Collins, Tyler Hicks and Bull Cooper hadn't all been staring so intently at her denim-clad backside. How the hell could he leave with those three idiots drooling over her?

He could still see her, her eyes flashing like blue fire when he'd told her he was taking her home. She'd argued that she'd come to town with Tammy and Jenny Campbell and she was leaving with them. Since neither Tammy or Jenny had been in sight, and Jordan had been in no mood to argue back, he'd simply picked Alexis up, tossed her over his shoulder, then tipped his hat to the other men and carried her out. No one had dared try and stop him.

No one but Alexis, of course.

She'd fought him, but it hadn't done her any good, of course. He didn't even bother to be gentle when he dumped her in the front seat of his truck, he just headed straight back toward her ranch.

She argued non-stop, and when he'd finally had enough of her mouth, he'd told her to shut up. She'd told him she'd shut up when she felt like shutting up and kept railing at him. Halfway home, he finally snapped. He'd pulled off the road, dragged her into his lap and kissed her.

That shut her up.

She'd tasted like honey and mint and though his mind told him to keep his hands off her, when she kissed him back, he stopped listening. From that moment on, there'd been no going back.

And the truth was, he hadn't wanted to go back.

"Allie."

She didn't turn when he moved beside her, just kept staring out across the lake. He frowned at her almost serene profile. He was used to her anger, knew how to handle her when she was in a snit. Quiet, calm Alexis, he didn't know what to do with.

Strangely, the longer she stayed silent, the more he felt his own anger build. "Dammit, Alexis. Say something."

"Say something?" She made a small sound of disbelief. "Eight years after the fact, you tell me that you never signed our annulment papers—"

"Your annulment papers." He moved in front of her, forced her to look at him. "Not mine."

"And that's why you never signed them?" Raising a brow, she met his gaze. "Because it was my idea, not yours?"

"I told you, they got lost in the chaos of the move."

"There is no chaos in your world, Jordan." She shook her head slowly. "Your world is orderly and neat and always in control. You don't lose anything."

I lost you, he nearly said, but stopped himself in time. He didn't want to tell her that anymore than she wanted to hear it. "I thought we should have at least given it a try."

"A try?" Her voice rose slightly. "Your idea of a try was me quitting school, moving to Dallas and setting up house, then popping out babies."

"That's not what happened." Rather than put his hands on her shoulders and shake her, he shoved them into his back pockets. "And you said you wanted children."

"After I finished school," she shot back. "After I'd worked for a couple of years."

"I suggested you didn't need to work." Lord, she was just as stubborn now as she'd been then.

"I was your husband. I had money, lots of it. I wanted to take care of you. What the hell was wrong with that?"

"You wanted to take care of me?" she asked quietly, furrowing her brow as if she'd never considered the possibility.

She closed her eyes on a long sigh, and when she opened them again, moved toward him, held his gaze with hers as she tentatively reached out to him. He stiffened when she placed her palms on his chest, felt his pulse quicken when her fingertips moved gently back and forth.

"If that's what you wanted," she murmured, "why didn't you just say so?"

"You never gave me a chance," he replied,

"So much time we wasted." She shook her head sadly, stared at him with those big blue eyes of hers. "If only I'd listened to you."

If he hadn't been so distracted by the soft tone of her voice, the heat of her fingertips and the closeness of her body, Jordan might have seen it coming. But because he hadn't, when she shoved him, he hadn't time to catch his balance or even better, take her with him. He stumbled, caught his boot on a rock and even as he fell back into the icy water, called himself an idiot.

"I don't need you to take care of me, Jordan Grant." Hands on her hips, she glared down at him. "I never did, and I never will."

With the grace of a queen, she turned and headed for the car. He'd barely picked himself up when she slid behind the wheel, started the engine, then spun the wheels and roared away.

Dripping wet from the waist down, he stared after her.

Son of a bitch.

He plucked his hat from the lake's edge, slapped it against his soaked jeans and jammed it on his head. It was a five mile walk back to the ranch. Not especially far, but distance wasn't the point here.

He'd tried to be nice. He'd even tried to be reasonable. He should have known neither would work. All's fair in love and war, he thought, and decided that when it came to Alexis Blackhawk, they were one and the same.

"You sure you don't want to come to town with us?" Alaina stuck her head in Trey's down-stairs office that Alexis had temporarily—to Trey's annoyance—converted into a sewing room. "Cookie's grocery list isn't that long. We can have lunch in town, do the grocery shopping, and be back in a couple of hours."

"I'm fine." Alexis plucked a straight pin from the seam she'd stitched, then glanced up from the sewing machine. "Besides, with you both gone, I'll get our dresses finished sooner."

Kiera had argued that the Four Winds hotel tailor could have handled the last minute alterations for the bridesmaid dresses, but Alexis had insisted on doing them herself. She'd been sewing since she was twelve, had a degree in fashion, and from time to time, for fun, she'd even designed a few outfits herself. She could take in a seam blindfolded or fix a hem with one hand tied behind her back.

And besides, since shoving Jordan into the lake yesterday, she'd needed a project to keep her hands, and her mind, busy.

The image of him sitting waist deep in the water as she'd driven away had been the one bright spot of her day.

"Are you sure you'll be okay here by yourself, sis?" Alaina fidgeted at the door. "I can stay here with you, if you'd like. Kiera doesn't really need me at the store, and she's the only one who can decipher Cookie's shorthand, anyway. It's not like I'll be much help picking out the perfect roast or choosing the right wine."

"Neither one of us would be much help there." Alexis leaned back in Trey's leather desk chair and smiled at her sister. While Alaina's life had always been about horses and Alexis's had been about clothes, Kiera's passion had been food. "Kiera was the only person Cookie ever let in his kitchen."

"Only 'cause I wouldn't go away." Kiera came up beside Alaina and slipped an arm around her shoulders. "Come on, Allie. You've been holed up in here all morning. We're beginning to think you're intentionally avoiding us."

"Don't be ridiculous." Alexis felt the anxious tug in her gut, then rolled her eyes in exasperation. "Why in the world would I want to avoid you?"

When her sisters exchanged a brief look, the anxious tug in Alexis's gut turned to a pinch. If Jordan had said anything to them, so help her, she'd have to seriously hurt the man. She would make Jordan Grant's life so—

"We were talking so much about weddings yesterday and you went missing," Alaina admitted sheepishly. "Then last night at dinner you were so quiet, and we were worried that, well, maybe we were being…annoying."

Guilt sliced through Alexis. She'd been so wrapped up in her own emotions and Jordan, she hadn't even considered what her sisters were thinking. Ashamed of herself, Alexis stood and walked to her sisters, put one hand on Alaina's cheek, the other on Kiera's.

"Being here," she said quietly, "being with you both, talking about your weddings, sharing such a special time in your lives, would never, ever annoy me. I am so sorry if I made you think that."

"You've been acting a little strange." Kiera stuck her hands into the pockets of her slacks and shrugged one shoulder. "When you don't talk to us, we don't know what to think."

They were right, Alexis thought. How could they know what to think when she'd never told them anything about Jordan? She'd carefully hid that part of her life from them. From everyone. Maybe it was time to tell them. Not today, of course, but maybe after Kiera's wedding. Or better, when she and Sam got back from their honeymoon. But then Alaina's wedding was right behind, so maybe she should wait until after the first of the year, or—

"She's doing it again," Alaina said to Kiera, who cocked her head and nodded.

"I'm not doing anything," Alexis denied. "Now go already. I'll have these dresses done by the time you get back and you can both fuss over me and my strange behavior then."

With a gentle nudge, Alexis scooted her sisters from the doorway and went back to her sewing. When she heard the front door close a minute later, she stopped and listened to the sweet, blissful quiet. Jordan and Trey had left after breakfast to look at some yearlings in the south pasture and Cookie had begrudgingly limped off to the bunkhouse to rest his hip.

Satisfied that she was finally alone, if only for a little while, she sat back in the chair and dragged both hands through her hair.

She knew she had to tell her sisters the truth, knew it was the right thing to do, but she just didn't know how to actually do it. To look them in the eye and tell them she and Jordan had impulsively ran off to Vegas and gotten married eight years ago?

And were still married.

She was still trying to fully absorb the enormity of Jordan's announcement, had laid awake tossing and turning most of the night. How could he have done this to her? And why? They'd both made assumptions regarding married life before they'd gone to Vegas, and they'd both been terribly wrong. The only difference was she'd been able to admit it, and he hadn't.

As if Jordan Grant, Mr. I-Get-What-I-Want-When-I-Want-It, would ever sincerely admit he was wrong.

Still, even for Jordan, eight years was a long time.

Obviously, they were going to have to talk about their situation sometime between now and the wedding, but as far as she was concerned, the longer they waited, the better. After all this time, she reasoned, a few more days hardly mattered.

On a sigh, she laid her hands on the desk and stared at them. As clearly as if it were yesterday, she could see the gold wedding band Jordan had slipped on her finger. Their simple matching bands had been part of the "Double Deluxe" chapel service package. They'd laughed about it, and after he'd carried her over the threshold in their honeymoon suite, he'd kissed her and told her that he'd buy her a proper ring when they got to Dallas. She'd kissed him back and said, "You mean New York."

That had been the beginning of the end.

Closing her eyes, she dropped her hands into her lap. She hadn't looked back after she'd thrown the ring at him and walked out—hadn't dared look back. If she had, she knew she would have done anything he'd asked her to, given up everything for him. Every hope, every dream.

And yet, over the years, there'd been moments she'd wondered what if. What if she hadn't left? What if she'd gone to Dallas? If she'd had all those babies they'd talked about?

Would life have been so bad?

"Allie."

Her eyes popped open and she saw him standing in the doorway, arms folded over that broad chest of his, watching her. Damn him! Couldn't she have even a few minutes peace without the man showing up?

"I thought you were looking at yearlings."

"I'm back."

No kidding, was her first thought. That was one hell of an understatement. "I'm busy, Jordan."

Straightening her spine, she turned her attention to the dress in front of her and with a flick of her wrist, snapped the pressure foot onto the seam. She hated that he'd walked in on her at such a vulnerable moment. That she'd been thinking about him, about their elopement. About those damn rings.

Hoping he'd go away, she ignored him. Focused instead on the hum of the sewing machine and the seam she was stitching, determined not to let him rattle her. When he moved in front of her, she kept her eyes on her sewing.

"You're standing in my light," she complained without looking up.

He moved away, but the smug sense of victory she felt was cut short when her machine suddenly stopped. She glanced up, saw him holding the plug in his hand.

"We're going to talk, Alexis."

"This is hardly the time." She glanced nervously at the doorway. "Trey—"

"Is in the bunkhouse, having lunch with the hands. We're alone, Allie. Just you and me. We might not get another chance."

"You had eight years' worth of chance." She narrowed a look at him. "You show up here unexpected, spring this news on me, then expect me to sit here calmly and talk? Well, I'm not ready to talk."

He flicked the plug aside. "Get ready."

"You're still bossy, I see."

"And you're still stubborn."

"I'm stubborn?" She put a hand on her chest, then started to laugh. "That's a real hoot, Jordan. Maybe when you want to talk serious, you can come back and—"

"We're talking," he said firmly. "You want to keep wasting time arguing about it, fine."

"The only time I wasted was time spent married to you," she sniped.

If she'd hadn't looked away for a split second, she might have seen him move around the desk, might have even been able to avoid his hands before they'd closed around her arms. But she'd been too intent on being glib, had let her guard down for a split second, and she'd missed the warning signs.

"Take your hands off me." There wasn't much heat in her protest and she knew it. Worse, she knew that he knew it, too. The best she could manage was an indignant lift of her chin.

She could have fought him. Broken away, yelled at him, stormed off. Instinct told her to do just that. *Survival* told her do that. But here she stood, instead, her body pressed up against his, her breasts crushed against his chest, and every last bit of logic and reason dissipated like smoke in the wind.

And where there was smoke, so the saying went, there was fire.

She looked into his narrowed gaze and saw the flame there, felt it ignite her blood. No other man had ever sparked feelings in her like Jordan. Love, anger, frustration, joy. Passion. When she'd been with him, every emotion had intensified. Obviously, eight years hadn't changed that.

Excitement raced over her skin when his gaze dropped to her mouth. She couldn't breathe with him so close, couldn't think. "I thought you wanted to talk."

"We will."

"No," she managed to whisper when his mouth lowered to hers.

"Yes."

Despair washed over her when his lips touched hers. Despair and desperation and intense longing. She told herself to pull away from him, or at the very least, not to respond, not to feel. She might as well have told the sun not to rise.

So familiar, she thought. His touch, firm and solid, his taste, dark and heady. Her fingers curled tightly into the crisp cotton of his shirt. The heat of his skin radiated through her hands, up her arms, all the way down to her toes.

"Kiss me back," he murmured.

When she shook her head, he smiled against her mouth. "You know you want to."

When his lips brushed over her chin, she drew in a breath. "I do not."

"Fine. Don't kiss me back." He nipped at her jaw, trailed kisses down her neck. "I'll just enjoy this for both of us."

She was crumbling fast. Breaking down into tiny little pieces of need. When his mouth covered hers again and his tongue swept over her bottom lip, she shuddered. She hated that he had this power over her, that he could make her feel things she didn't want to feel.

The realization gripped hold of her and gave her the strength to resist him. Flattening her palms on his chest, she pushed. When he didn't budge, she pushed harder and turned her head away. "Stop."

For a long moment, he didn't move, then

slowly he dropped his hands from her arms and stepped back. "You're my wife, Alexis."

"Was your wife," she said, shaking her head. "I filed the annulment papers. Just because you didn't sign them doesn't change a thing."

"Like hell it doesn't." Irritation sharply edged his words and his voice rose. "Right or wrong, like it or not, you're still my wife."

She opened her mouth to argue, but something from the doorway—a slight movement, or maybe a sound—caught her attention. She froze, turned stiffly and felt her heart stop.

Damn.

Alaina and Kiera stood in the doorway, their eyes wide, jaws slack. All things considered, Alexis supposed she could have dealt with them finding out like this. They were her sisters, after all, and at some point she'd been going to tell them the truth, anyway.

What she couldn't deal with, and most certainly didn't want to face, was the man standing behind them.

Dear God, please tell me I'm hallucinating.

Matthew met her gaze, glanced at Jordan, then looked back to her again. "Hello, Alexis."

Five

Alexis felt the blood drain from her head, and when the room started to tilt, put a hand on the edge of the desk to steady herself. She wasn't hallucinating. She wasn't dreaming. The man she'd been dating for the past few weeks stood less than ten feet away, looking very polished in his tan slacks and white Ralph Lauren shirt.

The question was, how long had he been standing there?

Based on the hard set of his mouth and the burn of steel in his eyes, long enough.

"Matthew." She dragged a shaky hand through her hair. "How did you, where…"

"He was pulling off the highway, heading for the ranch." Kiera's voice was cheerful, though a bit strained. She glanced briefly at Jordan, swallowed, then turned her stunned gaze back to Alexis. "We practically ran into each other. Imagine that."

"You should have called and told me you were coming." Alexis made her best attempt at a smile, but since she wasn't certain her knees were strong enough yet, didn't dare move. "I would have picked you up from the airport."

"My meeting in Los Angeles was rescheduled, so I thought I'd surprise you. Seems that I succeeded." Matthew stepped into the room, moved toward Jordan and held out his hand. "Matthew Langley."

"Jordan Grant."

Alexis felt as if she were having an out of body experience as she watched the two men look each other in the eye and shake hands, wondered if this situation could possibly get any weirder.

Didn't want to know if it could.

"Must be awkward," Matthew said evenly. "Meeting your wife's boyfriend."

"No more awkward than meeting your girl-friend's husband," Jordan replied with a shrug.

"You are *not* my husband." When her voice cracked, Alexis cleared her throat and frantically searched for an explanation. Couldn't find one that made any sense. "Matthew, this isn't how it looks."

"So you're not married?" Matthew asked.

"Well, yes, sort of. Technically." Alexis dragged air into her lungs, felt the walls of Trey's suddenly crowded office closing in on her. "But it's really more of a misunderstanding."

"You mean you really are married?" Alaina asked incredulously. "You and Jordan? To each other?"

"*Were* married," Alexis quickly corrected, felt the beginning of a dull ache right behind her eyes. "Past tense. Briefly, a long time ago."

"This is a joke, right?" Kiera looked around the room. "There's a camera hidden here somewhere. We'll all watch it later and have a good laugh."

Alexis seriously doubted this would be a moment she would ever want to watch again or laugh at, let alone record. And why wasn't Jordan helping her out here? Why was he just standing there, looking so damn smug? If Matthew wasn't standing here, too, watching this little family drama-comedy unfold, Alexis swore she'd throw something at Jordan.

Better yet, Trey kept a gun in his safe, she remembered, and tried to recall the combination.

"So it's true?" Alaina glanced back and forth between Alexis and Jordan. "But how…when?"

"Eight years ago." Alexis wiped her damp palms on her jeans. "One of those crazy summer things. An impulsive trip to Las Vegas, an all-night chapel. We came to our senses a couple of hours later."

"You were only married a couple of hours?" Kiera asked.

"If that." Alexis shrugged one shoulder, gritted her teeth so she wouldn't scream. "We realized we'd made a mistake, I flew back to New York, Jordan went to Dallas, and we filed for an annulment. Until yesterday, we haven't even seen each other."

"He called you his wife." Though Matthew's comment was directed at Alexis, he was looking at Jordan, holding the other man's gaze. "Present tense."

"That's the funny part." Somehow, Alexis

managed a dry laugh, and it scraped like sand-paper on her throat. "There was a little glitch with the paperwork, and it seems that, officially, the annulment never actually went through."

"We're your sisters," Alaina said quietly, furrowing her brow. "How could you not tell us something like that?"

The hurt on Alaina's face and in her voice cut through Alexis like a dull knife. "I'm sorry. I should have told you—" she looked at Kiera "—both of you. But it just happened, and then it was over and it was easier to put behind me. Jordan and I agreed it was better not to tell anyone."

"Let's get one thing straight here." Jordan narrowed a dark look at Alexis. "For the record, I never agreed to anything. You asked me not to tell your family we eloped in Vegas, and reluctantly, I honored that request. Furthermore, *we* didn't make a mistake, or file for an annulment—you did."

"You wanted me to quit school and play housewife," Alexis snapped. "Cook your dinner and greet you at the door each night with a pink ribbon in my hair."

"I asked you to change schools, not quit,"

Jordan said. "And housewives don't play, they work damn hard, Alexis. I wanted you to build a home, a life with me, and I'll make no apologies for that."

She opened her mouth to respond, then closed it again. Damn him! Eight years was suddenly like yesterday and they were standing in the middle of a hotel suite, nose to nose, same old argument, same old opposing points of view.

The only difference, of course—a huge one—was that her sisters and her boyfriend were now standing here, too.

Shaking his head, Matthew looked at Jordan, then Alexis. "So you are still married, then."

"Matthew, I'm so sorry. This is just as big a shock to me," Alexis said, but when he lifted a brow, she sighed. "Okay, well maybe not quite as big a shock, but it's still a shock. After Kiera's wedding, as soon as I get back to New York, I'll make sure the paperwork is straightened out. *We'll* make sure." Alexis shot Jordan a heated glance. "Won't we?"

Jordan's mouth pressed into a hard line.

"Where is everybody?"

At the sound of Trey's voice from the other

room, Alexis froze, then exchanged nervous glances with her sisters.

"I take it Trey doesn't know about this, either?" Alaina whispered.

Alexis shook her head. "Of course not."

"Could we please not tell him until after my wedding?" Kiera worried her bottom lip. "He's already grumpy about having to wear a tux on Saturday, and as the bride, I'd really appreciate it if our brother isn't aggravated any further. Mr. Langley—" remembering her manners, Kiera smiled graciously at Matthew "—if you aren't busy, I'd love for you to come to the wedding. As my sister's guest, of course."

"I appreciate the offer." Matthew looked at Alexis. "How do you feel about that, hon?"

How did she feel? With every pair of eyes in the room turned on her, how could she feel?

Trapped.

The walls in the room just kept getting smaller and smaller, but somehow, Alexis managed to move beside Matthew, slip her arm into his and smile up at him. "I think it's wonderful."

"Maybe we should ask Jordan if it's okay with him." Matthew looked at Jordan. "Him being your husband—technically and all."

Alexis heard the challenge in Matthew's voice, could see it returned in Jordan's hard, steady gaze. Good grief, as if she hadn't had enough problems with one man, she thought miserably. Now she had to deal with two.

"Where the hell is everyone?" Trey yelled out again, louder this time.

Make that three men, Alexis decided, turned as her brother stuck his head in the doorway and frowned at everyone.

"Look who we found," Kiera exclaimed, her voice a little too bright, a little too high. "Alexis's boyfriend. Isn't this fun?"

Fun? Alexis could think of several words, not one of them even remotely resembling fun. The dull ache in her brain turned to a sharp pound, but somehow she managed to make it through the introductions and the strain of pretending she was thrilled Matthew had shown up.

If not for Jordan, she thought irritably, she would be thrilled. It was sweet of Matthew to come all this way and surprise her. Romantic, even. He was handsome, funny, understanding. Open-minded. Everything a woman could want. Everything she wanted.

It meant nothing that her lips were still

tingling from Jordan's kiss. That her skin was still humming.

Nothing.

She managed to keep the smile on her face when they all moved into the other room for something cold to drink. As soon as she could find a moment alone with Matthew, she'd be able to explain about her very brief marriage.

And once those annulment papers were finally signed, she thought, it would be as if her so-called marriage to Jordan Grant had never happened at all.

Cigar in one hand, glass of whisky in the other, Jordan leaned against the porch railing and watched the sun slowly drop behind the trees. He'd declined Trey's offer to join him and Matthew on a tour of the stables and paddocks, preferring instead the comfortable solitude of the early evening.

The deepening shadows brought an edge of autumn chill to the warm evening air, carried with it the scent of honeysuckle and late blooming roses from Alaina's garden. From the creek behind the house, bullfrogs croaked a throaty chorus, while inside the house, the sounds of female conversation and laughter mingled with the clack of plates and silverware being cleared from the table.

If he closed his eyes, he could almost be seventeen again, though he wouldn't be standing here on the porch. He'd be behind the barn, sneaking a beer and cigarette with Trey, hoping like hell that Helena Blackhawk didn't come flying around the corner, ranting about the sins of tobacco and alcohol leading to the more erotic depravity of the flesh.

As teenagers, he and Trey had prayed that was true. Women were wonderful, mysterious, sweet smelling creatures that occupied most of their thoughts and a great deal of their time. Opportunities to explore the female gender up close and personal were sought after with enthusiastic and competitive imagination.

Jordan smiled at the memory, remembered he'd once overheard Betty Rutfield tell Lucy Overton that between Trey Blackhawk and Jordan Grant, no man's daughter was safe in Stone Ridge.

Jordan had known that everyone in Stone Ridge had scratched their heads over Richard and Kitty Grant's son hanging around with that half-breed, wild Blackhawk boy. There'd also been talk that Trey's father hadn't really drowned saving a little boy's life, but was alive and well, living in Houston, working on a dude ranch.

There were other stories, too, Jordan remembered. That crazy Helena Blackhawk had killed her husband and buried him somewhere in the hills. Or that young Trey, abused by a drunken father, had murdered the man in his sleep one night and let the bears take care of the body.

Since William Blackhawk rarely came to town and wasn't friendly when he did, the locals didn't really care much one way or the other. Gossip and hearsay was usually much more interesting than reality, anyway, most folks figured.

Even Jordan hadn't known what the truth was until the day after he and Trey had graduated high school. Following the ceremony on the football field, Trey's mother had cried and kissed him, told him how proud his father would have been, how she wished her Willie could have seen his little boy all grown up.

The next morning, with all the parties and high school behind them, Jordan remembered sitting on the hood of Trey's old black truck, the last six pack of longnecks between them, watching the sun come up over the lake.

"My father isn't dead," Trey had said quietly, staring at the sunrise while he tipped a bottle to his mouth. "He lives in Wolf River with his wife and a son, owns one hundred thousand prime acres of ranchland and has more money than God."

Trey threw his bottle into the circle they'd drawn in the dirt several yards ago and it landed dead center. "My mother was William Blackhawk's dirty little secret. When he got tired of her and the half-breed brats he'd never wanted, he paid her off and never looked back. My mom's been telling that story so long about her poor Willie drowning trying to save a child, even she believes it."

Jordan stared at the bottle in his hand, then finished off the last of his beer and tossed it into the circle, as well. It landed beside Trey's, broke in two. "My mom's sleeping with my dad's lawyer and my dad is sleeping with his best friend's wife."

Trey said nothing for a long moment, but then he started to laugh. Quietly at first, then harder. Jordan joined him and before long they were both falling off the hood, rolling in the dirt.

They'd moved on with their lives. Jordan to

college, Trey running his family's ranch, but William Blackhawk was never mentioned again.

Not until a few weeks ago, when Trey called to tell him that he and his sisters had inherited a bucket load of money from a grandfather they'd never known, and a conservative figure for each of them, by the time they totaled all the accounts and interest, was somewhere in the twelve million dollar range.

That was one hell of a bucket.

Funny how life could change like that, Jordan thought. He blew a smoke ring, watched it dissipate. Blink of an eye. You're heading south, then wham!—you're headed north.

Just like his relationship with Alexis.

He heard the screen door close behind him and without turning, knew it was her. He'd been waiting for her, savored the knowledge that for once, she'd have to come to him.

Glass of red wine in her hand, she moved beside him, rested her arms on the railing while she stared out across the yard toward the paddocks where a hand worked with a roan mare.

"Nice evening," she said as nonchalantly as if she were plucking a piece of lint off that pretty blue sweater she had on.

"Uh, huh."

"Kiera's got apple cobbler cooling for dessert." Delicately, she sipped at her wine. "I swear I gained five pounds just smelling it."

He turned his head, studied her through the stream of smoke slowly drifting up from his cigar. "Looks good on you, Allie."

She slid a glance at him, let the silence between them linger while she watched a hawk soar overhead, then disappear into the distant treetops. "I thought dinner went well."

"Kiera's always been an impressive cook." He nodded in agreement. "And the fact that Cookie actually let her prepare the entire meal in his kitchen is even more impressive."

"Not without his supervision," Alexis said. "Or grumbling that all those fancy cooking schools had turned her into a snooty show-off. But I'm not talking about the meal, Jordan, and you know it."

"You mean because your boyfriend and your husband sat at the same dinner table without ripping each other's throats out?"

"You are not my husband." Her eyes flared, then she pressed her lips into a thin line. "But yes, I appreciate that you managed to be civil through the meal."

"Do I get a reward for good behavior?"

She tilted her head at him in that familiar stance of exasperation. "I'll see that you get an extra helping of cobbler."

"Next best thing to my first choice."

"Jordan—"

"Tell me about Wolf River," he said before she could scold him. "All those Blackhawk cousins you never knew about."

"Not much to say." She shrugged, took a sip of wine. "I haven't met any of them yet. Trey doesn't say much, but Kiera and Alaina think they're all wonderful. It's just hard to believe they've all been so welcoming, especially considering who our father was and all the people he hurt."

Jordan knew that William Blackhawk had been a first rate bastard, a man without a conscience or scruples. He'd cheated and lied, stolen money from his brothers, then sold out his own niece and nephews when their parents were killed. He'd lived a double life, one in Wolf River, one in Stone Ridge, and they'd both been equally vile. When the man died in a small plane crash three years ago, Jordan figured the world became a better place.

"Anyway—"Alexis drew in a deep breath

"—I'll meet them all soon enough. Even Dillon is coming to the wedding."

"Dillon?"

"Just when we thought it couldn't get any stranger or more complicated," she said, shaking her head, "and we find out William's son in Wolf River—Dillon—was fathered by William's brother. So he's not our half brother, like we thought, but a cousin."

Trey had already explained the confusing family tree, but Jordan was still trying to digest it all himself. He stared at the smoke circling up from his cigar. "You told Matthew all this?"

She stiffened, and her eyes snapped to his. "Why would I?"

"I got the feeling you were serious about him," he said casually.

"What if I am?" She tossed her head. "It's been eight years, Jordan. That's a long time."

"Maybe it's just exactly the right amount of time."

"We were kids," she said quietly. "Is it really so hard for you to admit we made a mistake?"

"I don't believe in mistakes, Allie." He wanted her to look at him, was certain he'd know the truth if he could just see her eyes.

"Every step we take, every stumble, every fall. Even when it's wrong, it's still right."

She did look at him now, and he saw the mixture of disbelief and mistrust on her face. "Since when did you become such a philosopher?"

"When did you become such a cynic?"

"I'm a realist," she argued. "A happy realist. For the first time in my life, I have everything I've ever wanted. An incredible home, a fantastic job, money. A relationship."

Jordan didn't miss the fact that Alexis hadn't mentioned Matthew until he'd walked out of the stables with Trey. Even then, her voice had lacked conviction. He wasn't sure if she was trying to convince him, or herself.

The sound of a cell phone interrupted the peaceful country setting, and Jordan watched Matthew answer his phone while Trey spoke to the hand working with the roan.

"Sign the papers, Jordan," Alexis said when Matthew slipped his phone back into his pocket and headed back to the house with Trey.

"What if I don't want to?"

Her breath seemed to catch, then her mouth flattened. "I have no idea what game it is you're playing with me, but I want you to stop."

He shook his head slowly. "No game."

"Game?" Trey's boot hit the bottom step of the porch stairs. "What game?"

"Alexis just asked me if the Rangers were playing tonight." Jordan blew out a stream of cigar smoke.

Matthew furrowed his brow. "I didn't know you liked baseball."

"She can't stand it." Trey stomped the dust off his boots. "Always said it was only one snore away from watching bass fishing."

"You don't know what I like, Trey Blackhawk," Alexis said indignantly. "It just so happens I watch a game now and then. Especially if the Mets are playing."

"That's great." Matthew moved beside her, slid a possessive arm around her shoulders. "I've got season box tickets I usually just give away. We'll go when we get home."

The smile on Alexis's face didn't reach her eyes. "I can't wait."

Jordan grinned at her, was certain the only thing she couldn't wait to do was box his ears for starting this.

"So—" she looked up at Matthew "—you ready for some dessert?"

"I'm afraid I'll have to take a raincheck," Matthew said with a sigh. "I just got a call from my producer. He's managed to finagle an interview for me with Phoebe Jansen."

Trey's head came up. "The movie star?"

Matthew nodded. "She's in New York for the next few days, promoting her new movie. Her manager called the station and set it up. I've got a two hour exclusive with her at 8:00 a.m. tomorrow."

"A two hour exclusive with Phoebe Jansen?" Alexis raised her brows. "Actors of that caliber rarely give more than a five minute cattle call interview."

"That's why as much as I'd like to stay—" he pulled her close and smiled down at her "—I've got a ten-thirty flight I just might make if I leave now. I'll fly back Saturday for the wedding. Miss me?"

When Matthew brushed Alexis's lips with his mouth, Jordan's hand tightened on his glass and he downed the contents, focused on the burn of the whisky in his throat rather than the heat of jealousy in his gut.

"Of course I'll miss you," Alexis pouted.

"It's the day after tomorrow," Trey said impatiently. "Can we go have dessert now?"

"How would you guys like an autographed photo of Phoebe?" Matthew offered. "Something to keep you company on a cold night?"

Jordan didn't miss Matthew's jab, but refused to rise to the bait. "Sure."

"Forget the picture." Trey opened the screen door and wiggled an eyebrow. "Ask her if she wants to be my date at the wedding."

"I'll see what I can do," Matthew said, then looked at Jordan. "How 'bout you? You want me to see if I can get you a date, too?"

"Not necessary." Jordan held Matthew's gaze, then he looked at Alexis. "I'm sure I can manage to find my own."

Matthew's lips hardened as he returned Jordan's stare, then he pulled Alexis closer. "I should go say my goodbyes."

Jordan lifted his glass. "See you Saturday."

Six

"I think I'm going to throw up."

"Don't you dare." Alexis closed the last tiny silk-covered white button at the neck of Kiera's wedding dress, tightened the inside clasp, then stepped beside her sister and slipped an arm around her corseted waist. "You don't have time. You have a hundred and fifty guests waiting for you to walk down the aisle in fifteen minutes."

Frowning, Kiera stared at their image in the dressing room mirror. "Not helping, sis."

"One hundred and fifty-five, to be exact,"

Alaina said, kneeling at Kiera's feet to straighten the hem of her dress. "At least, that's what the wedding planner told me a few minutes ago."

"Definitely not helping." Kiera put a shaky hand to her stomach and closed her eyes. "I can't do this."

"You can and you will." Alexis squeezed her sister's waist. "Now open your eyes, look at me and breathe. Alaina, you too, stand here with us."

Framing the bride in long gowns made of midnight blue silk, they all breathed together, slow and deep, until the color finally came back into Kiera's cheeks and her shoulders relaxed.

"Was it like this for you?" Kiera asked, holding her gaze steady with Alexis. "When you and Jordan got married, were your palms sweating and your heart racing and you thought you might jump out of your skin?"

Good Lord, of all the things she didn't want to talk about right now, Alexis thought, it was her own wedding. "Kiera, you can't compare what happened with Jordan and me, and besides, we really haven't got time for this right now."

"Please." Kiera reached out and grabbed Alexis's hand. "Please. It's not that I'm having any doubts about marrying Sam, I'm not. I just need to know if all these feelings are normal."

Alexis glanced from Kiera to Alaina, could see they were both waiting for an answer, both needed to know. Kiera, who was standing on the edge of the cliff, and Alaina, who was walking toward it, were, oddly enough, looking to her for some kind of reassurance.

"My heart was jumping around like a bouncy ball," Alexis said, squeezing Kiera's icy fingers. "My hands were shaking so bad I could hardly sign the marriage license."

It was all so vivid in her mind. The scent of red roses in the tiny chapel, the stained glass windows, the somber, soft-spoken minister. The memory stirred in her blood, tumbled in her stomach, and for a moment, she was back in that chapel, candles flickering all around them, the instrumental version of "I'll Always Love You" playing softly in the background.

"I thought I was going to faint," Alexis said quietly. "And then Jordan and I were looking into each other's eyes, saying our vows, and suddenly I felt a calm inside me, a certainty I'd never known before."

The words had come so easily, she remembered. Without hesitation, without doubt. At that moment, she never could have imagined she'd be alone three hours later, on a plane home.

She blinked, brought herself back to the present and saw both Alaina and Kiera staring at her. "What?"

"You're still in love with him," Kiera said, her eyes big and wide and full of amazement.

Cursing her loose tongue and wandering mind, Alexis plucked Kiera's bridal veil from the stand on the dressing table. "Don't be ridiculous."

"You are," Alaina agreed with Kiera. "Every time you say his name, you get that look in your eye, and when you two are in the same room, there's this feeling, you know, like a storm is coming."

"That's not love, sis." Shaking her head, Alexis fluffed the veil. "That's frustration. The man makes me crazy."

"Oh, I know *that* feeling." Kiera clasped her hands to her heart. "Sam makes me crazy, too. Especially when he pulls that, 'I'm the man and I know better than you routine.'"

"Oh, that's definitely D.J., too," Alaina said, smiling. "Sometimes I can't decide if I want to deck him or kiss him."

"Stop." Alexis took Kiera by the shoulders and made her stand still, then jabbed the comb of the veil into her sister's updo. "We're not talking about this anymore. Whatever happened between Jordan and me is ancient history. As soon as he signs the annulment papers, it will be as if we never even existed."

"You don't really mean—"

"Not one more word," Alexis cut Kiera off. "This is *your* wedding day. You look absolutely stunning and Sam is out there waiting for you right now."

"Alexis, I still don't think—"

They all turned at the quiet knock on the dressing room door. The wedding planner, a pretty blonde the Four Winds hotel had recently hired, opened the door and stuck her head in. "Five minutes," she announced, then disappeared again.

Kiera stilled. Wide-eyed, she stared at her reflection in the mirror while Alexis finished adjusting the veil and Alaina handed her a bouquet of white daylilies and pink roses.

"I'm getting married," Kiera whispered, then looked from Alaina to Alexis. Her eyes filled with tears. "I love him so much."

"No, no, no." Alexis blinked back the moisture in her own eyes. "Don't you dare cry now. If you start, we'll start, and we haven't got time to fix our makeup. Just tough it out at least until halfway through the ceremony, then you can let loose it you really have to."

Kiera swallowed hard, then drew in a deep breath and positioned her bouquet at her waist.

Handel's Water Music drifted in over the speakers, signaling the start of the ceremony. Smiling, the sisters all looked at each other.

"Ready?" Alexis asked.

A calm settled over Kiera's face. She lifted her chin and straightened. "Ready."

The Imperial Ballroom of the Four Winds Hotel in Wolf River shimmered. Votives flickered on burgundy satin tablecloths, white lights twinkled over the dance floor, champagne and chocolate flowed from bubbling fountains. Four-foot high pedestals of elegant white flowers graced every tabletop, and the sweet scent mixed with the aroma of Beef Wellington and chicken marsala while a ten piece band played a blend of soft blues and slow country western. A few guests made their way to the dance floor while others lingered over dinner, talking, laughing. Smiling.

Everyone except Jordan.

Nursing his second beer, he stood by the bar, watching Alexis. She sat beside Matthew at the bridal party table—the same table Jordan had been sitting at until ten minutes ago. Jordan had tolerated Matthew's presence throughout the meal, had even managed to endure the reporter's detailed recount of his interview with Phoebe Jansen, which had seemed to fascinate everyone at the table.

Everyone except him.

While Matthew had discussed a behind-the-scenes story about Phoebe's new film, Jordan had been mentally writing a script of his own, one in which an entertainment reporter from New York suddenly ends up missing in East Texas after taking a wrong turn off the highway. Alexis was the female lead in Jordan's movie—the runaway bride kidnapped by an escaped convict, ultimately rescued by a rogue FBI agent. Played by himself, of course. Jordan was still working out the details, but all in all, he was happy with the basic plot, especially the ending when the heroine shows her appreciation to the hero.

He'd spent a lot of time imagining that part.

Taking a long swallow of beer, he looked at Alexis, watched her unconsciously fingering the sapphire and diamond necklace at her throat while she sipped a glass of champagne. He thought about those soft fingers, what her hands felt like on his bare skin. Time hadn't diminished his memory. If anything, it seemed to accentuate it. It might as well have been yesterday they'd made love, he thought. He remembered every whispered plea, every moan, every touch. Like a rare, fine wine, he'd kept those sensations and the feelings associated with them bottled up.

He'd known that coming here, seeing her, would stir things up. In fact, he'd counted on it. But he hadn't realized to what degree—how strong and how sharp those feelings would be.

When he'd watched her walk down that aisle before Kiera, her blue gown shimmering like rain down her long, slender curves, his throat had closed up on him. He'd been robbed of oxygen, of coherent thought, and all he could think, all he could see, was Alexis.

Her face had been lit with joy; her eyes shimmered like her dress. She'd had that same look eight years ago, the day she'd stood before him and promised to love him, to be his wife. Forever. The thought was like a sucker punch to his gut.

And then the wedding march began and Jordan had forced his attention to Kiera. Like an angel, she'd floated into the chapel. He watched her take Trey's arm, who then presented her to Sam. There seemed to be a collective sigh from all the women in the chapel when the bride faced the groom, and when they exchanged their vows, the tissues came out and there wasn't a dry, female eye in the room.

When Sam slipped the ring on his bride's finger, Jordan's gaze turned to Alexis and their eyes met. She'd looked away, but not quickly enough. Not before he could see that she was remembering the ring he'd slipped on her finger, the vows they'd exchanged eight years ago. He also knew she'd never admit she was remembering.

Damn stubborn woman.

He watched Matthew touch Alexis's shoulder and lean in to whisper something in her ear. When she smiled and nodded, Jordan felt the growl roll deep in his throat.

"So what do you think of him?"

Eyes narrowed, Jordan turned sharply at the sound of Trey's voice. "What?"

"I like him, I guess." Trey signaled the bartender for a beer. "Which is good, since it looks like he's going to be around for a while."

"Says who?" Jordan snapped.

"That's what getting married is, Jordan." Trey furrowed his brow. "At least it's supposed to. Something you don't like about my sister's new husband I should know about?"

Damn. Trey had been talking about Sam, Jordan realized, cursing the fact he'd been caught off guard, and yet relieved at the same time because he'd nearly walked across the room and pummeled Alexis's *date*.

"I like Sam just fine." Jordan shrugged and glanced at the happy couple currently on the dance floor. "Why wouldn't I? Seems like a nice enough guy."

"Should have been there the first time we met." Trey tipped his beer to his lips. "I'll have to tell you about it some time. Now that you're moving back to Stone Ridge, I might actually see you more than once a year. Hell, I might even let you play poker with us on Fridays. Give me a few hands and I'll own your ranch."

"Or I'll own yours."

Trey rolled a shoulder and leaned back against the bar. "We could, you know."

"Could what?"

"A co-op," he said, leaning back against the bar. "Combine land and assets."

"Trey Blackhawk? Mr. Lone Wolf, combining land and assets? Wait—" Jordan tapped his ear "—I must have heard wrong."

Trey frowned, but took the ribbing in stride. "I've got the money to expand now, so why not? Our ranches touch on the east, I figure if we can get Ambrose Tucker's place on the south, we'd be a force to reckon with."

"Not a snowball's chance Ambrose will sell." Jordan shook his head. "And the old coot is too stubborn to ever die."

"Can't hurt to talk to him." Trey finished off his beer, sighed when he saw the wedding planner motion for him. "Think about it and get back to me."

When Trey walked off, Jordan did think about it, for all of three seconds, until he saw Alexis on the dance floor. At least she wasn't dancing with Matthew, he thought, but Alaina's fiancé, D.J.

Needing a distraction, Jordan glanced around

the dance floor, putting names to faces. The elegant redhead dressed in green silk was Grace, and her husband, Rand Blackhawk, was Trey's cousin, though the man looked more like a twin brother, Jordan thought. There were more Blackhawk cousins, Lucas, whose wife was a tall, stunning blonde named Julianna, and Clair, who was married to Jacob. Clair owned the Four Winds, and Jordan had heard that she'd been instrumental not only in bringing the estranged Blackhawk family together, but Sam and Kiera, as well. Clair was also pregnant, Jordan noted, watching her and Jacob dance alongside Alexis and D.J.

When Matthew suddenly reappeared and took Alexis in his arms and smiled at her, Jordan's hand tightened on his glass. Dammit, how much of this was he supposed to take?

But the real question was, how much *could* he take?

He lasted exactly fourteen minutes. Long enough for Trey to give a toast, long enough for cake to be served, long enough for the dance floor to fill up again. He polished off the rest of his beer, glanced around the room for Alexis. He'd kept his distance from her tonight, given her space, but now he wanted her in his arms, wanted to hold her close—Matthew be damned. If the dance floor was the only way, so be it. When he didn't see her, he frowned and looked for Matthew.

He didn't see him, either.

Jordan's frown darkened. They would have had to walk past him if they'd gone to the restrooms. They also would have had to walk past him if they'd gone out on the patio.

So where the hell were they?

He spotted them on the other side of the room, felt the cold knot in his gut tighten when he saw them walk out of the reception. Setting his teeth, he slapped his empty glass on the bar and started after them.

Seven

Alexis stood in front of the private elevator for the suite level of the hotel, impatiently pushed the already lit UP button. Regret flickered through her, but she'd made her decision, was certain it was the right one. And whether it was or wasn't, her motto had always been "Don't Look Back." It had gotten her through the difficult times, kept her spirit strong.

It would get her through tonight, too, she thought, drawing in a deep breath to reassure and calm herself. It had to.

"Alexis!"

She froze, didn't even turn at the sound of Jordan's angry voice from the other end of the marbled hallway. Dammit. She couldn't face him now, couldn't look at him, couldn't talk to him. As it was, she'd barely been able to take her eyes off him all night, couldn't stop thinking how handsome he looked in his black tuxedo, couldn't stop the unwanted rise of jealousy when she'd seen the single women staring at him, smiling at him.

She told herself it was just the stress of the past few days and watching her sister get married that had stirred up all these emotions inside her. Weddings did that to people. All that happily-ever-after business made a person's insides go soft and their brain turn to mush.

When Jordan called her name again, something close to panic gripped hold of her stomach, and she pushed the UP button again, cursed the slow elevator.

Relief poured through her when the doors slid blissfully open. She rushed inside and pressed the Close Door button, then turned and watched Jordan hurrying toward the elevator. His long legs quickly closed the distance between them, but when the doors began to close and she felt confident he wouldn't make it in time, she smiled at him and waggled her fingers.

Her smile disappeared when he managed to get a hand inside.

Jaw clenched, he stepped into the elevator car and pressed a button. The doors whisked smoothly shut and she felt the hum of the hydraulics ripple up through her toes, heard the sound of Carlos Santana's "Smooth" quietly filter through the overhead speakers.

When Jordan turned to face her, his eyes had the fierce look of a caged animal. She could barely breathe knowing she stood in that cage with him and there was no place to go, no place to run.

"Where do you think you're going?" he asked tightly.

His question caught her off guard, but she recovered quickly, determined to hold on at least until the elevator doors opened and she could escape. She summoned forth a bravado that her pounding heart belied and shot him an icy look. "Are you conducting a survey, or is it just idle curiosity?"

"Enough with the smart answers." He backed her into the corner. "Just answer the damn question."

"It's none of your business where I'm going. I do what I want, when I want, Jordan Grant, and I certainly don't need your permission."

"Good." He moved in closer, until his thighs touched hers. "Because you're not getting it."

Hold on, she told herself, though it felt like the longest elevator ride of her life. Chin up, she held his gaze, gave him a look that would have had any other man backing up. Any man but Jordan. Jaw set, eyes glinting, he stared right back.

The cold that had slithered through her a moment ago began to warm. He stood so close she could feel the heat of his body radiating through her dress, through her skin. Could smell the masculine scent of his aftershave, the scent of desire.

She wanted to push him away, but she couldn't bring herself to touch him, wasn't certain what she would do if she did. *Fine*, she thought, changing tactics. If she couldn't control the beast, she'd reason with him.

"This is ridiculous," she said with a heavy

sigh. "Jordan, please, it's been a long day. I'm tired. Whatever it is you have on your mind, can we just do this in the morning?"

"No."

She pressed her lips together, simply wasn't in the mood to argue. When the elevator finally stopped and the doors slid open, she said a silent prayer of relief—then gasped when he snatched her arm and pulled her down the hallway.

"Jordan!" She stumbled after him, struggling to stay on her feet and keep the strap of her purse on her shoulder. If she could have managed to snag one of her four-inch heels off, she would have beaned him with it.

When he stopped abruptly in front of one of the suites, she collided with him. "This isn't my room," she argued.

Ignoring her, he swiped his key card in the door and opened it, pulled her inside the room with him and shut the door. When he flipped the door latch, her heart slammed against her ribs.

Obviously, this was *his* room.

"What do you think you're doing, dragging me in here like some kind of Neanderthal?" She tried to pull her arm away, but he held on tight.

"If you think I'm going to stand by and do

nothing while you run off to meet your lover, then think again."

Her lover?

It took a moment for Jordan's words to sink in. Alexis might have laughed, but that would have diffused her anger, and she realized she needed the anger, needed something she could sink her teeth in and hold on to.

"What makes you think you can be out of my life for eight years, then just suddenly show up and boss me around?"

Why didn't it seem like eight years anymore? she wondered. Why did it feel as if it were yesterday? Same emotions, same heat, same argument?

"Because you're my wife," he shot back. "Eight minutes, eight hours, eight years, I don't give a damn. I *am* your husband."

"I signed the papers, Jordan." She lifted her chin, pointed it at him. "Just because you didn't, doesn't mean I'm bound to you."

"But you *are* bound to me." He dragged her roughly against him. "Marriage or no marriage. Papers or no papers. You always will be. That's what scares you so much, doesn't it, Allie?" he said tightly. "Because you know no matter how long you wait, or how long you fight it, you always will be."

"No." She didn't want to hear this. Wouldn't listen to him. "You can't keep me here. Someone will come looking for me. It's Kiera's wedding, for god sakes. You really want to make a scene?"

"The wedding is over, and by now, Kiera and Sam are in a limo on the way to the airport. But since you're so worried *someone* will come looking for you—" tightening his hold on her arm, he pulled her across the room "—let's just make a phone call and put someone's mind at rest, shall we?"

He picked up the receiver on the phone beside the living room sofa and punched the button for the front desk.

Alexis tried to grab the phone from him. "What are you—"

"Matthew Langley's room," Jordan said into the receiver.

"Jordan, stop it!" She managed to wrestle the phone from him and slam it back down. "Are you insane?"

"Obviously." His eyes narrowed to cold, black slits. "A sane man wouldn't be wasting his time standing here arguing with the most stubborn woman in the world. A sane man would have given up when that woman walked out on him. A sane man would have signed the damn papers and found another woman."

His words sucked the air from her lungs, and she stilled. Why did those words hurt? she wondered. How *could* they hurt after all this time?

"Why didn't you?" she asked, her voice strained and tight.

"If you have to ask why, it doesn't matter." He released her, and when she stumbled back, raked his hand through his thick hair and turned away, cursing. "Just go, Alexis. Get the hell out."

Run, her mind screamed.

Run fast and far.

But her heart whispered something entirely different, and she couldn't move. Could barely breathe.

If only those damn elevator doors had closed, she thought in despair.

"I wasn't going to Matthew's room." Her quiet admission hung in the silent air. "I was going to my room."

Jordan turned back, watched her with those dark, angry eyes, but said nothing.

"I broke it off with Matthew." She rubbed her arms, hoped she could hold herself together. "Yesterday."

"Yesterday?" Jordan's furrowed his brow. "But why would he—"

"Come to the wedding with me?" Embarrassed by her admission, she looked down at the plush beige carpet. "Because I asked him to."

He stepped toward her. "Why?"

"To keep you away." She closed her eyes, wasn't certain her knees would hold her much longer. "I figured if I could just make it through the wedding, then get through the night, I could go back to New York tomorrow, back to my life, without—"

When she stopped, he reached out, cupped her chin in his hand. "Without what?"

Opening her eyes, she lifted her gaze to his. Pride slipped away, leaving only raw, sheer need.

"Without doing this."

She closed that small space between them. That huge gap. Slid her hands up his broad chest, around his neck.

No more running.

Not tonight. Every last drop of denial, of resistance evaporated. *We're both insane,* she thought dimly. But there was only this moment, only Jordan. Insane or not, it simply didn't matter.

His arms circled her waist, pulled her fiercely against him. His mouth slammed down on hers. There was no need for seduction, no reason to coax. She wanted. He wanted. And they would both take.

His mouth stayed on hers when he scooped her up in his arms and carried her into the bedroom, kicking the door wide as they passed through. His taste, his scent, were all so wonderfully, erotically familiar to her. Fire raced back and forth over her skin, through her blood, and when his mouth dropped to her neck and nuzzled, she moaned.

The drapes were open, and moonlight filtered in through the soft white sheers covering the floor-to-ceiling windows, casting a silver glow across the room. Beside the bed, he lowered her slowly down the length of his hard, muscled body. Even as her feet touched the ground, she still felt as if she were floating on a cloud of intense pleasure. She slid her hands inside his tux jacket, slipped it off his broad shoulders, let it drop from her fingers, then lifted her gaze to meet his. Raw need glinted in his narrowed eyes, made her knees weak and her pulse jump.

Arms at her sides, she shivered, dropped her head back when he lowered his mouth and trailed kisses from one shoulder to the other. His hands slid around her waist, found the zipper of her dress and slowly tugged it down.

"I want you," he murmured, raising his head to gaze down at her.

"I want you, too." She drew in a breath when his fingers slipped the straps of her dress off her shoulders.

Blue silk shimmered to the floor, lay in a pool around her feet. What little she wore was black. Strapless bra, lacy thong, four-inch high heels. She stood before him, exhilarated, terrified, excited.

"You're even more beautiful than I remember." His throat was thick and rough, his eyes dark and narrowed. "And I have a fantastic memory."

His lips brushed her temple, her cheeks, then found her mouth again. His kiss was impatient, demanding, and she wrapped her arms around his neck, gasped when he dragged her down to the bed. Her hands moved over the rippling muscles of his shoulders, then slid down and searched for buttons, opened each one until her hands were inside his shirt on bare, hot skin.

He moved over her, pressed her deep into the soft mattress, caught her wrists in his hands and held them still while he tasted, moved down her neck to her breasts. It was almost too much. The heat of his breath on his skin, the feel of his mouth teasing, tempting, then nipping through silk, tugging on one beaded nipple, then the next, all of it made her crazy with desire. She moved under him, impatient, wanting to run her hands over him, touch him, but he held on to her wrists, arousing her all the more, frustrating her until she moaned in protest.

And still he held her prisoner, pinned her beneath him, holding her arms over her head while he explored her body with his mouth and tongue. She was gasping, squirming with need, and when he finally let loose of her wrists to cup her breasts, she moaned again, slid her hands over his shoulders and down his solid, wide chest.

She tugged at his shirt, wanting desperately to feel his skin against hers. Somehow, her bra had disappeared and his tongue stroked one hard nipple, then sucked. An arrow of intense heat shot between her legs and she moved against him, wanting him inside her, needing him inside her.

Pleading, moaning, she raked her fingernails over his scalp, then down his shoulders. His hands moved to her thighs, ripped the tiny strip of lace from her hips and tossed it aside, and his fingers trailed over her thighs, caressing the sensitive inside of her legs, then moving upward to the most sensitive spot of all.

Trembling, she arched upward when he touched her, felt the heat and cold collide. How had she lived without this? she wondered. Without him? When he stroked her, the question and every other thought flew from her mind. She could only feel. Pleasure coiled and tightened, and she thought she'd go mad wanting him inside her. When she could stand it no more, she pushed at him until they rolled and she was on top, grappling with his belt. They struggled together, until pants and shoes and clothing lay across the bed and floor and they were rolling again.

He rose over her, kneed her thighs apart and gripped her hips in his large hands. Breath held, heart hammering, she closed her eyes, thought she might die from the sheer need fisting her body.

"Look at me, Alexis," he said raggedly.

"Hurry—" struggling for every breath, she reached for him "—please hurry."

"Open your eyes and look at me," he demanded, catching her wrists and holding them at her sides. "Say my name."

She knew why he wanted her to do this, what his intention was, but it didn't matter. At this moment, she would have done anything he asked, she realized with dread. Anything. There was nothing she could refuse him.

Slowly, she opened her eyes, locked her gaze with his. "Jordan," she whispered, heard the desperate need in her own voice, and the frantic beat of her heart. "Make love to me, Jordan."

He moved his hands up her arms, held her tight and slid inside her.

Her world shifted; there was only this moment, only Jordan making love to her. She bowed her body upward, whispering his name again and again. Eight years of need and want slammed together and meshed tightly as one, then tighter still. Gasping, she wound her arms around his neck, needing him closer still, deeper.

They moved, wild and raw and crazy, matched each other stroke for stroke, both giving, both taking.

The combined force of the explosion was blinding, deafening. Pure white light blacking out everything but that one shattering moment of sheer ecstasy.

Aftershocks rippled between their bodies, left them both shuddering and gasping. Together, still holding tight to each other, they sank back into the bed.

When he could move again, Jordan rolled to his side, bringing Alexis with him. She lay beside him, limp as a rag doll, her body molding to him like soft clay. They were both still breathing hard, and the sound mixed with the heavy beating of their hearts.

He pulled her closer, pressed his lips to her damp shoulder and tasted the salt on her soft skin. When she shivered, he lifted his head. "Cold?"

Eyes still closed, she shook her head, but he pulled the sheet up over them, anyway. He figured she'd find an excuse to escape sooner or later, and he was determined it would be later.

Much later.

When her breath evened out and her heart slowed to a steady thud, he tucked a lock of tousled hair behind her ear, then ran his fingertips over her cheek. Her eyes, still glazed and heavy with desire, lifted to his.

"We always were pretty good at that," she murmured.

He kissed the tip of her nose. "We were good at other things, too."

"Yeah?" She pulled away from him, searched his face. "Like what?"

He'd never really thought about it. Never put their relationship under a microscope and analyzed it. "I don't know. Just being together."

"That's not an answer." She rose on an elbow, propped her head on hand and studied his face. "We fought too much."

"I loved fighting with you," he said. "Loved making up. Loved listening to you whisper on the phone in the middle of the night so no one would hear you. Those looks you'd sneak me when Trey and your sisters weren't watching. That sly smile that told me you'd be waiting for me at the lake."

There'd been times over the past eight years

when he'd wondered if that summer with Alexis had been a dream. It had all happened so fast, with such intensity, such need and passion, that it didn't seem possible. Love, marriage, annulment papers. How could all that be real? He'd told himself at least a hundred times it couldn't have been.

But looking at her now, laying here beside her, he knew it had been real. He knew that every moment with her had been more real, that he'd felt more alive, than the rest of his entire life.

"We were good together, Allie." Lightly, he ran a knuckle over her jaw. "Then and now."

She closed her eyes on a sigh and started to rise, but he held her down, kissed her until her resistance faded and she was once again pliant in his arms. He rolled to his side, bringing her with him, reached for the bedside lamp and turned it on.

"No light," she complained, shaking her head.

"I want to see you," he murmured, and slid a hand over her hip.

"Use your fantastic memory."

He snagged her hand when she tried to turn the light off, then circled the curve of her backside with his fingertips. "Tell me about this."

"It's a tattoo. Not much to tell."

"When did you get it?"

"Alaina and I—" She drew in a breath when he kissed her neck, moaned when he cupped her breast "—turned twenty-one. New Orleans."

He raised his head. "Alaina has a tattoo?"

"You tell another living soul and I'll kill you." She gasped when his mouth moved down her side. "We have a pact."

Her words didn't have a lot of heat, but her skin did and he tasted it, tasted the need. "A unicorn," he muttered, and nibbled. "A mythical flying creature definitely suits you."

She would have argued with him, but he moved over her, slid an arm around her waist and dragged her against him, kissed her hard and long and deep, until she finally gave up and kissed him back, her body quivering with need.

Abruptly he ended the kiss, rose over her, watched the rapid rise and fall of her chest, then the fluttering of her thick eyelashes as she opened her eyes and met his gaze.

"There's an elephant in here with us," he said raggedly. "Sooner or later, we are going to talk about it."

She stared at him for a long moment, nodded

slowly, then reached up and dragged his mouth back to hers. "I choose later."

It was a small victory, he thought, getting her to agree. But when they tumbled across the bed again, Jordan wasn't certain if it was his or hers.

Alexis woke to the glare of sun and the sound of water running in the bathroom. A bullet of panic shot through her and she bolted upright, looked at the bedside clock, then closed her eyes in relief. It was only eight thirty—not a lot of time, but just enough to get back to her room, shower, throw her clothes in her suitcase and get downstairs to meet the hotel car waiting to take her to the airport.

And with Jordan in the shower, she couldn't think of a better time to escape.

He'd be annoyed, she knew. But his time, she wasn't running. She'd promised him they'd talk about their "elephant" and she would. She just needed a little more time to think, to get used to the idea of him being back in her life. It wouldn't be easy, especially with him in Texas and her in New York. But she was willing to give it a try. Give them a try.

Dragging a hand through her hair, she sat,

winced at the pull of sore muscles. Lifting her arms, she stretched out the kinks and aches, then raised a brow when she noticed a bruise on her thigh.

Not that she was complaining. She figured she'd left a few bruises on Jordan herself.

Smiling, she glanced back at the bed, smoothed a hand over the disheveled sheets. Last night, she'd been so certain the morning would bring regrets. Certain she'd be calling herself ten shades of stupid, along with a flurry of other names that would best describe a complete absence of intelligence.

How strange it was—as hard as she tried—she couldn't muster up even a sliver of remorse, and the realization made her uneasy. She'd been so sure she'd made the right decision leaving Jordan. And now, here she sat, in his bed, her body still humming from making love with him, her mind still reeling, and she wasn't so sure anymore.

Spilled milk, she thought with a sigh and stared at the bathroom door. At the moment, the past wasn't her problem. The problem was now. Right now.

No matter what had happened before, no

matter how much time they'd spent apart, she knew she loved him. She'd tried to deny it, of course. To him, to herself. But it was the truth. More than life itself, she loved him. She always had. She always would.

But could she be married to him?

That was the real question.

When she heard the sound of Jordan's deep voice singing she snapped out of her musings and quickly glanced around the room for her clothes, frowned when she didn't see them.

She knew exactly where her dress had been last night—on the floor, next to the bed—where Jordan had taken it off of her. Her bra she wasn't so sure about, and her thong, well, that she was certain she wouldn't be wearing again. Even her shoes were gone, though she was pretty sure Jordan had tossed them on the floor at the foot of the bed, right next to his own shoes and socks.

Wrapping the sheet around her, she dropped on her hands and knees and looked under the bed. Nothing. Come to think of it—she glanced around the room again—she didn't see his clothes, either. She hurried to the closet and opened the doors.

Empty.

Eyes narrowed, she stared at the bathroom door. It didn't take a genius to realize he'd taken both his and her clothes in the bathroom with him. Carefully, slowly, she turned the doorknob.

Locked.

Damn you, Jordan Grant!

She took back every nice thought she'd had about him this morning. Now all she wanted to do was strangle him. He'd known she'd leave and this was his underhanded, double-dealing, black-hearted way of keeping her here while he took one of his twenty-minute showers.

She resisted the urge to kick at the door, ground her teeth together instead. Even with her sense of style and design, she couldn't do much with bed sheets, and the idea of strolling down the hallway wearing a white duvet cover or beige striped drapes was more than her pride would allow.

Cursing Jordan, she glanced around the room one more time, then tilted her head and smiled.

He wanted her clothes so bad, she thought and dropped the sheet on the floor. Fine.

He could keep them.

Eight

"Where shall I put these, Miss Blackhawk?"

Alexis glanced up from the column she'd been attempting to write for the January issue of *Impression,* sort of an out-with-the-old-in-with-the-new resolutions guide for cleaning out a closet. The writing hadn't been going so well. In fact—she swung around in her desk chair so she wouldn't have to look at her flashing curser on a blank screen—it hadn't been going at all.

Mary Margaret, Alexis's assistant, stood in the doorway, holding a tall vase of white roses and soft yellow Dendrobium orchids that blended in with Mary Margaret's pale blonde hair. When Mary Margaret moved into the room, Alexis allowed herself to lean forward and breathe in the sweet, delicate scent of the flowers, but because she knew they were from Jordan, she resisted touching them. She was still ticked off over his stunt at the hotel three days ago and she wasn't ready to accept anything from him just yet. Not a phone call, not flowers, not even the Belgium chocolates or basket of muffins he'd had delivered.

As if I could be worn down so easily with flowers and sweets, she thought firmly, though yesterday, she'd nearly buckled when a box of brownies from the Fudge Factor had arrived. The man was playing dirty, she thought, but he'd at least had the decency not to sign any of the cards. Her staff already had enough fuel for the firestorm of rumors sweeping the office.

She took another sniff of the roses, felt a chink in her armor, then shook it off. "You keep them," Alexis told her assistant.

"I'd love to." Behind her horn-rimmed glasses, Mary Margaret stared at the arrangement with big moon eyes. "But my desk is filled with the other flowers. So is Tiffany's, Scott's and Sandy's."

Alexis glanced through her window at the sea of floral arrangements in the outer office. They'd started coming Monday morning and hadn't stopped, and though there'd been quite a bit of drama and speculation over all the anonymous deliveries, Alexis hadn't said a word. Which only created more drama and speculation, of course. Most everyone thought she and Matthew had argued and broken up, or the opposite, they'd gotten engaged. But even those bold enough to ask her straight out had come away with nothing, and it was driving them crazy.

Which was where she'd been since Jordan had strolled back into her life, dammit.

"Throw them away, then," she said, but the look of horror on Mary Margaret's face had Alexis rolling her eyes. "All right, all right. Put them in the ladies' restroom."

Her assistant smiled at that idea and started to turn away, then quickly turned back, set the flowers on Alexis's desk and pulled a large, padded envelope out from under her arm. "Oh, I almost forgot. This just came for you, too."

Alexis saw the Texas postmark, then turned

back to her computer and squared her shoulders. "You can have it."

"But you don't even know what it is," Mary Margaret argued. "Aren't you curious?"

She glanced at the brown padded envelope. Okay, so maybe she was curious—just a little. With a sigh, she put her fingers to her keyboard and pretended the contents of the package didn't matter in the least. "You open it."

Mary Margaret's gray eyes lit. "You sure?"

Not really, but she shrugged anyway and started typing, though nothing that made any sense, watched from the corner of her eye when her assistant opened the envelope.

"It's a strapless bra." Brows raised, Mary Margaret held the strip of black lace up and stared at it. "Size—"

Alexis leaped from her chair and snagged the bra, then the envelope. *Damn you, Jordan.*

"Incoming," Tiffany yelled from the outer office, which had become the staff's announcement that another floral arrangement or package had arrived for Alexis.

Enough already! Alexis screamed mentally, stuffing the bra back into the envelope, terrified what might come next. She had half a mind to fly to Texas just so she could give the aggravating man a kick in the shins. She watched an oversized arrangement of pink roses moving toward her office and decided to stomp on every single long stemmed flower until—

She froze as the arrangement came closer, felt the blood drain from her face. Tall, muscular men in black Stetsons and Armani suits didn't deliver flowers.

Unless their name was Jordan Grant.

She watched him head directly toward her, saw everyone in the office staring at him, too, their jaws slack. If her knees hadn't frozen and her brain completely shut down, she would have slammed her office door and locked it.

Though a little voice in her head told her to pick up something—a stapler would do nicely—and throw it at him, she refused to give him the satisfaction and the staff a show. Instead, she drew in a calming breath and watched him step into her office.

"Mr. Grant," she purred, her voice the embodiment of complete composure. "What a surprise."

"I was in the neighborhood." He set the roses on top of a filing cabinet, then looked down at Mary Margaret and touched the tip of his Stetson.

Mary Margaret slowly tilted her head back and met Jordan's gaze. Her mouth dropped open.

Alexis resisted the temptation to roll her eyes—and to throw Jordan out. A route of indifference was the better path, she decided and kept her face and tone casual.

"Mary Margaret Muldoon—" Alexis glanced at her assistant "—Jordan Grant."

Jordan smiled and offered a hand. "A pleasure, Miss Muldoon."

Mary Margaret didn't move.

Alexis shook her head, almost felt sorry for her assistant. Jordan had always had that affect on women. Lord knew she hadn't been immune herself.

She still wasn't immune, she thought, looking at him now. In jeans and a T-shirt he could make a woman's heart stutter; wearing a suit and Stetson, he could make it stop.

Top it off with that damn smile of his, Alexis thought irritably, and there wasn't a female alive who stood a chance. Especially young, inexperienced secretaries from Katydid, Kansas.

"Mary Margaret," Alexis prompted.

The assistant looked at Alexis and blinked. "What?"

Alexis raised a brow.

"Oh. Oh!" Mary Margaret's cheeks turned as red as the blazer she wore and she looked back at Jordan, shoved her hand into his. "How do you do, Mr. Grant."

"Fine, thank you." Jordan's fingers closed over the assistant's small hand. "And please, just Jordan."

Mary Margaret's blush deepened and spread down her neck. "Can I get you, I mean, would you like someone, I mean something, or are you—"

"Mr. Grant is in a hurry," Alexis said through a forced smile.

"I've got a few minutes." Jordan let go of the assistant's hand. "Coffee, black, would be nice, if it's no trouble."

It *is* trouble, Alexis thought, and frowned at Jordan, but didn't dare make a scene.

"One cup of black coffee coming up." Efficient with a capital E, Mary Margaret sprang into action. "Decaf or regular? Croissant or muffin? We have blueberry, poppy seed, banana nut—"

"Just the coffee." Alexis moved to her office door, put her hand on the knob.

"Right." Mary Margaret glanced at Jordan again, who smiled even wider, and Alexis could all but hear the other woman's heart slam against her ribs. "Right away."

When her assistant hurried out of the office, Alexis calmly closed the door and faced Jordan. "What do you think you're doing?"

"If you're busy, don't mind me." He sat on the edge of her desk, glanced at the envelope she still held in her hand. "I see you got my package."

"I got it." She considered tossing it into the trash, just to make a statement, but it didn't matter how much money she had now—too many years of being broke had instilled a sense of financial prudence in her. "There are a couple of items missing."

"Not missing. I know exactly where they are. In fact—" he grinned "—I currently have my favorite close to my heart."

Alexis gasped when she realized there was only one article of clothing she'd left behind that was small enough to fit into his jacket pocket. "You didn't!"

He reached inside his suit lapel. "Would you like it back?"

"No!" She put out a hand, realized how loud she'd said the word, and how thin her office walls were. When she glanced over her shoulder, every head in the outer office quickly snapped back to their work. Eyes narrowed, she looked back at Jordan. "That's not funny."

"Sure it is." He slid his hand back out, empty, and folded his arms comfortably. "Just depends on where you're sitting."

"You're sitting on my desk." She tossed the envelope beside him. "What am I going to have to do to get you to leave?"

He raised a brow. "That's a loaded question."

"Jordan Grant—" Alexis sucked in a breath through her teeth "—so help me, I'm going to—"

"I'll leave if you do two things," he cut her off. "One, tell me how you got back to your room without your clothes."

He surprised her with such a simple request, one she was happy to oblige. "There were sheers behind the drapes. I made a sarong, then left a hefty tip for the maid to return them after you checked out. What's two?"

He chuckled. "You always were clever."

"What's two?" she persisted.

"Have dinner with me."

"Dinner?"

"Yeah, dinner. You and me." One corner of his mouth turned up. "I'm asking you out on a date, Allie. You know, like in a restaurant."

A date? Why should that make her pulse jump? she wondered. They'd slept together, even been married. Why did a date suddenly feel so intimate?

"I have a meeting."

"Cancel it."

"I can't."

"Then I'll wait."

She saw the determination in his eyes, the need, and her pulse wasn't just jumping now, it raced. She closed her eyes, drew in a deep, fortifying breath. "You can't just barge in here, Jordan, and expect me to drop everything."

"I don't expect you to drop anything, nor have I barged," he said quietly, his gaze somber now. "I've waited eight years, Allie. Eight long years."

She felt her resolve weakening. It *had* been eight long years, she thought, though she'd never even admitted that to herself. Self-preservation told her to stop this right now, to run, but she'd done that once and this was where it had brought her.

Right back to Jordan.

She couldn't think of a worse place to be having this conversation, or a worse time. Any second now Mary Margaret would be walking back in, not to mention the entire office was watching, holding their breath in anticipation.

But suddenly none of that mattered. She met Jordan's gaze and the rest of the world fell away. *Eight years.*

If there was any chance for them to have a future, any chance at all, she needed to know.

"Why?" she asked softly. "Why did you wait?"

"Pride at first," he admitted. "And anger. My idea of marriage was a wife at home, kids. I needed to know you would do that, for me, for our children."

She shook her head. "You demanded it."

He shrugged. "I suppose I did. I had to learn patience, Allie. Eight years without you taught me that."

"And the annulment papers?" Dammit, why were her hands shaking? "Why didn't you sign them?"

"I couldn't sign something that said we never existed, that you were never my wife." He rose, moved close to her. "You were and you are."

She backed up, couldn't think with him so close, saying these things. "What's changed?" she whispered. "We're still the same people. We want different things."

"I want you, Allie." He leaned down, brought his mouth close to her ear. "I want my wife."

"Here we are." Mary Margaret burst happily through the door, juggling a mug of black coffee and a basket of muffins. "I didn't know what to bring, so I—"

The assistant stopped, caught the look on Alexis's face, then glanced at Jordan and swallowed hard. "I'll, ah, just leave this on the desk."

When Mary Margaret hurried out and closed the door behind her, Alexis let out the breath she'd been holding, couldn't decide if she wanted to laugh or cry. Or both.

As if it might protect her heart, she folded her arms and glanced down at the floor, hating herself for being so weak. "I'll end my meeting early."

Jordan stood at the hotel penthouse window and stared down at the flashing lights of Times Square directly below him. Though he didn't mind doing business here, or even taking in the sights on occasion, he didn't understand this kind of life, this frenetic flow and non-stop crush of people and traffic. He was used to living in eight-thousand-square-foot houses, surrounded by twenty thousand acres.

A man needed space, he thought. Room to breathe.

He glanced at his watch, figured he had just enough time to make a quick phone call to his secretary before he left to meet Alexis at the restaurant. He'd made reservations at the exclusive Furbeir's, and sent a limo stocked with Dom Perignon and eight bouquets of long stemmed red roses to pick her up at her office. One bouquet for every year they'd been apart, he'd signed the card.

Remembering the look on her face when he'd walked into her office this afternoon made him smile. Underneath all her indignation and protests, he'd seen the pleasure in her eyes, had felt her soften when he'd told her he wanted her. She hadn't even argued with him when he'd told her she was his wife.

It was a start, he thought. A good one. Tonight, whatever it took, he'd hear her say it, too.

He turned at the knock on the door, knew it was

time for the evening housekeeping shift to come in and turn down the bed—a bed he intended to share with Alexis. If not tonight, then the next night, or the night after that. However long it took to get her to admit they belonged together.

At least this time if she ran away in the morning, he wouldn't have to get on a plane to chase after her.

He already had an image of her spread out on that big bed, her arms reaching for him, calling his name. Those fiery blue eyes glazed over with passion.

When he opened the door and those fiery blue eyes were staring into his, he felt the ground tilt under him. It took him a heartbeat to realize it actually *was* Alexis standing there.

She'd changed from the black business suit she'd worn earlier to a long sleeved burgundy sweater dress. The neckline plunged, the hem swirled around her knees. His throat turned to dust at the sight of her and when he took in the black stilettos and dainty silver ankle bracelet, his heart slammed against his ribcage.

She held an open bottle of champagne in one hand, two glasses in the other. Pink silk peeked out of an oversized black purse slung over her shoulder. Unless he missed his guess, it was lingerie, and he couldn't wait to see it on her almost as much as he couldn't wait to take it off.

"I felt like staying in," she breathed, her voice as smoky as her eyes. "I hope you don't mind."

She strolled past him, the scent of her reminding him of moonflowers and magic and everything that was Alexis. He watched her walk from the foyer to the bar, forgot to breathe when she sat on a barstool and crossed those long, killer legs of hers. When her dress slid several inches up her thighs, the blood in his upper body rushed south.

He closed the door.

Damn. He could never quite get his footing with this woman. Every time he thought he had the situation, and his emotions, under control, she'd throw him a curve ball. And the woman could throw one hell of a curve, he thought, sliding his gaze up her body.

She poured two glasses of champagne, held one out for him. He moved toward her, took the glass. "Are we celebrating?"

She narrowed her eyes in thought, then shook her head. "More like a suspension of hostility."

He clinked her glass with his, would take

whatever she would give him, even though he wanted more—so much more.

But he'd already waited eight years, he reasoned. He figured he could wait a few more days.

"I should be mad at you." Alexis sipped her champagne. "My office was in such a stir after you left, no one could concentrate. I had to re-schedule our meeting."

"I'd say I was sorry—" He wanted to taste the bubbles that he knew would still be lingering in her mouth. "But it would be a lie."

"Honesty is good," she said with a nod. "A solid foundation for a relationship."

"Is that what we have?" He set his glass on the bar and moved closer. "A relationship?"

"I don't know what we have yet." She stared at her glass for a long moment. "Everything happens so fast with us, Jordan. Eight years ago. Now. I can't catch my breath when I'm with you. I can't think."

He took her glass from her hand, set it down, then lowered his head. "I don't want you to."

She laid her palm on his chest to stop him. "It frightens me, knowing you have that kind of power over me."

"Is that why you left me?" he asked quietly. "Because I frightened you?"

She nodded slowly. "You were older, experienced. Wealthy. You excited and terrified me all at the same time."

"Allie—"

"Honesty." She leveled her gaze with his. "Look me in the eye and tell me you didn't want everything your way. Tell me you didn't manipulate our marriage, then expect me to smile and nod like some kind of bobble-headed rich man's wife."

His first instinct was to deny it, but he knew that wasn't what she needed to hear. He laid his hand over hers, stroked her knuckles with his thumb.

"That was then," he said. "This is now. We're both older, both successful in business, and money certainly isn't an issue."

"No." She smiled. "That part is true."

"We're not the same people, Alexis." He cupped her chin in his hand, watched the blue of her eyes soften. "We can start over; just take it one day at a time. Figure out all the details as we go along."

"I want to believe that," she whispered. "I want to believe you."

"Believe this,"

He lowered his mouth to hers, kissed her gently, took his time tasting the champagne on her lips. He felt her resistance melt, knew that, at last, he'd broken through the wall she'd built to keep him out. It took every ounce of willpower he possessed not to rush her, not to make her agree right now that they belonged together. That she belonged to him.

He slid his hands down her shoulders, slanted his mouth over hers, deepening the kiss and exploring the taste of her more deeply. With a soft moan, she opened to him, moved her hands inside his suit jacket, stirring the need and desire inside him.

"I like you in a tie." She reached out, took hold of the strip of red silk and pulled him close. "You know every woman in my office Googled you after you left this afternoon."

"Is that so?" He'd found a tasty little corner of her upturned mouth and nibbled there.

"I even caught Mary Margaret running a search on you," Alexis murmured, worked the knot on his tie loose. "I think she wants to have your babies."

He smiled at that, slid his hand down to cup

her breast, felt her tremble under his touch. "What about you, Allie? he asked. "Do you want to have my babies?"

Her fingers stilled, then she pulled the tie from his neck. "Maybe. Right now, I'm still deciding if I want you."

"You do." He trailed kisses over her jaw, nuzzled the spot under her ear that always made her moan. "Tell me you do."

"Yes." The tie slipped from her fingers. She drew in a breath and dropped her head back. "I do."

He slid his hands down to her knees, then up, under her dress, up her smooth, firm thighs. The image he'd had of her in his bed, naked, reaching for him, blew out of his mind. Now he wanted her here. Right here. On the barstool, on the floor. As long as it was now.

When she leaned back, draped her arms on the bar behind her, offering herself, he nearly lost it. Need pumped like wildfire through his veins, his heart pounded, in his chest, his throat, his head. He reached for his belt buckle, realized the pounding was also coming from the door.

He swore under his breath, furious at the interruption, but realizing that it was better now than five minutes from now.

"Housekeeping," he said raggedly. "Don't move."

He dragged a hand through his hair, moved toward the door and opened it. His heart screeched to a halt when he saw who was standing there.

Tall, blonde, face-on-every-magazine-cover, Phoebe Jansen.

Not now, he thought. Good God, not now.

"Hey, Jor." Dressed in a black Versace pantsuit, Phoebe breezed past him. "Sorry I didn't call. I just got in from drinks with Eve. She's hounding me to take that part I told you about."

"Phoebe—" Jordan avoided looking at Alexis "—this really isn't a good time."

"Don't worry, hon. I'm not staying." Smiling, Phoebe leaned in and kissed his cheek. "This is just the first time I've had to thank you for setting up the interview with Matthew. If I'd have known how hot the guy is, I would have done it without you asking me."

Just put a fork in me, Jordan thought. He knew he was cooked and about to be eaten, could feel the heat radiating from the direction of the bar. He put a hand on Phoebe's shoulder and herded her back toward the door. "Let's talk later, Pheeb."

"I'm serious, Jordan." Phoebe pulled away. "I really like this guy. I think I may have an affair with him."

Jordan wasn't certain if this could get any worse, but when Alexis stepped into the foyer, he suspected it not only could, it would.

Phoebe's brow lifted when she spotted the other woman, and she glanced back at Jordan, her face apologetic. "Sorry. I didn't realize you had company. I'll just be on my—"

"Were you talking about Matthew Langley?" Alexis asked, her voice cool and even.

"Do you know him?" Worried now, Phoebe stared at Alexis. "'Cause I was kidding about the affair. I mean, I just met him. Jordan asked me to do the interview, so I did, as a favor. For a friend."

"You and Jordan are friends." Alexis slid a frosty gaze at Jordan. "He never mentioned that."

"That's all we are." Misreading Alexis's icy tone for jealousy, Phoebe did her best to reassure the other woman. "Really. Just friends."

"And it was Jordan who arranged the inter-view with Matthew?" Icecaps were forming on

Alexis's words. "The interview that had to happen last Thursday, the exclusive, two-hour, last-minute interview."

Phoebe glanced nervously between Alexis and Jordan, not sure what to say. "I better go."

"No." Alexis slipped the strap of her purse onto her shoulder. "I'm the one who's leaving."

Jordan recognized the look in Alexis's eyes, the hard set of her jaw. He knew there was absolutely nothing he could say to her right now, nothing she would listen to or hear. Short of tying the woman up—and for a long second he seriously considered the possibility—there was no way in hell he could make her stay.

She paused in front of him, narrowed her eyes as she met his gaze. "Sign the papers, Jordan."

She turned then, and white-knuckled, his gut twisting with frustration, he watched her walk through the door and out of his life.

Nine

Muscles straining, arms shaking, Jordan lay on his back and forced the bar into one more set. The extra twenty pound weights he'd added this past week had honed and strengthened his body, but had done little to help his mind. The fierce urge to spill blood gripped him like a fist.

When he lost count, he swore and started over.

New York had been a fiasco.

Seven days ago, he'd nearly convinced Alexis that they belonged together. Had come so damn close. He'd even gotten her to think about babies, for god sakes. In the blink of an eye, it all vanished like smoke in the wind. Alexis, marriage, children. Everything he wanted.

Just thinking about it had him forcing one more set with the weights, determined to sweat out the image of her walking away.

Phoebe had felt awful that her timing had been so incredibly bad; she'd also been mortified that she'd teased about having an affair with the man. She'd offered to talk to Alexis, but Jordan had nixed that idea. He saw nothing positive coming out of the two women sitting down to "chat." As it was, Alexis would probably never speak to him again, anyway. Especially after all that talk about "honesty."

He would have told her about the thing with Matthew, dammit. Eventually. It wasn't really dishonest. It wasn't like she really needed to know he'd arranged for Matthew to get the interview the Phoebe. Phoebe hadn't minded doing a favor for an old friend.

And what was so bad about it, anyway? Grunting, he heaved the weight up again. Matthew got a great interview with Hollywood's hottest female film star. Hell, he'd done the guy a favor.

Breathing hard, Jordan dropped the weight into its holder, sat on the bench and stared at his reflection in the surrounding mirrors. Sweat ran down his face and back, soaked his T-shirt. He hadn't shaved in four days or used a comb in two.

He frowned darkly at himself. What the hell did it matter?

"You look like hell."

Scowling, Jordan looked up, caught the towel that Trey threw at him. "I'm busy."

"This how you city boys keep from going soft?" Tipping his black Stetson back, Trey glanced around the fully equipped gym.

"You wanna pump something other than your jaw, Blackhawk?" Jordan dragged the towel over his neck. "I'll spot you at two-twenty."

"Shoot, I pick up calves weigh more'n that." Trey lifted a seventy-five pound free weight and curled it as easy as a piece of foam. "Speaking of, I've got fifty head you can take off my hands, dirt cheap, if you want. That is, if you ever plan on owning a real ranch."

Jordan's hand tightened on the towel. "What the hell is that supposed to mean?"

"Most ranchers with land like this have some

kind of livestock. You know, horses, cows." Trey curled the weight again in one smooth motion. "Unless you're planning on raising hay."

"You got a better reason to come all the way over here other than annoy me?" Jordan asked irritably.

"Yep." Trey set the weight down and moved to the punching bag, gave it a couple of jabs. "The annoying part is just a bonus."

"Dammit, Trey, I'm not in the mood."

"I suggest you get in the mood." Trey threw a solid right punch into the bag. "Lisa Jefferies and Sue Ann Potter are on their way here, bringing us dinner."

Jordan's head came up. "What?"

"Lisa called and invited me to a housewarming meal to welcome you back to Stone Ridge. They'll be here at seven."

Cursing, Jordan snatched his watch from the hook he'd draped it on. It was six-thirty. "Why the hell didn't you call me?"

"I did." Trey danced on his toes, feigned a left and cut with his right. "You should answer your phone."

After six calls from his office in Dallas, four from his refinery in Midland, then two from his accountant, Jordan had unplugged his landline and turned off his cell.

"You entertain them," he said, shaking his head. "I'm busy."

"Doing what?" Trey slammed a fist into the bag. "Signing my sister's annulment papers?"

Jordan stilled, then slowly narrowed a gaze at Trey. "What did you say?"

"You heard me."

"She told you?"

"Alexis tell me anything?" Trey gave the bag a hard right. "Hell, no."

Jordan felt as if he'd taken Trey's punch directly to his gut "Then how—when did you—"

"I've always known." Trey straightened and loosened his fists, shook out his shoulders. "I knew the summer it started, the Vegas wedding, even the annulment. Only reason I let it go on without saying anything was 'cause it was you. Anyone else would be picking their teeth out of their tonsils."

"Why didn't you say anything?" Jordan stared at Trey. "All these years, and not one word?"

"I could say the same about you." Trey stared at Jordan, his gaze dark and serious. "And if I'd ever thought for one second you intended to hurt her, friend or not, I'd have to lay you out."

"You could try, I guess." Jordan nodded, and though he didn't like it, understood where Trey was coming from. "It doesn't matter now, anyway. She won't even talk to me."

"Because of the Phoebe Jansen interview?"

Dumbfounded, Jordan stared at Trey. "How the hell do you know all this?"

"I figured that one out myself." Trey folded his arms and leaned back against a treadmill. "I knew you'd dated Phoebe a few years back, right before she went big. I seriously doubted it was a coincidence when Matthew suddenly had to leave for an interview with her right before the wedding. I'm guessing Alexis found out when you were in New York."

"She's my wife, dammit." Jordan dragged his hands through his damp hair. "I'll be damned if I'll look the other way while she plays footsies with some other guy."

"You looked the other way for eight years," Trey pointed out.

"No." Jordan shook his head and let out a breath. "God, she'll kill me for sure if she finds out, but I've always known what she was doing, kept an eye on who she was with. Matthew's the first guy that I thought might be serious."

"So you decided it was time to convince Alexis she needed to come to her senses and settle down with you?" Trey lifted a brow. "Man, I would have loved to see the look on her face when you told her you were still married. Did she hit you?"

"She pushed me in the lake," Jordan admitted reluctantly.

"That's Alexis," Trey said, nodding. "Never could rein her in. She always did the opposite of what I wanted, just to prove she could. The night William Blackhawk packed up his things and walked out on us, I told her to stay upstairs. She was only eight, but would she listen to me? Hell, no."

No one in the Blackhawk house had ever discussed what happened—what really happened—the night William Blackhawk left. A muscle jumped in Trey's jaw, and his dark eyes narrowed, staring blindly at his reflection in the mirror.

"My mom was hysterical," Trey said. "Begging my father not to go. I didn't give a damn, I hated him. Kiera was too little to understand or even remember, but she was crying anyway, so Alaina held her, comforted her. Alexis just paced, kept saying that our daddy wasn't really leaving and never coming back. She said that daddies didn't do that."

It wasn't difficult for Jordan to imagine Alexis at eight years old, her chin lifted, her little back held straight, determined that her will alone would make her world be exactly as she willed it to be. It was that fierce resolve and un-wavering belief in herself that had drawn him to her in the first place.

"I should have known she wouldn't stay put. Alexis never listened to anyone." Trey's eyes turned to black stone. "It was my fault, what happened to her."

Jordan's hands tightened on the towel. "What happened?"

"When the yelling got louder, I went down-stairs," Trey continued. "Found my mother huddled in the corner of William's office while he finished clearing out his desk. He told me to get out, I refused. It would have come to blows right there except Alexis came flying in the room. Before I could stop her, she'd flung herself at William, grabbed on to his leg, pleading with him not to go, that she'd be good if he stayed, she'd mind him and do all her chores. He shook her off like a piece of dirt."

It was like a fist around his gut, around his heart, and Jordan couldn't stop the thought that if William Blackhawk were still alive, he'd want to kill him himself.

"I managed to get one swing at him," Trey said, satisfaction and hatred glinting in his eyes. "But I was only fourteen and he was a big man. He laid me flat and walked out."

The curse, raw and gritty, shuddered out with Jordan's breath. "She never said anything to me. Not a word."

"My mother isn't the only one who lives in denial." Trey rolled a shoulder, then sighed as he straightened. "Might as well sign those papers and be done with it, Jordan. That's what Alexis wants, you might as well give it to her."

"What the hell kind of thing is that to say?" Anger narrowed Jordan's eyes. "She's my wife."

"She doesn't seem to think so." Trey shrugged. "Once that girl makes a decision, there's just no changing her mind. Why don't you just go shower and we'll have us a nice evening with Lisa and Sue Ann?"

"Why don't you shut up." Jordan threw the towel at Trey and turned. "Damn you, Trey, just shut the hell up and get out of my house."

"Hey," Trey yelled after Jordan when he stomped out of the gym. "What about Lisa and Sue Ann?"

"Not my problem," Jordan shot back over his shoulder and headed for the shower.

At the moment, he had a much bigger, much more important problem to deal with.

Halfway home, the rain started to fall.

It didn't matter to Alexis. The walk from her office to her new apartment was only seven blocks, and after twelve hours sitting at her computer, it felt good to stretch her legs and clear her mind. It was more of a mist than a real rain, anyway, she thought, just enough to dampen the streets and freshen the air. Fall had moved into New York City these past few days, but no one seemed to mind the chill in the air. Joggers still ran in the park wearing T-shirts, nannies pushed strollers, vendors hawked their wares.

The world didn't stop because of one broken heart.

On the outside, Alexis thought she probably

looked like any other New Yorker coming home from work. She moved with the flow of the people on the sidewalks, kept her gaze straight ahead, her face impassionate. On the outside, she looked like she knew exactly where she was going, exactly what she'd do when she got there.

On the inside, she felt like shattered glass. Every breath, every beat of her heart, cut a little sharper, a little deeper.

It hadn't been easy, keeping up this front for the past week. She'd seen the curious glances, heard the whispers. There were hounds in the office, and they could smell weakness, would pounce at the first scent. She'd busted her butt to get where she was, to earn the respect of her peers. Sniveling around the office, all weepy and despondent over a man, was more than weak, she thought. It was pathetic.

She preferred the privacy of her own home, lights out, under the covers, to cry her eyes out.

All these years she'd convinced herself they didn't belong together, that they were completely wrong for each other, the chasm separating them too deep and too wide. She'd been angry enough at first, self-righteous, and those feelings had kept her sane. Kept her from

running back into his arms and giving up everything she'd ever dreamed.

Across the street from her apartment house,
she stopped, looked at the fancy, forest-green
awning, the uniformed doorman, the elegant
glass doors. She'd closed escrow and moved in
four days ago. Sixteen hundred square feet over-
looking Central Park. Marble bathrooms, sleek
granite kitchen counters, twelve-foot ceilings
and two fireplaces. She hadn't opened one box
yet, hadn't hung up her clothes or even put
sheets on the bed.

Her big, empty bed.

People would kill for everything she had. The
job, the house, the money. She should be
dancing with joy, running through the park,
skipping in the fountains. Why the hell was she
standing out here, in the middle of the sidewalk,
in the rain, feeling so completely and utterly
alone?

So completely and utterly miserable.

Because she loved him. She *loved* him,
dammit. Beyond life itself. Beyond every
painful breath and beat of her heart, she loved
him.

She watched the rain drops slide down her

black cashmere coat, heard the cars passing, the bump of music from an unseen radio. All she needed to do was cross the street. Pick one foot up and put it in front of the other. Just keep moving. Why was that suddenly so difficult?

People walked around her. A man dragging three Pomeranians on leashes. Two teenagers talking, not to each other, but on their cell phones. A businessman flagging down a taxi. Daily routines, she thought. Everyone going about their mundane, ordinary, run-of-the-mill activities.

And she couldn't even make herself walk thirty feet to her apartment entrance.

The rain increased, but she didn't care. Closing her eyes, she sat on a park bench. Go inside, a voice of reason chastised her. Shut up, she replied.

She didn't want reason anymore. Didn't want logic.

She wanted Jordan.

She didn't want to want him. But she did.

He'd refused to sign the annulment papers, created turmoil at her office, used Phoebe to get Matthew out of the way. And still, she loved him.

Honesty, she thought with a sigh. There was hers.

From the park, she heard children laughing, a mother's warning not to step in the puddles, then the distinct plop of small feet splashing. She turned toward the sound and opened her eyes, almost smiled at the four little boys jumping in the pooling water.

"Mind if I share your bench?"

When she turned, it was her heart jumping.

Jordan.

She blinked, afraid that she really had gone crazy, and this was her imagination messing with him mind. She almost reached out to touch him, just to be certain.

When he sat down beside her and leveled his gaze with hers, she didn't need to touch him to know he was real. It was Jordan, no question about it. He looked a little tired, she thought, noting the tension crinkling the corners of his deep green eyes.

He looked wonderful.

She was still trying to find her voice when he spoke.

"I signed the papers today and filed them, Allie," he said quietly. "Tomorrow morning you'll no longer be a married woman."

Her heart, the little pieces that were left of it,

dropped. She stared at him. He'd done it. He'd really done it. Wasn't this what she wanted? What she'd asked him for? What she'd insisted on? Be careful what you wish for… The words flashed into her brain, bounced around like pinballs. She now had everything she'd ever wanted and realized it wasn't what she wanted at all.

For the first time in her life, she understood what her mother had felt. Why she'd gone crazy. Love could do that to a person, Alexis thought. Was doing it to her right now.

But she wouldn't fall apart here. Not in front of Jordan, in front of the world. She still had her pride—a thread, and she was hanging on to it for dear life. All she had to do was stand, say goodbye, and walk those thirty feet across the street to her big, beautiful apartment.

And she would. In just another minute, as soon as she was certain her knees would hold her.

She swallowed hard, held her chin up. "It was hardly necessary for you to come all the way to New York to tell me that."

He shrugged. "Some things need to be said in person."

"How civil of you." She managed to stand, forced the corners of her mouth upward and tried her hand at being cheeky. "Maybe we can be friends, Jordan, now that we're not married."

He kept his gaze on hers, shook his head slowly. "I don't think so."

She hadn't thought it possible to hurt any more than she already was. Once again, she'd been wrong. She prayed the dampness on her face was the rain.

"All right." She nodded stiffly, turned. "See you around, then."

"One more thing, Allie."

She wasn't certain she could handle one more thing without crumbling, but she hesitated, glanced over her shoulder. He rose from the bench and closed the short distance between them.

"Will you marry me?"

"What?"

"Like I said, some things need to be said in person." He reached for her hand, lifted her fingers to his lips. "We can go out on a few dates first. We never really had a chance to do that before. Please, Allie, just give me that chance."

"Jordan—"

"Let me romance you. Let me tempt you,

seduce you." He brushed his lips over her knuckles. "Let me love you."

She shuddered at his touch, but fear caught hold of her, had her snagging her hand away. "If this is your idea of a joke, so help me—"

"I love you, Alexis. That's no joke." There was an urgency to his voice now. "I loved you eight years ago, but my pride kept me from going after you. I was so certain you'd come back to me, and when you didn't, I was angry."

If he knew how many times she'd almost gone back to him, how many times she'd packed a bag. How many times she'd actually made it to the airport before her own pride turned her back around. And still, she couldn't tell him. Not yet.

"Not signing those annulment papers was my way of hanging on to you, of having the last say." He shoved his hands into his trouser pockets. "Having control. You're right about that. I did want control. I was certain if I let you go out and do all the things you wanted to do, you'd realize you didn't need me."

That had been the problem, she knew. That she'd needed him so much, had loved him so much, it had scared her.

"What's changed?" She looked into his face, felt her bones melting with that need and that love, wanted so badly to lean into him. "Why would now be different for us? I have a home here, you're at Five Corners. And children—"

"When you're ready." He glanced at a woman pushing a stroller across the street, hurrying to get out of the rain. "I won't lie to you, I want kids—yours, ours. But I need you, Allie. More than my next breath. Everything I have means nothing without you, including Five Corners."

"Are you saying you'd live here, in New York?" She shook her head in disbelief.

"That's exactly what I'm saying." He reached for her hand again. "My heart is with you, wherever you are. Wherever you say. Just be my wife. Love me."

"And Five Corners?" she asked, her voice breathless, her chest strumming as the pieces of her heart pulled together and swelled.

"Trey and I are forming a co-op between Stone Ridge Stables and Five Corners and hired a management company to run it. We bring in a couple more ranches, and we'll have the largest in the entire state. I—we—can spend as little or as much time there as we choose."

"You and Trey?" Good Lord. Two of the strongest, most powerful, most obstinate men she'd ever known—partners? It made her head spin.

But she couldn't think about that now. It didn't even matter. All that mattered was Jordan. Standing here, in the rain, telling her that he loved her. Asking—not telling—her to marry him. To be his wife. To have his babies.

And she *did* want his babies, she knew. Soon.

But first, she wanted him. Wanted to pack eight years' worth of love and life into as short a time as possible. She wouldn't regret the years they were apart, she decided. She would simply look forward to the future. Together.

She watched as he pulled his hand out of his pocket, opened his fingers. She was certain her heart stopped when she saw what he held.

Her wedding ring. The one she'd thrown at him eight years ago. He'd kept it. All these years, he'd actually kept it.

"I love you," he whispered. "Marry me."

She stared at the ring, the simple band of gold. Love and hope and need consumed her. Overwhelmed her.

"Allie, for god sakes," he said raggedly. "Say something, please."

She lifted her gaze to his, felt the tears sliding down her cheeks, mixing with the rain.

"It's about time," she murmured, touching her lips to his. "It's about damn time."

* * * * *

BAD BLOOD

A POWERFUL
DYNASTY,
WHERE SECRETS
AND SCANDAL
NEVER SLEEP!

VOLUME 1 – 15th April 2011
TORTURED RAKE
by Sarah Morgan

VOLUME 2 – 6th May 2011
SHAMELESS PLAYBOY
by Caitlin Crews

VOLUME 3 – 20th May 2011
RESTLESS BILLIONAIRE
by Abby Green

VOLUME 4 – 3rd June 2011
FEARLESS MAVERICK
by Robyn Grady

8 VOLUMES IN ALL TO COLLECT!

www.millsandboon.co.uk

BAD BL⬭⬭D

A POWERFUL
DYNASTY,
WHERE SECRETS
AND SCANDAL
NEVER SLEEP!

VOLUME 5 – 17th June 2011
HEARTLESS REBEL
by Lynn Raye Harris

VOLUME 6 – 1st July 2011
ILLEGITIMATE TYCOON
by Janette Kenny

VOLUME 7 – 15th July 2011
FORGOTTEN DAUGHTER
by Jennie Lucas

VOLUME 8 – 5th August 2011
LONE WOLFE
by Kate Hewitt

8 VOLUMES IN ALL TO COLLECT!

MILLS
BOON

www.millsandboon.co.uk

Intense passion and glamour from our bestselling stars of international romance

Available 20th May 2011

Available 17th June 2011

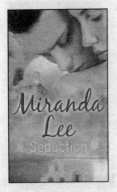

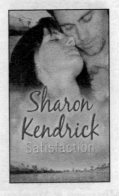

Available 15th July 2011

Available 19th August 2011

Royal Affairs – luxurious and bound by duty yet still captive to desire!

Royal Affairs: Desert Princes & Defiant Virgins

Available 3rd June 2011

Royal Affairs: Princesses & Protectors

Available 1st July 2011

Royal Affairs: Mistresses & Marriages

Available 5th August 2011

Royal Affairs: Revenge Secrets & Seduction

Available 2nd September 2011